LIZ MISTRY moved to West York[...] late 1980s. Her gritty crime fiction [...] dural novels set in Bradford embr[...] she describes as 'Warm, rich and fe[...] exploring the darkness that lurks beneath. Yet, her heart remains in Scotland, where childhood tales of bogey men, Bible John and grey lady ghosts fed her imagination.

Her latest work, The Solanki and McQueen crime series is set around West Lothian, where she uses the distinctive landscape, historic heritage and Scottish culture as a backdrop to her hard-hitting yet often humorous stories.

Struggling with clinical depression and anxiety for many years, Liz often includes mental health themes in her writing. She credits her MA in Creative Writing from Leeds Trinity University with helping her find a way of using her writing to navigate her ongoing mental health struggles. The synergy between creative and academic writing led Liz to complete a doctorate in creative writing researching the importance of representation of marginalised groups within the genre she loves.

Her husband, three children and huge extended British Indian family are a constant support to her. In her spare time, Liz loves visiting the varied Scottish and Yorkshire landscape, travelling, listening to music, reading and blogging about all things crime fiction on her website blog, The Crime Warp.

You can connect with Liz here:

Website: lizmistry.com

𝕏 : (Twitter) LizMistryAuthor

f : www.facebook.com/LizMistrybooks

◙ : @lizmistryauthor

Also by Liz Mistry

Last Request
Broken Silence
Dark Memories
Blood Games
Dying Breath
End Game

The Solanki and McQueen Crime Series

The Blood Promise

The Revenge Pact

LIZ MISTRY

ONE PLACE. MANY STORIES

HQ
An imprint of HarperCollins*Publishers* Ltd
1 London Bridge Street
London SE1 9GF

www.harpercollins.co.uk

HarperCollins*Publishers*
Macken House, 39/40 Mayor Street Upper,
Dublin 1 D01 C9W8

This paperback edition 2024

1
First published in Great Britain by
HQ, an imprint of HarperCollins*Publishers* Ltd 2024

ISBN: 9780008686482

To my beautiful extended family as always!

'*Vengeance taken will often tear the heart and torment the conscience.*'

~ Arthur Schopenhauer

Prologue

As always, Ricky got off the train at Haymarket and made his way down the alley behind Hamish's boxing club, off Morrison Street. He'd more on his mind than updating the terms and conditions of his deal with the dirty copper from Edinburgh who enjoyed lording it over the criminal scum. Fuck's sake only someone who thinks they're better than everyone else would insist on being called the Gaffer, right? Stuck-up bastard!

Glad of the cover of darkness, which he planned to make good use of, Ricky arrived early, making sure he'd time to scope the place out. There had been a time when he'd trusted the Edinburgh crew – but no more. He'd gambled all his money on their partnership – but then the bastards had betrayed him in the worst way imaginable. Worse than stealing his investment, worse than stabbing him in the back over a smack deal gone wrong. Even worse than screwing his missus. Christ, if *that* had been all they'd done then he could have lived with it. Licked his wounds and got on with it, but this was so much fucking worse and 'The Big I Am' Edinburgh bastard was about to pay for being part of what had gone down.

Ricky ignored the nagging wee voice that sat on his shoulder gabbing in his ear, telling him it was his own fault. That he'd been seduced by the Gaffer's false promises of fame and fortune. Like every other Gorbals boy, Ricky had wanted to scramble out of destitution and give himself, his wife and the bairns a better life than he'd had. He didn't want them growing up with empty bellies and a clout round the ear on payday from a dad who drank to forget the misery of his tawdry existence. It wasn't a bad ambition for a laddie with a growing family and few options, and Ricky was prepared to do whatever it took to succeed. He'd never had a good relationship with the polis, so taking a step further into the darkness wasn't a big deal. Not when the potential to rule his city was his for the taking. Besides, he had brains and, more importantly, the gift of the gab. He already had a following of criminals with similar ambitions, but without the nous to capitalise on the opportunities presented by the heroin that was flooding the market.

The other Glesca gang lords were complacent. Too bloody old to see the prospects a canny liaison could bring. Too blinkered to see potential from abroad. Their territory was ripe for the picking and, with all the gallusness of youth, Ricky was ready to step in. He couldn't get enough of the white stuff for the city's demands and there was no prospect of it drying up the Gaffer's plans to oust the increasingly complacent career criminals from their respective cities, the sincerity had been encouraging, the lightness of tone appealing. 'A Tale of Two Cities, eh, big man? Edinburgh and Glasgow. You and me.'

Ricky hadn't been sure about the posh voice, big ideas and ready smile and he was hesitant about throwing his lot in with the polis. Wee Frankie, the right-hand man – with his gruff approach, stony silences and mangled puss – was more relatable to Ricky. *He* was what Ricky's ma would call 'a braw-looking chookie'. 'Ugly sod' would've been Ricky's choice of words. Frankie was building up a reputation over in Pilton for being tough. Christ!

Even Ricky over in Glasgow had heard of him. Wee Frankie and the Gaffer combined had connections and weren't afraid to use them. Word on the street was that by using the Gaffer's intel, Wee Frankie and a couple of stooges executed a few successful post office raids.

It had been the similar raids that Ricky had organised in Pollokshields that had attracted the Edinbugger crew's attention. It had shown he wasn't afraid to get his hands dirty – unlike the Gaffer, he'd been in the thick of it. Got a buzz from the action, Ricky did. He couldn't understand the appeal of going to all the bother of planning the action, but staying in the shadows. He'd soon learned the Gaffer's motivations for being a ghost – *deniability.* Never in the firing line, the Gaffer could hold both hands up saying, 'It wisnae me, guv,' and of course, it held a ring of truth, because it *was* the truth. The Gaffer *was* never there. It was just Ricky in Glasgow and Frankie in Edinburgh who were in the firing line. The Gaffer was the puppet master pulling strings in both cities. Ricky appreciated the genius of it all.

Although he was on the Gaffer's territory now, he wasn't scared. They'd been on each other's territory often enough, so it wasn't unusual to arrange a meet in Edinburgh.

Over the past year the Gaffer and Wee Frankie had become extensions of Ricky's family. Then, that wee fucker had gone over the line. Completely over the fucking line and the Gaffer had let him. That's when Ricky'd started to do a bit more research. Should've done that before he got in tow with them, but hey ho, hindsight's a wonderful thing, is it not? That's when he realised that the Gaffer had as much to lose as him, if not more. That's when Ricky realised just how connected and just how corrupt the fucker really was. He wouldn't be the only one glad to see the bastard get shafted. Not by a long shot.

The smir of rain in the air soaked through his coat as he chased some tramps away and took his place in the shadow of the bins. He threw his fag into a puddle and shoved his hands in his pockets as he waited. Hunkered down, the stink of urine and excrement – some of it human – was nauseating. Adrenalin fizzed through Ricky as the Gaffer's words echoed in his head. 'It's all right there, Ricky mate. I'm telling you, this smack's going to make us rich quick and *we'll* be in at the start of it. We can create our own markets, make sure the stuff flows between the two cities. It's a genius idea. A no-fucking-brainer and with my connections, it's as guaranteed as a good shag round at Dora's in Stockbridge on a Saturday night, ken?'

Ricky had laughed at that. The threat that Dora Noyce might expand her prostitution empire to *Glasgow* had the pimps and punters grabbing their balls in anguish. Yet, here was the Gaffer bandying her name about like she was a personal friend. Ricky was in awe and despite being nervous, he was wholly intrigued. Although, he had more to lose than the other two, Ricky was aching to take on the world. What a fucking gullible wanker he'd been! Visions of ousting the kingpin Arthur Thompson from his throne were too tempting. Before long he was up to his smelly, wee oxters in it. *A Tale of Two Cities indeed.* In hindsight he should have stuck to his gut instincts and minded what his dad said. *Never trust an Edinbugger, Ricky. They're all slithery wee bampots* – and he'd been right. Now it was up to Ricky to get it sorted and move on.

It was time now and as per the arrangement they came alone. That was the deal. Whistling, the Gaffer entered the alley. The theme from *Shaft*, would you believe? Like the Gaffer was on *that* stratosphere. Some bloody big 'I am'. Ricky nearly jumped up there and then, with his knife in his hand. He wanted to shaft the fucker, but something made him hesitate. A spark of light flickered as a smoke was lit. The pungent smell wafting through the drizzle. 'I know you're there, Ricky.'

He froze, hand tightening on the knife. How the hell did the dobber know he was here? Did one of those wee Edinbugger goons see him getting off the train? He'd been careful. Kept his wits about him as he left the station.

4

'Get up, man. What the fuck do you think you're doing hunkered down in the shit like Lipton's bloody orphan.'

Ricky got up and edged from the shadows. Standing there, smoking, eyes narrowed, smirking, the Gaffer said, 'Looks like you and me have got to the end of the road, eh?'

With a step towards him, well-toned arms reached up, circling his shoulders. Ricky shrugged them off and twisted so they were face to face. Blood whooshing through his veins made him dizzy and without thinking he thrust the knife hard, aiming for the bastard's gut. The Gaffer sidestepped it and tutted. 'For God's sake, son. Maybe no' do that, eh? Neither of us is going to die here tonight, you get it? We've worked well together. Made a load of dosh and now it's time to part ways amicably like. Put this minor event behind us.'

The half-smoked fag flicked over Ricky's head into the darkness beyond and an amused laugh filled the air, making his blood fair boil. 'I'll make an agreement with you, okay? You and your crew will never set foot in Edinburgh again, and me and mine won't trade in Glasgow. We'll both still be quids in.'

Ricky lunged again, but the cocky fucker dodged out of his way. Two figures sidled into the alley – Wee Frankie and Fat Boy Gibbsy. The Gaffer didn't even glance at them. 'Just hold up a minute, lads. We're just coming to an agreement here, me and Ricky.'

Ricky bowed his head like a subservient slave. The Gaffer slapped his back and thrust a wad of twenties towards him. 'That's the boy. Now, I heard about what's gone down with you and I regret it. That should never have happened, but c'est la vie, as the frogs say, eh? No point in getting all aerated about something that can be easily sorted, is there? Here's something for your trouble.'

As the flutter of notes landed by his feet, a forceful yell left Ricky's throat. 'Now.'

From the other end of the alley Ricky's men appeared. Did the eejit really think he'd not come prepared? All three of them hesitated and that's when Ricky made his move and rammed his knife up to the hilt in the Gaffer's gut and twisted it. 'Take your fucking money and shove it up your arse. You'll need it. Mark my words, I'll bring you down for what happened. I'll bring you down in the only way that'll hurt you. In your fucking pocket. But just you remember.' He jabbed the Gaffer's shoulder with a bony finger as the blood pumped from the stomach wound. 'Glasgow belongs to me and, before long, so will Edinburgh.'

Ricky yanked the knife out, and he and his men ran like shadows from the alley and made their way back to their own territory.

Ricky hadn't expected to read the Gaffer's obituary in the *Daily Record*. That had never been his plan. It was always about lessons taught, threats made and fear instilled. It was about showing the Edinburgh underbelly that Glesca wasn't that far away and that hiding behind a badge might not be enough. Not even for the Gaffer.

Present Day

Tuesday 14th February

Chapter 1

*'As warfare between gangs in Edinburgh and Glasgow peaks,
a new report into the extent of criminal gang activity in our
cities and proposals to combat it will be published today by
the Scottish Government. Later on we'll have an MSP spokesperson to comment on the impact of the report as well as . . .'*

The drive from Livingston police station to the Lang Whang –
otherwise known as the A70, which stretched between Edinburgh
and Ayr – should have taken no time, but it *was* rush hour and
it *was* February in Scotland.

'Bloody gangs!'

DS Jasmine 'Jazzy' Solanki waited, knowing full well that her
partner DC Annie 'Queenie' McQueen was just getting started
on a rant that had become ever more frequent in recent weeks.
And cue . . .

'Bloody clarty wee toerags, that's what they are. Mucky wee
scumbags, filthy wee bawbags who need a sharp kick up the
jacksie. Bloody Loanie Gibbs and Jimmy Nails, who the hell
do they think they are? The eejits in Holyrood, with all their
proposals and reports and committees, haven't got a bloody
scooby.'

9

Couple of lowlife gangsters? Jazzy hadn't had the pleasure of meeting either the Edinburgh gangster Loanie Gibbs nor the Glasgow one Jimmy Nails, although their reputations were known to everyone in Police Scotland. Gang warfare had become a regular occurrence over the past few months and it seemed that no one – not even with their ears on the ground – could pinpoint what had caused it. For decades now, only minor scuffles had arisen between the two cities' criminal underbellies and those had been swiftly squashed, diverting police attention away from the respective gangs' covert criminal activity – drug dealing, prostitution, fraud, money laundering and such like. Talk of turf wars, possibly involving gangs from outside Scotland or from the north of the country, had been mooted, but no concrete motivation appeared to have been established.

Jazzy didn't disagree with Queenie. How could she? The gangs were becoming the bane of Lothian and Borders Police's life and the all-out antagonism between the two cities' gangs was diverting valuable policing away from the more rural areas. Livingston was only one of the stations feeling overworked and getting the sharp end of the local folks' tongues for delays in responding to their demands. Only the previous week a known Edinburgh criminal had turned up murdered in Peebles and that had landed in Lothian and Borders Police laps. Thankfully not Livingston, but still it had implications for the entire division.

'. . . *the Scottish Cold Case Unit are repeating last year's appeal for information regarding the unidentified male, dubbed Cairnpapple Man, who was found in a shallow grave near the prehistoric burial site near Bathgate over three decades ago. Forensic artist, Dr Hazel McLeod, from Glasgow Caledonian University, has expressed her optimism that the rerelease of this facial reconstruction created using techniques like those used on the Woman in the Bin might finally result in Cairnpapple Man being identified.*'

10

'Barlinnie! That's what they deserve. A stretch in the BarL, a wee incarceration in the Big Hoose, a length o' time in the Bar, eh? What do you say, JayZee?'

Again, Jazzy couldn't disagree. Things were becoming intolerable for officers on the streets and the sneaking suspicion that the crime scene they were heading to was an extension of the open warfare that had leached from the cities' borders and into the surrounding areas was preying on her mind. Since her near-death experience last year, Jazzy had been reinstated to her previous role of sergeant. It had come with the proviso that she, Queenie and the rest of D team remain on office duties at DCI Dick's convenience. Of course, the dickless wonder – as D team not so affectionately called him – had rubbed his hands in glee, and, despite the obvious need for more detectives working active cases, he'd kept them relegated to desk duty.

This small taste of freedom sent adrenalin rushing through Jazzy's system. Should she have deflected DCS Afzal when he directed her and Queenie to take the call? Was she storing up a shedload of grief by defying her DCI's specific instructions to 'stay in the office and leave the policing to those who are able'? She exhaled and tried to ignore Queenie's relentless chuntering. She'd acted on a direct order from the big boss, so DCI Dick could swivel on it. Besides, she'd been cleared by her consultant to return to her role as a detective, providing she stuck to observational and light duties.

'. . . Here at Radio Lothian, you're listening to Kirsty Ndibanje and now here's one from our very own Paolo Nutini. "Through the Echoes", one of my favourites . . .'

As Queenie pulled the Land Rover onto the grass verge behind a line of police cars and CSI vans, Jazzy turned the radio off. Her physiotherapy was going well and she hoped, albeit without much conviction, that her appointment later in the week would confirm that she could drive again. Much as she appreciated Queenie's help, Jazzy preferred to engage in some downtime as she drove to and from work, but with her partner around, downtime was impossible. Besides, Jazzy couldn't quite let go of feeling ill at ease at being beholden to someone. Her issues around being in control made it hard to navigate that fine line between accepting help from a close friend and the accompanying feeling that she was selling her soul.

Jazzy cursed her partner when she was forced to slither on sleet-covered grass between the car and a marshy ditch. Behind them, the mortuary van pulled up and, in deference to the black ice that had developed overnight, braked to a gentle stop. The gloominess of the occasion was intensified by freezing weather. Further away, beyond the flapping police tape of the outer cordon, was a second tape that stretched across the road. Just visible through the lightly swirling snow was yet another string of tape. Within this inner cordon, a group of white-clad figures erected the crime scene tent, whilst others searched the areas for forensic evidence. Already yellow markers were dotted around the verge and on the concrete itself.

Jazzy took a moment to remember the last major crime scene she'd attended. It had been before Christmas, in an office in Armadale, and was responsible for the nightmares that featured continually in her sleep. She rolled her shoulders, feeling the movement pull on her arm. She'd injured it whilst trying to catch a serial killer and had been lucky to survive the encounter. Although her luminous pink neon stookie had been replaced by another identical one, Jazzy still needed the accompanying sling to support its weight. However, to get into the crime scene suit, she'd have to dispense with the support bandage for a short while.

Jazzy braced herself against the chill breeze and watched on as Queenie rummaged in the boot looking for fresh unopened crime scene suits and cursing the jumble of junk that had become muddled with her work equipment – toys, wellies, changes of clothes, snacks, a buggy, courtesy of her granddaughter Ruby. Queenie and her husband Craig had cared for their grand-daughter since their daughter's murder and Ruby was the light of Queenie's eye.

'There ye are, ye bugger!' A mottled-faced Queenie emerged from the chaos with two crime scene sets and waved them in the air. 'Got the bastards. Let's get going.'

'I'm still half expecting Dick to get wind that we've been freed from captivity and turn up, that damn moustache of his twitching, as he banishes us from the scene. You know we only got it by default because the idiot had left his phone in his office whilst he went to the loo.'

Queenie snorted. 'He'll still be in there. He took the sports pages with him. That man wasn't for having a quick crap – oh no. He's in there for the long haul. Besides, wasn't it your— I mean, the chief super who ordered us to go?'

A red bloom flashed across Jazzy's cheeks. 'For God's sake, Queenie, shut up, okay?'

In a moment of weakness, she'd confided to her colleague that the chief super was her biological father and she was loath to acknowledge the relationship, much less have it become common gossip, even if Waqas Afzal was keen to mend bridges. *Not going to happen!*

For once Queenie looked abashed. 'Sorry, but I'm right, aren't I? He outranks the dickless wonder, so we're good to go, yeah?'

'Yeah, I suppose so, but don't expect to be on this investigation for long. I bet Dick will allocate B team to this one. He's got a bee in his bonnet about all the gang stuff going on.'

They were an unlikely pair. Jazzy, tall and slender, her long, waist-length hair tied back in a ponytail, and Queenie, short and stumpy with hair not dissimilar to Oor Wullie's. But they worked well together. *Who'd have thunk it?* Jazzy gripped Queenie's arm and lightly squeezed to take the sting from her words. 'Although, maybe it'll be harder for him to bounce us once we're in? So, no puking, Queenie. No compromising the scene, okay? No matter *what* we're confronted with, you can't throw up. We can't give Dick any ammunition.'

'Aye, okay. You've made your point, JayZee, but, as I've told you before, it was just a dodgy pasty, that's all.' Queenie, nose in the air and crime scene suits tucked under her arm, marched past Jazzy, heading towards the cordon. Jazzy's warning yell came a second too late as Queenie, unaware of the black ice in the shadows of the trees, found herself hurtled into the air, crime scene suits in their plastic bags scattered to the wind. She tried a mid-air backpedal and a sort of twisty desperate manoeuvre while cartwheeling her arms in the air, but the inevitable crash landing was unavoidable as she ended up on her substantial bahookie, glaring at the officer who'd stepped forward to help her to her feet. 'Jeez, oh, JayZee. Could you no' have warned me? I'm no Torvill, you know?'

Jazzy swallowed her laughter. 'You're right there and – just for clarity – you're no Dean either. Come on, let's see if you can make a more dignified entrance.'

Still grinning, Jazzy used her left arm to howff Queenie to her feet.

'I'm not usually so clumsy, like.'

Jazzy hid her smirk. 'Och, don't say you've already forgotten about the scene with the homeless lad? Remember, you slid on the ice and tumbled down the hill, nearly landing in the River Almond. Or what about the time you managed to find the only moist cow pat in a field with no coos and ended up skiting on your arse, or . . .'

'Aye, aye, all right, you've made your point. But, you know, I'm not sure you should be parading about out here in these conditions Not with your arm.'

Jazzy ignored her friend's concern and gingerly walked over the icy road. Flashing her warrant card, she ducked under the first tape. She suited and booted herself in crime scene overalls – her hair bundled on top of her head, which pushed the top of her hood out like a malformed rhino horn – and ducked under the inner cordon tape. After signing both herself and Queenie into the scene she followed the treads laid out by the crime scene investigators to avoid contaminating or damaging any possible evidence and headed towards their victim, who had been conveniently dumped by the side of the road.

Franny Gallagher, the crime scene manager, was standing beside the body as her team finished erecting the tent over it. 'Good to see you, Jazzy. How's the arm?'

'Och, you know? It's all right. Getting better.'

That wasn't strictly true. Her arm was still painful and she'd had an operation a fortnight ago to insert some pins to increase her eventual mobility. But she'd learned that showing weakness in this job was a sure-fire way to lose the respect of some of the more Neanderthal officers she had to work with – her boss, DCI Tony Dick, being a prime example of that. Although Franny wouldn't judge her, habit made Jazzy downplay her injury. 'What have we got, Franny?'

Before the CSI manager could respond, Queenie, huffing and puffing like a reluctant pig on a treadmill, joined them. Her face, nipped as it was by the hood elastic of her overall, looked like a scowling, whingeing turnip. One scary enough to frighten the life out of any bairn on Halloween.

'Bloody ice. Bloody criminals. What the hell were they thinking, dumping a body on the Lang Whang? You know, we might get away with palming it off on Lanarkshire. Keep those lazy sods busy for a change, eh?'

Queenie was right. This crime scene probably fell under Lanarkshire's remit, but with no physical boundary between the two police divisions at this point and the likelihood that this body was linked to ongoing Lothian and Borders investigations, it would be prudent for them to take the case.

'Two.' Franny looked from Jazzy to Queenie and back again.

15

'What?' Jazzy and Queenie had almost identical frowns on their faces.

Franny's eyes crinkled above her mask. 'There are *two* bodies. Did nobody tell you? There's another one less than a mile up the road.' She hesitated, then winked at Jazzy. 'And that one's *definitely* in Lothian. The paramedics have confirmed death but we're still waiting for Dr Johnston to arrive – he's at the other crime scene – so we've not moved either body yet. You know Lamond, he likes to be thorough, especially with suspicious deaths. Says that seeing them in situ can contribute to a stronger assessment of cause of death during the post-mortem.'

With a recent increase in bureaucracy after a couple of malpractice incidents, Jazzy couldn't blame him for being thorough. 'It's his signature on Form 11 at the end of the day.'

Medical Certificates of Cause of Death, commonly called Form 11, were subject to random review. However, that wasn't the reason Lamond Johnston was so particular about his work. Over the time she'd been working with the pathologist, Jazzy had learned that, like her, he felt a duty of care about the deceased. He'd confided that when someone's life had been snuffed out prematurely through an act of violence, it made him determined to use every scientific and forensic tool at his disposal to bring the culprit to justice. The fact that he – very subtly and briefly – employed the unscientific power of prayer, had initially made Jazzy uncomfortable, however, until she realised his few words of supplication before he commenced his examination were mostly to maintain his own sanity. They all had to cope with their trials in whichever way they could, after all.

With Queenie muttering and moaning beside her, Jazzy approached the body.

The deceased was male, maybe late teens or early twenties, wearing jeans and one of those oversized hoodies. The lad's clothes were stained – a combination of blood, muck and shit. Whether the kid had voided his bowels at time of death or beforehand would be ascertained during the post-mortem. After studying the position of the body as it lay on its side with its back to the road, Jazzy exhaled. 'Shoved from a moving vehicle you reckon, Franny?'

'That's my best guess.' She moved a few metres away from the body and pointed at some tyre tracks on the road. 'Here you can see evidence that the vehicle braked abruptly, but didn't completely stop. Then, presumably after pushing his nibs here out of the vehicle it accelerated again, leaving skid marks on the road. We've already processed the treads and sent them to the lab for identification. Hopefully, if you find a vehicle we'll be able to match it.'

'Any ideas on that?'

Franny grinned. 'You know that all of this is just educated guesswork at this stage, Jazzy.'

'I'll take anything to kick-start the investigation. We're pretty much going in blind at the moment. There's no CCTV in this area but we'll release an appeal, just in case someone happened to be out and about and saw something. So, until the PM is complete, anything you can offer might help.'

'Well, judging by the width of the treads, you're looking for a large car, but as I say until I've run the treads through our database, I can't be more specific than that. What I *can* tell you, though, is that the skid marks indicate that the vehicle was heading *towards* Carnwath, which tells us that the other victim was dumped first – just this side of the Wester Crosswood Hill Farm.'

Jazzy looked along the road and tried to visualise it. She'd seen the farm before and had a rough idea of where the first body had been dumped, but of course that prompted many questions. Why had no attempt been made to hide the bodies? It was almost as if the killer wanted them discovered sooner rather than later. Whilst Queenie jotted down the information, Jazzy crouched beside the boy. She sighed. 'What did you do to warrant this?' Although she couldn't tell which of the boy's injuries had been caused when he'd been rolled from the moving vehicle, she guessed that at least some of them would have been inflicted peri-mortem. What the hell was going on? Were these two more casualties from whatever war seemed to have spilled over into her territory from the two major cities in the area?

'Well, hallo, hallo, hallo, officers and forensic scientist, how are we today?' Dr Lamond Johnston approached them and, although his smile was obscured by his mask, the crinkly lines by his eyes showed he was smiling. Jazzy wouldn't have expected anything less from the pathologist. Lamond was an optimist and tried to bring that to his work, no matter how awful the scene he'd been called to was.

'Hi, doc. Just the man I wanted to see. I'm hoping you've got some information I can use. We need to ID the bodies to notify next of kin. Any thoughts?'

'Well, Jasmine, I've just been to the other crime scene.' He paused and met her eyes, his smile dulling as he continued, 'And before you ask, you can rest assured that a crime – murder to be specific – has been committed.'

Jazzy hadn't been in any doubt that this was an act of violence. In her years in policing she'd never come across anyone who'd fallen out of a moving vehicle by accident, never mind two people one after the other. If it had been accidental, then it would have been phoned in straightaway. However, Dr Johnston was a pedant who liked to dot his i's and cross his t's. As he studied his second corpse of the morning, he exhaled and then with a tut straightened his shoulders. 'My first impressions of this unfortunate young man indicate that he too has been the recipient of a severe and deadly beating prior to death.'

The pathologist made a quick cross sign before hunkering down onto one knee. It sometimes made Jazzy uncomfortable that he did that. She had been brought up by her aunt and uncle from the age of twelve and understood the power of faith to heal and soothe. It wasn't for her, though. The destructive force of religion – like that between her mum's Hindu family and her biological dad's Muslim one was not something she could ignore. And then in her job, she found it hard to reconcile the depravity she witnessed with belief in a higher being. Surely if there was a God, then these atrocities wouldn't happen?

'The other victim was quite a bit older than this one and, despite the facial bruising, I suspect you'll find they are related.' He glanced up at Franny. 'I think the other CSI team found ID in his back pocket as I was leaving.'

As he spoke, Franny's mobile vibrated. She opened an image of a driving licence and showed it to Jazzy.

'Marcus Jones? Any idea who he is?'

Chapter 2

Vengeance

I am Vengeance! Vengeance with a capital V.

I've not always considered myself that way, but, well, sometimes things happen and radical changes are necessary. I know it's a dramatic name – some might say over the top – and many of my acquaintances would be surprised because, despite my many faults, I've never been a flamboyant person, but that's how I consider myself now.

So much time has passed since it all began and in truth there are many stages to my story, all of which I want to share so that – just in case I leave it too late – it's all documented. I'll rest easy knowing this.

It was November last year when I realised I was actually going to go through with this. After all, when you've got nothing to lose, there's no real risk, is there? So, here we go . . . my story.

Before I embarked on this journey, I'd entertained visions of being made whole on my return to my homeland. I'd been convinced that an overwhelming warmth would suffuse me, body and soul, reassuring me that my decision to return wasn't based purely on hatred. That some iota of fondness lurked there deep inside me, awaiting this great reunion to be enacted, like a fledgling chick on its first solo journey. I'd hoped that the hollow void that had always occupied so much space in my heart and my head – a millstone weighing more than the sum of all my parts – would melt away. That the gnawing, festering rage would shatter and disperse into the ether with all my failed, fragile hopes and dreams, past and present.

What a bloody fool I was. What a bloody fool I am.

So much for that rush of familiarity washing over me the moment the plane hovered over the city of my birth. So much for those endless prayers that my broken heart would be miraculously mended. That I can be whole again, not the shell of a person masquerading as a human.

I allow my mind to take me back those few short months. I feel nothing as the plane descends. Not a sodding jot of emotion! Maybe it's because the view is obscured by clouds and rain, or maybe it's because I've never seen an aerial view of my home town before. I mean, the jet lag's bound to be playing its part, right? It's understandable, isn't it? Of course, a long-haul flight including two stopovers and two delays would set me off kilter. Then there's that indefinable apprehension that filled my gut before we even took off from Auckland all those hours ago. It still lies there, rotting inside me, as we circle the airport in ever-decreasing loops. It'd been slowly leaching into my stomach lining the entire journey – as tart as the rhubarb we used to dip, as kids, into our little cones of sugar as a treat, and as heavy as the massive tumshies Dad used to carve for Halloween.

With my insides churning, I avert my gaze from the window and stare straight ahead, uncomfortable with the memories of my past. A childhood of false promise and dubious safety. A childhood that had been happy – until it wasn't. That had been safe – until it wasn't. I slip the folded paper from between the pages of my book and, glancing round to make sure my fellow passengers aren't looking, I flip it open. It's tattered now after

21

being opened and closed like this so many times. Tears prick the backs of my eyelids and I inhale to stop them slipping from my eyes. That starts off the coughing.

Christ, just get a grip. Stop drawing attention to yourself.

Head bent, trying to stifle the racking coughs, I fold the paper, slip it back into my book and reach a shaking hand for my water bottle.

'You okay there, eh? You need some more water, like? I can ask the flight attendant, if you want?'

I shake my head and instead begin tapping the fingers of both hands against my thumbs one at a time, starting with my index fingers. One, two, three, four. Two, two, three four. Three, two, three, four. Four, two, three, four.

The bloke next to me misinterprets it as anxiety about the landing. 'It'll be okay. Don't worry. We're on the home stretch now.'

His accent is pure Glasgow and it adds to the sensation of me slowly losing my shit. The desire to punch his smiling, reassuring face is strong. I want to yell at him to mind his own sodding business. To remind him that he doesn't know me. Knows nothing about me. For all he knows I could be an axe murderer off on my jollies to disembowel a few Glaswegian nosy bastards. I paste my usual bland smile to my lips and resist the temptation to take my unfathomable rage out on him – but only just. Instead, I nod and turn my eyes back to the window, close them and keep up my slow, measured counting and tapping. One, two, three, four. Two, two, three four. Three, two, three, four. Four, two, three, four . . .

The air pressure changes as we begin our descent and my ears pop. I check my seatbelt and watch the tarmac loom closer and the airport vehicles grow larger. The plane judders as the wheels hit the runway at Glasgow International Airport and it begins its last few bumpy metres of my journey home. *This* is a significant moment, a pivotal one. I could disembark, stay the night in an airport hotel and forget all about my reasons for being here. I could take the next flight back to New Zealand. However, that ship has sailed. I smile at my mixed metaphors. Nothing like a good metaphor – especially a mixed one – to make the point, eh?

The jet glides to a standstill and my fellow passengers begin grabbing cabin bags and gathering up their things, desperate to make a speedy exit. I flick back to my earlier thoughts, managing a smile as the Glaswegian, oblivious of my nasty thoughts, passes me my small bag from the locker above. Being realistic, though, the main reason I'm so disconnected, so flat and emotionless, is probably a combination of everything I've just itemised in my mind's eye.

I'm one of the last to leave the plane and weariness makes my movements slow and laboured. I decline the flight attendant's offer of a wheelchair. My first steps back on Scottish soil will be on my own two feet, no matter how difficult that will be.

I finally reach the baggage reclaim area and prop myself against the wall as I wait for my luggage. I'm sweating and a little dizzy too, but there are no seats available. As I wait, the unflattened vowels and Glasgow burr that fills the concourse transports me back fifty years. No, it had been more than fifty years since I'd been back home. *Home?* Now there's a word I didn't think I'd ever use about Scotland. Not ever.

A smile twitches my lips. What's that they say? *You can take the wean out of Scotland, but you can't take Scotland out of the wean?* Well, I'd hung my hat on that one. Hell, I'd hung everything on that single – and in hindsight – fragile and completely unrealistic hope. I'd been ripped from Scotland yelling and screaming and transported halfway around the world. Yet, despite my current nostalgia, it felt like Scotland had been ripped from *me*. The dialect floods back like a long-lost lover returned to my bed. Even the folk are familiar – their gestures, their good-humoured chaff, their ready smiles and jokes – all of it is contagious. I'm too knackered to join in, too knackered to insert myself with my weird hybrid accent into their scenarios, even if I wanted to. Which I don't. It's like an alien culture – familiar only because

I've seen it on the TV or read about it or something. Not real. Not part of *me*. Not anymore.

A lad, basketball cap flipped backwards, glances at me from his plastic chair and within seconds he's jumping to his feet, grabbing my hand luggage and guiding me over to take his place on the flap-down seat. 'Here, sit yourself down there. Take the weight off your feet. They'll take forever to get the baggage carousel up and running, like.'

As I thank him and fall onto the seat, he smiles and nods before joining a group of youngsters a bit further down. I wonder what he sees when he looks at me. A grey-haired, pale, emaciated elderly tourist? Maybe I remind him of his grandparents? Maybe he thinks I've not got long for this world. I smile. He's not wrong there. I'll shuffle off this mortal coil before too long. But *not* before I've done what needs doing. Not before I've righted the wrongs – *all* of them. Those from fifty years ago *and* those more recent.

The Glasgow chill infiltrates right into the heart of the airport as I settle in for the long wait the lad promised. Pulling my jacket tight round my chest, I close my eyes, rest my head on the wall and allow my mind to wander. I've got four things to do before I die and I'm determined to complete all of them. Four obsessive aims that propelled me across the world and I will not fail in my quest. By the time I die, I will have found what's mine, taken my revenge, destroyed my enemies and committed at least one murder.

I *am* Vengeance.

Chapter 3

Unobserved, Loanie Gibbs studied his archenemy, Glasgow gangster Jimmy Nails, from across the restaurant. The tenuous semi truce that had existed for decades between the two had been going down the pan for months now and Loanie was determined to discover why. His bullshit radar told him that nothing was quite as it seemed. He could think of no inciting event that might have triggered such unwarranted violence from Jimmy's crew and he knew that whatever was behind the violence attributed to his Edinburgh gang, he hadn't sanctioned it, nor had any of his team. Which left him wondering if all the argy-bargy, and the deaths and violence were a skilfully engineered plan by an external force – a takeover bid to oust Jimmy in Glasgow and Loanie in Edinburgh.

Jimmy's family had been ruling the roost in Glasgow since the Seventies. Loanie's family, starting with his departed dad and followed by his uncle, Wee Frankie, had functioned the same way in Edinburgh. In fact, a deal between the two sides had been mutually beneficial until something happened that blew the whole lucrative pact in the air with both sides going their own ways. Although they avoided confrontation with each other within their cities, both had continued to grow their criminal enterprises throughout the rest of Scotland, the North of England and abroad.

There was no need for the pact to be broken. No need at all. Over the years, the younger generations on both sides had become more savvy and had on occasion rubbed shoulders when the financial benefits were high enough. Still, their mutual distrust ran too deep to withstand anything more than a transitory accommodation of the other's interests. Besides, it wasn't likely that Nails was leading this turf war. He had his own demons to deal with, having until recently been imprisoned. Word was that he'd come back to a shithouse of internal wrangles so the timing was wrong for him to go on the radge with Loanie. No, something else was afoot, and even though he hated doing it, Loanie had to reach out to his nemesis to find out what.

For all he'd not long been released from the Big Hoose, Jimmy Nails looked remarkably well. Loanie grinned. Amazing what a few sessions on a tanning bed could do to eradicate that uncooked jailhouse pallor. In fact, if he hadn't known the man, he'd have thought the wee Glasgow bawbag had just got back from the Maldives, not a four-year stretch in the Bar L.

They'd agreed to meet on neutral territory and the Inn on the Loch was an ideal location, besides which, their haggis burger was to die for. Jimmy had chosen a table facing out over Lanark Loch and now with it blowing a hoolie outside, whipping up the loch and sending ferocious ripples over its surface, it was a sight to behold. Not that Jimmy was watching the view – he was too engrossed in his phone.

Jimmy 'Hardass' Nails – as he liked to be called – had lost a bit of weight since Loanie had last seen him. That looked good on him too. But the swirls of grey threading through his dark hair indicated that it hadn't all been a walk in the park in Barlinnie for him. They were both in their fifties, so the salt-and-pepper look was also an age thing. Which was why Loanie shaved his off completely. He preferred to look the tough guy rather than the auld guy.

As Loanie pulled out a chair and slid into it, Jimmy glanced up and, in pure Glasgow, deadpanned, 'Thought you'd got cold

26

feet there, Lionel son. The amount of time you spent gawping at me before you came in made me wonder if you were feart?'

Loanie shrugged when Jimmy showed that his phone had been on selfie mode to check out his entrance. 'Aw, you're too smart for me, Jimmy. Too damn smart. So, what do you want to do first? Business or food?'

The lines on Jimmy's face deepened as he smiled. He shook his head. 'And what makes you think I want to break bread with you, Loanie Gibbs? After all, you and your little Edinbugger fuckers took advantage of my absence when I was in the nick, didn't you? Nah, man, this isn't a social occasion.' He smirked. 'It's not a bloody date, if that's what you think, with it being Valentine's Day and all. Nae chance.'

Loanie grinned. 'You're not my type, Jimmy.' He gestured to a passing server. 'Coffee please, son. Cappuccino, eh, extra sprinkles and one of your brilliant haggis burgers eh? Extra chips with that.'

When the server looked at Jimmy, he relented. 'Oh, go on, then, I might as well join you. Can't have you on your own on Valentine's Day now, can I? I'll have the homemade steak pie, please, extra gravy.'

The lad walked off with the menus, and Jimmy winked at Loanie. 'Nothing like a homemade steak pie to celebrate your freedom, is there?' He lifted his half of bitter and took a swig. 'What's with the cappuccino, Loanie? Extra sprinkles, tae? That how it is, eh? You going up in the world, like? You a cut above the rest of us now, eh? Bonnie tells me you're in Morningside now. Too posh for the likes of us, maybe?'

'Och away with you, man. That carry-on with your brother-in-law and nephew wasn't down to me, as well you know. That was . . .' he circled two fingers in the air '. . . shall we say a rogue enterprise among the ranks on both sides. Our break got dealt with, which is more than I can say for the break in your ranks, from what I've heard.'

'Aye, well, I've only just got out of the Big Hoose, but it's in hand. Nothing for you to worry your wee head about.'

Loanie shrugged and leaned forward, elbows resting on the table. 'But I *am* worried, Jimmy. This is bigger than what those wee toerags got up to. You do realise that don't you? It's like there's an orchestrated attack on us and on our businesses and I'm not entirely sure where it's coming from. On the one hand it seems arbitrary – like some Sassenachs are casting a net around, looking to snag themselves a big cash cow, and then on the other it's like it's . . .' he shrugged '. . . I don't know – targeted?'

'Aye, that's why I agreed to meet. We need to squash them like fucking ants before they get their nasty wee pincers up our arses.'

'So, we're agreed. It's some new outfit yanking our chains? Trying to set us off against each other so they can swoop in and take our businesses?'

'Aye, it seems that way. Putting aside the whole Ned and Dan business and your two stupid fucking cousins Tommy and Markie – and their nonsense – it's too organised. First one of your shipments goes missing and then one of my containers.'

'One of your blokes gets his knees capped, then a couple of my employees get duffed up.'

'Yeah, one of your illustrious establishments gets firebombed, then one of mine. It's too neat. Too premeditated. Definitely targeted.'

'You heard anything from the Glasgow end?'

Jimmy finished his beer then gestured for another. 'I'm hearing nothing. Getting heehaw from my sources, which is why I'm here. Since my time in the nick I'm persona non grata among our boys and girls in blue. Wondered if you still had any influence with the Edinburgh pigs? The Gaffer maybe?'

Loanie's snort was loud enough to draw the attention of a couple on the next table, but one look at the two men had them focusing back on their meals in no time. 'Fuck off. You're not serious? The Gaffer. No, that boat's long sailed. The Gaffer's retired and I'm the big man now.'

A gust of wind rattled the windows and Jimmy sighed. 'Well . . .'

'Aye, well . . . You know as well as I do that the reason you're here is to reinstate that fucking agreement from when we were weans. We're both struggling to keep on top of things. Both struggling to work out if it's the bloody Scousers or the Geordies. Hell, I'm worried it might even be the Aberdonians. We need to work together on this.'

'Aye, you got that right. You don't think it seems personal, do you? I mean, if I was wanting to expand my business enterprise, I'd look towards Dundee, or maybe even Aberdeen. Neither Gordy Mac in Dundee nor Alfie in the granite city are as tight as we are. It'd be easy to usurp their contacts.'

'I don't think this is going to be solved in the short term, Jimmy. I think we'll need to be hypervigilant and tighten our inner circle to weed out the weak links. Whoever is doing this, they're like a corbie mithering a dead rat. It won't give up till there's no meat left on the bones.'

The server set two steaming plates before them and Loanie unwrapped his cutlery from the napkin. 'Well, fingers crossed this tit-for-tat shite isn't a bad omen, Jimmy. But, if I'm honest, it feels like it is. You know that Hitchcock film, *The Birds* – well, that started off with just a few crows, didn't it and look how that ended.'

'Aye, everybody covered in bird shite and a whole load of dead bodies.'

Chapter 4

'Noooo!' Queenie's response to seeing Marcus Jones's name on the driving licence of victim number one sounded more distraught than sorrowful. A beetroot flush flashed over Queenie's round face as she jiggled on the spot like she desperately wanted to run from the scene, climb into her Land Rover and head back to the station.

Jazzy frowned and laid her hand on Queenie's arm. 'You know him, Queenie?'

Lifting a shaking hand, Queenie yanked at her tight-fitting hood and nodded. 'Aye, I know him and let me tell you, if the body up the road really is him, then a planeload of shite is about to land on our heads.' Wafting a hand in front of her bright red face she glared at Jazzy. 'Should've hammered on the bog door when we got the call, like I told you. Should've sent Haggis or Geordie in to drag Dick away from his "me time". Should've got Hobson to make an announcement over the tannoy, but, oh no, *you* wanted to get back in the action.' Her glare intensified. 'Well, let me tell you, JayZee Solanki, never have I been more disappointed in one of our Jazz Queens. No' even that wee Smurf Haggis has disappointed me as much.'

'Eh, I think you'll find it was me who made all those suggestions, Queenie, and *you* were the one who vetoed every one of them.

In fact, you were so keen to get out of the station that you ver' near yanked my good arm from its socket.'

Queenie shrugged. 'Aye well, let's no' split hairs, eh? We'll agree to dual responsibility on this, is that no' right?' She paused. 'Unless Dick's likely to sack me. In which case you'll have to take sole blame. After all, you *are* the sergeant these days.'

That was the most Jazzy could hope for from Queenie, so she moved on. 'Who the hell is Marcus Jones?'

'Marcus, goes by Markie, is Loanie Gibbs's cousin. A wee tyke from Edinburgh. Not one of Loanie's most dependable employees, but, well, he is family. This could be more of the crap that's already going down.'

Now it made sense. Jazzy had come across Lionel, or Loanie as he was known, Gibbs on a case last year when they'd discovered he'd once been wrongly suspected of murder. Loanie was a bigwig in the Edinburgh underworld. The question was, would he intensify the violence in response? That would definitely exacerbate the ongoing wars between Edinburgh and Glasgow. Loanie would suspect the Glasgow Nails family and violence was bound to escalate. Of course, she'd suspected these two murders were gang-related. Most crimes in the area were these days. She just hadn't expected the victims to be this high-profile. 'How close are Loanie and Markie?'

'Aye, well, that's where I'm not entirely sure. Markie's older than Loanie, but he's a bit of a daft bugger – or rather he was. He's always been on the periphery of anything major. Do anything for a quick buck, but certainly not the mastermind. Nah, after his dad, Wee Frankie, stood down, Loanie took over and rumour has it neither Markie nor his brother Tommy, who's a good bit younger than Markie, were right bothered by that. They still got their lifestyles but no pressure. Still, family is family, isn't it?'

Franny had remained silent, but now she pointed to the younger, yet unidentified victim. 'You reckon that's the younger brother, Tommy?'

Queenie, holding her breath, leaned over to view the victim close up. Springing up, she backed away from the body, hand clamped over her mouth. She made a few gippy sounds, but shut her eyes and managed to control the reflex to hurl all over the scene. Poking her chubby fingers under the elastic of her hood, she dragged it off and took another few deep breaths. 'It's been a while since I had the pleasure, right enough, but aye, that looks like Tommy. Same colouring and they do look alike.'

Jazzy leaned close to Queenie and lowered her voice. 'Well done, you did that without a single vomit. Now, off you go, back to the car and phone Fenton and Geordie to be ready when we get back. Get them to run the driver's licence through the database. I don't want to do a death notification without being certain. I won't be long, but we should just run by the other crime scene to touch base, and we can do that on our way back to the station.'

Chapter 5

Rather than update her immediate superior DCI Dick, Jazzy chose to update the chief super, Afzal, telling herself that because Afzal had directed her to the scene, it was only right that she feed back to him. That she chose to engage with her biological dad – with whom she still had several unresolved issues – rather than her line manager was telling. To give him his due, he didn't insist on her reporting to Dick directly.

Jazzy suspected that despite the work her team had already started, they would once more be edged out of the action in favour of A or B team. Dick was nothing if not predictable in his hostility towards Jazzy and her team. For now, though, she would focus her energies on progressing the investigation as efficiently as possible.

With today's murders spilling into Lothian, the division would have to be more vigilant. Who knew what Loanie Gibbs or Wee Frankie Jones's response on hearing about the deaths of their cousins and sons would be? In view of the ongoing open investigations in Lothian, South Lanarkshire had agreed to waive their claim to the murder of Markie Jones. Although it was the logical decision, they seemed a wee bit *too* keen to pass the baton. Not her problem, though.

With the IDs confirmed, Jazzy was keen to keep the deceased men's identities from the press until the next of kin, Frankie Jones, had been notified, and she wanted to do that as soon as possible. That breathing space gave those higher up the chain of command more time to determine their strategy. *Good luck with that.* For now, though, Jazzy had her team gathering background information on the victims and canvassing for dashcam footage or sightings of a large vehicle. DC Fenton Heggie was trolling through both Markie and Tommy's social media accounts, whilst DC Geordie McBurnie was battling with the phone companies for access to their records to plot their last known whereabouts. The post-mortem was scheduled for later in the afternoon and, if DCI Dick didn't show up before then, Jazzy would attend it.

Jazzy was scrutinising the results filtering through from the lab when the incident room door crashed against the wall, making everyone jump. DCI Dick swept towards her, his eyes flashing and his moustache quivering at the prospect of a confrontation. The wind was taken from his sails when, at a more sedate pace, the chief super followed him into the room and took over.

Afzal looked tired. His ready smile was absent and the salt and pepper of his hair seemed more salt than pepper. Deep grooves lined his brow and his shirt hung loosely from his shoulders. Jazzy averted her gaze, busying herself with her computer work. It had been only a couple of months since he'd tried to rekindle their relationship. She'd told him then that she could never forgive him for the hell he'd left her in. How could she? Without a backward glance, he'd left her to the mercy of an abusive alcoholic mother and now he wanted to build bridges, make her part of his family, introduce her to his wife and daughter?

Yes, Jazzy had done her research on DCS Afzal's perfect family – the one that *didn't* include her. It had been hard looking at the online images of him with his arm round his beautiful and successful paralegal wife, gazing adoringly at their equally radiant teenage daughter, *her* half-sister. *God how many half-siblings can one girl rack up?* How could they possibly accept her into their lives? A damaged woman with few social skills and a chequered past. They'd run a crooked mile. The only reason he'd connected with her now was because some twist of fate had brought them together when she joined Police Scotland and she had no intention of inflicting herself on his shiny new family. No intention of making her parentage public knowledge and no intention of forgiving him. Still, Jazzy would work with him, for she was always the consummate professional.

However, their acceptance of *her* wasn't the main issue. It was her father's betrayal that she couldn't let go. It burned in her mind every time she saw him, prompting her to wonder if he was as perfect as he portrayed. Chief Super Afzal raised his voice and smiled, making eye contact with each of them. Jazzy's cynicism won out as she stubbornly refused to meet his gaze. *Your Mr Nice Guy act doesn't wash with me, matey.*

'Firstly, I'd like to thank you all for your work on this case so far. In Tony's absence, DS Solanki stood up to the mark at short notice and got this investigation moving forward. As you know Police Scotland are up against it at the moment. Finances are tight and this ongoing war between the Edinburgh and Glasgow gangs is taking its toll.'

He cleared his throat and perched on the edge of Geordie's desk. 'That said, DCI Dick – Tony – reminded me that Jazzy is still in recovery after the recent operation on her injured arm and that the rest of D team are still undergoing counselling following incidents in December. With that in mind, I have only one choice. It's with reluctance that I'm splitting the team up on a temporary basis and diverting DCs McBurnie and Heggie to A and B teams, whilst Jazzy and Queenie manage the day-to-day public interface from the office.'

Jazzy jumped to her feet, her face flushed. She glared at DCI Dick, eyes flashing, uncaring if he recognised the extent of her anger, then directed her venom towards Afzal. 'You can't—'

Before she could end her sentence, he cut her off, his tone curt, his face uncompromising. 'I can and I have.'

He stood, and left the room without a backward glance, leaving a stunned silence in his wake. His words were like a slap in the face. So much for wanting to build bridges – it seemed Afzal was much better at tearing them down. *That* was his special talent.

The dickless wonder stared at her, fiddling with his moustache, daring her to push him a little more. But Jazzy was too savvy for that. This was yet another lesson learned. Her birth father was not to be trusted. Not as her father and *not* as her boss.

'So . . .' Dick had the audacity to rub his hands together like a gleeful gnome, as he addressed the chastened little group. 'Heggie you're on B team. McBurnie, you can pirouette along in your stilettos to A team.'

Geordie's face reddened. 'If that's a reference to something I do in my personal life, sir, then I want it noted that I take offence. Derogatory remarks like that are against policy.'

Dick looked him up and down, eyes narrowed. 'Really? You're taking offence at a turn of phrase? Get a grip and man up. We've no time for this – we've got criminals to catch.'

Jazzy, bristling for a fight, moved to stand beside Geordie as did Queenie and Fenton. 'Actually, sir, that *is* offensive and clearly a reference to Geordie being a drag artist. I suggest you think very carefully before using such comments in the future or we'll have no option but to put a complaint into human resources.'

Dick glared at the quartet of officers. 'You continue with this sort of antagonism towards a senior officer and *I'll* have no option but to issue my own formal complaint.'

He spun on his heel and headed from the room, pausing by the door to issue one final jibe. 'Looks like your hold on the chief super is loosening, Solanki. If I were you, I'd be careful. Very careful.'

Chapter 6

Vengeance

I shove a painkiller in my mouth and take a long swallow of the single malt I bought in the Scotmid earlier. That had been a fiasco. I'd still been out of it after my treatment and should have stayed home. But I needed the fresh air on my face – to feel alive. For Christ knows, I'm not long for this world, so it makes sense to make the most of every second I've got. I can feel the cancer eating into me every day and I'm exhausted most of the time. The desire for revenge carries its own powerful energy and as well as all the preparations I made prior to my return to Scotland, I've managed to set many things in place since being here. My focus wavers between being razor sharp and being wrapped in cotton wool, but I play to my strengths and maximise the times when my brain is running on full power.

I'm lucky, I guess. If my circumstances had been different, I wouldn't have been able to do this. I'd have died a dried-out old prune, filled with self-hatred and unable to redeem myself. It's quite amazing what you can do when you've got money to smooth the process.

That wee fainting spell in Scotmid has made me more visible, though, and I can't work out if it will be my saving grace or if that little slip will cost me dearly. From my comfy armchair, positioned just so I can see out the living-room window to the houses across the street, I can see the Land Rover that brought me home. The woman driving it insisted. 'I'm parked just behind the shop. We can manage. We'll do it nice and slow. I'll get you to my car and then I'll drive you home.' Her concerned chatter had made me smile.

'I've seen you before, in your window. You live opposite me.'

She was gruff but kind and so I gave in. It was like I already knew her – well, in some small way I did. I'd been watching her and her family for weeks now.

'Come on now, I insist. Wouldn't hear of you getting a taxi. Not when I live nearby.'

I was glad of the lift, but at the same time I wished we hadn't connected. Now I've found myself obsessed with seeking out movement in her home – laughing at the wee lassie's tantrums, smiling at the way her husband snatches a kiss over the top of their child's head. It's bittersweet. Like watching a video of how my life should have been and I'm vicariously reframing my past through her. Makes me regret the breakdown in my relationship with my own child. Then, I dismiss my maudlin thoughts and focus on the information I've just received. It's done. A major escalation that just can't be ignored. It's exciting and very, very exhausting.

After the notification arrived, adrenalin swept through me, bolstering me. Now, though, as it drains away, I'm shaky and weak. I want to curl up in bed, pull the duvet over my head and block out everything – just for a while – till the nausea has gone. Instead, I pull up the images I've been sent. At every step of the way I require proof positive. I've learned the hard way that blind trust can be treacherous and although my money has supposedly 'bought' their trust, I won't take it for granted.

I don't get off on the pictures of the two dead men. I targeted them to send a message and because I've seen the abuse they've already been responsible for – two chips off the old block, but with none of their father's brains. I'm not doing this because I enjoy violence. I've never been a violent person. Well, only really towards myself and only when things got too much for me and I hit that self-destruct button. However, I do feel duty-bound to look at each of them. It's only polite considering I ordered their deaths. I consider it a necessary evil that serves to keep me in touch with reality. At a push, I could have forced myself to be present for the torture, but why? Those men mean nothing to me and their deaths only push my cause forward.

Maybe it was weakness that made me instruct them to go ahead in my absence? Some would say that the desire to keep my distance – to sanitise myself – from the evil I've ordered is self-preservation and I tend to agree. After all, they are being paid well for their work. Others, no doubt, would accuse me of wanton disregard for humankind. My answer would be that humankind gave up on *me* a long time ago. Why should I succumb to softness when I have a bigger picture in mind? I'm not a great saviour. I know that, but I *am* prepared to go the extra mile to stop the cycle of depravity that has prevailed for over half a century.

The photos are worse than I imagined – bloodier and more graphic, taken from all angles. I suppose my contractors think they gave me my money's worth, but the *degree* of suffering is irrelevant. It's the final product I'm interested in and they reassure me that my orders have been carried out. The mercenaries have completed their side of the bargain and that makes me optimistic for our continued relationship.

As I close the images, I'm relieved to extinguish the sight of so much suffering and pain. My sympathy must lie with the innocent, not those two pieces of vermin. Before long none of the guilty will know who to trust and that will make my plans so much easier to navigate. They won't suspect me. Why would they? I'm not on their radar. An anonymous threat taking jab after jab at them – they'll be spinning on their heels.

I open my email and pause to consider what my next communication will say. This is my chance to ensure that my message has been driven home and it's important it arrives before they find out exactly what I've done. I have it. My fingers are swollen and clumsy with all the meds being pumped into me. Every word is an effort to type, but I do it with a light heart.

Subject: Vengeance is coming for you!

Hi Frankie,

Long time, no see. I would offer my condolences for your loss, but that would be hypocritical.

   However, thought you might like to see what was done to your boys in the name of Vengeance. Check out the attachments. Expect a visit. Expect the worst and expect more of the same, for I AM VENGEANCE and I'm coming for you!

Chapter 7

Silence followed the departure of the two senior officers. It was Jazzy's job to rally her team, but right then, all she wanted to do was scream. She exhaled and counted to ten. 'All right, you lot, I know we're all a wee bit shellshocked, but you know, it might not be as bad as we think.'

'What the hell are you talking about?' Queenie slumped into her chair and glowered at Jazzy. 'Those bampots are splitting up the Jazz Queens. What could be worse than that?'

Whilst Geordie, for once not vetoing the Jazz Queen tag, nodded, Fenton looked vacantly into space, as if dissociated from what had just gone on. *Has the news floored him completely?* The lad found it difficult to meet new people and he and Geordie had become close over the short time they'd worked together. Fenton was a brilliant IT expert, which any team would be lucky to have. Besides, they wouldn't be working on different planets. She squeezed his arm. 'It's only temporary, Fenton.'

Startled, he jumped and blinked up at her. But before he could respond Queenie butted in, her voice wavering. 'Aye so *you* say, JayZee, but you know as well as I do that these things have a habit of becoming permanent. It's not like Dick's going to be mad keen on letting us work together when your arm recovers. He wants us out. We're like bugs in his bed – irritants, vermin he wants to exterminate, cockroaches to be annihilated.'

Geordie shuddered. 'Eh, you can't actually annihilate cockroaches, Queenie. They're indestructible.'

'That's my point, son. *We're* going to be the cockroaches. We're going to have to be indestructible. Forget the wishy-washy Jazz Queens, we're the Cockroaches. *That's* our new name. That's what we'll call ourselves until we're reunited as D team.'

Scratching his arms and then his legs, Geordie shook his head. 'Nah, that doesn't work for me, Queenie. Can't stand beasties. Spiders, flies, ants – hate them all, but especially cockroaches. I mean, have you even seen the size of them? And those sticky-out bits on the top of their heads? And the way they skitter about as soon as the light goes on.'

His scratching intensified. 'Nah, I'm happy to stick with the Jazz Queens. I'm comfortable being a queen, jazz or otherwise, but definitely no' a cockroach.'

Name aside, Queenie had a point. They'd have to fight to be reunited as D team and that would involve some covert machinations. Jazzy cleared her throat. 'Right, we're stuck with the decision for now, but that doesn't mean there's not a way back. I mean, what's the single biggest problem facing us right now?'

With his trouser leg pulled up to the knee, Geordie applied aloe vera cream to his self-inflicted scrapes. 'The bloody war between the Edinburgh and Glasgow gangs.'

'Aye, that's right, and if us four make a sizeable contribution to ending this, then nobody can say we're ineffective. Nobody can label us the dunces anymore.'

Queenie rubbed her hands together. 'Now you're talking, gal. What have you got in mind?'

Jazzy hesitated as an idea began to form. 'You two' – Jazzy pointed to Fenton and Geordie – 'will be right in the middle of the investigation, whilst me and Queenie are sidelined, which means we're in a prime position to set the Jazz Queens up as a sort of covert operation working behind enemy lines.'

Still allowing the idea to roll, Jazzy grinned at her colleagues. 'Fenton and Geordie will divert any useful information – any anomalies that you reckon are being ignored by your respective new teams – to me and Queenie. We'll follow up alongside doing the paperwork shite that Dick will pile on.'

Geordie began pacing the room, whilst Fenton looked like he was on Mars not in Bonny Scotland. 'Aye, I think that'll work and then we can meet up at yours or Queenie's when we need to. Preferably Queenie's because Craig always has food in. What do you reckon, Fent?'

Fenton jolted and looked at his mate. 'Eh, aye. Okay. Whatever you think.' Then he retreated inside his head as the others discussed the various avenues they wanted to explore.

Finally, plans made and future actions decided, Queenie frowned and glared at Fenton. 'Hey, you, Haggis, you've not contributed your usual pointless drivel to the conversation yet. Come to think of it, you've got a face like a slapped arse and it's been like that since before all this shite with Afzal and Dick. What's up? Something bothering my wee Haggis? Come on noo, son, you can tell Queenie.'

She moved closer and raked her beady eyes over his face. 'Aw no, it's bad, isn't it? Dinnae tell me, that supermodel you've been dating has dumped you, has she?'

Fenton huddled further over his laptop and ignored Queenie, but if he expected *that* to deflect her, he was mistaken. Jazzy grabbed Queenie's arm and shook her head, warning her to leave it well alone. But Queenie was on a roll.

'Got herself a wee date with some actor, has she? Not that wee Martin Compston, I hope. He's far too short for her.' She clicked her fingers. 'Aw, but wait a minute, are you and Compston no' aboot the same height?' Finger tapping her top lip, she frowned. 'But, nah, it cannae be him. I'm sure he's married.' She looked at Geordie. 'He married, do you know? That Martin Compston from *Line of Duty*, is he hitched?'

Geordie shrugged, fingers working his phone. 'Google says he's five foot seven. That's not short.'

Queenie snorted. 'Here speaks the Gangly Green Giant. How tall are you? Like eight feet tall or something?'

Geordie grinned. 'It's Jolly.'

'What? What's jolly? Nobody here's in the slightest bit jolly, son. Read the damn room.' She flung her arm wide to encompass everyone and sent a full cup of coffee flying off the table onto the floor.

With a sigh Geordie grabbed a kitchen roll and began to mop up the mess. 'The Green Giant – he's jolly not gangly.'

'Aye, but you *are* gangly. You can't deny it. You're on the lanky side, So, how tall are you?'

'If you're that interested, I'm six foot three. About half a foot taller than Jazzy and about three feet taller than you.'

'Don't you gi' me that cheek, son. I'm a solid five foot four.'

Jazzy cleared her throat.

Arms in the air, Queenie tutted. 'All right, all right, I'm five foot one and a half, okay? You all bloody happy now, making a point of mentioning my lack of height when the laddie's in turmoil? Insensitive bastards that you are.'

Fenton lifted his head, a slight frown marring his brow as he glared at Queenie. 'She's not dumped me. God, if only that was all it was.'

Queenie lowered her voice. 'Is it something sexual? Is she into some weird fetish? Because I once had a boyfriend who . . .'

With Geordie and Jazzy now making no attempt to hide their laughter, Fenton rolled his shoulders, all bristly and indignant. 'No, it's not that. And even if it was that, I wouldn't share it with you lot.'

Queenie put both hands over her heart. 'I'm hurt. Wounded to the core. Course you'd confide in us. We're your mates, why wouldn't you?'

Jazzy could think of many reasons, but she was rather enjoying the show, so she sauntered over to Geordie and settled in to watch as Queenie persevered.

'So, don't keep us in suspenders, Haggis. None of this leaving us dangling on a thread of anticipation. Keeping us on our tippy-toes with excitement. What's the problem? Just spit it right oot and your Auntie Queenie will sort it.'

With a huge intake of breath, Fenton puffed his chest out, exhaled and got to the crux of the issue. 'Rebecca wants to get married.'

Queenie groaned and slapped the desk with her palm. 'Aw, no! I'm sorry about that, son. What a way to dump someone, eh? Telling them you're getting wed to someone else? That's just rubbing the dog's balls in salt, isn't it?'

Geordie sniggered. 'She wants to get married to *him*.'

'Eh, really? She wants to wed oor wee Haggis?' Queenie's face contorted like a deflating balloon. 'Now *that's* a right dilemma you've got yourself there. I mean, how old are you? Like nineteen? No *way*, do you want to get hitched at nine . . .'

'I'm twenty-five.'

'Aye, like I was saying, there's no way you want to get hitched at twenty-five. If I was you I'd dump her. I mean, I always thought she wasn't good enough for you.'

The scowl faded from Fenton's face. 'Really? You think I'm too good for her.'

Geordie groaned and Jazzy bit her lip, waiting for Queenie's punchline to hit.

'Are you bloody mad? Course I'm not serious, you absolute numpty. She's bloody gorgeous and she's far too good for you.'

Fenton's draw dropped, his bottom lip trembling.

'But . . . you clearly love her and from what my Spidey sense told me at Christmas, the woman – God alone knows why – clearly loves you. So, just get hitched, eh? Go shopping for a nice wee – not too wee, mind – engagement ring. Drop on one knee

45

in a fancy restaurant and pop the question. You know deep down that's what you really want to do. It's no' bloody rocket science.'

Fenton bit his lip, his face scrunched up in concentration, looking like he was about twelve, not twenty-five, and then he nodded. 'Aye. You're right, Queenie. Dead right. I do love her and she loves me, so what am I getting all het up about? I'll do it. I'll bloody do it. I'll pop the damn question.'

Queenie, a tear in her eye, leaned over and hugged him. 'Oh, you've got me all emosh with your nonsense. But congratulations, you and that lanky bint will make a lovely – if a wee bit lopsided – couple.' She flattened his hair with her hand and pinched his cheeks. 'But for now, can you no' just sit down and focus? We've got plans to put into action.'

Chapter 8

Loanie nursed his whisky as Wee Frankie sat silent beside him on the couch. The fifty-inch TV blared some inconsequential crap about life in a US penitentiary. When the plods came to give the death notice – all false solicitude and eyes everywhere, checking out Frankie's gaff like they expected blocks of cocaine or packets of pills to be scattered around – Loanie hadn't known how Frankie would react. He'd half expected the wee man to go ballistic, but his uncle had surprised him. After agreeing to formally ID the bodies, he'd ushered them out the door with a quiet, 'Thank you.' He hadn't even asked what had happened to the lads. He seemed content to know they'd been discovered on the Lang Whang, but hadn't asked for specifics. The gormless wee police nyaffs had stood half-smiling, unable to fully conceal their pleasure that another two thugs had bitten the dust. Loanie had been itching to get in their smug faces and bombard them with questions. But Frankie had shut the door in their faces and turned to him. 'I think a wee dram's in order, son.'

Like it was any other bog-standard day, Frankie poured them both a whisky, plonked himself down in his favourite spot on the reclining sofa and flicked through channels on the telly. It was almost as if this news wasn't a surprise to him. As if he'd known about it. Or at the very least, expected it. But that couldn't be right. Maybe he was in shock. Maybe it hadn't registered with him that Markie and Tommy were dead. He sneaked a glance at his uncle, wondering how the older man could be so calm in the face of the news he'd just received.

Drink cradled in his hands, Frankie shook his head as the US penitentiary governor on the TV waxed lyrical about the way the prisoners were offered training, allowed privileges, treated well. 'Aye, that'll be right, son. You'll be telling us next the tooth fairy's real. That not right, Lionel? That them Yank gangbangers are treated like royalty in there? I don't think so. Nae bloody chance.'

'Frankie, do you not want to talk about Tommy and Markie? About what happened to them?'

Frankie shrugged. 'What's there to say, son? We've got enemies. You know that. Like the rest of us, Tommy and Markie skirted outside the rules and that gave them a good life – wads of money, plenty of high jinks, benefit of all the good things in life, top-notch cars, classy women, decent houses and now they've had their comeuppance. Thing is, Lionel, the life choices we've made over the years, the things we've done, the people we've wronged – all of that has made every one of us a target. I'm surprised I got to this age without my chickens being brought home to roost.' He sipped his whisky, took the cigar from behind his ear and sniffed it before returning it to its place. 'I'm sad. Course I am. They were my boys, and when you've seen the things I've seen, you live your life half expecting shite to happen. It's karma, that's what it is, and there's nothing we can do about it.' He flicked through the channels until he landed on a cartoon featuring a cat and a yellow bird, and began laughing like he'd not a worry in the world.

Loanie was unconvinced. There was something odd about Frankie's reaction. His explanation, whilst logical, didn't ring true. The Frankie of a decade ago – not even that long – a few years ago, would have already been phoning the boys, sussing out the word on the street, tracking down the bastards who'd done him and his family wrong and slaughtering them. This Frankie was new. All this shite about karma was completely uncharacteristic. Frankie was a fighter – a boxer, for Christ's sake. He'd never roll over and allow a wrong to go unavenged and especially not the murder of his two sons – his own blood.

With the telly in the background Loanie tried to figure out what was going on. Had someone got to him? Maybe one of the gangs that were already causing them so much grief? Christ, Loanie had heard they were tough bastards. Maybe they'd cut Frankie in but only if he'd sacrifice something and, let's face it, Markie and Tommy were about as much use as a butter knife at a fight. Neither of them contributed to the business, so, from a business perspective, they were the logical sacrificial lambs. Would Frankie really betray the Gaffer by offing his sons for the sake of earning more dosh from another gang? They'd worked together for years. It was the Gaffer's business acumen that kept their enterprise raking in the cash through recession after recession. 'Junkies always need their fix and perverts always want to get laid' was the Gaffer's mantra. If Frankie had chosen the path of betrayal at this late stage, then that was a worry.

Maybe it wasn't one of the new gangs though. Maybe Frankie had thrown his lot in with Jimmy Nails. That made more sense in some ways. Frankie might have decided the Gaffer was weakening and that Loanie wasn't up to the job. Hell, maybe that's why he retired in the first place, so he could set up an alternative partnership. Loanie replayed his earlier meeting with Jimmy Nails. There hadn't been a whiff of deceit from the other man – although Loanie knew better than to leave his back exposed. Still, he'd thought they'd reached a détente where they'd work together on a temporary basis to protect their mutual interests.

The last option was worrying. What if Frankie had ordered the hit himself? What if he'd decided to lop off the dead wood to fund his retirement? What if he was using all the rest of the crap going on to gradually get rid of his liabilities? Then another thought, worse than the previous, struck. What if the Gaffer and Frankie had come up with this plan together? What if they were behind the entire shebang? If they'd ordered all the violence? Now, *that* was a distinct possibility. Perhaps they'd decided to reel in their assets and skip ship.

Loanie sipped his whisky. It was too early for him and its bitterness was like acid going down his throat. Something was off and he wasn't entirely sure who he could trust. The man sitting next to him had been his mentor since he was twelve and the idea that he might not be able to rely on his uncle saddened him.

He thought about his cousins. They'd grown up together. Been best mates, and even if Frankie couldn't summon up a tear for them, Loanie felt their loss. They were kin. *His* kin and, when your kin were slaughtered, you did something about it. A blood killing required revenge and the fact that Frankie hadn't mentioned that was worrying. That he wasn't planning payback already and that he was giggling away to bairns' cartoons on the box when his two sons lay in body bags, angered him. Loanie glanced sideways at his uncle. Frankie was focused on the cartoon, the silence between them disturbed only by an occasional laugh. Maybe he was doing his uncle a disservice. Perhaps Frankie *was* planning it. Perhaps he'd already set wheels in motion. He might have known they were dead even before the pigs arrived.

Loanie set his glass down and tried to convince himself that the auld boy – despite his earlier talk of karma and such like – was on top of things. But the more he sat and the more his uncle watched mindless TV, the more the rage which Loanie mostly kept bottled up began to fizz and ignite.

Frankie might not be sharing things with him, but he wasn't the only one who could keep secrets. He wasn't the only one who could make plans, he wasn't the only one with contacts to watch his back and he certainly wasn't the only who could be ruthless. Loanie would bide his time. He'd collect information, he'd keep an eye on the Gaffer *and* Frankie. He'd get to the bottom of this and, if the Gaffer and Frankie were culpable, then he'd make sure they knew the real meaning of revenge. And if Jimmy Nails was playing him then he'd pay too.

Chapter 9

Exhausted by everything that had happened that day, Jazzy flopped back in the chair by her desk and inhaled. Today had been difficult emotionally as well as physically. Every time she moved her arm, a sharp piercing pain assaulted it. Removing her sling at the crime scene earlier had been a mistake. She should have put it back on after donning her crime scene suit. *Woulda, shoulda, coulda, Jazz.*

She wanted to go home, run a hot, therapeutic bubble bath and soak in it till the painkillers kicked in, then go to bed with a wheatie and Winky purring beside her. That wasn't in her immediate future, though. She had something to do before she left work and then, afterwards, she had one of her scheduled visits with her brother at the State psychiatric hospital in Carstairs and she dreaded both things. Her friend, DI Elliot Balloch, as per their carefully constructed protocol for such visits, would accompany her. So, for once, her temporary chauffeur, Queenie, had been able to go home alone.

Using her good arm, Jazzy pulled her chair closer to the computer and signed into her work email. As she waited for them to load, she held her breath, dreading seeing the one that was certain to be there. *How had things come to this?*

Before Christmas, Jazzy and her team had investigated a series of murders that ended up being the work of a serial killer. Even worse she turned out to be Jazzy's half-sister, working with her twin brother Simon. Whilst Simon had been apprehended, diagnosed as clinically insane and was now safely incarcerated. Jazzy's sister Mhairi had escaped.

With Mhairi – whom Jazzy now referred to only as the Bitch – still at large, and Simon claiming to have information he would share only with his older sister, the task force, named Operation Birchtree, had reached out to Jazzy. She'd wanted to put the whole sorry thing behind her, but, until the Bitch was behind bars, she and her friends would not be entirely safe. With little option and despite her mixed feelings, Jazzy had agreed to weekly meetings with Simon to try to extract information, with the proviso that Elliot accompany her.

And then there was this. The Bitch took great pleasure in contacting her sister at regular intervals. Although she'd been expecting it, Jazzy's shoulders tensed, sending a deep, sharp pain through her biceps when she saw it. The very innocuous subject heading made it even more chilling.

Subject: Say hi to Simon from me!

There was no need for Jazzy to open it. Regular as clockwork, within an hour – two hours tops – of her arranged meeting with her brother an email from the serial killer would pop into her inbox. She'd no need to inform the team – after the first one arrived in January, the IT team had been granted access to Jazzy's account and they monitored it. Each email's VPN was encrypted and bounced around the world like a Spacehopper on speed and, to date, the only useful information they'd gained from the communications was that Simon still had contact with his partner in crime.

Of course, they'd vetted the staff at Simon's facility, interviewed his lawyer, scrutinised other patients' visitors and searched his room for any communications means. Each time they'd come up with nothing and the emails kept coming in, regular as clockwork. The Bitch had developed a means of communication either with Simon or with someone involved on the task force, the hospital or Jazzy's team and they were no closer to identifying the leak.

With her finger hovering over the mouse, debating whether to open the email or not, Jazzy was unaware of Elliot entering the room until the familiar scent of his aftershave registered. She kept her eyes on the screen as he slid into the seat beside her. 'Go on, Jazz. No point in waiting. You might as well see what she says.'

Jazzy half turned towards him. A frown furrowed his brow. Tension radiated from his tight-lipped smile to the clenched fist that rested on the desk. 'When's this going to be over, Elliot? When will this end? When someone I love is dead? Is that when?'

Elliot exhaled and shook his head. 'God only knows. This must be torture for you.'

Jazzy swallowed the lump that was in her throat. She'd known Elliot since he'd rescued her when he was on his first day on the job and she was a kid. Somehow, they became inextricably linked. Apart from her adoptive parents, her aunt and maternal uncle, Elliot had been the only other person she trusted implicitly – until she inherited D team. Now, with even more people to feel responsible for, the burden of keeping them all safe was sometimes too much for her. 'Let's just not go today, Ell. Let's not give them the satisfaction of seeing me dance to their tune. I'm not a puppet. I never have been and I won't be theirs.'

Even as she said the words she was aware she was kidding no one. Elliot knew her too well. If there was the slightest chance that enduring a weekly hour of purgatory would bring the Bitch to justice and end this debacle, then Jazzy would keep going. She clicked the mouse to open the email and there in black and white was her latest communication from a serial killer.

Hey Jazzy

Just so you know, I'm still watching, still waiting, still biding my time. Patience has always been one of my virtues.

Watch your back. You never know when I'll come for you!

Till next time,
Your loving sister

Thursday 2nd March

Chapter 10

'I'm a dead man.'

Jazzy, who had been in the process of sending a sneaky text to Fenton asking for forensic updates on the latest gang-related crime scene – a body dumped on the banks of Linlithgow Loch, looked up at the unfamiliar man. Tall, slender, probably in his early thirties with a riot of floppy brown hair that he had tucked behind his ears. He was going prematurely grey at the temples, and judging by his rapid blinking, he was nervous. She turned to the uniformed officer standing beside him. 'Sergeant Hobson?'

Wullie Hobson smirked and splayed his shovel-like hands before him. 'This is well above mah pay grade, DS Solanki. Think it's more of a *detective* sergeant's job than a beat bobby's. So, if you don't mind, I'll leave you to it. Loads to do downstairs and I'm off shift in . . .' backing towards the door, he glanced at his watch, his smile widening as he saw the time '. . . fifteen minutes and twenty-five seconds.'

Jazzy got to her feet and in her haste to reach the sergeant before he left, managed to bang her cast on the edge of the desk. A sharp pain radiated right up her arm, through her elbow, and settled in a ball of tension in her shoulder. 'Wait, Wullie.'

With a wiggle of his fingers and a large wink, Wullie allowed the door of the Major Incident Team's shared office space to close between them. *No bloody respect.* A quick glance round the room told her that, for once, she was alone. *Trust everyone to be absent when I want to palm a civilian off on them.* With a fixed smile, Jazzy gestured to an area to the side of the room, designated for these sorts of civilian visits, then rolled her eyes. Queenie had been at it again, using the desk as a picnic table and not bothering to clean up after herself.

As Mr Nervous settled into one of the two chairs, Jazzy found a bin and, uncaring that Queenie would give her laldie later on, swept the entirety of her colleague's lunch into it. Sitting opposite him, Jazzy rested her arms on the table and, head to one side, smiled. 'I'm Detective Sergeant Solanki and whatever's bothering you, I'll see if I can be of assistance, although really, here in the Major Incident Team we don't usually see walk-ins.' She paused as a flush made its way up Mr Nervous's cheeks, then relented. 'That's quite a statement you made there, Mr . . .?'

'Mackie.' He extended a hand across the table, then reconsidered and let it fall into his lap instead. 'Sidney. I mean you can call me Sid. Most folk do, but Sidney is my proper name.' He grimaced, blinking again, before focusing on his hands in his lap.

Unsure what to make of him, Jazzy allowed the silence between them to grow. He was well presented and, despite his jittery behaviour, she didn't get any unstable or druggy-type vibes from him – not that she was qualified to make either assessment, but experience and instinct made her pretty sure she was right. Besides, Wullie would have screened him before bringing him up here.

'So, Sid, would you care to elaborate on what you mean about being a dead man, for if you don't mind me saying, you look pretty alive to me. Do you feel endangered? Is that why you've come here today? Has someone threatened you?'

Sid inhaled a breath so deep it threatened to suck all the air from the room, but it also seemed to settle his nerves because his eyes lifted to meet Jazzy's. He swallowed as if preparing to speak, and then stopped, but in the end, shook his head and thrust a crumpled and folded wad of paper at her.

Intrigued, Jazzy accepted the sheets, but placed them on the table unopened. 'I'll get you some water, Sid. Maybe that'll help. I can see you're rattled, but at some point, you're going to have to speak to me, so let's just see if we can calm you down a little.'

As she walked over to the water cooler, she considered phoning DC Geordie McBurnie. He was far better at calming people down than she was. Hell, even the normally abrasive Queenie – when in the right mood – was better at it than Jazzy. She handed the recyclable cup of water to Sid, resumed her seat opposite and flicked the papers open. It was a newspaper article printed from a computer but although the headline itself was attention-grabbing, it was the image that made Jazzy's breath hitch in her throat. For long seconds, she studied it, her eyes darting from it to the man before her trying to make sense of what she was seeing in the context of the article. *Now I understand why you're so upset.*

She read the headline again.

CAIRNPAPPLE MAN'S FACE RECONSTRUCTED: DO YOU RECOGNISE THIS MAN?

Jazzy remembered hearing about the case when she was training at Tulliallan. Cairnpapple Hill was such a well-known local Neolithic site, that the discovery of human remains buried in a shallow grave nearby had created quite a buzz. The victim had been murdered and, despite an extensive investigation, was never identified, thus making it one of the most significant cold cases in the region. How tragic that someone could remain unidentified for over thirty years. Had no one missed him? Many theories had circulated at the time – that he was an illegal immigrant, that he'd come over from Ireland, that he'd come from London and some even wondered if he'd travelled from as far afield as the United

States, but none of those theories had borne fruit. Finally, with nobody coming forward to identify the man, his case had been referred to the Scottish Cold Case Unit at Glasgow Caledonian University, where it appeared that at last some progress had been made on the decades-old investigation.

Sid leaned forward, his voice hoarse and stilted. 'You see it, don't you? That man in the photo is me. I'm that dead man.'

Jazzy took a moment to compose herself. Clearly, the dead man in the newspaper wasn't Sid Mackie; still the resemblance between the two was disconcerting. 'Look, let me read the article and we'll go from there, okay?'

Sid closed his eyes as if to block out the image of the dead man who could have been his twin. Out of consideration, Jazzy lifted the copy so that the image was no longer in his line of vision. The article had been dated three months ago, which explained why it had flown under Jazzy's radar. She'd been up to her ears chasing down a serial killer at the time. She began to read the short article.

Cairnpapple Man's remains were discovered, partially buried, in a shallow grave in a copse on the edge of the prehistoric site over three decades ago. Forensic examination confirmed the young man had been hit repeatedly over the head and narrowed the date of his murder to sometime between 1988 and when the remains were discovered in 1990.

Despite numerous appeals by Police Scotland no one has come forward to identify the man who is believed to have been between five foot ten and six foot one and aged between sixteen and twenty-five at the time of his death.

However, this new reconstructed image of him, released by the Scottish Cold Case Unit breathes new life into the stalled investigation. Police Scotland are hopeful that this might jog the public's memory and result in a positive identification.

Police Scotland have provided a list of items discovered with the man. (Turn to page 3 for more details.)

If you recognise this man or his possessions or have relevant information that may help police with their inquiries then contact us on the number cited below.

This is not only a missing persons investigation, it is also a murder investigation.

Jazzy flipped to the next page to find a list of items found with Cairnpapple Man and pictures of his clothing. There had been no identifiers – driving licence, passport, library card, credit cards – in his wallet, which indicated that the killer had removed anything related to their victim's identity. He'd been wearing Lee brand jeans and a short-sleeved denim jacket – also Lee brand – over a well-worn black leather jacket with no label. The jacket was similar to that worn by Bruce Springsteen on the cover of *Rolling Stone* magazine in 1984. On the denim jacket pocket was a square yellow enamel pin with BORN IN THE USA on it. Each letter of USA was coloured like the American flag. A picture of Springsteen in said jacket was beside the one taken of the clothes removed from the deposition site. Jazzy's eyes lingered for a moment on the healthy, smiling rock star before drifting to the stained clothes retrieved from the body of the unidentified young man.

By the time she'd finished, Jazzy's head pounded. Why would Sid Mackie come here rather than phone the helpline cited in the newspaper? True, Cairnpapple Hill was under Lothian and Borders jurisdiction, being situated near Bathgate, but why not approach the Cold Case Unit handling the investigation? Sid slouched in the chair, shoulders hunched with his arms folded protectively across his middle, looked like a sudden gust of wind would knock him to the floor.

'Sid, do you have any idea who this man is?'

But Sid was already shaking his head. 'No. I've no clue who he is and that's what's freaked me out so much. It's spooky having a doppelganger murdered near to where you grew up.'

'You grew up nearby?'

'Yes, Torphichen, but I was only little in 1988.'

Torn between fascination and the knowledge that this case didn't fall within her remit, Jazzy tapped her fingers on the table. The Scottish Cold Case Unit were better placed to extract any pertinent information from him and, of course, to complete a DNA comparison. So why was she hesitating? *Because I'm a nosy bugger, that's why.* That wasn't the only reason, though. Since the personal nature of the investigation before Christmas combined with her resultant trauma and physical injuries, she had been forced to undertake compulsory counselling and the D team had been tasked with routine busywork. The boredom was excruciating. Even though Jazzy had been reinstated to detective sergeant, DCI Dick had clipped their wings. Only last week Fenton had heard the dickless wonder describing them to the A team as 'misfits and fuck-ups'. Jazzy glared in the vague direction of the offices where the Dick and the other 'high heid yins' from Edinburgh, Glasgow and Lothian and Borders were strategising solutions to deal with the accelerating all-out violence in Scotland's central belt.

'His similarity to you is so pronounced, it's safe to assume there must be some familial link – although, of course, that would have to be officially confirmed. Have you contacted any of your relatives? Do you know of anyone – no matter how distantly related – who may either know this bloke or possibly be able to identify him?'

Sid ran trembling hands through his hair. 'There's nobody left. Grandparents are long gone – I never even met them – as are my parents and both of them were only children. There's only me.' He sighed and pointed at the discarded printout. 'And him. Well, sort of him.'

All sorts of scenarios flitted through Jazzy's mind, and although fascinated by the mystery of it all, professionalism insisted Jazzy refer Sid to the appropriate department. Still, the fact that he had chosen to turn up here at Livingston police station puzzled her. 'Why didn't you contact the number in the paper?'

'I know. That's what I should've done, but I was just so tired after travelling all this way that I just wanted to see where he was found and then' – he shrugged – 'I came here. Couldn't bear speaking to someone on the phone. Wanted to speak to a human. A real person. I wanted to make sure that the person saw *me* and then saw . . .' He pointed a shaking finger towards the sheets of paper that Jazzy had placed face down next to her tablet.

Travelling? She'd assumed that he lived locally. 'Where have you come from, Sid?'

He blinked a couple of times as if trying to keep himself awake. 'Avanos, Cappadocia.'

Jazzy hadn't been expecting that. 'Cappadocia? In Turkey?'

He nodded. 'We moved there – all of us – Mum, Dad and me when I was a nipper. Dad could run his business from there and the heat was good for Mum's rheumatoid arthritis. After they died three years ago – a car crash – I stayed. I'm settled there, speak fluent Turkish, got dual citizenship, a good job. Dad's business takes care of itself, I'm financially independent and I've no family ties to Scotland anymore. Nothing to bring me home – until now, that is.'

Jazzy smiled at his use of the word 'home'. *You can take the laddie from Scotland, but you can't take Scotland from the laddie.* From the strength of his accent, Jazzy would have bet he'd never left the country. 'What do you do in Avanos?'

His shrug spoke volumes. 'I'm a marketing director for a tourism company.'

'Not tempted to take on your dad's business, then?'

'What, exporting kilts to the rest of the world? No chance. I've no desire to learn the intricacies of kilt manufacturing, so I'm selling it.'

'How did you find out about this? I doubt it made headline news in Turkey.'

'No, you're right there. I was browsing the other day and found this *Daily Record* article from last year and when I saw how much that guy looked like me, I had to come. To be honest, it freaked me out. It was like coming face to face with my own mortality.'

'You saw this article online and instead of phoning or emailing, you took a flight from Turkey to Edinburgh, checked out the deposition site of your lookalike's body and then turned up here?'

'Like I said, it shook me. Shite, that guy could be my twin. He was murdered and dumped in a woody area, like a bag of rubbish. Course I wanted to see where he was buried. I mean . . .' he looked at Jazzy, a frown tugging his eyebrows '. . . what if we *are* related? That would mean I could have other relatives out there. Other people who might have known my mum or dad. Livingston just seemed less anonymous somehow than Glasgow.'

Jazzy understood that, but there was nothing more she could do. With reluctance she picked up the landline and phoned the contact number in the paper. 'We have a walk-in here in Livingston who might be able to help identify Cairnpapple Man. It would be best to speak to him in person. I'll organise a car to bring him to you.'

After hanging up she said, 'I wish I could help you more, but this really is outside my remit. I hope you find what you're looking for. Every unidentified victim deserves to be named.'

'You're just palming me off?' As quickly as Sid's anger rose, it dwindled away and he slumped back in his chair. 'I'm sorry. That was unreasonable of me. This isn't your case and I appreciate your kindness. It's just . . .'

'All a bit much? Especially after a long flight?'

'Yeah, something like that.'

Her phone rang – Hobson letting her know the car she'd requested was waiting. Jazzy stood. 'Good luck with everything, Sid.'

Chapter 11

'*The Cold Case Unit at Glasgow Caledonian University are on the cusp of revealing valuable new information that could lead to finally identifying the unnamed Cairnpapple Man, who is believed to have been murdered around thirty years ago. Cairnpapple Man was so named because of the proximity of his final resting place to the Neolithic henge and Bronze Age burial site, Cairnpapple Hill. On this dreich March morning, you're listening to Kirsty Ndibanje here on Radio Lothian and if you're still suffering from end-of-winter blues, here's Scotland's very own Lewis Capaldi with "Forget Me" to cheer you up.*'

Whilst Lewis Capaldi sang, Jimmy 'Hardass' Nails took a moment to consider the news report, then shook his head and dismissed it. It was a habit he'd got into in the Big Hoose – listening to the local news and analysing it to see if it might impact him or his interests on the outside. It rarely did, but it was a worthwhile discipline to employ. Following routine and being methodical were the props that got him through his time inside, and besides, on the few occasions he gleaned some relevant information, it allowed him to give instructions despite his incarceration.

Now, he was in his sister Bonnie's front room with the curtains shut tight, the too sweet flowery air freshener irritating his throat and her overpriced and overstuffed furniture covered in plastic sheeting. Knowing from experience the unpredictability of these situations and, in deference to her plush new carpet, he'd spread more plastic over the floor before tying his nephew and brother-in-law to the chairs. Jimmy was ready to exact his revenge on the two wee nyaffs who had fucked things up in his absence. Today was Judgement Day.

Irked by the music, Jimmy tutted. 'Bloody Lewis Capaldi? What's wrong with "Big Country", eh? Quality tunes, like? Christ, next it'll be the sodding Bay City Rollers.'

Jimmy's nephew, Dan Moran, ignored the warning head shake from his dad, Ned Moran, and blurted out, 'Bay City what?'

Jimmy spun round and glared at the two men, before settling a scowl on his nephew. 'You bloody simple or what, you dipstick? Does the way I've got you trussed up naked like a bagged grouse on the Glorious Twelfth not give you a wee hint that you should keep your damn trap shut?'

When Dan lowered his head, his mouth drooping in a sulk more befitting a toddler than a teenager, Jimmy exhaled. 'Bloody idiot. *Bay City who?* I ask you, do they no' teach you about Scottish culture at that fancy school I footed the bill for? Next you'll be telling me you're a Lewis Capaldi fan too.'

Dan opened his mouth to reply, but one glance at his uncle's hard stare had it snapping shut again.

'That's more like it, son. Using your nous. I like that. Shame the pair of yous didn't think of employing that strategy whilst I was banged up. Then we wouldn't be in this fucking mess.'

Whilst Jimmy had been rotting in Barlinnie, he'd left Bonnie in charge. She was tough as buffalo hide. But she'd got pregnant and there had been complications, which is when she took her eye off the ball and trusted these two and that's when things had started to go wrong.

'Hey, Ned, remember when Bonnie offed Jessie Dalgleish?'

Ned glared at him with flashing eyes, but Jimmy was on a roll. 'You know I thought when they found her floating in the Clyde that you'd got away wi' shagging her. That Bonnie hadn't known about it.'

He flicked Ned on the forehead and laughed. 'Soon as I saw you on crutches and with a black eye, I knew Bonnie had offed her.' Another flick to the forehead. 'Ye cannae say I didn't warn you though, can ye? But no, no no. You were all full of "I can handle Bon, Jimmy. You just leave her to me." Aye how did that work oot for ye?'

Jimmy stroked his chin. 'What aboot, I get Bonnie in here instead of me? Do you think she'd be more lenient, eh?' He kicked his brother-in-law in the shin, and as Ned jerked back, his eyes wide and panicked, he leaned in and whispered, 'No' bloody likely, you absolute scrotum. She'd fucking annihilate you. There's naebody more loyal than oor Bonnie and it's safe to say she's pissed as fuck wi' you for fucking up when she was out of commission.'

His mind drifted to his meeting with Loanie Gibbs the other week. Despite Loanie's belief that the attacks on their networks were the work of external forces, Jimmy couldn't entirely shake the idea that it was more personal, which brought him right back to the two numpties sitting in front of him. Could they be in cahoots with Loanie as part of a big takeover bid? Although it seemed unlikely, their betrayal in leaking info to Loanie was too big a coincidence to ignore. The fact that there had been no reprisals after the murder of Loanie's cousins, combined with years of antipathy between the Edinburgh and Glasgow criminals, added to Jimmy's confusion. His dad's deathbed warning had guided Jimmy through the last thirty-odd years – 'Don't trust those Edinbugger bastards, son. They'll screw your sister or your daughter soon as look at you, but . . .' Ricky Nails had grabbed Jimmy's arm tight, his skinny scrabbling fingers digging into his flesh '. . . don't diddle them either, Jimmy. They're mean bastards and not breaking the status quo has served us well. *Don't* mess with the Gaffer and *don't* mess with Edinburgh. You promise me, son? No' Edinburgh – at least not till the Gaffer and Wee Frankie are dead, okay?'

Jimmy had promised and he'd stuck to that promise, but over the years faint ghostlike memories niggled just outside his consciousness, but he couldn't pin them down and that made him uneasy.

He turned his attention back to the trussed-up pillocks in Bonnie's large living room. Ned shivered, his peely-wally skin all goose-bumpy, his voice all whiney and grating. 'We've learned our lesson, Jimmy. No need to go ballistic. Besides it's freezing. Let us go, man. We go way back, you and me. I'm your brother-in-law, for Christ's sake. It was just a wee mistake. Nothing to get in a stoorie about.'

Jimmy glared at Ned, whose shrivelled-up cock bore testament to how cold he was. He'd told Bonnie to shut down the heating in this room and with both his captives chittering, he smiled. Every wee discomfort for them carried an exponential increase in pleasure for Jimmy. The very sight of them made him want to shove their heads down the toilet and flush – preferably after he'd taken a huge dump in it. But, in the absence of an available loo, he'd make do with watching their skin turn blue.

Having deliberated long and hard before coming to his decision, Jimmy allowed the rage simmering in his belly to inflate and fill his chest, but he wasn't quite ready to let loose with it yet. Whilst Ned looked petrified, Dan was too fucking stupid to realise the desperation of his situation.

Now, with Adele's 'Rolling in the Deep' as a background track, he glared at them, their stupidity oozing from their bodies in waves. How the hell had he inherited such useless pieces of shite as relatives? He'd never asked Bonnie why she'd got hitched to Ned Moran, but he suspected it was because she thought she could control him. *How did that work out for you, Bon?*

While his nephew and brother-in-law waited their fate, Jimmy prowled the room. 'You know, everything would've been fine if Bonnie hadn't "got caught". Fuck's sake, pregnant at forty-seven. No wonder she had complications.' He paused and smirked. 'What do you think of the bairn, eh, Ned? Judging by the bairn's skin colour and her intelligence, she's no' yours, is she? That piss you off, Neddy boy?'

Despite the chill an angry flush bloomed over Ned's face. 'Shut the fuck up, eh?'

Jimmy tutted and turned his attention to Dan. 'What about you, son? Piss you off to have a wee sister in the nest eh?'

After a glance at his da, Dan shook his head. 'Nah, I like Crystal. She's cute.'

'Aye, thank fuck for that. Imagine yer ma having to put up with another eighteen years of the same shite she put up with you. When she was laid up wi' the bairn, you two should've supported her, but instead you stupid brainless wee turds decided to go rogue. What a pair of bampots you are.'

'It wisnae us, Uncle Jimmy.' Dan's voice was all high and squeaky. Jimmy had a sudden urge to yank out his tongue and ram it down his throat, but the sound of Bonnie's bairn's laughter drifting through from the kitchen grounded him. Hands clenched into fists and breathing heavily, he allowed her glee to wash over him until his thundering heart calmed.

Dan, misinterpreting his uncle's change in demeanour, put on a wheedling tone. 'You gonna let us go now, Uncle Jimmy? I've got an appointment with the bookies later. Besides, wee Crystal's here. You don't want her to see or hear this, do you?'

If there was one thing Jimmy hated above all else, it was someone whingeing at him. Still not ready to fully open the doors to his fury, he reached over and slapped the lad across the head so hard he thought Dan's brain might have escaped through his ear. Now the whingeing was replaced by high-pitched sobbing. *Aw, for fuck's sake!* He raised his hand as if to strike the lad again. 'Button it, right?'

Tears tripping him, snot dripping from his chin, and the huge red palm print on his face glowing like a tomato, Dan nodded. *At bloody last, the stupid wee bastard's got the message.*

Satisfied now both his captives were more subdued, Jimmy continued his reflections. 'Did neither of you have the nous to understand that she'd realise what you'd done? That yous had fucked up?'

Heads bowed, Dan's sniffles were annoyingly loud but Ned was silent. Their shoulders slumped as if for the first time they realised that Jimmy might not go easy on them because they were related. His anger surged again; he'd not be able to control it for much longer. His loyalty lay with his sister – family first – and those two had taken liberties. Bonnie had dealt with it the best she could and managed some damage limitation, but not enough to broker more than an uneasy peace whilst he'd been banged up. Now he had to sort it, before he lost control of his empire.

Although the actions of the two numpties sitting before him might have resulted in Jimmy's balls being caught in a virtual vice, the reality was they'd caused only a minor inconvenience. Yes, he'd had to reassert himself as the Glasgow boss and quash the rumours on the street that he was losing control, but that was easily done. He'd decades of proven leadership behind him and everybody knew not to get on the wrong side of Hardass Nails, but there were whispers on the street that he was 'going saft' because he'd let them get away with it.

'Now, for a blast from the past with the Beatles' "Love Me Do" . . .'

Jimmy rolled his eyes. Radio Lothian was getting on his tits big time. That Kirsty lassie hadn't played a decent tune yet. What was wrong with folk? After years of being subjected to Big Jockey Crossan, singing Elvis Presley in the next cell every damn night, he'd been looking forward to hearing some decent tunes. Maybe Dan was right about one thing. Maybe it was time to get himself signed up to Spotify. His rage got redder – flickering crimson flames engulfed him so, fed up with his nephew's stupidity and his brother-in-law's whingeing pleas, Jimmy picked up two pairs of stinking socks, liberated from the laundry basket. With his huge fingers he prised open their reluctant gobs before shoving the socks in. For good measure, he wrapped a scarf round their heads to keep them in place. 'That's better. Now I can hear myself think.'

As Jimmy set out his tools on the wee card table he'd set up in view of his captives, Dan's awareness of his current predicament kicked in and he evacuated his bowels. For once, Jimmy was grateful for Bonnie's overuse of air fresheners. He picked up a vice and weighed it in the palm of his hand. 'Seems fitting, does it not? My balls are in one of these wee beauties because of your mistakes so . . .' He let his words trail off, relishing the tension radiating from the other two men. If they thought a bit of cold and a slapped puss were bad enough, wait till they saw what was coming their way.

Crystal's laughter drifted again from the kitchen, her innocent singing punctuated by his sister's harsher voice. She was negotiating with a supplier in her toughest Weegie brogue. 'You get ma' drift, son? You dinnae deliver the goods on time and your bollocks will be in severe danger of being emancipated from your crotch, like. So maybe no' cheek me, eh?'

Jimmy grinned. Bonnie always cut to the chase.

'You two not only betrayed *me*, you betrayed her too and, more than that – in fact, *worse* than that – you took advantage of her vulnerability at a time when you should have been right by her side, smoothing out the creases and making things easy for her. You're a useless pair of bawbags and nobody, not *one* person, will miss you. What does that say about you, eh?'

Ned struggled against his ties as muffled whingeing noises got lost against his mouth gag. Jimmy ignored him, instead slapping the vice against one hand as he perused the rest of the tools he'd laid out. 'In our world *we* rely on family and *they* rely on you,

you get me?' He moved closer, the vice swinging in his hand 'Family is like a finely oiled machine – each cog has its job and when everyone does their bit things run smoothly. That right?'

He opened the vice and moved it towards Ned's balls. Squirming the man tried to close his legs, but Jimmy touched the metal to his ball sack, making him jump as if he'd been electrocuted. 'I asked you a question. Is that right?'

Ned's head moved up and down like a pneumatic drill and Jimmy moved the vice away from his groin.

'So, that being the case, would I be right in saying that you two deserve to be punished?' Jimmy, vice at the ready, sidled over to Dan.

Rocking back and forth, Dan trembled like a newborn deer, his eyes darting everywhere but at his uncle. When Jimmy touched the vice to his balls, the lad shat himself again and in disgust Jimmy slapped his face and stepped back coughing. 'You fucking disgusting wee runt.'

Gobbing onto the plastic sheeting, Jimmy resumed his questioning. 'So, the big question is, just how big a punishment do you deserve? The vice?' He waved it in the air, before raising his other hand. 'Or my fists?'

He paused to let his words sink in, enjoying their reactions. Ned had closed his eyes and was whispering the Lord's Prayer like the lapsed Catholic he was whilst Dan's shivering had reached an entirely new level. In one smooth movement Jimmy threw the vice on the floor, clenched his fist and rammed it into Ned's squishy belly, then repeated the action on Dan's much firmer one. For ten minutes, he worked himself up into a lather and gave them the pasting they deserved. He released every burning pocket of rage, allowing the anger to drive his bare fist again and again into every part of their bodies. He didn't care if they lived and he didn't care if they died. They were just human punchbags to him and he kept going and going and going. His sweat mixed with their blood as he pummelled them to two pulpy lumps in the plastic-covered living room of a posh house in one of the poshest areas of Glasgow. Maybe, despite his wealth, he hadn't come too far from his Gorbals roots after all.

Finally, with his breath coming in heavy pants, blood dripping from his knuckles and sweat drenching his T-shirt, Jimmy stopped and studied the swollen lumps of meat before him. He didn't care if they were alive or dead. Either way, they'd be dealt with. Not by him but by one of his minions who'd make sure to spread the word that Jimmy was back and wouldn't tolerate betrayal.

Neither of them twitched. The persistent gurgle in Ned's throat indicated he was still alive – just. But the lad was still, blood dripping from his chin, his face a morass of gunge. Good job Bonnie had Jimmy's ability to compartmentalise. She wouldn't care if they survived or not. They were dead weight and she'd be happy to cut them loose in a very final way. He smiled as he left the room. If necessary, when that time came, he'd be sure to take his time with them – for Bonnie. The promise of that almost made him hope they survived – but only almost.

After a shower and with the sounds of Ed Sheeran following him down the hallway, he joined Bonnie in the kitchen.

'Done?' Tall and raven-haired, Bonnie could pass for being in her late thirties rather than the fifty-year-old she was. Despite the hard life she'd lived and the things she'd done to keep ahead of her competitors, her complexion was clear and unwrinkled. Her part of the family business usually worked as smoothly as a stripper on a greased pole, so Jimmy was happy to cut her a little slack. None of what happened had been within her control and, to give her credit, she'd tried her best to rectify things. Now, it was his job to take over and sort things for good. He kissed her cheek and ruffled the wee lassie's dark hair. 'For now. Not to say that's a final decision, mind.'

A flicker in Bonnie's eye was the only indication that she was disappointed that they were still alive. She shrugged, hauled her daughter onto her knee and smiled. 'You're the boss, Jimmy. I'll do whatever you need but I'm no Florence Nightingale, you know?'

'Don't expect you to be, Bon. Just leave them be for a few hours.' He grinned. 'Call it reflection time, eh? Then, if they're still breathing later on, get them upstairs. No point pampering the fuckers. You know who to phone if we need to clean ship, don't you?'

Bonnie laughed. 'Maybe not tell me what to do, eh? Not my first rodeo and no doubt it won't be my last.' She paused and licked her lips, holding his gaze. 'I'm glad you're home, Jimmy. Glesca hasn't been the same without you.'

Chapter 12

Jazzy's thoughts kept drifting to Sidney Mackie's visit earlier and she wished Queenie would hurry up and get back so she could share the strange meeting with her. It had been almost two weeks since DCI Dick had split up the D team and they were all feeling it. Queenie was restless and had taken to making up excuses to mooch around the corridors in the vain hope of catching sight of Fenton or Geordie, but worse than that, without the other Jazz Queens there to distract her, she'd become tetchy and spent a lot of time analysing Jazzy's shortcomings. Her latest 'JayZee' gripe was about Jazzy's 'trust issues' and she'd spent ages analysing the root causes of her partner's 'prickliness'. Of course, she was right. Still, that didn't make her constant suggestions and observations any more palatable. Jazzy understood that it all came from a good place and that was why Jazzy tried so hard not to lose it with Queenie. It wasn't like she was oblivious to her lack of trust issues. Christ, with both her therapist and Queenie on her case how could she be?

What really got her, though, was that she *was* working on them. She really was. She was loads better than she'd been even a few months ago. Hadn't she – in and among the chaos of a serial killer investigation – let her guard down and revealed her deepest secrets to people she hardly knew? She'd bought Christmas presents for her new friends, the co-workers who had wormed their way under her skin, hadn't she? Most years, she barely remembered to buy her mum and dad Christmas gifts, but this year she had, and the warm fuzzy sensation that filled her chest told her she'd do it again.

The biggest addition to her life though was her friendship with the two teenagers from Stùrrach. Benjy and Ivor had got right under her skin and concern over their welfare was as important to her as the welfare of her cat Winky and her parents. After Ivor nearly died at the hand of Jazzy's sister and the ongoing trauma, Benjy struggled to cope and Jazzy felt responsible for them. Then, there was *the* big one. She'd attended her first ever works night out to see her colleague, Geordie McBurnie, perform in drag as Misty Thistle and, more importantly, she'd had fun. She'd enjoyed dancing with Elliot. She'd giggled, in a very unJazzy way through her and Queenie's Killer Queen theme tune. She'd worn a dress and make-up and let herself go. For the first time in a long time, she felt connected to people other than her parents and Elliot. Her life was enriched by all her new connections, but especially her work ones. That was why Dick splitting up her team was so cruel. In such a short space of time they'd become closer than Jazzy could ever have imagined.

The enormity of that realisation floored her, for she didn't know what to do with all this emotion and the addition of this large, often unruly extended family. Her interactions with them sometimes felt cumbersome – like she wasn't sure quite how familiar to be, how much concern over their welfare she was supposed to express. It was a conundrum but, on balance, Jazzy was doing okay.

She glanced round the room, looking for a distraction from scrutinising the limited CCTV footage of vehicles caught near the various deposition sites in the vain hope of seeing a familiar vehicle, and was glad when her phone buzzed, with a WhatsApp notification. Seeing it was from Geordie to their Jazz Queens group, her lips spread into a wide smile.

Misty Thistle #DragQueenExtraordinaire:

Update! Surveillance on LG associates in Edinburgh and JN associates in Glasgow was stepped down as of this morning. I'm still on admin duties. Nothing else to report. Queenie, thanks for the tablet. From Thistles, I presume? Loved it! Still on for meeting later?

Jazzy sighed. They'd been expecting that, but still it was a blow. Had Jazzy been in charge she would have argued that after the murders of Markie and Tommy Jones, both sides in this Glasgow/Edinburgh chaos would keep their heads down. The funerals had been only at the tail end of the previous week and Jazzy credited both sides with being savvy enough to realise that, in the current climate, Police Scotland would be keeping tabs on them at least until then. A further couple of weeks' surveillance might have provided useful information. But she wasn't in charge and budgets were tight.

Alternating with Geordie and Fenton, she and Queenie had, for the past week, spent time scoping out known associates of Loanie Gibbs and Jimmy Nails, but so far there had been nothing fruitful. Looked like now that there were no CID toes to tread on they could divert their surveillance to the big guns instead.

Thanks for update, #DragQueenExtraordinaire. We'll just have to take up the slack! Yes, okay for tonight. That Queenie and her homemade tablet! Yeah from Thistles, where else? Already scoffed mine.

She added a smiley face and shut down the video footage. If she didn't meet her paperwork quota she'd be in bother, so she picked up the next form from the pile in front of her. Brain-deadening form-filling wearied her and soon her mind drifted from their lack of progress on identifying any leads on the Tommy and Markie

Jones murders to her brother, Simon. She'd had another of her 'task force sanctioned' early morning visits with him in the hope of shaking something loose about the whereabouts of her sister, and was exhausted. Being in his presence was soul-destroying. Each visit was fraught with innuendo, insults, manipulation and guilt-tripping, and although it was hard for her to completely subdue her feelings for the brother she'd once known, she left him in the psychiatric facility feeling traumatised and empty. It wasn't just navigating through his warped machinations either that had her on edge, it was the taunts from her sister. This morning's visit, like the previous ones, had been preceded by the usual email from the Bitch.

Subject: Say hi to Simon when you see him today!

Hey Jazzy,
Simon says you're desperate to find out how we're communicating. Good luck with that. In the meantime, in case there's any doubt – I'm still watching, still waiting, still biding my time. Watch your back. You never know when I'll come for you!
Till next time,
Yours truly, sister dearest.

With continued pain from her arm and the constant threats from her sister combined with feeling obligated to undergo these weekly traumas with her brother, Jazzy felt brittle and ready to crack. No matter how much she rolled her shoulders or cricked her neck, she couldn't shake the weight that bore down on them. She knew it wasn't real. That it was the after-effects of seeing her brother. He was so different from the little boy she'd taken care of. Cruel and nasty, he delighted in taunting her about their inability to find his partner in crime. Visit after visit, she'd listened to his rantings, desperate even in his erratic behaviour, to recognise the child she'd once known. However, he wasn't her brother anymore. Not the one she'd loved, anyway, and this weekly torture was affecting her mentally and physically.

The previous night, Jazzy had been visited in her dreams by her dead mother who armed with shears had attempted to shave off all her hair, like she'd done when Jazzy was little. She'd woken up sweat-sodden and shivering, tears streaming down her cheeks. In the cold light of day, she recognised that the reason she refused to cut her hair as an adult was attributable to that one incident when she was twelve. She was also self-aware enough to realise that lack of sleep, poor diet and living on nervous energy was why her arm was taking so long to heal. She was exhausted and if Queenie didn't get back soon, she was in danger of laying her head down on her desk and snatching ten minutes.

The only positive she could take away from the long and stressful day was that DCS Afzal had agreed that something had to change and had expressed this to the task force – Operation Birchtree – responsible for apprehending the Bitch. So, instead of regular slots, they would now vary the time and day of her visits and limit the officers privy to those details. The IT team continued to track her and Elliot's email accounts. Both her home and her work area had, for the umpteenth time, been swept for bugs, and a deeper dive was being done on anyone who could possibly be leaking information between Simon and his mentor. So far nothing had come up, but Jazzy was hopeful that these new measures would be effective.

Just then, Queenie swept into the room like a whirling dervish on speed and braked to a halt inches from Jazzy. 'Idiots. Bloody idiots. Just a couple more weeks' surveillance and they'd have had the bastards. But no . . .'

So, Queenie had seen Geordie's WhatsApp. Jazzy rolled her shoulders and let Queenie bang on about Dick's incompetence till she ran out of steam. Then, hands on hips, Queenie studied her friend in the solicitous way she'd adopted since Jazzy's injury and although her words came across as less than caring – she was Queenie, after all – her expression oozed anxiety. 'What's up with you, JayZee? You've got a face like a slapped bahookie – all red and twisted, like. You know, all mottled and aeriated? Chapped like nappy rash on a bairn's arse?'

Although grateful for her partner's concern, it irked Jazzy big time. It was hard putting everything that had happened behind her when she'd had no option but to interact with her manipulative brother in case he revealed some useful piece of information that might lead them to locating the Bitch. It was even harder to focus on the present like her therapist advised, without Queenie's concerns about her mental state being a constant worry. Her concern was like a neon sign emblazoned across the woman's forehead flashing out a warning every time anyone so much as looked in Jazzy's direction. TREAD CAREFULLY, SERIAL KILLER'S SISTER RECOVERING FROM TRAUMA! YOU HAVE BEEN WARNED. BE PREPARED!

So what if she was dwelling on things. Hardly surprising was it? The visit earlier from Sid Mackie had intrigued her and had momentarily distracted her from the thoughts that were never far from her mind these days. Alongside that was the knowledge that, although she'd been reinstated to detective sergeant, she was responsible for her little team of four Jazz Queens being split up. DCI Dick hated her and so it was her fault they were lumbered with busywork. The entire station was buzzing with it, especially now some more of the fallout had landed in Lothian and Borders backyard.

Since the Jones brothers' murders, another couple of low-level criminals' bodies had been dumped in Linlithgow Loch and the discovery of a new synthetic amphetamine in a nightclub in Bathgate all spoke of increased activity requiring more feet on the ground. Yet, DCI Dick still refused to allow her and Queenie any involvement in the investigation. It was all a ploy. She'd never felt so hedged in before and was champing at the bit to get out and do something that would burn off her excess energy and with it the constant anxiety that made her edgy and irritable.

She'd even bought herself a treadmill so she could run at home, because she didn't trust herself to run on the ice in case she fell and damaged her arm again. Waste of money that was, as every step was agony. She'd ended up relegating the useless piece of equipment to the spare bedroom. Now, a fireball of anger ignited in Jazzy's chest and threatened to explode in a diatribe of hurtful words that she'd regret later. It was only the strength of her willpower and the knowledge that Queenie's attitude came from a good place that extinguished the flame as she swung her chair round to face her partner, rolling her head to ease out the cricks that computer work had left her with. Queenie's persistence, combined with her combative stance, finally brought a half-smile to Jazzy's lips.

'We've had a visitor.'

'Ooh, that's new. Who was it?' Queenie's eyes sparkled as she rubbed her hands together. She was as bored as Jazzy and was desperate to get back into a meaty investigation.

'You'll never guess. Not in a million years.'

Queenie settled her backside on the side of Jazzy's desk, nabbed a handful of crisps from the packet Jazzy had been nibbling on and scrunched up her face in concentration. Now it was Jazzy's turn to study her friend. Jazzy hadn't been the only one to come out of their last investigation emotionally and mentally drained and carrying a whole load of baggage she'd prefer to dump in the sea so the tide could wash it far away. Of course, that wasn't likely to work. Nothing could eradicate the damage that had been done the previous year. Now, with Queenie focused on her crisps, she noticed the changes in her friend. Queenie's spiky hair had always been a bit grey, but now that grey was more prominent, as were the lines meandering across her brow. Those at the edges of her mouth were etched deep and the crow's feet extending from her eyes had lost their gentleness. The perpetual dark bags under her eyes indicated that Queenie, like Jazzy, still had interrupted sleep and no wonder.

Whilst Jazzy's memories were sharp, they would become fuzzier over time. Queenie's, by contrast, would remain with her for life. Her friend had hyperthymesia or highly superior autobiographical memory, which meant that every crime scene she'd ever visited was forever stored in her mind, in vibrant Technicolor. In their previous case, Queenie's condition had been crucial to their investigation, but Jazzy had seen the toll, both mental and physical, that hit had taken on her friend. Some might say that with her responsibilities at home, Queenie should consider early retirement; however, Jazzy suspected that what kept Queenie on the job was that it gave her access to police records, which meant she could keep on top of the unsolved investigation into her daughter's murder. Each day was a struggle for Queenie to keep the memories locked into the imaginary cubbyholes she'd created in her mind. Jazzy suspected that at night, like her, the older woman had little control over those that surfaced in her dreams – and that would account for her swollen eyes.

With a mouthful of crisps that splattered over the desk, Queenie, sniffed the air. 'Well, I reckon we can discount the dickless wonder because a) I can't smell his aftershave and b) I'd have slipped on his slug trail on the way in.'

Jazzy grinned. In just those few words, Queenie had summed up his character almost perfectly.

'On account of your slapped-arse face, I'm going to go for the chief super? Am I right? I know you can't stand the smarmy git. Although to be honest, if it wasn't for my Craig being such a catch, Afzal would be getting a wee bit of Queenie attention, you get my drift?'

'Yuck, Queenie. Just yuck.' Jazzy shook her head, trying to dispel the image of Queenie amorously pursuing the chief super. Still, she enjoyed the little game with Queenie. It felt good to lighten the atmosphere, to indulge in a bit of teasing. Especially when her heart still felt so brittle sometimes.

'Nope. Besides . . .' she pointed to her frowning face '. . . this is my concentrating expression, not a slapped-arse one. Which I'll have you know, unlike you, I never wear. Look, I'm just going to tell you, Queenie.'

She flipped over the wad of paper Sid Mackie had left behind and prodded it. 'That was my visitor.'

Queenie grabbed the sheet, her greasy fingers leaving splodges on it, and tutted. 'You taking the piss, JayZee? This is Cairnpapple Man.'

'Exactly and *that's* who came to visit.'

'You all right, hen? Feeling a bit wobbly? Been at the gin, have we? A wee bit out of sorts, today?'

Jazzy shook her head and snatched the sheet from Queenie's fingers before it was completely covered in greasy paw prints. 'Nope. This guy, who could have been Cairnpapple Man's twin, waltzed in off the street stating, and I quote – "I'm a dead man" – and Hobson brought him to me. Weird, huh?'

For once, Queenie's gob was smacked. She opened her mouth, then closed it again, before finally managing a sceptical, 'Nah, yer taking the pish, like.'

Whilst Queenie ate, Jazzy filled her in on her strange morning.

Chapter 13

DCI Dick slithered into the office in a wave of aftershave and barked at them. 'Don't know what the bloody hell you were thinking, DC Solanki.'

He glared at her, but before he could elucidate, Jazzy raised her eyes to meet his unflinchingly and said, 'DS.'

DCI Dick frowned, his huge moustache wobbling so much Jazzy wondered if it was about to slide off his upper lip. The thought that it might be stuck in place with Velcro or something similar made her lips twitch. 'What?'

'Detective *Sergeant* Solanki. That's my rank. Detective *sergeant*. I'm surprised you've forgotten already. I was reinstated after my, and I quote, "outstanding work in uncovering and identifying the existence of an active serial killer operating in Scotland, which resulted in the exoneration of five wrongfully convicted prisoners".'

He wafted his hand at her, his face an unattractive shade of beetroot red. 'You might want to remember your recent reinstatement to DS is still only probationary. Some of us are sceptical that you have the necessary experience for the job and, I've heard it mooted – not by me, you understand – that they wonder whether your original promotion was more a case of positive action than merit. We all work hard at what we do. Just because *you* got the credit doesn't detract from the work the rest of us did. After all, it's not rocket science to understand why your face got bandied about the news channels, is it?'

Jazzy's chest tightened. The bastard was alluding to one or both of two common misconceptions: that Jazzy was in some sort of sexual relationship with the chief super, which got her unfair recognition, or that the colour of her skin was the only reason she was propelled into the limelight. Jazzy didn't need to defend herself, though. Not with Queenie in the room.

'Aye, you're right there, sir. It's not rocket science at all. Oor Jazzy here risked life and limb to catch a team of serial killers whom we still wouldn't know existed without her input. She provided valuable information and when other senior officers . . .' Queenie looked at Dick, her mouth a sneer, her eyes unwavering '. . . were content to follow the easy and, sadly wrong, investigative route of focusing on a single suspect, DS Solanki widened the investigation, which resulted in one of the two being apprehended.'

The ball of tension in Jazzy's chest loosened and whilst DCI Dick glared at her friend, Jazzy sent her a bright smile. *This* was friendship. Jazzy only wished she'd been able to find friends like Queenie before now.

'Of course, no one is saying Detective *Sergeant* Solanki didn't get what she deserved.' The emphasis on 'sergeant' was more of a sneer than an acknowledgement of her rank. 'However, perhaps, she needs a little refresher course on protocol.'

Protocol? Jazzy racked her brains, but couldn't come up with any protocol she'd broken – there weren't many to break when all you did day in and day out was sit behind a sodding desk. Unless of course he'd somehow found out about them moonlighting in Edinburgh and Glasgow. Or maybe he'd discovered she was going over the CCTV footage. 'Not sure I know what you're referring to, sir.'

'No? Are you certain? I mean, you just had to, didn't you?' His beady eyes bored right into her, but since Jazzy had no idea what he was referring to, she said nothing.

'Going behind my back and contacting the Cold Case Unit in Glasgow about that Cairnpapple Man. Don't even *think* of denying it.'

Ah, someone from the CCU had contacted Dick already and he'd been caught on the hop because he hadn't read the report she'd sent him. 'No intention of denying it, sir. I actually sent you the report ninety minutes ago, so—'

But Dick was on one. 'You know, as your superior—'

'Senior, sir. We don't use superior anymore. It's not PC, according to that course you sent us on last week.' Queenie, wide-eyed, smiled up at him whilst holding her crisp bag with her middle finger extended.

'Oh, for . . .' Dick closed his eyes, swivelled on his heel and began marching out of the room. 'Well, even though we're up to our oxters in dead drug dealers from Glasgow and Edinburgh, it looks like someone high up wants *my* resources directed else-where – bloody tossers bringing their gang war into West Lothian, makes my blood boil. Why can't they do the decent thing and off them in their own backyard? Let Greater Glasgow or Edinburgh divisions deal with it.'

He glared at Jazzy as if it was her fault. '*Your* efforts with the Cairnpapple Man have landed you with babysitting duty because *they've* decided, in their infinite wisdom, to conduct a televised reconstruction next week and the lookalike has insisted on *you* being on board.' He grinned like he'd just delivered a death sentence, but inside Jazzy was cheering. Anything that got her out of the station was a bonus, but she wouldn't let Dick know that. Besides she was already intrigued by the whole mystery.

'As for you.' Dick glared at Queenie. 'You needn't think you're getting out of it, either, DC McQueen. You're going too.' He paused, allowing his smile to widen, whilst Jazzy and Queenie attempted to look suitably subdued. Seemingly satisfied with their contrite expressions, he backed from the room, throwing his final words at them as if they were arrows to their hearts. 'And don't fuck it up. Now, if you'll excuse me, I've got important people to schmooze with.'

As the door swung closed behind him, Queenie wiggled her hips in a shoogly sort of dance and grinned. 'We're going out to play, JayZee. Well done, girl. You played a bloody blinder with Cairnpapple Man's twin.'

But Jazzy was too busy watching DCI Dick's interactions outside the office to share Queenie's enthusiasm. She narrowed her eyes. Three of the most senior officers from Glasgow and Edinburgh were congregated outside the incident room and accompanying them was another group of people who, Jazzy assumed – based on their obvious 'I'm a detective stature' – were the retired officers Fenton had told them were being brought in to assist. With decades worth of specialist historic expertise in criminal activity in both cities, it was expected that their input might help progress the investigation into the escalating turf wars.

Jazzy didn't recognise all of them, but she was pretty sure Dick had shared a Mason's handshake with the larger of the three high heid yins from Edinburgh. What was that all about? She watched as the man leaned in close to Dick and whispered something, his large hand slapping Dick's back like he was a long-lost friend. Dick glanced round, as if checking that the others were out of earshot, then nodded and handed the older man something. Jazzy craned her neck to see if she could identify him and when he turned away from Dick she found she *did* recognise him, for he was Elliot's boss, DCI Dougie Shearsby, who was about to retire.

She wasn't surprised. Elliot didn't rate the bloke and was pulling his hair out with the added layers of bureaucracy Shearsby had brought to the post. In Elliot's mind, less red tape and more feet on the streets was the best way forward in their current situation. And was that a bow? Had the stupid sod *actually* bowed to two of the ex-officers? *Sycophantic prick*. Jazzy would rather trust a man-eating tiger not to kill her than Dick. Those two were up to something. She was sure of it, she just had no idea what it could possibly be. Not yet anyway, but maybe when they put their heads together later on, the Jazz Queens would.

Sensing that someone was watching her, Jazzy switched her gaze from Dick's guffawing sycophancy and met the gaze of DCS Afzal. He stood a little apart from the group and his smile was hesitant, but Jazzy ignored him, allowing her gaze to drift to the only woman in the small grouping. Now this was someone she *did* recognise. This was Elliot's now-retired big boss ex-DCS Emily Hare, from Edinburgh division, and what *she* didn't know about criminal activity in her city wasn't worth knowing. The older woman regarded the backslapping bonhomie shared by the men with a stiff smile. She'd have the mark of the men around her, and Jazzy had no doubt that she'd recognise DCS Afzal as the only one worth her attention. It was unfortunate that Jazzy shared that opinion because she'd much rather be able to hate her father unconditionally. It would be so much neater.

Chapter 14

Vengeance

'A spokesperson from Police Scotland has today issued a statement requesting information about the torture and dumping of two Edinburgh men on the A70 – known as the Lang Whang on Valentine's Day. The men had previously been identified as brothers Tommy and Markie Jones and, as yet, the police have not arrested anyone in connection with the crime. DCS Waqas Afzal has issued a plea for anyone with information about the murders to come forward.

'In other news, there's been a record number of . . .'

The sickness has been bad. I laugh – almost as bad as the damn Scottish weather. Anyway, I'm not complaining. Not really, because the pain relief is adequate and the enforced thinking space much needed. Besides, I've put my time to good use.

My rented house is an Airbnb in a bustling wee cul-de-sac and being able to watch my neighbours' comings and goings from the comfort of my reclining chair has helped pass the time. It feels good to connect with other peoples' lives – albeit as an unnoticed observer – especially when I know mine is nearing its end.

When I've felt able, I've kept myself busy researching and planning my next big move. Of course, the low-level stuff I've commissioned is still ongoing and it feels good to hear the effects of it on the news.

'And finally, as a result of heightened publicity around the digital facial reconstruction of Cairnpapple Man last year, a member of the public has come forward providing important information that may lead to him being identified. Next week, the Cold Case Unit in conjunction with Scottish TV are to televise an imagined reconstruction of the man on Cairnpapple Hill itself . . .'

I pause for breath as the newsreader ends the bulletin. Breathing is increasingly difficult, but the antibiotics are kicking in. It's not a cure, but if it helps me to stay alive till my work is done then I'm all for it. I look at the main wall. I've filled it with photographs. Not the torture porn images of the bludgeoned Jones brothers that my associate sent me: those were merely for confirmation purposes – well, that and to torture Frankie a wee bit too – no more than he deserves. Instead, I've divided the wall in half.

The first half has a few photos from my childhood, which allows me to revisit my memories. My eyes are drawn back, time and again, to a group of us kids in hand-knitted cardigans, sitting atop a couple of old crates. It must have been the tail end of winter, for none of us are wearing coats. The tenement I lived in with my family looms behind us. It's a bittersweet memory, for every one of us boasts huge grins, despite the poverty that was our life. Of course, that photo was taken when I was about eight or nine – before things changed, before we moved and I lost touch with my friends. Increasingly, I find myself yearning for that time – for that innocence. Things could have been so different if we hadn't moved. Then again, would I want everything to be different? Would I deny myself the suffering – and everything that suffering brought me – to be happy like that again? On balance, I reckon not. Despite everything there are some things I can't bring myself to regret fully.

The other half of the wall looks more like a Wanted board than anything else. Essentially, that's exactly what it is – a Wanted board. My list of criminals against whom I seek revenge. I've arranged them in a triangle. The biggest target – the most hateful, the guiltiest one at the top. Underneath are the next two and beneath them the final three. All around the central triangle are photos of other guilty targets – the casualties of the war I wreak. Two of them – Tommy and Markie Jones – have a huge red cross through their faces; the others will get their comeuppance for their reckless lives, their senseless crimes and for the misery they inflict on others.

If everything goes to plan – if I survive long enough – the last one standing will be my final victim and that one – and one other – I will take care of on my own – with a little help from my friends.

By the time I get to them they will expect me, for I am Vengeance and they will *not* survive.

Chapter 15

The Black & Blue boxing club in Gorgie used to be one of Loanie's favourite haunts. It had been around for decades and he remembered his stocky wee da bringing him here when the pungent smell of the coach's cigars battled for dominance against the heady mix of adolescent sweat mingled with the heavier, meatier stench of old men past their best and the equally distinctive nip of metallic tanginess that hung like a stark, ever-present warning in the air – *If you dare to set foot in the Black & Blue boxing ring then prepare to bleed. Prepare to sacrifice some of your blood to the litres spilled by boxing heroes of the past.*

When Loanie was a kid, the big rumour was that Ken Buchanan, the former world lightweight champion, had trained in Black & Blue and that was why black-and-white photos of the boxer with gloves on, fists up, hung slightly tattered around the grimy grey walls. There was even a rumour that crime writer Ian Rankin named a book after the club – though Loanie doubted that Rankin even knew of its existence.

The club made him think of his auld man. Fat Boy Gibbsy, everybody called him to his face, but behind his back it was Fucking Bastard Boy Gibbsy. Loanie's dad was a scrapper. A nasty piece of work. Loanie reckoned his dad's lack of height made him even nastier than he otherwise would've been. It was said that Fat Boy Gibbsy could have been as good as any of the great Scottish boxers – Kenny Anderson, Vernon Sollas, Tancy Lee – if he'd just kept off the sauce and if he'd had the nous to realise that boxing was a discipline to be exercised in the ring, not an excuse to obliterate every demon, real or imagined, outside it. Fat Boy Gibbsy's special brand of evil went before him and there were few daft enough to cross him outside the ring and even fewer prepared to take him on inside it.

Loanie's ma had no choice in the matter. She was his dad's punchbag for all their married life, until – when Loanie turned twelve – she wasn't. Every day he blamed himself for her death. He still had visions of the blood spewing from her mouth, her swollen eyes, her arm stretched towards him, her words a hiss of blood bubbles and fear. 'Now he's killed me, he'll come for you next, Lionel. He needs someone to batter. You've got to run. Run, Lionel, run.'

As her hand fluttered to the ground and her chest stopped moving, Loanie had released a feral yell that had been building like a huge clot in his diaphragm for years, increasing in size with every punch, every slap, every kick his dad inflicted on his mum. And now it was out – released into the world – the monster within him was awakened. It would never cower in silence again. When the polis finally arrived at their tenement building in Leith and found Loanie holding his dead mum, her head resting in his lap and his dad lying motionless in a pool of his own blood and excrement, they'd both been dead for hours. Forty years ago, response times to Leith tenements were slow, which played in Loanie's favour. All that time he'd sat rocking his mum's lifeless body to and fro in his lap and trying to coax her back to life meant the scene had been well and truly compromised.

Countless neighbours testified to Fat Boy Gibbsy's violent nature and countless others testified to the quiet, placid nature of wee Lionel Gibbs. Whatever the polis thought about what had gone down in the Gibbs' home that murky summer's evening, no one had pointed the finger at wee Lionel and so neither did the police. Lionel carried no guilt over what he'd done to his dad. He'd loved him – course he had – what wee laddie doesn't love his da? But he'd also hated him.

His mum's sister was married to Wee Frankie Jones and she'd taken him in with her own wee boys. Wee Frankie was a right character. A boxing expert all his life with a sideline in criminal activity, ably abetted by a childhood acquaintance who had seen that the grass could be that much greener if they as a respected police officer used their position for criminal ends. With Wee Frankie – a respected boxer and coach – as a figurehead for the Gaffer's less-than-legit activities, there was always a ready supply of henchmen to enforce his will. And, with inside knowledge from his old mate clearing away any obstacles that arose, Wee Frankie had an easy time of it. He considered himself the conduit for the Gaffer's operations and that suited him, for he could still focus almost completely on his one true love – boxing. Boxers looking to earn their fortune and take on the big-name fighters looked to Wee Frankie for guidance and, in return for their physical backup when necessary, Wee Frankie was more than happy to run them.

Of course, Frankie had sussed out Lionel's involvement in his father's death and had never held it against the lad. With his own kids being thick as shit, Frankie focused on Loanie and taught him everything he could and vouched for him with the Gaffer. Loanie owed them both big time – and he was happy to repay their faith in him numerous times over the years. When Wee Frankie had retired before Covid, Loanie had become the Gaffer's right-hand man and neither of Frankie's sons had objected. Whilst happy to reap the monetary benefits of being on the payroll but with no responsibility, they let Loanie take the lead. He had all the skills they didn't, plus he had the ability to blend into situations. He didn't draw attention to himself unnecessarily and as a result, the coppers thought he was too low-level to be bothered with – well, some of them thought that, which was why he was usually left to get on with things unhindered.

Now, though, after spending time with Jimmy Nails a few weeks back, discussing the conflict between their respective businesses and the subsequent murder of his two cousins, it had become clear that everything was so much more complicated. Of course, he didn't fully trust Jimmy and no doubt the feeling was mutual, but keeping a communication channel open with the Glasgow kingpin might pay dividends in the long run. Suppliers from south of the border and from Europe were a constant threat and seeking out new ways to compete was increasingly difficult. In recent months, the Gaffer too had been talking about easing away from the business side of things and that worried Loanie. He was sure that something was going on with the boss. Was it a health concern or something more insidious? Loanie would have to get to the bottom of that, because the Gaffer and Frankie were both behaving recklessly and that meant more risk for Loanie. *As if I don't have enough shite to deal with!*

Uncertainty was never good for any business and the result had been a shedload of folk jumping ship. That, in turn, left their flanks open to attack from outside gangs with an eye on acquiring new business territories. But it was worse than that, because Loanie was convinced it wasn't the Scousers or Geordies he had to worry about, so if not them then who? He didn't want to consider that he was being double-crossed by the older men but what else could explain their uncharacteristic behaviour?

For the first time ever, Loanie felt uneasy and out of his depth and now the Gaffer had insisted on a course of action Loanie was reluctant to follow, which was why he'd come to consult his uncle. Deep down he felt that Frankie would always have his back – regardless of his behaviour since his sons had died. He was hoping that a man-to-man chat with Frankie might reveal what was going on with the two men. His hopes were pinned on his uncle's behaviour being down to grief and that he'd be the voice of wisdom in Loanie's ears, like he'd always been before. And if it was worse than that, then Loanie would just have to take the auld fucker out.

He pushed open the creaking gym door, releasing an unfamiliar, more sanitised aroma than the one he remembered: citrus-with-only-a-hint-of-sweat. The echoing thud of feet pounding the rings and the thwack of leather gloves hitting the punchbags was as it had always been. The pang of nostalgia made him smile, but only for a second. Loanie Gibbs wasn't one for smiling and right now, he had less cause than usual for good humour.

Although his uncle ran the gym, it was Loanie who owned it. Both his cousins, Markie and Tommy, had regularly told him to get rid of the dump, but Loanie was loath to do so. It was Frankie's passion – his pride and joy – and he couldn't take that away from the man who'd brought him up and treated him like his own son. Besides, Black & Blue was also a tangible link to his past – to his auld man. Yeah, his dad had been an animal, but nowadays, with a list of violent actions to his own name, Loanie wondered if he wasn't just as bad as his old man. The business enterprises he ran for the Gaffer were diverse – drugs, prostitution, a bit of trafficking from Eastern Europe, illegal gambling, organised illegal bare-knuckle fights, financial scams and weapon selling. Of necessity, keeping a handle on all these operations required a tight fist and a low moral threshold. Loanie wasn't afraid to go the extra mile to protect what he considered to be his firm and he was savvy with it too. Though recently he'd begun to wonder if he was getting too old for this game. He'd decided that when the Gaffer signed the businesses over to him, he'd hang on for a year, eighteen months tops, then, if it felt like the right time and if things had settled down, he'd consider passing the mantle to one of the younger kids.

His cousin Markie had a couple of sprogs dotted around Edinburgh but neither of them were suitable. Maggie B was a bit too much like Loanie's auld man for him to feel comfortable leaving her in charge. He wasn't squeamish, not by a long chalk, but Maggie B took too much pleasure in her work for his liking. On more than one occasion, he'd challenged her about how she treated the women in her brothel and she'd laughed in his face and ordered one of the girls to be beaten. Loanie had shrugged and let it go. Her business, her rules.

Maggie B's sister, Gloria, on the other hand, would be the ideal choice. However, Gloria had long since turned her back on, in her words, 'her dysfunctional amoral rabid family'. Loanie laughed. She was a one, was Gloria. Stupid bint had even changed her name by deed poll to Bertram. Fucking Bertram? Where the hell had that come from? What Gloria had yet to realise, though, was that you could change your name, you could turn your back, you could walk away, but somehow, somewhere, sometime family connections would jump up, bite you in the arse and drag you back to the Leith tenements in a heartbeat. Maybe now was the time to drag the cowbag back, force her to take her responsibilities seriously.

Loanie wasn't quite there yet, though. That's why he had kept a low profile for the past few weeks, snooping round and spying on the down low, keeping his activity secret from the Gaffer. Calling in favours only from those he trusted most – or those who owed him the most or feared him the most. Either way, loyalty was at a premium and it was costing him big bucks to maintain that loyalty.

And that's why he was here. Although he hadn't mentioned it to Jimmy at their meeting, he'd heard rumours about Ned Moran and his kid being targeted. He hadn't ordered it, so who had? In the two weeks since his cousins died, the rumours about a hit on the Morans had intensified and he couldn't put it past the Gaffer to have ordered it without telling him. But nothing was confirmed. It was all speculation and whispers, and it was doing Loanie's nut in.

The familiar thud, thud, thud of leather on the ring, the twang of the ropes, the low thrum of country music in the background and the harsh guttural tones of Wee Frankie barking out instruction as he coached his newest protégé were reassuringly familiar. For all the fact that over forty-five years had elapsed since Loanie first stepped into this gym with his dad, Wee Frankie looked the same now as he did then. Lithe and light on his feet, Wee Frankie still danced round the ring barking out instructions to his boys, 'Raise your right hand', 'Protect your face', 'Keep your left up.' The overhead lights shone on his bald pate as he skipped, like a young thing, hardly breaking a sweat himself round the ring. Engrossed in his work, Wee Frankie's eyes never missing a trick, he ignored the droplets of sweat that splatted onto his face. It would be easy to forget he'd buried his sons only the previous week.

Heart tight with an emotion he didn't want to think about too deeply, he just watched him. He swallowed hard to remove the lump in his throat. Wee Frankie had been the one to tempt him back into the ring after he'd killed his da. He suspected the coach had wanted to teach him how to channel his anger in a more controlled way. To an extent it had worked. Frankie's expert tutelage gave Loanie a focus for his darkness, however unlike the other laddies. Loanie took those skills outside the ring and into his work. He wasn't like his dad though because he could control the darkness, allowing it to surface only when he'd been wronged and when he had no other choice. From what he'd heard about Jimmy Nails, he was the same. Maybe being contemporaries, they were the new breed of gang bosses. Firm, fair but with an edge when it was necessary. *Fuck knows what the next lot will be like.*

'Aw, Lionel, son. I didn't see you there. Ye'll be wanting a wee word, is that right?'

It had been over a week since he'd visited his uncle – since the wake – yet the old man received him like he'd only nipped out for a pack of fags. Frankie, groaning a little as he ducked under the ropes and jumped down onto the ground, rubbed his lower back. 'Getting too old for this, son. Too damn old.'

100

For as long as he'd known the old man he'd uttered those exact same words every time he exited the ring. Now, though, Loanie noticed a tightening of Frankie's lips and the slight frown that tugged his eyebrows together. Pain? Grief? Guilt? Loanie couldn't decide.

Frankie slapped an arm round his shoulders and guided him through to his office. 'What's on your mind, son?'

'It's Luke Pollard. He was supposed to be providing wheels for a disposal job in Fife. He's gone AWOL . . .' Loanie shrugged, leaving his sentence unfinished.

Wee Frankie took a moment to digest this. Although Luke was one of his best mates, not so much as a twitch flickered over his face. Maybe he'd seen too much death over his lifetime. Perhaps all the things he'd lost over the years – all the friends who'd died, the loss of his wife, his sons, his brother-in-law – had left him immune to worry. Or maybe it was something else? Loanie tried to quash the treacherous thought, but it niggled just behind his sternum. His eyes narrowed, searching for any indication that Frankie already knew Luke's fate, but he couldn't decide.

'Aye, I know what ye mean. With all these murders and gangster shite going off you'll be keeching it. I hear that wee nyaff, Bertie McEwan, was tied up by the ankles and his throat slit only the other day.'

Loanie couldn't suppress the smile that twitched his lips. It was Bertie McKewan's body that Luke had been tasked with disposing of in a friendly pig farm across the Forth Road Bridge. Bertie's death wasn't common knowledge yet, although it soon would be. It paid to make a show of what you could expect if you double-crossed Loanie Gibbs. Whatever emotional trauma Frankie was going through, he still had his ear to the ground.

'Aye, the wee bastard deserved what he got. Disposing of Bertie was the job Luke blobbed on.'

He waited for Frankie to respond, but his uncle allowed a silence to gather between them until Loanie had no option but to continue. 'There something going on, Frankie. Something more than just a tussle wi' the Weegies, ye know? I mean Hardass Nails isn't stupid and it's not that long since he got out of the Bar L, so I think it's all a bit odd. It all started before then, though, didn't it? Just can't quite put my finger on when. You any ideas?'

Wee Frankie sat behind his desk, chewing on his lip. He had a cigar behind his ear, even though when the smoking ban kicked in, he'd given up, just like that. He took the cigar and rubbed it under his nose, inhaling its pungent aroma.

'Ye know, Lionel, see in that drawer.' He pointed to his top drawer. 'In there I've got a cigar that's worth a grand. One of Fidel Castro's own, I'm told. It might be over fifteen years since I quit, but mark my words, I'm going to sit here and smoke that fat cigar right here behind my desk before I retire fully. That's about the only thing I've got to look forward to these days.'

Loanie assumed his uncle was referring to his grief at losing his sons. But Frankie went on.

'See, Lionel, I'm not as fit as I was and it's almost time for me to hang up my boxing gloves. Things will get bad, really bad before they get any better and I'm sorry.'

He met Loanie's gaze. 'I've done bad things in my life – worse things than you can imagine and now it's time for me to pay for that. It'll not be long for me now, son. There's a target on my back, but before I pass, I want to tell you this. That lassie – my granddaughter Gloria, Markie's bairn. She'll be your salvation, son. She'll be the only one who can sort this mess out. It's bigger than you think and the only way to end this is to bring in new blood.'

'What the hell are you on about? We'll protect you. *I'll* protect you. I won't let anything happen to you – you know that. I'll get some men out here right now.'

Frankie smiled, his eyes sad. 'Sometimes, son, you just can't escape from your past. I owe a debt – a big one and I'm over fifty years too late paying it. If I'd been a man in those days I'd have behaved better, but I didn't and now those sins have come back to bite me on the arse. The worst thing is, I didn't learn from those mistakes. I kept repeating them again and again, using my position as the Gaffer's right-hand man to pave the way so I could do what the hell I liked. Take what the hell I liked. There's a cumulative weight on some sins, you know, Lionel, and I've got so many to my name I can scarcely distinguish one from the other. Victim after victim after victim all built up like bricks one on top of the other, growing higher and higher. I don't remember half of their names. Never saw the need to take a note. But now I am taking note, son, because now, it's not only me paying for the debts I have racked up. My actions have caused pain and death for those I love and the Grim Reaper has come to call.'

Loanie frowned. He didn't understand. It sounded like Frankie thought Tommy and Markie had been murdered to pay him back for some long-ago grievance – that he knew who was responsible. So why the hell wasn't he going after them?

Every movement heavy, Frankie pulled himself forward and moved his computer mouse. 'When I say the Grim Reaper, I mean Vengeance. Vengeance is coming to call and there's not a thing anybody can do about it. Look . . .' Frankie swivelled his screen till Loanie could read the email dated the morning Markie and Tommy were found.

Subject: Vengeance is coming for you!

Hi Frankie,
Long time, no see. I would offer my condolences for your loss, but that would be hypocritical.
However, thought you might like to see what was done to your boys in the name of Vengeance. Check out the attachments Expect a visit. Expect the worst and expect more of the same, for I AM VENGEANCE and I'm coming for you!

103

Frankie clicked the mouse and an image of Markie and Tommy's bodies filled the screen. It left no doubt that they'd suffered and that their passing had not come easily. A sound started in Loanie's gut and worked its way up till it escaped his lips as an angry howl. He pushed himself to his feet, stumbled a little and tried to control his hammering heart as Frankie removed the image. 'What the fuck? Who did this, Frankie?'

Fingers steepled at his mouth, Frankie exhaled. 'I've no idea. It could be any one of hundreds of people. And before you ask, I've tried to get a location for the sender, but apparently, it's encrypted. It's not an idle threat – we've seen what this person's capable of.'

'So, what are you saying?'

'I'm saying that it has got to be linked to all the other stuff and because it seems that it's Jimmy Nails's business in Glasgow and ours here, it's someone that we've both wronged.'

Loanie scoffed. 'Yeah, right. You and Jimmy Nails haven't dealt in the same circles, have you?'

'No, we haven't, but me and his dad and the Gaffer did. Maybe it's related to that. Maybe our interaction with this Vengeance bastard goes back fifty years ago or more.'

Loanie wasn't convinced. 'Why would someone wait fifty-odd years for revenge?'

'Aye, that's what I was wondering. I've no idea and that's why I haven't mentioned it to the Gaffer yet. Anyway, let's give it some thought. See if I can narrow it down, eh? Now, there's a reason you've come to visit, isn't there? Let's get that dealt with.'

Loanie forced himself to focus on Frankie's issue. His problem would have to wait. In the meantime, he'd send a couple of the lads over to look out for his uncle. 'Aye, the Gaffer's becoming . . .' he exhaled as he tried to come up with a word that might fit '. . . unpredictable.'

Frankie laughed. 'Aye, that's true, right enough. Always been a bit erratic, has the Gaffer. Thought they were made of that Teflon stuff they go on about. Me? I thought it was a superpower – the ability to make your shit smell like roses.'

'I think the old fucker might be losing it, though, Uncle Frankie. Our presence has been requested in Stoneyburn tonight and in Bathgate next week. As backup, would you believe? Seems there's a plan, but the canny wee bastard's not for telling me what it is. Maybe you'll have more luck finding out than me, eh?'

'The pigs still got eyes on us, Lionel?'

Loanie shook his head. 'Nah. As expected, soon after the funerals they moved on. We're in the clear for now.'

Frankie sniffed his cigar then returned it to its place behind his ear. 'In that case, I'll go with you, Lionel, and I'll try to find out what the auld bugger's up to, but you know as well as I do that that nugget can be a tight-lipped bastard at the best of times.' He got up. 'I'll also put out the word that I want to know where Luke is, but, if I were you I wouldn't hold out any hope on him being returned to us in one piece, if at all. This is bigger than me and you and bigger than Jimmy Nails too. Christ, I think it's even bigger than the Gaffer. Hell, who knows, maybe Vengeance has Luke. Maybe he's another innocent being used to deliver a message to me.'

Chapter 16

It had been a long fortnight since DCI Dick had disbanded the team and, in that time, the Jazz Queens had been careful not to have any interactions in the station that would make anyone suspect that they were unofficially still working together. Jazzy suspected that DCI Dick had spies throughout the station and keeping contact between them to a minimum would deny him the chance to rollick them.

It had been Queenie's suggestion to make their meeting an occasion so, here they were at Harburn golf club, eating at Bistro 19. Having stuffed their faces, they were ready to share the week's news. First up, and the most joyous was Fenton's. His beaming smile from the minute they met and all through dinner was a giveaway. 'I did it. I proposed and Rebecca said yes.'

'Good man.' Queenie was on her feet and bashing him on the back, before Jazzy and Geordie could issue their congratulations. 'You get down on one knee, like I told you, aye?'

'Eh, well, not exactly. Didn't quite make it to one knee. On my way down, I wobbled a wee bit and grabbed hold of the tablecloth. It and the bottle of champagne I'd ordered ended up on the floor.' For a moment a frown marred his face. 'But she still said aye, which is all that matters.'

Queenie raised an eyebrow. 'Why am I not surprised? Not so much that she said aye, although I think we're all surprised by that. Nah, the tablecloth thing. *That* doesn't surprise me.' She shook her head in mock sadness. 'There's a reason everybody calls you Haggis, you know? A reason . . .'

Jazzy spoke before Queenie could gather momentum. 'You're the only one that calls him Haggis, Queenie. Nobody else on the planet calls him that.' She turned to Fenton and raised her glass of Coke. 'Congratulations. I'm sure you'll both be very happy.'

Queenie, glass in hand, said, 'Aye, if he manages not to yank the tablecloth every time they're out for a meal.' She nudged him. 'Aye, congratulations, son. You've played a blinder there. Well done.'

Geordie grinned, raised his glass and offered his good wishes too with a few questions about dates for the wedding. But it was a short discussion and they soon got down to business.

'How is the investigation into the Lang Whang murders going?'

Geordie kicked off on that one as he was temporarily part of the investigating team. 'Well, apart from what I said earlier about the surveillance on both Loanie Gibbs and Jimmy Nails's crews, not a lot really. Dr Johnston's report came back as expected. Cause of death for both was heart attacks brought on by the torture. They were dead when they were rolled from the vehicles. I won't detail all their injuries or we'd be here till next Christmas, but the poor sods suffered.' He rearranged his gangly frame so he could lean closer. 'Overheard Dick talking about one of Loanie Gibbs' contacts – a Luke Pollard. Seems he's AWOL and Loanie's looking for him. So many crims from both Glasgow and Edinburgh are going missing and that's not counting the ones who turn up minus their hands or feet, or in one instance, one of Jimmy Nails's guys turned up minus a tongue.'

Everyone was aware of the escalating violence. Such previously unheard of levels of violence landing in their backyard was fair game and everyone seemed to be pulling their hair out, but nobody seemed to have a handle on it. 'No active leads being followed, Geordie?'

'Thing is, boss, I'm not actually doing a hell of a lot on A team. They've got me on admin stuff mostly. However, from what I pick up in the incident room, there's bugger all to go on. No forensics that we can use unless we find the vehicle to match carpet fibres with. No DNA apart from the victims and those tread marks came back as ones used by a range of vans. Word is Dick's pulling his hair out. Frankie Jones has clammed up and, according to the detectives who did the death notification, he couldn't get them out of the house quickly enough.'

'Known associates, enemies?' asked Fenton.

'Plenty, but nobody from the Edinburgh crew is talking. They interviewed Loanie Gibbs, the victims' cousin and the big man in charge in Edinburgh, but he said nothing either. Funeral was the other day and nobody who wasn't expected or didn't have an alibi showed up.' He frowned and rasped his fingers over his chin stubble. 'The only weird thing I've found is that Loanie's alibi for the time the bodies were dumped was that he was in a business meeting. He wouldn't tell us who with, but CCTV and GPS pinpointed his location. Upshot is, you'll never guess who he was meeting.'

'The Dalai Lama?' Queenie bounced on her chair and clicked her fingers. 'No, wait a minute, I've got it, the Easter Bunny . . . no, definitely Rick Astley. It was definitely one of those three he was meeting.' Queenie nudged him in the ribs. 'Bloody idiot! Get on with it, we've no' got time for guessing games. Spit it out. Who was he with?'

'Jimmy Hardass Nails.'

Jazzy's forehead puckered. 'Jimmy Nails? From Glasgow?'

'The very same and, before you ask, although neither would verify it, CCTV at Inn on the Loch did.'

'So, unless either one of them ordered a hit on the Jones brothers, they're not responsible for the dumpings.'

'But that's not to say that either or both of them didn't do the torturing.'

For a moment the four officers contemplated Geordie's information, then Fenton sighed. 'And I've got nothing to report either.' His earlier good humour had dissipated and now his shoulders slumped. 'It's awful in B team. They're a bunch of wankers. They're liaising with Fife polis on the possibility of a pig farm near Kirkcaldy being used as a disposal site for human remains. Turns out the slaughterhouse discovered a load of jewellery in the guts of some of the pigs and when they handed it in, the jewellery owners were from Shotts and were on the missing persons list. But they won't let me near that. Instead they've got me archiving crap from their previous case – where an old man threw a toaster into his wife's bath after years of suffering domestic abuse. Can't wait to be back in D team.'

'The pig farm's interesting though, isn't it? Not the first time a pig farm's been used for body disposal. Maybe keep an eye on that, Fenton. Try and check any CCTV footage they've managed to grab, eh? Or any other persons of interest they're monitoring. It's too coincidental not to be linked.'

'On it!' He took a note on his phone and then sighed before continuing. Jazzy empathised. It was slow work and they were at a disadvantage, working in the dark to glean snippets of information. 'It's not that they're not working the case. They are. Phone calls to the polis in Newcastle and Liverpool have been a dead end. I think Dick's resigned to the fact that these attacks aren't the work of English gangs and there's been no sightings logged of any of the key players from south of the border. Same for the northern gangs – zilch. I overheard Dick on the phone to the chief super. Gist of their convo was that because whoever was controlling things was always a step ahead, they were considering the possibility of a leak from our side. Have to say, it makes sense, doesn't it?'

It made perfect sense and Jazzy questioned wisdom, if that was the case, of bringing so many ex-coppers – experts or not – into the investigation. Now was the time to close doors and focus the investigation as a cohesive unit, not divide it up among different teams. It was frustrating not to have access to every area of the investigation, but there was nothing they could do about that. It wasn't within Jazzy's current remit and the reality of the situation was that the D team's hands were tied, but they'd still follow up where they could.

She lowered her voice and gestured for them all to lean in. 'So, all these meetings with current and ex Glasgow and Edinburgh DCS are happening and as you can imagine, Dick's all over them. Some of them are retired, but the other day I saw Dick exchange a dodgy handshake with one of them – soon to be ex-DCI Dougie Shearsby.'

'If you're thinking they're Masons then I'd be surprised.' Geordie grinned. 'Their handshakes are designed to be secret, so maybe it's just a tawdry chat-up attempt by Dick?'

'Yuck.' Jazzy shuddered. The very idea of Dick and chat-up in the same sentence was disturbing. 'If that was all, then I'd concede the point, Geordie, but they were acting suspiciously and were whispering to each other. It was dodgy. Plus, Dick handed him something that he made sure no one else could see. It wasn't and now with the rumour mills suggesting that someone must be leaking information about police countermeasures and that conversation Fenton heard between Afzal and Dick? Well, I think it might be worth our while checking up on them. Can either of you two access information on Dougie Shearsby? See what his personal life is like, find out what sort of a copper he was? I'll see if I can dig a bit – maybe get more info from Elliot. If not, Queenie and I can do another run by our contacts. They've mostly kept schtum till now, but it's worthwhile seeing if we can shake anything loose.'

Fenton raised a hand. 'I'll do that. There's only so much archiving you can do without going mad.'

'Thanks, Fenton. There were a couple of others at the meeting but apart from Elliot's ex-boss Emily Hare, I didn't recognise them. I'll ask around and see if I can get their names and get back to you. On the subject of Elliot – his informants have come up blank in Edinburgh and he reports that they're feeling uneasy, more reluctant to speak to him, harder to get hold of. Even the low-level criminals are running scared because they don't know where the threat is and they don't want to put themselves at risk. Some of them are already skipping ship.'

For a long moment the four of them pondered the information that had been shared, then a smile lightened Queenie's expression. 'JayZee's got something exciting to share.' Queenie wiggled her eyebrows like one of the Marx Brothers. 'Go on, tell them about your dead man.'

The thought of her and Queenie's outing with the TV company the following week made her smile. At least that was something to look forward to. She proceeded to tell them all about Sid Mackie turning up, which at least was a diversion as they contemplated the possible identity of Cairnpapple Man, then Queenie called for the bill. 'Well, if that's us done, then I want to try to make it back in time for story and bath time with Ruby. Come on, JayZee, let's get this show on the road.'

Chapter 17

Benjy Hendry hadn't felt himself for weeks now. It didn't matter that he knew *why* he didn't feel right or that he knew the immediate danger was over. It made no difference to how his body and his head felt. He wasn't thick. Course not. Benjy had read up on it all and he knew what it was. Post-traumatic stress disorder. He even knew that professionals – using the World Health Organization's International Classifications of Diseases 11 – characterised all the symptoms that had begun plaguing him before Christmas as being directly attributable to the horrific series of events he'd witnessed and been part of. For fuck's sake, he'd seen his cousin, Ivor, nearly die at the hands of a serial killer. He'd seen his new friend, Jazzy, blow up before his eyes – he'd thought she was dead. He'd thought Ivor was dead and all he wanted was for him to be dead too.

There'd been blood. So much blood. So much noise – that damn stupid ice-cream van tune plagued his nightmares, made him want to scream as he relived the horror again and again. The images of what had been done to Imogen Clark's parents that the journalist Ginny Bell had uploaded to her blog were with him constantly. The sight of Ivor, head yanked back, her eyes screaming at him to help her, her throat so pale and throbbing, then the blood. The blood everywhere and Ivor falling to the frozen ground, her eyes flickering shut. Everyone went on auto drive and that bloody tune – *'Girls and boys come out to play'* – kept playing on and on as Ivor's life drained onto a bloody manky farmyard. *'The moon doth shine as bright as day.'*

The words mocked him. *'Leave your supper and leave your sleep.'* Then the crash and Jazzy sailing through the air, landing on a heap in the field with the bike on top of her. *'And come with your playfellows into the street.'* When the explosion came it rocked the air, sent a premonition round the group. A premonition that had never left Benjy. The weight of it pressed down on him. It surrounded him, like a blanket of wire wool, making it impossible for him to sleep, to focus, to be calm.

Beside him in the driver's seat, Ivor moved, her hand reaching out and gripping his arm tight to tell him that she was there with him. To ground him in the here and now. To transport him away from the hell they'd shared before Christmas and reassure him that she would always be there for him. The tightness that had crept almost imperceptibly into his chest eased a little and his breathing slowed, the rasps becoming fainter as he patted her arm, to let her know he was coping.

Ivor, whose real name was Ivory, always had a calming effect on him. Whilst on the surface she appeared to be regaining her old confidence, sometimes she looked so sad and scared. Often, she'd stroke the scar on her throat, like she had to remind herself of what she'd nearly lost. Then she'd nod, straighten her shoulders and smile at him. If her eyes were a bit less full of life and her smile not quite as wide as before, Benjy hadn't the heart to mention it. Ivor was doing *her* – coping and dealing in her own way and Benjy had to learn to do the same.

He turned his head to scan the road, looking for anything untoward, anything suspicious. He'd already done it loads of times – one hundred and three times, to be exact – one for every minute they'd been stationed here. As with each of the previous scans, he'd identified nothing to be concerned about, yet his anxiety didn't abate. He was on high alert and nothing he did seemed to reduce it. It was weird. The sleeplessness, the need to go over everything that had happened again and again and again hadn't started immediately after the events. It had crept up on him gradually. At Christmas he'd been pulling a cracker with his dad when the image of Ivor on the ground hit him, leaving him whimpering at the dinner table. They came regularly now. They robbed him of his sleep, they stole morsels of happiness from him, they killed his desire to live. Like tinnitus but in 3D with moving images – and that damn song.

He'd begun to accept the new soundtrack to his day when the panic set in. The foreboding, the sense that nothing was right in the world. The heavy weight of fear and darkness prevailed and he was sure that evil was there waiting in the shadows for an opportunity to steal someone he loved from him. Which was why he was here, with Ivor, parked outside Jazzy's home waiting for her to return home safely. He had to know she was safe. Something, he didn't know what, compelled him to keep watch over her. She wasn't home yet, and although this was later than usual, that fact didn't concern him. Queenie would be with her and she'd keep her safe. She picked her up, because Jazzy still couldn't drive with her arm in its cast, and she dropped her back home.

During the day, Jazzy had confided she was confined to desk work, which reassured him, although he could tell it infuriated his friend. For him, though, it was the thought that Jazzy's enemy might turn up and ambush her in that short space of time between her leaving the safety of Queenie's car and entering the security of her home.

Ivor never told him his fears were irrational. Instead, she nodded and sat beside him, playing random songs on Spotify and not griping about the cold. Ivor didn't talk much anymore. Not as much as before. Her injury had made it touch and go whether she'd lose her voice altogether and she'd been lucky – not that luck had anything to do with it. It was Uncle Pedro who'd saved her. Still, nowadays she seemed content to listen and draw rather than speak. Benjy missed her chatter. The long rambling conversations about nothing and everything. It was another thing that had been stolen from him that night.

Headlights lit the street and Benjy, heart thudding wildly in his chest, peered through the gathering dusk, the thudding only receding on a wave of stagnant air when he saw Queenie's Land Rover draw into the kerb. Seconds later, Jazzy got out, her ponytail bobbing behind her, and Queenie pulled away in her usual heavy-on-the-accelerator manner. With long strides Jazzy marched towards them. Her face was stern, but Benjy could see the concern in her eyes when she rapped her knuckles on the passenger window.

'Come on, you two. You need to stop doing this. I'm safe. You're safe. Well, you would be if the pair of you stopped slipping away from the officers we've got looking out for you. You need to let this go. You need to move on with your lives.'

Benjy shook his head and refused to meet her gaze. 'Last time, Jazzy. I promise, this is the last time.'

'Humph, I'll believe that when I see it. You said that yesterday and the day before. And the . . .'

Eager for information, Benjy cut her protestations short. 'You heard from her, Jazzy?'

His eyes bored into hers. Was that hesitation on her part? Did she glance behind her like *she* was afraid of the shadows too? But when she looked back at Benjy, her lips curved into a smile. 'Don't be daft. She's long gone, Benjy. Long gone. She won't come back. She won't risk her skin. Not now we know what she's capable of.' Jazzy slapped her hand on the door, leaned in and smiled at Ivor. 'Take him home, Ivor, and you need to stop him coming here every day. Can you do that?'

Ivor shrugged and started up the car as Jazzy jogged up her path and opened her door. They waited till she was inside, with the door closed, before Ivor pulled away from the kerb and drove slowly past house where Jazzy, like she did every other night, stood at the living-room window, her cat, Winky, in her arms, waving them on their way – reassuring them that she was locked up safely at home.

As they drove towards Stùrrach, Benjy wondered about that little pause he'd detected when he asked about the escaped serial killer. He hadn't imagined the way Jazzy's smile didn't quite make it up to her eyes. She wasn't telling them everything. Of that he was certain. His chest tightened and the damn tune echoed in his head, slow and taunting.

'Girls and boys come out to play
The moon doth shine as bright as day
Leave your supper and leave your sleep
And come with your playfellows into the street.'

They were the playfellows. Him and Jazzy and Queenie and Elliot and Fenton and Geordie. Every one of them were her playfellows. A cast of puppets to be manipulated at her will. It was no wonder he couldn't sleep. No fucking wonder!

Chapter 18

'Shite. Those bloody kids are going to get themselves killed.' Jazzy watched as Ivor drove out of Bellsquarry before casting a last glance down the street. Satisfied that the street held no threat, she closed her curtains, double-checked her security before pulling out her phone and calling Elliot. 'Those kids are still acting out. They ditched their minder again tonight and were waiting for me when I got home. What if the Bitch is around? What if they get caught. I'd never . . .'

The words of her first communication from the Bitch were never far from her mind and again now they beat a tattoo in her head.

Justice is never far away. It might take months, it might take years, but trust me, we'll meet again. For now, though, watch your back and make sure those you care about watch theirs too.

That note had been left on her car windscreen outside her house whilst she'd been at her team's Christmas do. It had thrown her, big time. She'd known then that until the Bitch was safely behind bars, she and everyone she cared about were targets. She could just about cope with the uncertainty . . . but her friends?

117

Her team? *That* was a different matter. Her inability to catch the killer when she had the chance had left them all at risk and there was nothing she could do about it. Apart from infrequent meetings with Simon, at the State psychiatric hospital, Jazzy had been excluded from the ongoing investigation.

'It's okay, Jazz. It's okay.' Elliot's voice was reassuring – as if he sensed her anxiety. 'Let me think about it. I'll pull in some favours and get someone who owes me to keep them safe.'

Jazzy's laugh was hard. 'You mean you're going to get one of your CIs to watch those kids? Really? With everything that's going down with the gangs in Glasgow and Edinburgh, do you really think you can trust your informants? Get real, Elliot. You told me they're scrambling over each other trying to keep their throats intact and their limbs attached. Give them a juicy assignment and who knows who they'll sell you out to. You said it yourself, it's lawless out there. Doesn't it tell you something, Elliot, that dickless wonder and DCS Afzal are cosying up with the chief supers from Edinburgh and Glasgow as well as retired ex-bosses too? If they're bringing in ex-coppers to sort out their gang problems, what hope do we have of them catching the Bitch, *or*, more to the point, protecting anybody.'

The silence between the two was contemplative rather than angry. Elliot was a realist and he'd be aware of the fragility of his carefully nurtured relationships with his CIs. After all, the worst *he* could do was throw them in the nick, but the gang leaders – well, they were an entirely different breed of human. Sometimes Jazzy wondered if they were indeed human at all. The number of bodies littering the streets these days seemed to indicate that their lack of humanity was escalating and the streets seemed to be running red with blood and nobody was able to work out why things were intensifying right now.

'You're right Jazzy. Remember Dukesy?'

'Your CI? Shuffles when he walks?'

'Aye that's right. He wanted protection. Protection that I couldn't offer because Edinburgh division is as stretched as

Greater Glasgow. I saw him earlier and he said he was heading up north to avoid being embroiled in the shite that's going on down here. Can't say I blame him, either.'

'So, no money to protect innocent kids who got caught up in something evil? Is that what you're saying?' Jazzy's tone was harsher than she intended and she bit her tongue, regretting her outburst. It wasn't Elliot's fault after all. He always bent over backwards to help when he could. 'I'm sorry. That was unfair. I'm just so frustrated. Frustrated and worried to death for them. I can't have any more deaths on my conscience. I just can't.'

Elliot's tone when he replied was subdued – despondent even. 'You got an idea, Jazz? Because I'm all out of them.'

Jazzy plopped down on her sofa and allowed Winky to jump onto her lap. Elliot was the eternal optimist and his glum affect and the flatness of his words showed just how difficult things were in Edinburgh, which meant that the fallout on the surrounding areas would continue to escalate.

When Jazzy didn't respond, he continued, 'We need someone who'll blend in with the Stùrrach villagers. We need someone they'll not clock as polis and I just don't have anyone free. I hate to say it, Jazz, but Benjy and Ivor are on your turf. It's up to you to try to sort it out. Maybe have a word with DCI Dick and if that fails – which knowing the dickless wonder, it will – then go above his head to the chief super.'

Now it was Jazzy's turn to sigh. Neither of those two options was remotely acceptable. Firstly, although DCI Dick hated Jazzy, the reality was his budget was severely stretched, which meant that he had a genuine reason to ignore any requests regarding ongoing protection for the two teenagers. Which left DCS Waqas Afzal. Jazzy's heart sank at the prospect of having to go with her begging bowl to the big boss. Of course, he'd listen to her. Perhaps he'd even see things her way, but that didn't mean she wanted to have an interaction with him. Not with their troubled history and certainly *not* if it risked their true relationship becoming common knowledge.

'Leave it with me. I'll have a think about it.'

A companionable silence stretched between them for a few moments and then Elliot said, 'So, you said some high heid yins were in your neck of the woods. Which ones? Any ideas what prompted that visit?'

'Joint task force would be my reckoning – not before time too. Neutral territory and all that. You're soon to be ex-boss, Shearsby, was there.' She filled him in on her observations of Shearsby's interactions with DCI Dick.

'That wouldn't surprise me. Guy's a right todger. I'll keep an eye on him.'

The venom in Elliot's words drew a smile from Jazzy. 'Geordie reckons that a Mason's handshake is undetectable to an observer, so maybe I'm wrong.'

'Mm, maybe, but I wouldn't put anything past Dick, or Shearsby for that matter, if he thought it would give him a leg up. Who else was there? Anyone else I'd know?'

'Another of your ex-bosses was there too. Emily Hare. What's she like?'

'Aw, Emily's all right. Got her head screwed on. Very efficient. I enjoyed working with her. Was sad when she retired. We could do with more like her.'

'Dick was in his element. Right up their arses – all loud guffaws, moustache in constant motion and back slaps, he was so eager to please.'

Elliot's laugh made Jazzy smile. She liked it when he laughed. Liked *making* him laugh, but that was a phenomenon she wasn't keen to examine, not until things were less unsettled. Not until the Bitch was locked up and the key thrown away. Not until everyone was safe. She cleared her throat. 'You all right for next week?'

Immediately, the shared moment of camaraderie between them vanished. Elliot's response was slow to come and was accompanied by a sigh. 'Of course, I'm all right for next week. No way would I let you go through that on your own. You know that, Jazz. But . . .'

Again, he paused and Jazzy visualised him pinching the bridge of his nose. His jaw would have tightened in frustration and he'd be doing that weird twisty movement with his neck to try to release the tension. Although she anticipated his next words, she waited. She owed him the chance to verbalise his concerns, even if she'd ignore them. He'd still come with her. Still have her back. Still help her pick up the pieces, so she owed him that much at least.

'You don't have to keep doing this, Jazz. Simon is playing you. Using you as a distraction from his being incarcerated. It gives him a buzz to feel that you're playing his game. You know that. Plus, we don't know who is feeding the two of them information. I worry that we've got an enemy close to us. I'm pissed off that they're still using you to do their dirty work, if I'm honest.'

Everything Elliot said was correct. Simon was a manipulative sociopath and he enjoyed yanking her chain. However, every other investigative avenue had led to a dead end. The Bitch was a ghost and Jazzy was convinced her brother's hubris would eventually make him share details that might help them. Jazzy also suspected that the Bitch would be aware of Simon's loose tongue. In fact, she was counting on that.

'I know that. I know it's a long shot, but I've got to take it. I've got to try anything to put an end to this. Besides, now we've increased the IT checks and are taking those other precautions, I feel more reassured, don't you?'

'I think "reassured" is pushing it, Jazzy. We've got to continue to be vigilant. We can't rely on others to protect us. We've got to keep our heads in the game and I, for one, will be relieved when I don't have to visit that place again or see that little bastard's smug face.'

'I'm sorry Afzal is making you accompany me, but I'm also glad he is. You being with me helps. It makes it just a bit more bearable.' Aware that her voice had wobbled on the last word,

Jazzy injected some warmth to her tone. 'Look, did I tell you about the rather interesting day I had. A dead man walked into the station and next week Queenie and I are having a day out because of it.'

Chapter 19

It had been a while since Jazzy had last visited the Argy Bargy pub in Stùrrach, but it was well worth braving the elements to be there. She wasn't driving and after her phone call with Elliot earlier, she could indulge in a glass of wine for once. The taxi driver had looked a bit dubious when she gave her destination and, in the end, Jazzy reckoned it was only the sight of her banged-up arm and the fact that she said she was happy to walk from the end of the road that had convinced him to take the fare. They were in the snug, the fire was lit, the lighting dim and for once Jazzy felt safe, cocooned in the security of this strange, but loving village.

'So, Jazzy – or should it be DS Solanki tonight? – what can I do for you?'

Jazzy tipped her glass in Uncle Pedro's direction and winked. 'Best if we keep it informal tonight, Pedro.'

The big man's ever-present smile widened and he raised an eyebrow. 'Ah, it's like that, is it? Well, crack on, hen. You know I'll help you if I can.' His voice got a bit gruff as he continued, 'We owe a lot to you and your friends. Us Stùrrachers have long memories. We won't forget it.'

Jazzy's take on things differed wildly from Pedro's. Whilst the villagers saw her as some sort of saviour who'd risked life and limb to save Benjy and Ivor, Jazzy couldn't shake the belief that she'd put the teenagers in danger in the first place. But that wasn't why she was here tonight. Tonight, she wanted a favour. Since Christmas, she and Pedro had become friends. They'd shared a few drinks in the Argy Bargy. They'd also shared a few war stories. Jazzy had found it easy to talk to the big man. His gentle strength sort of drew her in and made her trust him.

It hadn't happened all at once. Rather, it had been a gradual lowering of her defences as she realised that, like her, Pedro had his own demons to exorcise. He'd shared stories about his life as an army doctor in Iraq and his subsequent nomadic, less-than-predictable one since he'd been discharged from the army. Tongue in cheek, he often described his past as being 'textured not chequered'. He'd confided that he had many friends from many walks of life, some of whom lived completely off the grid. It was this network Jazzy hoped he'd utilise on her behalf.

'I've two favours to ask you, but I want you to know that you don't have to agree. I won't hold it against you if you say no. Is that clear?'

'Ach, away with you, Jazzy. Whatever you want doing, consider it done. Now, let's get the business part out of the way, so we can catch up on real life. How does that sound?'

Wishing they could cut to the catching-up part, Jazzy took another sip of her wine. She placed her glass on the beer mat. 'Let's get the easy part out of the way first. I'm worried about Benjy. He's not coping and he needs help. I think he's suffering from PTSD and that's not something that will go away without professional guidance.' Jazzy knew from first-hand experience. 'He keeps turning up at my place to check that I've got home all right and . . .' She rubbed her hand over her brow.

'Say no more. I know a thing or two about post-traumatic stress myself. Nobody who served in a battle zone got off scot-free and what that wee laddie witnessed was as bad as a battle zone. I'll keep an eye on him. See if I can't have a wee word with him.'

124

'It's not just that, though, Pedro. You've heard of all the gang stuff kicking off?'

Pedro nodded.

'Well, the consequences of that are that resources are being directed towards those investigations, which means . . .'

He wafted his hands in the air. 'Aye, I get that too. There's nobody free to keep an eye on those two kids, and the Bitch – as you so aptly call that killing scumbag – is still at large. Don't you worry yourself. I'll be their bodyguard till you catch the serial-killing bastard who tore a hole in Ivor's throat. That's not a problem. Now, what else?'

'I need you to do more than that, Pedro. I need you to find her.'

'The Bitch?'

Too nervous to speak, Jazzy nodded.

Pedro downed the last of his pint and signalled to the bloke at the bar for another drink for them both. 'Looks like we might need this, eh?'

When the drinks arrived, he took a long swallow of his before speaking. 'I take it we're not talking through legal channels.'

Still hardly believing she was going through with this, Jazzy shook her head. 'The legal channels aren't working. We're no further forward and the pair of them are taunting us. It has to stop. For all our sakes. It must end before someone else gets hurt.'

Pedro's eyebrows pulled together. 'And what exactly do you mean when you say "end"?'

That was the part Jazzy struggled with the most. Just how far was she prepared to go to keep everyone safe? Edging into minor illegalities to find a serial killer was one thing, but was that *all* she wanted or did she want more?

The silence between them was tense, then Pedro said, 'In my experience, being responsible for the death of someone – friend or foe – whether by action or one degree removed, is too big a burden to carry. You're not that person, Jazzy Solanki. You'd never forgive yourself if you gave me carte blanche tonight to arrange for the death of another human being. Let's opt for locating the Bitch and once we've done that, we'll trust that your lot don't fuck up the capture, eh?'

She closed her eyes for a moment to hide her sudden tears. When she opened them again she was composed. 'Thanks, Pedro. Thanks for this.'

'No bother. I've got a few contacts who owe me, so I'll get them on the case. Before long, that Bitch will be behind bars and we can all get on with our lives.'

Monday 6th March

Chapter 20

Jazzy had almost ignored the call from DCS Afzal, but something made her hesitate. She lifted her finger to disconnect the call, then reconsidered. What if it was about Simon? Or maybe they'd apprehended the Bitch. At that thought, Jazzy's heart hiccupped in her chest before continuing at a faster pace. She had no option really.

She pushed her chair back and as she headed for the door she mimed an 'I'm taking this outside' gesture to Queenie, who was busy throwing rolled-up paper balls into the bin.

Once she was in the corridor, the ringing stopped. Damn! She'd been too slow, now she'd have to phone him back. But before she could do so, it began ringing again. *Thank God!*

She answered with a curt, 'Yes?'

Afzal hesitated as if surprised that she'd answered. 'Something's come up and I need you to come to my office, right now.'

'Is it Si . . .?'

But her question hung half-uttered in the air as Afzal cut her off. *Arrogant bastard!* Tapping her phone against her lips, she contemplated ignoring his summons, but that was just her obstinate streak kicking in. If she wanted to know what his abrupt call was all about then she had no option. She'd have to bite the bullet and head up there.

The chief super's office was on the top floor and thus afforded more privacy than those on lower floors. When she arrived there, Jazzy hesitated outside his door, willing herself not to do or say anything stupid. At times like this, Queenie would be a good person to have by her side, for she could always be relied upon to demand answers in her own indomitable way while deflecting attention away from her. As she exhaled, tightened her ponytail and knocked firmly, Jazzy wondered who else would be present – hopefully not the dickless wonder.

His reply was instant. 'Come in.'

As she entered, her eyes swept the room and registered that they were alone. Afzal moved round his desk as if to greet her, then stood, arms clasped awkwardly in front of him as he nodded to three comfy chairs in the corner flanked by a coffee table. Jazzy's eyes drifted to the informal set-up and back to Afzal. Instead of complying, she moved to a chair in front of his desk and perched on the edge. With a shrug, Afzal ran his fingers through his hair, straightened his tie and returned to his earlier position behind his computer.

Ramrod straight, both feet on the floor and her fingers linked loosely in her lap, Jazzy waited. Her face had become flushed as she wondered what the hell this was all about. Perhaps something *had* happened to Simon? She wasn't sure how she'd feel about that. He might be her brother, but he was also responsible for countless deaths. Then, as Afzal's steady gaze fastened on her face, her eyes widened as another thought occurred. Was it Elliot? Or Benjy or Ivor? Or her parents? Had something happened to them? Had the Bitch got to them?

As if sensing her thought processes, Afzal wafted a hand in the air. 'Everybody's okay, Jazzy. That's not why you're here.'

He leaned forward, elbows propped on his shiny desk and fingers steepled at his chin. With the news that everyone was fine, relief flooded her body, but Jazzy, not prepared to give Afzal an inch, maintained a dignified silence. True, this cloak-and-dagger stuff had piqued her curiosity, but now an insidious thought wormed its way into her head. *What if it was a ruse?* She dreaded discovering that he'd brought her up here on false pretences. That this was personal, not professional. The very idea that she might have been duped made her hands clammy. A fiery ball rose from the pit of her stomach up into her chest and began to expand there, making it hard to breathe. She began to rise, ready to walk out before he could get started, but again, as if interpreting her innermost thoughts, he waved her back to her seat.

His voice held an edge of annoyance. 'It's not . . . about . . .' He shrugged and didn't finish his sentence, 'It's work, DS Solanki. I asked you to come here on a work-related issue.'

Relieved to have that clarified, she nodded and sank back onto the chair. She could cope with work-based things. She was a professional, after all. A light knock at the door had Jazzy's heart beating again. Clearly someone else was invited to this meeting and she braced herself for the dickless wonder's abrasive onslaught.

The door opened. Not DCI Dick, but ex-Chief Super Emily Hare from Elliot's turf. *What the hell is going on?*

'You've met DCS Emily Hare, I believe?'

Jazzy shook her head. 'No.'

Afzal frowned. 'No? Well, then let me introduce you. This is ex-Chief Super Hare from Edinburgh division. We're using her expert knowledge of Loanie Gibbs's activities in Edinburgh to assist in Operation Towpath. This is DS Jasmine Solanki.'

This was intriguing. Jazzy hadn't realised that an official task force had been created, let alone what it was called. The two women nodded at each other and Hare, with a glance towards the less informal seating arrangement, shrugged, and took the vacant chair next to Jazzy as Afzal spoke.

'This is sensitive, Jazzy. We're going to ask you to do something. Take on a huge responsibility and until I know that you'll accept it, I want your word that what we speak about won't leave these four walls.' Afzal maintained eye contact, his brow furrowed and his lips tight. His hands – now clenched together so tightly his knuckles had turned white – rested on his desk. To her left, Jazzy was aware of Emily Hare's scrutiny. She'd years of experience on Jazzy and who knew what she thought of Afzal recruiting a mere DS to whatever clandestine operation he had in mind. Elliot would be much more suitable for this, wouldn't he?

Tension radiated from him until Jazzy nodded. Whatever this was, it must be huge. It was a no-brainer for Jazzy. If she could be a part of the investigation – even on the periphery – then of course she would agree. Nothing could be worse than being stuck in an office doing busywork at DCI Dick's constant beck and call. 'Go on.'

With a brief smile, Afzal nodded at Emily, before launching into his speech. 'I don't need to tell you how bad things are. Apart from the murder of the Jones boys, throughout the region and beyond there are people being kneecapped, forced to drink bleach, beaten up, raped and generally terrorised. And so far, Police Scotland haven't had a handle on it. Until now, that is.'

He sipped from a glass of water on his desk. 'You won't be aware of this, because D team has been excluded from the investigation, but we've had conflicting information about the source – or rather sources – of this violence. As you'd expect, both Jimmy Nails's crew in Glasgow and Loanie Gibbs's in Edinburgh are responsible for some of the more minor tit-for-tat responses – often without the direction of the bosses themselves. Our sources have gleaned that there is someone else at play, though, and that neither Gibbs nor Nails are behind the more extreme acts of violence. At first, we suspected a hostile territorial takeover from the North of England, but in working with our friends south of the border we've deduced that not to be the case.'

This was exactly what Jazzy and her team had thought for a long time so nothing he'd said so far was a surprise to her. 'So, you're saying that it's confirmed that neither Loanie, Jimmy nor the English gangs are responsible for what's going on?' She paused, frowned and then corrected herself. 'Or not *entirely* responsible.'

'Exactly. We've had undercover officers working round the clock, but until this morning, despite the input from Emily here and others like her, we've been pissing around in the dark.' He paused. 'And that's where you come in.'

'Me?' Jazzy had never done undercover work before.

Afzal's grin took years off his age. The creases by his eyes became laughter lines rather than signs of the stress he was operating under. 'Oh, no, Jazzy. I think we both know that with your public profile, undercover work is not for you. Besides, there's nothing subtle about that pink cast of yours either. If you agree, I want you to be a minder for a longstanding covert operator. You already know him in his covert role, so that should make it easier for you to build a relationship at short notice.'

What? I know an undercover officer? Jazzy could count the number of non-police people she knew on both hands. Maybe Afzal meant 'know' as in be vaguely acquainted with. Now, *that* was more like it.

'I won't reveal his identity until you know exactly what will be expected of you and you agree to it.'

Jazzy leaned forward, all signs of her earlier tension and animosity gone. 'Tell me.'

'After the murders of Wee Frankie Jones's boys, a few red flags went up among our confidential informants. Although Frankie retired a few years ago, everybody expected him to seek revenge for their deaths, but he didn't. Not a sausage. We've been monitoring him, but there's no indication that he's reached out to any of his known enforcers, which made us wonder why not? That, in turn, brought to our attention the fact that Loanie Gibbs – Frankie's nephew and the man who inherited his business empire on his retirement – had reached out to Jimmy Nails. Again, curious. Why would those two feel the need to meet up unless they were convinced they were *both* under threat from the same source?'

None of this was news to Jazzy, but she managed to maintain a neutral expression. 'Long story short, we've been monitoring Frankie, Loanie and Jimmy Nails's activities and discovered that two out of the three – Frankie and Jimmy – have both felt the need to employ a hacker. Whilst we're not sure exactly *who* they want to hack or *why* they want to hack, this was enough to get us the go-ahead to do a bit of hacking of our own. Emily and I have been working on putting this together and *that's* where you come in.' Afzal paused. 'Coffee? I was up all night and I could do with a caffeine boost.'

'I'd prefer a whisky, Waqas, but coffee it is.' Emily Hare's smile was wide as the coffee machine buzzed in the background and then she turned to Jazzy and addressed her in her husky voice. 'This could be a really productive operation, DS Solanki.' Her grey eyes studied Jazzy as if she expected her to refuse. For someone in their early seventies, Jazzy thought Emily Hare had exceptional skin, before realising that the lack of reaction wrinkles on her face when she smiled was a result of Botox, not good genes.

Jazzy nodded. This was huge. Did Jimmy and Frankie believe they were being hacked or did they need an expert to find information on who was behind the violence? It was strange that Frankie was seeking digital help. She would have thought he was old-school. Perhaps their business infrastructure was under attack? But that didn't explain why Loanie wasn't leading on this. Perhaps he was behind it all? Were relations between Loanie and his mentor splintering?

Afzal placed both women's frothy coffees on coasters on his desk and sat down with his own. 'We have an undercover officer working in Edinburgh. He's been there for a while now, but as well as being skilled at nosing out pertinent information on the ground and developing sources, he's a skilled hacker. Over-the weekend we've set the wheels in motion for him to infiltrate Jimmy Nail's set-up. He's jumped ship from Edinburgh, like other low-level criminals in Edinburgh, and pretended to head up north – that seems to be where those who want to stay alive are heading. But, he's actually going to move to Glasgow, offer his IT services to Nails, in light of his IT expert going AWOL, and invent some beef with Loanie Gibbs as a cover story. I want you to be his contact here – his handler. He's doing this beneath the radar. Nobody knows he's working undercover, not even his CI handler in Edinburgh, and we want to keep it that way. With Lothian and Borders being dragged into this mess and with no real clue who the enemy is, we've decided to keep this card close to our chest. Just to be clear, this is only between you, me, the undercover officer and Emily here. Nobody else. We're keeping it tight. There's been too many leaks for us not to suspect that we've got a bent officer in our midst. This is a West Lothian operation only. So, what do you think?'

Every covert operative needed someone trustworthy to be on hand twenty-four hours a day and Jazzy was sorely tempted. 'Why me? I'm not exactly flavour of the month, am I?'

Afzal grinned. 'No, you're not, but you've been a handler once before and reports say you excelled in the role. Come on, Jazzy, you in or do I have to ask one of those wankers from B team?'

Emily Hare laughed and winked at Jazzy. 'There're always wankers from A or B team willing to trip you up. I know how hard it is to hold your own as a woman moving up the ranks. Take this opportunity, Jasmine. It will be the making of your career.'

Ah, so that's why Afzal brought Hare in. He thought she might refuse him, but he hoped a well-respected female senior officer would convince her. He underestimated Jazzy. No way would she allow her personal issues with Afzal to affect her professional decisions. 'Yep. I'm in. Give me the details, sir.'

'Ah.' Afzal cringed. 'This is where it gets tricky. The thing is the officer you'll be handling is a bloke known as Dukesy although he'll be in disguise as a Cockney hacker called Spaceman. Not sure even his current handler would recognise him. Have you heard of him?'

Jazzy's heart sank. *Dukesy, Elliot's CI?* They'd only been talking about him the other night and Elliot had said he was skipping town till things settled down. Now she knew why.

'Aye, I met him a while back. He's one of Elliot's, isn't he?'

'That's right. Will that be a problem for you?'

'Just not sure why you wouldn't use the officer he's already working with?' As the words left her lips, realisation hit her like a kick in the gut. 'You think Elliot might be the leak?'

Afzal scratched his forehead. 'We don't think that, Jazzy. On the other hand, we don't *know* that he's not.'

Emily Hare frowned and leaned forward. 'We hope it's not Elliot, Jasmine. We really do, but we can't discount him. He had a close relationship with another ex-DCS who we suspect may have used his position for criminal gain, so of course we must be scrupulous. Ex-DCI Shearsby is being monitored, as is DI Balloch. We're covering all our bases – with things as severe as they are, we've no other option.'

'Aw, for God's sake, this is Elliot we're talking about. He's not corrupt.' She turned to Hare. 'Surely *you* know that. He worked for you too. You must know he's not on the take.'

Hare, hands splayed before her, shrugged. 'He wouldn't be the first, dear, and I'm quite sure he won't be the last.'

Rage unfurled in Jazzy's chest and fire reddened her cheeks. She opened her mouth to respond, but Afzal intervened. 'Don't let this get personal. The reason we're keeping this operation in house in West Lothian and so low key is because we just don't know which of our officers to trust in Edinburgh *or* Glasgow. We're not targeting him. We're just being canny.'

Jazzy exhaled. What the hell would Elliot think when he found out she'd snatched his CI from right under his nose and hadn't had the courtesy to tell him? That she was working on an investigation to ascertain whether he was corrupt or not? Would he hate her? After everything he'd done for her, this felt like betrayal.

'Come on, DS Solanki, I need to know if you're in or out.'

A dull throb started at her temples and her vision blurred. She blinked a few times, trying to dislodge the shimmering mirage of Elliot that had appeared behind Afzal's shoulder. Elliot's arms were folded across his chest, his lips pursed in disgust as his head moved slowly from side to side in silent rebuke. Squeezing her eyes shut, she pleaded with the vision to understand, and when she opened them again, Elliot turned and faded to nothingness. Sweat pooled in her armpits and her heart tharrumped in her chest as she tried to swallow the acid in her throat. She was letting him down big time and it didn't take one of her stupid day visions to tell her that. What if, when he found out, Elliot thought that *she* believed he was corrupt? Would she live to regret her decision? Probably. Would she be racked with guilt every time she told him a lie to conceal the truth? Definitely. But she knew she had to agree. This was her chance to make a difference – albeit a small one. Besides, if anyone could prove Elliot's innocence then it was her.

'I'm in.'

Chapter 21

The fucking email that arrived on Saturday had got to Jimmy. Got right inside his head. At first, he'd thought it was a prank, but he'd soon dispelled that idea. Things were too precarious at the moment to dismiss threats like this as a bit of high jinks. Besides, it was disturbing. *Vengeance is coming for you!* That had been the subject heading. What sort of sick fuck sends an email like that? But if he'd thought that was ominous then the email content took ominous to a whole new level.

Dear Jimmy,
Long time, no see. I wonder if you remember me? I remember you. How could I forget?
I know what you did and I'll make you pay. You took something I valued from me, now I'll take something that you value from you. Can you guess what?
Beware, though, Jimmy, I won't stop there, for I AM VENGEANCE and I am coming for you.

Normally he wouldn't worry, but after the murders of the Jones boys in Edinburgh and a couple of other violent attacks on his men, he knew better than to ignore it. After Bobby Cassily had

138

missed their meeting in the chapel on Ecclefechan Street yesterday and hadn't answered his phone since and by all accounts no one had seen him since Saturday, Jimmy's anxiety levels had escalated, which was why he'd spent most of Sunday trawling the streets looking for him. He'd been round all his mate's known haunts and put the word out that he was looking for him, but so far nada.

Now, it was Monday and he'd had to adapt his plans. As he huddled over a coffee and a bacon roll slathered in brown sauce in Auld Ma Broon's café, wee frissons of anxiety pattered up and down his spine, and his shoulders were tensed. He'd had two very specific tasks in mind for Bobby and the wee bugger's absence had thrown a spanner in the works. *Where the hell is he?*

Jimmy had spent his time since his release from the Bar L reacquainting himself with his business, getting on top of things that had lapsed during his absence and making sure the message that Jimmy Nails was back in charge was out there. That email, however, had made him adjust his priorities. If anyone could find out who this Vengeance character was, then it was Bobby Cassily. If the fucker was shacked up with some whore, Jimmy would be right pissed off. But deep down, he knew that Bobby was no more shacked up with a bird than Jimmy was Mr Universe. Which could only mean one thing: Bobby was another casualty in the war that was going on around them.

He picked up a copy of the *Daily Record* that someone had discarded. The headlines were all about that Cairnpapple Man and a witness that had come forward. Jimmy skim-read the article, but decided there was nothing new in it. Just the same old rehash of the stuff from the other week. He flipped through the pages, checking for anything that might relate to his business interests but there was nothing, thank fuck! Granted, the arrival of that message had set him on edge, but that wasn't the only thing that made his teeth itch – the unpredictable carnage was more than worrying and although Bobby being offed wouldn't be more than a minor inconvenience to Jimmy, it still rankled.

He slurped a mouthful of coffee to wash the roll down, but it left a bad taste in his mouth – or maybe it wasn't the coffee. He'd been relying on Bobby to keep tabs on Loanie Gibbs, but now that idea had been kyboshed, he'd been forced to find an alternative. Flinging his napkin on top of his empty plate, Jimmy scraped his chair back, flung a twenty on the table and left.

The cool air hit him as soon as he left the café and rather than huddle away from it like other pedestrians, Jimmy leaned against the café window and waited, his head tilted back and with his eyes closed, he savoured the icy breeze washing over his face. He'd been banged up for too long not to appreciate a crisp fresh morning like this. With his next best option due to arrive at any minute, Jimmy considered what he knew about the man he was about to trust with his secret email. Although this hacker had defected from Edinburgh, Jimmy was sure the man's loyalty could be bought – at the right price. That was how things worked in his world and Jimmy had plenty of dosh to buy what he wanted.

At the sound of an uneven gait shuffling along the road, Jimmy opened his eyes and straightened. The man – known only as Spaceman – shambled towards him, a cigarette hanging from the corner of his mouth, his greasy, sparse hair flapping in the breeze. Spaceman was a Cockney who'd lived in Scotland for decades, yet had never lost his accent.

'Hey up, boss. Heard you wanted to see me.'

'You heard right, Spaceman. Walk with me, eh?' Jimmy took off along the street, his long legs eating up the pavement, but noticing that Spaceman lagged behind, he slowed his pace. For the length of the street the two men walked in silence, Spaceman puffing on his cigarette and Jimmy wondering if he was putting his trust in the right man. The fact of the matter was, he needed to know three things. He had to learn who had sent that email, he wanted to know if Loanie Gibbs was involved and lastly, he needed a breakdown of what Loanie was getting up to in Edinburgh. There was no one else who possessed the specific skills that he required and who could also blend into the Edinburgh scene as easily as Spaceman – well, Bobby could have, but fuck knew where he was. 'I've got a proposition for you. You up for that?'

Spaceman tossed his fag into the gutter and stopped. 'Well, son, that very much depends on the extent of the recompense for my bother.' He smiled, his teeth nicotine-stained, his ocean blue eyes seeming to penetrate right into Jimmy's soul. 'I mean, we all know just how dangerous being involved with the Nails or the Gibbs families is at the minute. I'd expect my fee to reflect that danger, you get me?'

Jimmy expected this, so he offered a fee that was less than the one he'd been prepared to offer Bobby and, after a few minutes of genial wrangling, they shook on a largely inflated fee.

With a satisfied grin, Spaceman squinted at Jimmy. 'So, what's the job?'

Jimmy explained about the anonymous email and Spaceman nodded along. 'Aye well, I'll need access to your email account.'

Jimmy grimaced. He'd been expecting that, but allowing a stranger – albeit a professional – access to his emails was a bit like opening the front door and welcoming the whole city in for a free-for-all. 'I need guarantees, Spaceman. That's my private stuff you want access to.'

Spaceman grinned. 'You know, I only asked as a courtesy, man. I don't need your passwords and suchlike to access your accounts. I'm a hacker – accessing folks' accounts is sort of in the job description.' He laughed a throaty, fifty-a-day laugh. 'You have my word, though. I have a strict client confidentiality rule and I've never yet broken it. You know that, otherwise you'd never have contacted me in the first place. Am I right?'

Of course, he was right. That's why he'd been near the top of Jimmy's list. His services had been recommended *and* his discretion vouched for.

'Regarding the other stuff, I expect detailed nightly updates, Spaceman. None of this checking in as and when you feel like it.

I want the information forwarded to me as you acquire it. I want times, places, names of the people he interacts with, and I expect you to get into his computer and phones too. Everything bugged. I want the lot, got it?'

'Aye, I've got it. I might look like a cabbage but I'm not green. I know what happens to them that cross Hardass Nails. I'm not daft, mate.'

He saluted Jimmy and shuffled off in the direction of the nearest bus stop without another word. It never ceased to amaze Jimmy that this middle-aged tramp-like figure could hide such a talented hacker.

Turning in the opposite direction, Jimmy shoved his hands into his pockets and whistled as he walked. Now he could relax for the rest of the day and crack on with untangling the mess his bastard brother-in-law had made of his 'not for the taxman' business accounts.

Chapter 22

'What's with all the cloak-and-dagger stuff, JayZee?' Queenie licked at the brown sauce oozing out the side of her sausage roll. 'Not that I'm complaining, mind. No, not at all. You know me, I like a free flat sausage in a floury roll, don't I? And I don't mind sitting on a bench in Cauther Square in the freezing cold, either – not when there's the food of the gods on offer.' She took a huge bite and washed it down with a slug of extra strong builder's tea.

Jazzy glanced round, making sure no one was in earshot and leaned closer to her friend. 'You've got to promise not to tell anyone.'

Queenie yawned, revealing a delightful mouthful of mashed-up bread and meat. 'Aye, whatever.'

'I'm serious. This is important. You can't tell anyone, okay?'

Queenie placed her half-eaten roll on the wrapper beside her, wiped her mouth with a napkin and studied her friend. 'Okay, hen. I'm all ears.'

With a big sigh, Jazzy took a swig of her water. 'Afzal called me up to his office this morning.'

'I wondered where you'd pissed off to. What did he want? A family reunion, eh? A tête-à-tête with his oldest daughter, an invitation to award him father of the y . . .'

'*Queenie!*'

'Sorry. That was bang out of order.' She lifted her disposable cup and waited for Jazzy to continue.

'I thought he'd sussed out that I'd asked Uncle Pedro for help.'

Queenie glared at Jazzy. 'You asked Uncle Pedro for help and you never ran it by me first? What the hell, JayZee? I thought we were partners in crime, us two. You know, BFFs. Trusted confidantes who shared their deepest darkest secrets. *That's* what I *thought* you and me were.' Queenie swung her finger between the two of them, her lips all pouty, disappointment clouding her eyes. 'Seems I was waaaay off the mark.'

Jazzy rolled her eyes and groaned. 'We *are* all of those things, Queenie. Well, not exactly *all* of them, but close enough. I had good reason not to tell you . . .'

'Oh, you had a sudden case of laryngitis, did you?'

'Eh, no, that's—'

'A bout of amnesia . . . forgot who your partner was, that it?'

'No, course n—'

'Then it can only be because you don't trust me.' Queenie took a bite of her roll and chewed, all the while shaking her head morosely.

'If you'd let me get a word in, I'll tell you.' Jazzy nudged Queenie and grinned. 'But only if you want to know, of course. I mean I'd understand it if you felt too betrayed to listen now.'

Queenie swallowed a lump of bread and sausage and shrugged. 'Hmph.'

'I'll take that as a yes, shall I?'

'Just get on with it, JayZee. What did you ask Pedro to do that you didn't want Afzal to get wind of?'

'What I asked him to do isn't exactly legal. I mean, it's really skiting on the very edges of legality, Queenie. That's why I wanted to keep you out of it.'

'Like a wee bit of illegal activity ever put me off catching a criminal. I mean, think needle-gate. You think I "forgot" I had a

144

knitting needle in my hand when I brought that wee tosser down? Did I fuck. He got what he deserved, that's all I'm saying.' With her fingers, she made a button action near her lips.

'Yes, but if there were consequences—'

'Then we'd go down together, you and me – we're the Jazz Queens and we have each other's backs. Anyway, what did you ask the big man to do?'

'Well, I asked him to keep an eye on Benjy and Ivor. I'm worried sick about their mental health – especially Benjy's.'

'Aye, I can see that. The pair of them have been through a lot, but that's not it, is it? That's not what you asked Pedro to do, is it?'

Twisting her fingers together, Jazzy shook her head.

'You asked him to use any means at his disposal to find Mhairi, didn't you?'

'Aye. I *had* to. I *have* to keep everyone safe, and that won't happen till the Bitch is locked up for good.'

Queenie nodded. 'Good move, hen. With all Pedro's contacts, he'll come up trumps, so I wouldn't worry about it.' Queenie slapped her hand to her forehead, leaving a smudge of brown sauce there. 'Unless of course Afzal got wind of it. He did, didn't he? One of Pedro's sources triggered an alarm; Afzal put two and two together and dragged you in. Shite, I'm sorry, JayZee. Has the bastard demoted you again?'

A flush filled Jazzy's cheeks with telltale colour. She shouldn't have mentioned Afzal. She should have led with her agreement with Pedro and kept the whole Afzal meeting out of the conversation. Now Queenie would be like the proverbial dog with a bone – only think velociraptor, not poodle.

'Nah, he didn't know anything about what I'd asked Pedro. It was just me being daft.'

'Oh, that right, hen?' Queenie's penetrating gaze sent more colour into Jazzy's cheeks. 'So, what *did* he want?'

Shite. Jazzy shrugged, aiming for nonchalance, but in the face of Queenie in interrogation mode, she fell far short. She'd have to come up with something convincing if she was going to divert Queenie from discovering her other secret. 'Nothing really. I mean, it was just a bit of a chat.'

'A chat, hmm?'

In the face of her friend's scrutiny, Jazzy floundered. She could face down the most hardened criminals, challenge the scariest, biggest, most violent perpetrators, battle with serial killers, yet Queenie was her kryptonite. Lying to her was as hard as gnawing off her own leg. The only way to deal with this situation was to employ a few half-truths and hope Queenie would swallow them. 'He was pumping me for information.'

'Information?'

Jazzy massaged her temple. Queenie's one-word questions were doing her head in. *Stick to as near the truth as possible, Jazzy.* 'You know the rumours going around about a corrupt officer in Edinburgh feeding information to the gangs about our operations? Well, Afzal wanted to see if I'd vouch for Elliot. With him being privy to some of the Operation Birchtree investigation – which almost certainly has someone within the ranks leaking info to the Bitch or my brother – *and* my minder when I visit Simon, he wanted to be sure he could trust him.'

Queenie, eyes wide, tossed her empty tea mug into a nearby bin. 'Jesus! That's low. Even for Afzal, that's low. What did you tell him?'

With some relief that Queenie had bought her half-lie, Jazzy shrugged. 'I told him I'd trust Elliot with my life.'

'But . . .? There's a but in there somewhere, JayZee. Something else you're not telling me.'

God's sake, Queenie, can't you just let it lie? Defeated, Jazzy came up with the only believable half-truth she could think of in the moment. 'He asked me to keep an eye on Elliot. You know, just to confirm that he's not corrupt.'

Queenie cast a side glance her way, then tutted. 'But that's no' all is it, hen?'

Jazzy couldn't meet her partner's gaze. This was crap. Queenie was her partner and she could trust her, so Afzal and his secrecy could go and do one. She took a deep breath and confided everything about her meeting with Afzal.

When she'd done it, Queenie shook her head. 'Aw, JayZee, you agreed, didn't you?'

'I'd no real choice, did I? Besides, we *know* Elliot's no bent copper, so all I'm really doing is confirming his innocence.'

'By going behind his back? By betraying his trust? By pretending to be his friend, but all the while you're doing Afzal's dirty work? This isn't you, JayZee. This isn't you.'

If Queenie were to find out the extent of Jazzy's treachery she'd be even more furious than she already was, so Jazzy lowered her head and let Queenie rant.

'Do you think you could fuck up your friendship with Elliot any more?'

'I know. It's crap, but what could I do?'

'You could have said no. Let one of the arse-wipes from A or B team do it.'

'Really? You'd rather I'd turned Afzal down? Let someone who doesn't care investigate him instead?'

Queenie shook her head and thumped Jazzy's good arm. 'Don't be a damn numpty. Course you couldn't say no.'

'But it's Elliot.'

'You know what your problem is, hen?'

Jazzy waited, for the inevitable . . .

'You're too uptight. Got the weight of the world on your shoulders. Take too much responsibility for things you can't control. You should be more like me.' Queenie jabbed herself in the chest. 'You need to get laid every now and again. Me and Craig, regular as clockwork get out the nipple lick and the—'

'No, just no, Queenie. This conversation is over.'

Chapter 23

Vengeance

Money is no object to me. Not anymore. Not after all this time. Over fifty years of hush money just sitting there doing nothing till now. Sometimes I try to work out how it makes me feel. Regular as clockwork every month for over fifty years that money landed in my account. Not sure how it was supposed to make me feel, but to me it was tainted. Completely and utterly tainted. Dirty money. Money that couldn't replace the warmth of family life, the familiarity of my home, the love of my kith and kin. So, no matter how far I fell, no matter how much I grovelled in the dirt, I wouldn't touch that money. Maybe even then, I realised that at some point, I'd have real need of it. A need that went far beyond the craving for another drink or another pill.

I don't kid myself that I thought this at the time. How could I? Most of my late teens and early twenties were spent stoned or trashed – blootered, as my Scottish family might say. Out of my head on whatever substance could provide the escape I craved. In those days, I'd have done anything to make the self-loathing fade for a short time – happy to substitute my self-respect for fleeting caresses and false promises. But how would I know what they might say? What their word choices might be?

The only thing I know about them with any certainty is that they considered *me* dispensable. Worthless – a piece of trash to be sent away, never to darken their doors again. Did they ever wonder how I was? Or was their shame so absolute they excised me from their memories with clinical precision? How did they explain my absence? They probably didn't. Maybe nobody noticed I was gone. Maybe they shared out my things and pretended they were never mine. Or did they just chuck them in the tip? Over fifty years in the shadows tells me I wasn't missed. So, even those memories on my wall – the ones I've cherished for so long – must be false. An illusion that my sick, vulnerable brain clung to because those small indications that I mattered, that I was once important, once perhaps even loved, were the only hope I had.

I'm rambling. The email I sent this morning has taken its toll. It's opened doors I'd thought were locked tightly shut and forced me to think of things. I've spent a long time looking at my photos, scrolling the internet and remembering. It's been exhausting.

I drag myself over to the photos I've stuck up on the back wall. Even though there are not many, there's a lifetime's worth of memories in them and only some of them good. There's me as a toddler clinging to my mammy outside our tenement flats in Easterhouse with a squad of other weans and their mothers, all grinning like idiots at the camera. All scrawny legs, skinny arms and hand-me-down raggy clothes. I wonder who took the photo. I wonder how it ended up among my things when I was exorcised from our family so abruptly. I study my mum. Wonder what she thought about it all. Did she ever miss me? Did she know the story behind my disappearance or was I just another casualty of Seventies Glasgow? She's dead now. So many of them are – but not all of them. Not the ones who've committed the biggest act of violence against me. Not the ones on my triangle of hate. Not the ones who will feel my wrath before too long.

I'm only just starting. Only just beginning my war against them, but they *will* be obliterated by the end. Every one of them.

One of the burner phones rings and I drag myself over to the wee table beside the gas fire, wishing I'd had the foresight to keep them beside me. 'Yes?'

The voice on the other has a Geordie accent. 'We're accelerating as you instructed. Creating chaos, flushing out those who need to be targeted. Things are progressing. Also, my team have got the surveillance equipment installed on the premises as per your request. You can tune in whenever you like.'

I smile. It's not a happy smile. More of a resigned one. Things are moving ahead well, but right now I'm too knackered to appreciate it in the way I had anticipated. I slip the folded paper from between the pages of my book and open it. My fingers shakily trace the words and then the image. Again, that involuntary tear springs to my eyes and my resolve to continue is hardened.

My revenge may not be sweet, but it will be complete, for *I Am Vengeance*.

Chapter 24

Shuggie Fratelli sat on a wobbly bar stool in the Tartan Sporran, nursing the dregs of his pint and wondering how lame he'd look if he ordered a half instead of a pint. He cast a sideways glance at Jeanie, who was serving auld Costa down the other end of the bar. Apart from him and Costa, the bar was dead. Hardly worth staying open, really, but this was usual for this time of the night and it was the reason he was here. He had a wee thing for Jeanie, although he doubted she'd even noticed him. She was pure dead gorgeous. Shuggie didn't usually go for girls with red hair, but there was something about Jeanie's that made his belly flip like a pole dancer on too much Red Bull. It wasn't that orangey-red like a bloody Belisha beacon. No, Jeanie's was darker, more luxurious – and thick. Just the sort of hair Shuggie could happily spend an eternity running his fingers through.

He scowled into his glass, his shoulders slumped as he acknowledged the hopelessness of his situation. There wasn't a snowball's chance in hell that Jeanie would give the likes of him a second glance. Why would she? It wasn't like he could take her anywhere posh, was it? Not like he had the dosh to even take her to Wagamama's – not that he was one hundred per cent keen on eating in a place that didn't do chips and offered you chopsticks as a matter of course. Still, for Jeanie . . .

He sighed again, still trying to work out if the half-pint option was a goer or not. Probably not. Then, he saw Matty coming in the door and heading straight to the bogs to shoot up. Maybe, when Matty came out, he'd be able to cadge a fiver off him. Maybe even a tenner, eh? Then again, having a convo with Matty wouldn't do his street cred with Jeannie any good.

Jeanie drifted up the bar and flicked a smile in his direction. 'You needing a top-up there, Shuggie?'

She knows my name, she knows my name, she knows my name. Shuggie's mouth went dry. Colour flooded his cheeks as he searched for a series of words to make an intelligible sentence – nothing. Not a one entered his daft gowk of a heid. *Fuck's sake, can you no' be cool for once in your life, Shuggie?*

The smile faded from her lips and she drifted back down the other end of the bar. *What the hell is it with you, Shuggie Fratelli? You can act the clown, you can stand on a stage and entertain folk for hours on end, but coming up with a solid chat-up line is beyond you? Get a bloody grip.* He risked a keek at her, but she was talking to some geezer in a suit wearing a knock-off TAG Heuer Formula 1 watch. He knew it was a knock-off because he'd seen the poser flogging them for twenty quid around Bathgate earlier in the week. *Should've dobbed the bastard in; that's what I should've done.*

'Hey, Shuggie, ma boy! You all right there, eh?'

Aw no, just when things couldn't get any worse, Matty was yelling his name from one end of the pub to the other. Jeanie's head darted up and swung between Shuggie and Matty, her expression leaving no doubt that he'd just dropped to negative numbers in Jeanie's ratings. *Fucking Matty!* What made it worse, though, was that as Matty weaved his unsteady way towards Shuggie, it was clear from the darkened patch at his crotch, that he'd pished himself. Shuggie closed his eyes and resigned himself to the fact that he'd no chance with Jeanie. Not in this lifetime anyway.

Maybe the heavens intervened, or maybe it was the fact that Matty's attention span – sporadic without the drugs, but completely non-existent when he was high – switched as he noticed the jukebox. There was a shuffling sound, followed by a gleeful clap and the unmistakable sound of the ancient jukebox swinging into action. 'Hey there, Jeanie, hen. Just put a wee song on for you. Come and dance with me. Come on, you know you want to. Who the hell wouldn't want a piece of this, eh?'

Shuggie opened his eyes as 'Oh Jean' by the Proclaimers filled the bar and was in time to see two things. The first was a sight he never wanted to see again – Matty thrusting his hips in Jeanie's direction whilst groping his sodden groin with one hand. The second – which he'd happily replay ad infinitum – was Jeanie calmly raising the flip-back bar hatch, retrieving a sodden tea towel from the bar and using it to lash Matty right on the hand that was cupping his gonads.

'Get the hell out of here, Matty Nicholls, before I use this towel as a cheese wire on your balls. You hear me?'

Yelping like she'd already castrated him, Matty sidled backwards towards the door with Jeanie – a full foot shorter than him – following, using the wet towel like she was in an Indiana Jones tribute act. Her laugh rang out clear and loud when someone opened the door before Matty reached it and he fell backwards through it, landing on his arse on the soaking wet pavement. For a second, Shuggie's grin was wide. Then Jeanie turned caught his eye. 'You that loser's mate, Shuggie?'

Her tone was more pity than anger and, as Shuggie opened his mouth, knowing that the words wouldn't come out like he wanted them to, an arm landed round his shoulders and the overwhelming smell of something fruity and old-fashioned clagged up his throat. 'Gie the man a break, hen. Just cos he went to school with that wee bawbag doesn't mean they're joined at the hip, does it, wee man?'

Shuggie, not exactly enamoured with the 'wee man' tag, stiffened and tried to edge away from the source of the scent, but the grip was unrelenting. *Who the hell is this?* He looked up and was rewarded by a reassuring smile. *Nope. Never seen this chookie before in my life.*

Shuggie's rescuer released him and slid into the nearest stool. Catching Jeanie's eye, and with a hand wave in Shuggie's direction the chookie said, 'Whatever the wee man's having and I'll have a hawf and a hawf – yer best Uisge Beatha, mind, none of that Bells crap for me.'

Shuggie settled back into his chair, downed the last mouthful of beer from his glass and sent furtive glances towards his unfamiliar benefactor, waiting for a flicker of recognition to hit. The more he thought about it, the more certain he was that he'd never seen the chookie before – tall, wavy hair and a smile that was too white to be natural. *Nope, not ringing any bells.* But the chookie's proprietorial attitude made Shuggie nervous. Was he after something? With his mind set on becoming the next Martin Compston on *Line of Duty*, he didn't want to end up with a record – squeaky clean seemed to be the requirement of thespians these days and although Shuggie's 'clean' might be less squeaky than some, he wasn't a bad lad.

'Do I know you?' Shuggie kept his tone respectful, but inside he wanted to pull his hood up, pop his earbuds in and walk away. As she poured their drinks, Jeanie kept casting wee not-so-subtle glances in their direction. *Well, I got what I wanted didn't I? I'm on Jeanie's radar now, just a bloody shame it's for having a druggie mate like Matty and accepting drinks from someone who was probably after something dodgy. Fucking life's a pile of dog turd sometimes, eh?*

With a nod and a smile for Jeanie when she deposited the half-pint of beer and the wee nip on the bar, the stranger raised the beer, pinkie ring catching the bar lights and took a long swallow. 'Ah, that hit the spot,' before nodding towards the untouched pint on the beer mat in front of Shuggie. 'Drink up, son.'

Thinking it would be a shame to waste a good pint, Shuggie lifted the glass and took a sip.

'In answer to your question. No, you don't know me, but—' The wink was all salacious bonhomie and Shuggie's stomach churned. Last thing he wanted was to be forced to avert the advances of a fat old pervert. 'I know your old man and I think it's time he – or rather *you* – repaid his debt to me.'

Shuggie had expected something like this. It had happened before and it would happen again. Why did he have to deal with the consequences of his dad's past sins?

'Aw, sorry, you're out of luck there. My da lives on benefits. Only got one leg on account of the diabetes and me, well, I've got nothing.' Shuggie scrambled in his pocket and flung the last of his coins on the bar between them. 'See, I can barely afford a half of lager.'

The chookie smiled. 'Och, no. You misunderstand me, Shuggie. I know all about your auld man's predicament and I also know you've got your sights set on a wee acting job. Well . . .' there was that wink again, all knowing and insincere '. . . you scratch my back and I'll make sure you get an audition for that *Shetland* series. You'll have heard of it, no doubt.' The finger tap on the side of his nose was overly dramatic. 'I've got contacts, you see.'

Shuggie fidgeted on his seat. Shuggie might not be the brains of Scotland but his head wasn't full of mince. This was well suspect and he wanted nothing to do with it. He slid from the chair, plastered on his widest smile and began edging towards the door. 'Aw, thanks and all, but I think . . .'

Two figures appeared from the shadows by the entrance. Although, neither of the men was tall, they loomed over Shuggie. The fruity old folks' scent was replaced by a sort of leathery smell, mingled with something younger – Invictus, maybe. With the instinct of someone who'd had to keep one eye behind him every day of his short life to date, Shuggie knew he was fucked. He studied them – a muscly wee ancient guy with a grin like he was about to snap your head off and a slightly younger, taller bald guy with tattoos and eyes as cold as ice. They stared him out.

'Aw, Shuggie, let me introduce you to my mates, Frankie and Lionel.'

Shuggie nodded and raised his palms in the air. 'Okay, I'll listen to what you've got to say, but no promises, like. I'm no' a criminal.'

'All I want, Shuggie, is to put you on retainer. That's all. Nothing illegal about that, is there?'

Shuggie shrugged. 'S'ppose not. But what will I be on retainer for?'

'Just to be on standby, son. Just to be on standby. Might need you to do a wee bit babysitting in the not-so-distant future, that's all.'

Shuggie's head wasn't zipped up the back. He knew the sort of babysitting they had in mind didn't involve minding a bairn. But he was out of options. With only Jeanie and Costa in the bar, there was nobody there to help him should he object. 'I don't even know your name and you're wanting me to do something for you?'

'Nae worries, Shuggie, my boy. You can call me the Gaffer.'

The Gaffer pulled a brown jiffy bag from a concealed inner jacket pocket. 'Here. That's to keep you on board, okay? There's a burner phone in there. Always keep it charged and with you. When it rings, answer it and follow the instructions. Easy-peasy, lemon squeezy, eh?'

Nothing was ever easy-peasy in Shuggie's world, but when the two minders took a step closer, crowding him, there was only one thing he could do, so he nodded, picked up the jiffy bag and spirited it away in the front pouch of his hoodie.

The Gaffer took out a leather pouch and extracted a wad of purple notes before shoving them into Shuggie's hand. 'Same again, when you've done your babysitting stint, son. Okay?'

Shuggie nodded, but the three older folk were already walking towards the door of the pub. The Gaffer turned, tipped two fingers to his temple and then, accompanied by the henchmen, left the pub, pausing only to say, 'You'll be hearing from me, Shuggie.'

Chapter 25

It had been a while since Jazzy had been a confidential point of contact for undercover work and despite her misgivings about going behind Elliot's back, a frisson of excitement warmed her gut and made her ultra-focused. Contact protocol between Jazzy and Dukesy, or Spaceman as she tried to think of him now, was simple. They each had access to the same email address and would use a series of unsent emails which sat in drafts to communicate on a nightly basis – unless imminent intel necessitated direct or urgent contact. The unsent emails – each one deleted after being read – ensured that intel between handler and undercover agent remained secure and secret. However, whilst Afzal and Hare were intent on identifying corrupt officers, Jazzy was intent on proving Elliot's innocence. Without a shred of doubt in her mind about her friend's honesty, Jazzy's suspicious nature had led her to implement a few covert strategies of her own to double-check the credentials of other players in the field. With this 'turf war' between the two cities escalating, her instincts were to doubt everyone – after all, the person orchestrating all the violence must be devious, have access to intel and also be above suspicion.

With that in mind, she'd tasked Fenton who – although lacking Dukesy's expert hacking standards – was skilled in IT with doing some digging on the QT. She'd asked him to operate covertly to ascertain as much intel as he could on Dukesy. As his handler, Jazzy didn't want to be blindsided by incomplete information about him. Plus, the way he'd deceived Elliot for years – acting as his CI whilst actually doing undercover work and then convincing him that he was splitting when in fact he was investigating him – had raised her hackles. She wanted to be sure of where his loyalties lay. The fact that she herself was behaving in an equally hypocritical way wasn't lost on her.

The other individuals she'd asked Fenton to scrutinise were Elliot's boss DCI Dougie Shearsby – the weird interaction with her nemesis DCI Dick had set off alarm bells – and both Emily Hare and DCI Afzal. As she delivered the last two names on her list, she'd held her breath awaiting Fenton's response, but other than a sharp intake of breath and a puzzled look, Fenton just nodded and said, 'Am on it, Jazz.'

His complete faith in her had brought a tear to her eye and on impulse she'd reached over and squeezed his arm.

Covert communication between Detective Sergeant Jazzy Solanki and undercover operative, Spaceman

Spaceman
Time 22:05
Subject: JN bit and I'm in.

Jazzy's heart hammered at the enormity of the job she had undertaken. Now that Jimmy Nails had enlisted Spaceman, she was the covert officer's only contact with the outside world and with him working a double-cross on Loanie Gibbs, his safety was at risk.

Draft email deleted and replaced

Jazzy
Time 22:07
Subject: Focus on finding out more about Jimmy's business dealings. Also, possible links between ex-DCI Dougie Shearsby – he was in a prime position to set DI Balloch up for a fall as his ex-boss – or any other possibly corrupt officer – and either of the two gang leaders. Take care. Keep me informed.

Draft email deleted and replaced

Spaceman
Time 22:09
JN is concerned about an email he received from a mysterious person calling himself Vengeance. See copy pasted below. So far no progress on locating sender as it's encrypted, but I'll keep on it. Worry not. I'm like Teflon. I'll report tomorrow.

Copy of anonymous email to Jimmy Nails

Subject: I am Vengeance and I am coming for you!

Dear Jimmy,
Long time, no see. I wonder if you remember me? I remember you. How could I forget?
I know what you did and I'll make you pay. You took something I valued from me, now I'll take something that you value from you. Can you guess what?
Beware, though, Jimmy, I won't stop there, for I am Vengeance and I am coming for you.

Jazzy read the threatening email twice. No wonder Nails had employed Spaceman. Who knew if this Vengeance was all part of the ongoing chaos or something completely different? Either way, it was good intel to have. She copied it and pasted it to a Word document, which she saved on a USB, which she then slotted into the hollowed space of her living-room door wedge.

Draft email deleted and replaced

Jazzy
22:10
Subject: Good work. Thanks.

But still she wasn't happy. Knowing she was breaking all the rules, she pasted the Vengeance email into another draft using the email address she had set up to communicate with Fenton and added the subject heading CHECK THIS OUT, before signing out.

A pang of unease made her flinch. Now, as well as being duplicitous with Elliot, she was being duplicitous with the other Jazz Queens and worse, she was dragging Fenton into it too. She exhaled and rolled her neck, desperate to release the tension that was making her head throb. This wasn't how the Jazz Queens worked. They were a united team. She pictured Queenie's irate face and the sad droop of Geordie's eyes when they discovered she'd enlisted Fenton behind their backs. She groaned – then Fenton, all sad eyes and childlike disappointment, would stare at her like she'd slapped him when he discovered that Queenie knew about Jazzy's undercover task and he didn't. And all of that was without considering Elliot's reactions. What a frigging mess.

Jazzy took the small Ganesh statue from her pocket and gently rubbed her forefinger over his round belly. 'Come on, Ganesh, how can I erase all these obstacles?'

She looked at the small glass statue for a moment or two then sighed. The only solution was to hold a Jazz Queen meeting and admit her bad decisions and update them. She stood and went over to the shelf, which contained her wider collection of Lord Ganeshes and after lighting an Agarbatti incense stick, and selecting a track on Spotify, she sat crossed-legged on the floor, eyes closed, and allowed the relaxing meditative music and the Gulab or rose scent to soothe her.

After ten minutes most of her tension had abated and, having decided to take her team fully into her confidence, she felt as relaxed as she had done for a while. It was the right strategy to take. Working together was what made the team so strong. Together they pushed the boundaries, their different skills and ways of analysing information maximising their chances of success. The only slight pang she felt was that she couldn't bring Elliot into the mix. To make sure he was fully exonerated she had to be circumspect and that meant trusting her team and Dukesy to come up with the goods.

Jazzy sat for a moment pondering the email Jimmy Nails had received. There was no doubt it had been threatening, but what did it mean? Who was the mysterious Vengeance and how did it impact on their ongoing investigations?

Tomorrow, she'd report back to the chief super and recommend a deeper dive on Jimmy Nails's enemies. Identifying this Vengeance character could blow the entire investigation wide open.

Tuesday 7th March

Chapter 26

The previous night had been filled with sweaty dreams featuring motorbike chases and ending in petrol-fuelled explosions. In between, the serial killers taunted Jazzy – their bodies covered in blood, their grinning, almost manic faces testament to how much they were enjoying their work before slitting Benjy and Ivor's throats. Bound in chains, Jazzy struggled in vain to escape her ties and rescue them. Ivor's screams filled her ears, flooding her already over-sensitised mind with guilt. Then, the kids' faces morphed into a maniacal Elliot's. His eyes flashed and as he took his turn with the knife he jeered, 'This is what happens when you betray me, Jazzy.'

When she finally managed to break out of her nightmares, it was with a deep sense of dread, an aching tiredness and certainty that the upcoming day would be a long one.

Should she just come clean to Elliot and clear the air? She couldn't, though. Maybe she did harbour a niggle of doubt about him. Angry with herself, she thrust those thoughts aside. Food and reassuring herself that Benjy and Ivor were okay were her top priority.

She picked up her phone and fired off a text to both Ivor and Benjy.

You okay?

Her leg jiggled as she waited for a response. When both replied within seconds of each other – a thumbs-up from Benjy and a smiling face from Ivor – a wave of relief swept over her. She'd been stupid to allow her dreams to affect her morning mood, but she wouldn't have been able to relax without reassuring herself they were okay.

Not that she could fully relax when there was the guilt at keeping her operation with Dukesy from Elliot. If he discovered that her remit was to ascertain whether he was corrupt, he'd be furious. Jazzy's involvement in the whole operation could be the last straw for their friendship.

Afzal's suspicions, based – from what Jazzy could work out – mainly on gossip and weak intel from an ex-chief super were ludicrous. She'd never met a more honest man than Elliot, but again that niggle prevailed. How many tales had she heard of good polis succumbing to the lure of making a quick buck, helping a friend out of a charge, or turning a blind eye to a crime? It left them open to blackmail and susceptible to pressure from criminals. Often, they'd get drawn deeper and deeper into a cess pool of crime from which there was no hope of escaping intact. But not Elliot. He was her hero. The man who'd swept in and rescued her from a horrible situation when she was only a child. She didn't want to consider him flawed or less than the hero he was in her eyes.

Some officers eventually broke under strain of trying to stop a never-ending river of crime and resorted to vigilantism. Could the extreme crime wave they were encountering now have made Elliot break? Had he been tempted to thwart the gang lords by taking the law into his own hands? Could he countenance providing information to both sides so they would kill each other off?

Jazzy smiled. She couldn't imagine Elliot succumbing to that sort of behaviour. However, she wasn't so sure about herself and that made her uneasy. In recent weeks she'd wondered what she'd do if confronted by the Bitch. Would she do the legal thing or the 'right' thing? Before she'd come face to face with two serial killers, she'd have denied the possibility that she could ever betray the oath she took when she joined Police Scotland. Now though, she wasn't so sure. Legal, police-approved channels had proven inadequate to protect her and those she loved and that made her question everything she'd always believed about herself. Maybe *she* was the one who should be scrutinised by Dukesy.

She ran her fingers over Winky's fur, leaned over and kissed his head. 'What am I going to do, Winky? How can I act normal around Elliot when I'm sneaking around behind his back?'

Elliot would suss out that something was wrong – he was bound to. Jazzy could only hope he'd put it down to the anxiety of her meeting with Simon. For now, though she had to put this business with Elliot on the back burner and prepare for that. Every week she rode an emotional roller coaster when it drew near to her visitation time and normally the only thing that kept her sane was Elliot. Today, she dreaded seeing him. She'd even gone so far as to ask Afzal to divert him elsewhere, just for today. The DCS had refused telling her that, except for being accessible round the clock for Dukesy, she was to stick to her normal routines as much as possible.

After throwing some stuff into her bag, Jazzy took a moment to text the Jazz Queens to set up a meeting later, then glared moodily out the window.

Life's a bloody bitch!

Chapter 27

As Jazzy waited for Elliot, Fenton phoned her. 'Hey, boss. Just a quick update about Shearsby. Seems he's floated between Edinburgh and Glasgow for decades – puts him in a prime position to have dealings with Gibbs or Nails. Plus, he's had a few black marks for being a bit too rough with prisoners and complaints from other officers regarding racism and misogyny. Pity the powers-that-be didn't see fit to cut him loose. I'll dig deeper, but wanted to keep you in the loop. Should have more by the time we meet up later. I've done an initial sweep on Elliot and Dukesy and haven't found anything concerning about either. To be fair if they were up to anything it'd be well hidden, so I'll do a deeper dive and see if I can rake anything up.'

Although relieved that Fenton had found nothing incriminating on Elliot and Dukesy, she was concerned about the information he'd given on Shearsby. Was he leaking information to Nails and Gibbs? Sounded like he was in a prime position to do so.

Normally, the beauty of being picked up by Elliot for their appointment at the State Hospital was that Jazzy had time for reflection on the drive over. Today, though, the journey couldn't go fast enough. Jazzy was all thunk out and just wanted the visit over with. She was surprised by how easily she blocked out her own duplicity and greeted Elliot as breezily as she normally did. *Maybe I should reconsider my career choices and take up acting.*

During the twenty-minute journey, through a miserable blizzard that didn't bode well for the scheduled TV shoot on Cairnpapple Hill later, Jazzy flexed and unflexed the fist of her sore arm, savouring the slightly uncomfortable pulling sensation as every sinew, muscle and tendon protested at the unaccustomed movement.

Elliot seemed in a subdued mood too, yawning and nipping the bridge of his nose, focused on his driving and his own thoughts, so Jazzy turned her thoughts to Simon.

He enjoyed playing games and had enjoyed the twistiness of the murders he and his twin had committed. Now he was incarcerated, he was caught up on wreaking revenge on Jazzy. Because she was a thorn in the Bitch's side and if the serial killer could destroy Jazzy bit by bit then that's what she would try to do – and she'd have no qualms about using her twin to do so.

When DCS Afzal had made the proviso that Elliott accompany her every time, she'd been thankful. Now, with the knowledge that she was keeping secrets from him she wished she'd argued for Queenie's company instead. Every visit took it out of her mentally and physically. A complicated quagmire of emotions erupted every time she saw him and Simon was fully aware of this and used his manipulation skills to extort every emotion he could. Sometimes, he portrayed himself as vulnerable and at other times, as some sort of sage or guru. If Queenie was here with her right now, she wouldn't have to think about how she was betraying Elliot. Besides, Queenie could always lighten even the darkest of Jazzy's moods. It was her super power.

Simon made her skin crawl, but then insistent memories would intrude, leaving her at sea with her emotions and that damn anchor yanked her back to the past. On the one hand the urge to protect him was never far from the surface, yet she was repulsed by what he'd become. Jazzy shuddered. He was as sick and disturbed as the Bitch, but he was the key to finding the Bitch.

He got a buzz from taunting her with snippets of useless information, but what kept the powers-that-be convinced she should continue her visits was the fact that he clearly, despite all their efforts, still managed to communicate with his partner in crime.

The fact that the emails from the Bitch always arrived before her scheduled visits was worrying. Despite all their precautions, she was always one step ahead of them. The psychiatric facility had agreed to increased security measures and more detailed protocols, but it was a mystery how the pair communicated.

As they pulled into the car park, Jazzy's phone rang. Afzal!

'There's been another email. Don't go in till we've decided on a plan of action.'

He hung up before Jazzy could respond. *Fuck, fuck, and double fuck! How the hell is this happening?* She flung her head back and released a low moan.

'What's happened?'

'The bastard knows we're here.' And with clumsy fingers she opened the email and, angled her screen so Elliot could read it too. The time stamp showed it had been sent only ten minutes earlier.

Subject: Say hi to Simon, will you?

You can't beat me, Jazzy. Why bother even trying?

Jazzy swallowed, but then Elliot said, 'There's an attachment, Jazz.'

She opened it and stared at the image, of her getting into Elliot's car in front of her house wearing the same clothes she had on now and with sleet swirling around them. For a moment neither of them spoke. This was devastating. Jazzy had hoped that switching up her visits would thwart the Bitch, but it hadn't worked. The only ones caught off guard were Jazzy, Elliot and the task team. They'd not informed his solicitor about it until an hour ago, yet still the Bitch had bested them. Was the communication directly from her half-sister or someone being paid by her? If it was the

Bitch in person then that meant that – contrary to the investigative team's intel – her nemesis was closer than they thought. She cast her mind back to when she'd left her house to get into the car. Had there been anyone around? That was irrelevant. There were so many ways these days to get sharp images from a distance.

'It can't be her. Not in person, can it? I mean, it's too big a risk to take, isn't it? To come back here?' Jazzy couldn't keep the slight tremble from her voice.

'No, it's much more likely to be some numpty happy to follow you for a quick buck.'

That didn't reassure Jazzy. The thought of someone stalking her yanked her right back to the events before Christmas and that wasn't a happy place to be. She thrust those memories to the back of her mind and focused on the important stuff. Whoever had taken the photo must have known in advance that she was visiting Simon today. 'You see anyone when you parked outside mine earlier?'

Elliot shook his head. 'I didn't see anyone and – because of where we were heading – I was keeping an eye out.'

'Same, so . . .'

'A neighbour?'

Elliot shrugged. 'Possibility, but let's not go there yet. Let's see what the team discovers when they go through their protocols.'

Whilst they waited, in the car park, IT experts had been dispatched to her home to scour it for bugging devices – again. Had someone listened in to her and Elliot's conversation the previous night? She wasn't using her own car for now, but they searched it and Queenie's Land Rover for bugs too. Both had come up clean. Afzal scheduled a team to scan Elliot's vehicle and to temporarily take possession of both their phones for testing to ensure that nobody had got through their security measures. Jazzy was glad she'd had the presence of mind to hide the one she had been issued to communicate with Dukesy right at the bottom of her bag.

On edge, she glared out at the clamouring clouds rolling in on a wind that had whipped up overnight. They were expecting thunderstorms later in the day, which reflected her current mood. The Cairnpapple shoot later with Queenie wouldn't be enjoyable – maybe it wouldn't go ahead.

With her scheduled meeting with Simon delayed to allow security checks inside the hospital, Jazzy and Elliot were confined to his car until the all clear was issued. She had to clear her head space of anything other than her plans to force Simon to give something useful away this time. She'd been sure that their unscheduled visit would put the kybosh on illicit communication between her siblings and she'd counted on flaunting that small win in Simon's face. Now, though she'd have to reconsider. She was fed up playing the softly-softly approach favoured by her bosses. She was fed up playing by her brother's rules and allowing every visit to be the Simon Says show. Today was the day she would take control. Today she was going to rattle Simon big time.

'Hey, Elliot. You think we need to devise a new strategy?'

Elliot grinned. 'Damn right I do.'

Chapter 28

Shuggie's dad was already in the kitchen when Shuggie shuffled in after a night spent tossing and turning, trying to work out the best way to confront his dad about the Gaffer. The auld man wheeled his chair back from the table, whammed four slices of bread into the toaster and glared at him. 'What the hell's wrong wi' you, laddie. You look like a skelpt arse this morning *and* you smell like a bloody midden. Away and get a shower, eh?'

Shuggie had a quick whiff of his oxters and had to agree – they were honking. 'I want my breakfast first, Da.' He skirted his dad's wheelchair, took margarine and jam from the fridge and tested the teapot. The side was scalding hot, so he popped two mugs down next to it alongside the milk.

'Breakfast chez Fratelli,' he announced with a flourish and a deep bow to his dad, using the French accent he'd been practising for the past few days.

'Och, away w' ye, you nuisance. Grab that toast and get it slathered with butter. I'm starving.'

Shuggie did as he was bid, wishing that, for once, instead of supermarket own brand marg and jam, they could afford a fry-up, but – unless he told his da about the five hundred pounds burning a hole in his gym bag under his bed – that wasn't going to happen. Besides, chances were with the gambling habit his da' had developed recently, the bookies would swallow it up nae problem. Now Shuggie kept as much of their paltry joint income away from his dad as he could. If he had to work for the Gaffer, he was going to make sure the money was put aside for his own prospects – his career – well, that and seeing if he could wangle a date with Jeanie.

'Bumped into some folk last night, Da. Say they know you from way back. Only name I caught was the Gaffer.'

If Shuggie hadn't been watching, he'd have missed the tightening of his dad's lips and how he glanced away, a peppering of sweat dotting his forehead. For sure, his dad knew exactly who the Gaffer was, but convincing him to tell Shuggie could prove difficult. Antonio Fratelli had a lot of secrets he didn't share with his only son and although Shuggie knew about his da's time in Saughton nick, he was savvy enough to realise that a minor drug deal gone wrong wasn't the only infraction his dad had committed before he moved to Bathgate and met his ma. Now it was just the two of them, his dad was even more determined to keep Shuggie on the right track.

Antonio stuffed a slice of toast into his gob, then followed through with a swallow of tea, but Shuggie was used to his avoidance tactics and was having none of it. 'So?'

'So, what?' Still not meeting Shuggie's eye.

'Do you know this Gaffer chookie? Looked like a rich fucker. All jewellery and posh clothes and all. Too posh for the likes of the Tartan Sporran. Wondered what would bring the likes of them to our neck of the woods.'

Slamming his mug on the table, tea sloshing onto his remaining toast, Antonio Fratelli pushed away from the table and with more will than dexterity swivelled out of the kitchen and into his bedroom. 'You keep away from the likes of the Gaffer, Shuggie. I'm telling you, that bastard's like a fart in a sealed room – deadly. Deadly as fuck.'

174

Without a backward glance, Antonio slammed the door behind him, leaving Shuggie with only the sounds of his dad repeatedly running his chair into the wall.

Shee-ite! Shuggie hadn't been expecting such an extreme reaction. Maybe a bit of mild consternation. A wee bit of bitching about the Gaffer's obvious financial success, but definitely not one of his dad's full-on meltdowns. Fuck, the auld man hadn't had one of them in going on six months. A cold chill settled around Shuggie. The thought of the £500 hidden away in his bedroom took on the threat of an unexploded bomb attached to the lavvy – like in that scene in *Lethal Weapon*. Why had he taken the damn money?

He was still crumbling his slice of toast into wee bits when he heard a faint ringing. He frowned and looked round, wondering if his dad had changed his ring tone. Then it hit him. The fucking burner. Shit a brick! He jumped up, ran to the door then stopped. He needed to get his act together. His only option was to answer the phone and try to blag it. Do do do, do do doo. Dodododo. Dodododo. *Mission Impossible theme tune.* That was it! Ethan Hunt would be his salvation for now. Then he'd whang the phone in the Bog Burn and leg it to London. That's what he'd do. Be all calm and quiet and react to each thing as it happened.

Next door, his dad was still at it, lunging his chair with increasing force into the plaster board – the neighbours would be hammering on the wall in a minute – bastards! With a sinking heart Shuggie realised that legging it wasn't an option. How could he leave his old man behind to deal with his mess?

He zoned out the banging, took a deep breath and grabbed the phone. 'Yeah?'

'I expected a prompter response, Shuggie. You're not going to be one of these dimwits who regrets the bargain they struck, are you?' The voice was cool as cucumber – smooth and posh Edinburgh and instantly recognisable as the Gaffer. 'Hope you're not thinking that legging it to London will create enough distance between you and me, Shuggie.' The laugh was all grit and fifty a day rasps. 'No, not you Shuggie, man. No, you're the real deal. A lad with principles, am I right?'

'Aye, yer right, eh. I mean, eh, Gaffer. I was in the shower that's all. Won't happen again.'

Honey laced with bitter lemon this time. 'No, you're right, Shuggie, it *won't* happen again.'

Shuggie swallowed hard as his bowels loosened just a wee bit. He decided biting the bullet might be the best policy. Least that way he'd know just how much shit he was in. 'You need me for something, Gaffer?'

The reward for his bravery was a deep rolling laugh. 'Och no, Shuggie. This was just a courtesy call. Just to make sure we were still on the same wavelength. I'll be needing you, right enough, but not right now. I was just checking you'd no plans to leave the country, like. For when it's *your* turn, I'll expect a speedy response. Understood?'

'Aye, understood. I'm yer man. I'll no' let you down.'

'I know you won't, Shuggie. Give my regards to your dad, now won't you. Me and him go way back. I'm sure he'll be proud that you're following in his footsteps.' That raspy laugh again. 'Or should I say foot*step*, eh? You get me, Shuggie? Foot*step*?'

Shuggie's face burned. How fucking dare that posh entitled git slag off his auld man? Bastard had no idea how hard life had been for Antonio Fratelli, bringing up a young son on his own after losing his wife. Keeping himself out of bother after his spell in the nick, rebuilding his life.

'Oh, you don't find my wee joke amusing, son? Never mind. Just so long as you remember who's holding all the cards in this wee relationship of ours. Keep the phone on you. I'll be back in touch.'

Shuggie collapsed on the side of his bed. The bangs from his dad's room were less frequent, but that only meant that his dad's anguished weeping was audible. Shuggie bit his lip. His auld man had tried so hard to keep him on the straight and narrow. Didn't want his son to make the same mistakes he had.

Of course, to Antonio, Shuggie's acting aspirations were pie in the sky. He was convinced Shuggie would be better employed doing an apprenticeship at West Lothian College – 'Maybe in plumbing or electrics, son'. Maybe Shuggie should've just accepted that job at Tony Macaroni's, like his da wanted. Shuggie could do the whole maître d' role no bother. He was an actor, after all – a thespian. But a waiter in a pizza palace held no thrall for him. On stage, he could be anybody – Danny from *Grease*, Shylock from *The Merchant of Venice*, the narrator in *Jesus Christ Superstar*. The world was Shuggie's oyster and he wanted to do that for the rest of his life. It was only on the stage, in character, that Shuggie felt truly alive. Like he was better than a wee laddie frae Bathgate, with mince between his ears. The Proclaimers song with that bit about the laddie leaving Bathgate behind was Shuggie's mantra and with that promise of a role in Ann Cleeves' *Shetland*, the Gaffer had played right into his every desire.

Despair washed over him as he curled into the foetal position on his sweaty bed and screamed silently into his pillow. He'd bide his time and see if he could come out with an alternative solution. One that didn't involve his dad losing his other leg – or Shuggie losing his balls.

177

Chapter 29

Jazzy's brother, Simon, was slouched in the lounge where they had their visits, facing the window. His back was to her, head flung back as he watched the freezing mist whirl past. Jazzy made sure he couldn't catch her reflection as she observed him. He looked benign – a normal, relaxed person enjoying the view. But she knew he would be buzzing. That sense of one-upmanship that his partner in crime had managed to prevail, even at this late hour, would be written all over his face. Her hand – the one not wrapped in its pink cast – twitched. A memory of Simon as a child, gripping her hand and looking up at her so trustingly, came to her. So serious, so beautiful, with his pale skin and light brown hair, she'd loved him with the same ferocity with which she hated their mother. He was the epitome of the very things child Jazzy had wanted to be, for then, maybe, she wouldn't get called Darkie or Paki or stinky arse or any of the other names her peers flung at her, each one as sharp as a stone and twice as hurtful.

She hadn't had to protect Simon from the other children when they started school – the *twins* fitted right in with the other kids. *They'd* been the normal ones – the white ones, she the strange creature that had to be feared and ridiculed and taunted. Not for the first time the tragedy of that struck Jazzy. How normal would those childhood bullies consider her beautiful, not-so-innocent brother now?

The person she'd had to protect him from was the two-faced monster that lived with them in their house – their mother – and she'd tried as best she could to keep him safe from her. From the moment they were born, Jazzy had loved them. The twins' dad had gone the same way that Jazzy's own father had and, like her dad, he hadn't thought twice about leaving the three bairns at the hands of such a cruel woman. As their mother had spiralled into deeper despair and neglect, fuelled by alcohol, six-year-old Jazzy had warmed the babies' bottles, changed their nappies and rocked them to sleep. She'd been both mum *and* sister. Maybe the twins were a replacement for the doll her mother had so cruelly thrown onto the fire that time.

Caught up in memories, Jazzy – not for the first time – tried to see through her brother's childish, trusting expression and into his soul. Had the darkness been there even then? Had his sweet smile and dimpled hands hidden it? Had the way he picked daisies for her been an act to throw her off the scent? Was she to blame for the evil quirk in his nature – that sadistic streak that he so revelled in? All those questions danced around in her mind, but the big one was always there at the front. Could she have prevented all those deaths?

He blamed her for what he'd become and it had taken Jazzy a long time and a lot of work to realise that she'd done her best. That she had been a child herself and therefore no responsibility lay on her shoulders. There were others who should carry the blame – social services, the school, her mother, her dad, the twins' dad, neighbours, Jazzy's grandparents – any adult who had turned a blind eye to the suffering of Hansa Solanki's children – the list was endless. However, ultimately, the crimes he'd committed were Simon's own responsibility.

Elliot stepped closer, placed a hand on her shoulder and squeezed, his voice low and comforting. 'You ready?'

A shudder racked her body as child Simon receded to be replaced by the man sitting by the window. 'No, not nearly, but . . . Let's do it.'

As they did on every visit, Elliot hung back and let her take the lead. He was there as backup and as another pair of ears, but they'd established early on that if he spoke or appeared interested in the siblings' conversation, then Simon clammed up. Jazzy reckoned her brother enjoyed Elliot's presence. He wasn't merely another pair of ears to listen to his warped meanderings, he was also the person who'd rescued them almost sixteen years ago.

She pulled up a chair and positioned it so she faced Simon, but could also look out the window at the swirling clouds. Of course, their conversation was recorded by audio and security cameras, in the hope that scrutiny of their interactions might give a clue – a micro-expression, an involuntary movement – something that she might miss.

'Sorry for your wait, sis.' Simon's smile was wide, expressing the exact opposite of sorrow. 'Seems your plans to surprise me with an unscheduled visit were foiled.' His sideways glance was gleeful. 'We'll have to wait for Auld Misery Guts to arrive, but in the meantime, maybe you could just visit me like a normal sister for a change, eh?'

Auld Misery Guts was the nickname Simon used for his solicitor. To be fair, it was an accurate descriptor, as Clive Warren rarely smiled and always smelled musty. Mind you, who wouldn't be a grumpy old bastard if they had to regularly listen to Simon's grandiose imaginings? Simon's distorted grip of reality often made him play the 'aggrieved brother deserted by his sister' card and sometimes Jazzy was convinced he believed it. At others, she knew it was just another tool in his manipulation toolbox.

Today, though, she was playing him at his own game. Even the slightest tell in her demeanour could give her brother the edge, so she schooled herself to remain motionless, her eyes focused on the sleet outside. She allowed the silence between them to lengthen and then delivered her message in a calm, matter-of-fact voice.

'I'm not playing Simon Says anymore, Si. I'm not indulging you in your petty little power plays. I agreed to sit here week after week, in the faint hope that you'd give me a clue to her whereabouts, but you know and I know that you're too smart for that – and so is the Bitch.'

She waited for her words to sink in. The desire to glance his way was enormous, but she resisted. He had to feel that he was losing his sway over her. He had to believe that she could walk away from him. If this hastily prepared strategy with Elliot had any chance of working, then she had to convince him of something she herself remained unconvinced of – that she'd washed her hands of him.

He laughed, and turned to study her, his eyes raking over her face like red-hot lasers.

'Not sure what you're talking about, sister dearest.'

Jazzy gave a throaty laugh and kept her tone light and breezy – like each word leaving her mouth didn't feel like yet another betrayal. As if she had no qualms about her decision. 'Oh, come on, Simon, that would *definitely* be a first for you. Course you know what I'm talking about. Someone as smart as you? You must have anticipated that this day would come.' Jazzy lowered her voice. 'Between you and me, this day would have come a lot quicker if I'd been able to convince my bosses that you were getting off on this. That the Bitch was the brains of the operation and you were just playing her game. That you had exactly zero information to give us.'

She nudged him, then grinned as she stood up. 'Thing is, Simon. Today, I convinced them that you're a sad little sicko whose only joy in life is taunting them through me. So, guess what?'

Simon's frown deepened; his fingers clutched sporadically at his jeans. *She* was the one in control. She injected as much glee into her expression as she could.

'That's right. I'm here to say bye, Si.'

Smile still intact, she turned and marched towards the doors. Simon jumped up and made to follow her, but the nurses were too quick for him. Each of them grabbed an arm and held him in place. Behind her, he struggled to free himself, his voice raised and his words spattering out like bullets from a Gatling gun.

'Who do you think you are, Jazzy? You think you're so special, do you? Well, you're not. You're just a *bitch* who lets people down. A whore. You're worthless, Jazzy. You always were. Just a piece of shite keeping everyone down. You'll never catch Mhairi without *me*.'

Jazzy continued walking. Elliot had fallen into step with her. No slumping shoulders for Jazzy Solanki, no hesitant stumbles, no wistful backward glances – not today. Face front, refusing to watch the skirmish that played out behind her, she strode on. Her heart hammered so hard she was sure it would explode. The sounds of the scuffle behind her brought tears to her eyes and sweat gathered under her jacket. She wanted to run from the hospital, but she kept her steps measured, just as she and Elliot had agreed.

Simon raised his voice. 'You'll be back, Jazzy. I *know* you'll be back. Simon Says you'll be back. Your guilt won't let you desert me. You can't move on. Not you, Jazzy. You can't move on because you're still that wee lassie with the head lice and the shorn hair. The wee lassie who pushed her mum to her death. You're no different from us. No different at all. We share the same wonky genes, Jazzy. The three of us – we share the same genes. That's what our mammy gave us. Wonky warped genes.'

Keep on walking. Don't let him get in your head.

'We share blood, Jazzy. All three of us. We made that promise and you can't bring yourself to break it fully. Not you, Jazzy. You need me. *Jasmine?*'

Nearly there now. Nearly there!

'She'll kill you, you know. If she thinks you're betraying her again, she'll kill you.'

The door's just there. Just within reach! On the home stretch.
'Did you hear me? She'll kill you. Jazzy. She'll KILL YOU!'
Keep breathing. Keep moving!
'Do you FUCKING hear me, BITCH? She'll KILL YOU. Fucking *KILL YOU*. She'll punish you, Jasmine. She knows you so well. She knows how you tick. She knows what's important to you. *SHE'LL FUCKING EVISCERATE YOU AND ALL YOU HOLD DEAR.*'

Chapter 30

Vengeance

I spent the night alternating between looking at my photo gallery and dozing on my reclining chair by the window. And when it began to get light and the central heating kicked in, I managed to nibble my way through half a slice of toast as I watched my neighbour through the window. With my blinds half shut, she won't spot me – she wouldn't even expect someone to be watching her. I feel like a bit of a stalker, but I mean her no harm. Watching her cute little family makes me feel warm inside, but then there's that shameful envy. But that's not really the whole story, is it? It's not all my fault because the magnitude of the blame lies with others – those who should have known better. Those I should have been able to trust. It's not just about vengeance, it's about justice.

I pull out the printed sheet of paper and study the image that had started me, all those months ago, on this journey. My eyes fill with tears and I rub them away with the back of my hand. No time for being a pussy. No time for crying. It had been by chance that I'd seen the article – on a visit to the oncologist, would you believe? I didn't normally look at the newspapers in the waiting room, but the man sitting along from me was weeping into a tissue – big, heart-wrenching tears and I wanted to give him privacy. So, I sifted through the pile of international newspapers– and selected the *Daily Record*. In all those years since I'd last seen one, you'd expect it to have changed in format or size or something, but it hadn't – not really and, in a fit of nostalgia, I'd been drawn to it.

As the other patient wept, I flicked through the pages, nostalgic with the familiarity of it all. My mum and dad had had a *Daily Record* delivered every day. My dad swore by it and now, a million miles from Scotland, I was reading it and all the memories flooded back. The sense of unjustness at the events that had banished me to another continent merged with guilt and disgust and fear and anxiety and then . . . a face I'd not expected to see stared back at me. My throat clogged up as I tried to make sense of what I was seeing. I desperately tried to remember the last time I'd seen that face or heard that voice – and what was really frightening was that I couldn't put a date or time to my last memory of it. All I knew was that, despite my fear, despite what the consultant might say, I had things to do.

That happened on the same day as I got my diagnosis. It seemed serendipitous to me. Another day, a different time, an alternative appointment and my last days on this planet would have taken a different course. I would have gone to my death oblivious of the ultimate wrong that had been committed.

A bang draws me back to the present, followed by high-pitched squeals of delight pealing out over the street as my neighbour's door slams shut. The little girl, in wellies and a bobbly hat, holds her daddy's hand whilst her mum climbs into the car and waves her goodbyes. They're off to the little park near Hermand Estate, no doubt, and Mum will be off to her work. I wonder what she does. I hope she's not got far to drive because those roads are treacherous, and according to Radio Lothian there's no prospect of the weather letting up anytime soon, just more black ice and crappy driving conditions.

One of my phones rings as I see the flash of taillights at the junction of our wee cul-de-sac and I pick up. 'Done?'

The voice on the other end is matter-of-fact. 'Done and in situ as agreed. Your message has been sent and the next part of your plan is about to begin.'

'What's the word on the street?'

Now his voice takes on an amused tone. 'Fear, confusion, trepidation. Chaos. Just what you wanted.'

As I hang up I smile and look at the printout again. It feels so good when things go to plan. I am powerful and nothing can stop me, for I am Vengeance.

Chapter 31

A flicker of unease settled over me. No rest for the Gaffer, eh? I'm not getting any younger and the last thing I'd anticipated when I reached retirement was to have to become more hands-on again. More and more often, recently, I've wondered if I've lost my edge. Yes, it had been fun locking horns with that wee Shuggie Fratelli – particularly because the wee bastard's dad still owed me big time. But it had left me exhausted. It wasn't the interplay between me and the young pup – no, that had been easy. It was the underlying niggle that I was missing the point somewhere along the line. That all this violence and bloodshed was more than a tussle over territorial rights. None of my sources – both in the force and among the criminal fraternity – had anything worthwhile to share.

I took another sip of my dram, rolled it around my mouth, savouring its peaty flavour, and thought about Jimmy Nails. He was a different breed from his dad, no doubt about that, and Loanie said he'd seemed sincere, but of course Loanie had been wrong before. Not often, granted, but still . . . Jimmy's dad had been a duplicitous wee bastard and no doubt Jimmy – or as the fud liked to be called, Hardass Nails – was equally lacking in the honesty department. So, although it seemed that Jimmy was as perplexed as us, I wasn't about to take that as read.

The problem I'd been wrestling with since the early hours was how much I should bring Loanie into my confidence. I trusted Wee Frankie and he'd vouched for the lad and, after all, he did have form. I'd never forget the mess that boy made of that bastard of a dad of his. Served him right, but my was that some anger at play there – vicious it had been, pure vicious – but I liked that. It showed promise. The lad had stepped up seamlessly when Frankie wanted to step back. I had no qualms about Loanie's ability to move forward with the business, none at all. What I did have concerns over was his ability to deal with something that might bring the entire lot tumbling down around our ears.

I've no intention of ending my days banged up in Shotts jail at His Majesty's Pleasure. I'd not survive five minutes in there. So, I have to work out what the fuck's going on. What the hell had pre-empted this hurricane of destruction?

I opened my desk drawer and extracted a piece of paper – a printout of an email sent from an anonymous and untraceable VPN address. I'd got my best techie hacks – not the polis ones, mind you – on the case, but no joy. I sighed and reread it for the umpteenth time.

Subject: Vengeance is coming for you!

Long time, no see, Gaffer. I've always believed in giving fair warning. So here it is, your fair warning. Your days are numbered. I'll take my revenge any way I can. Watch your back.
  I AM VENGEANCE and I am coming for you.

The whole 'vengeance' thing *has* thrown me, and the reference to a past acquaintance is ominous. I reread the words, trying to convince myself they mean nothing. If this anonymous sender expects me to know who they are, then they're sorely mistaken. I've no idea. True, the number of people who might want to take revenge on me was stratospheric, but the email wasn't specific enough for me to pinpoint anybody. It could be any one of hundreds of bastards I'd fucked over through my fifty-year career. I couldn't begin to fathom it out.

Still, I had options. Despite Loanie's conviction that we're missing something, my gut tells me this is all one big takeover bid from Glasgow. Maybe Hardass carrying on his dad's grudges – and to be fair, there were plenty of grudges the boy could choose from. His stint in the nick had probably toughened him. Made him thirsty for revenge.

With a shrug, I slipped the sheet back into the drawer and lifted my glass. Nothing like a wee dram to calm the nerves when the going gets tough, is there? Besides, I'd already set my counterattack in motion. Things were about to get ugly for a couple of lowlifes, right about now. Payback and a warning wrapped up in one big present with a bow on top. Jimmy Nails wouldn't know what had hit him.

Chapter 32

On their way to the medieval burial site the weather had cleared a bit, which made it likely that filming could go ahead as scheduled. As Elliot had driven past, Jazzy had pointed out the faux modern-day stone circle that a local farmer had built for his father years earlier. By her reckoning, the mock stone circle might have been constructed around the same time that Cairnpapple Man's body had been left in the field just beneath the historic burial site. She shivered. Somehow that made the circumstances around this reconstruction even more tragic. The digital forensic reconstruction of his face was amazing and Jazzy hoped that seeing a living, moving, three-dimensional person dressed like the victim, might be the jolt needed to encourage someone else's memory.

The roads leading to the site were narrow and temporary blockades had been set up at either side of the site entrance, allowing access only to those involved in proceedings. It was just as well because with all the vehicles necessary to transport the equipment and personnel, the road was rendered impassable. As the film crew and experts from Glasgow began unpacking their stuff, Jazzy started walking up the steps leading to Cairnpapple Hill. She welcomed the driving wind that slashed against her cheeks as she climbed. It felt cathartic – as if the weather was exorcising the lurgy that remained with her after seeing her brother earlier. The field to her left was fenced off and, after entering the small wooden gate that demarked the Cairnpapple site, Jazzy paused, taking in the fantastic views. If she squinted through the smirr of rain, she could make out the three bridges linking Edinburgh to Fife – the Forth Bridge, the Forth Road Bridge and the Queensferry Crossing. On a clear day these three bridges were a sight to behold. On a wet and drizzly March morning, they were still pretty damn impressive.

It was in this field that the remains of the fifteen to twenty-one-year-old Cairnpapple Man were discovered in 1990. According to experts, he had lain there undiscovered for between two and five years. Despite extensive media coverage at the time, no one had claimed the body or ID'd him. Of course, DNA analysis was in its infancy in the Eighties and Nineties so that proved an ineffectual avenue to follow then and, unfortunately, over the years samples that may have produced conclusive DNA at the time had become compromised.

It was only the physical similarity between Sid and the reconstructed face of the murdered man that made this a viable operation. This reconstruction – with Sid dressed in replicas of the clothes worn by their unidentified corpse, accompanied by a massive media campaign – might be their last shot at not only identifying Cairnpapple Man, but of solving his murder and bringing his killer to justice. The hope was that a positive ID would breathe more life into the decades-old murder investigation.

The crew trudged up the hill with their equipment, and the journalists, who'd been issued with passes, trekked up behind them. Jazzy continued towards the small cabin where Sid awaited her. To her right, the ancient burial mound rose from a circle of pits, sodden and eerie against the backdrop of modern paraphernalia. Jazzy considered the contrast between the ritualistic burials that had taken place here over five and a half thousand years ago and the unceremonious deposition of a young murder victim.

The Neolithic and Bronze Age rituals seemed respectful. A fitting way to mark the end of a life, and although not a religious person, Jazzy appreciated the importance of the Hindu funeral cremations she'd attended with her mum and dad. The ceremonial homage to a departed loved one seemed fitting to Jazzy. It signified that their life had mattered. That they'd mattered, that they'd been loved and valued and, perhaps most importantly, it allowed loved ones the chance to express their appreciation of the way in which the deceased touched their lives by respectfully sending them on their forward journey.

By contrast, Cairnpapple Man had been murdered and discarded in a shallow grave, stripped of his identity. His family had been denied the solace of grieving for him. It was so wrong and Jazzy really hoped that the facial reconstruction combined with his similarity to Sid Mackie and would give the dead man back his name. Perhaps reunite him with grieving relatives and that his story would be known.

'DS Solanki?'

Jazzy had been so lost in thought that she hadn't noticed Sid Mackie approach, holding an umbrella and wearing the replica clothes. For a second, Jazzy imagined that it was an older living version of the man she'd seen in the newspaper. It was as if Cairnpapple Man had been brought back to life, so strong was the likeness.

'Hi, Mr Mackie. I'm sorry our Scottish weather isn't going to make this reconstruction any easier for you.'

Sid grimaced and focused on the view. 'Aw, Sid, please. It is what it is. You know, right until I spoke to the investigative team, I'd managed to half convince myself this was a fluke. Just a weird coincidence or something. I know we don't have definitive DNA proof yet – they say there are a few more tests they can do – but I *know* we're related. It's strange but it's like I'm grieving. Although I've never even met the man, it's as if I've lost a relative.' He ran his hands through his hair. 'I can't get over how wrong it is that his life was snuffed out on a bloody forlorn hill near Bathgate and nobody – not a single sodding person – has put a name to him after all these years.'

They stood, side by side in respectful silence, contemplating the site where Cairnpapple Man's remains had been discovered. From nowhere, the wind calmed and a shimmer of sunlight broke through the clouds. A loud yelp, followed by muffled curses, drifted up the hill. Jazzy rolled her eyes. *Bloody Queenie! You can always rely on her to make a damn entrance.* Struggling to catch her breath, Queenie gasped her way towards them. Her trousers were japped with mud and the grass stain on her knee showed that she'd already fallen at least once.

'Meet DC McQueen – Queenie, my partner and, regardless of how she might appear right now, she's usually a lot more together than this.'

Queenie, wearing the thick hat with the ear flaps that Jazzy had got her for Christmas, peched up the rest of the incline, as if she were approaching the Everest summit. Red-faced, she drew to a dramatic pause before them and wiped her gloved hand across her brow. 'Bloody trek that was. Give me a minute to catch my breath.'

After a few moments punctuated by exaggerated sighs and laborious pants, Queenie stuck a dripping wet, muddy hand towards Sid. She pulled it back, studied it for a moment then wiped it down her jacket and inspected it again. It hadn't helped. With a shrug she gave up on the handshake and smiled. 'Pleased to meet you, Mr Mackie. This can't be easy for you. I know you've not met the deceased, but still it must be a shock. You have my very sincerest condolences and if you want anything, and I mean anything at all, then just you let me know.'

Right at that point, Jazzy could have scooped Queenie up and hugged her. Her partner's caring side always came through when it was needed and her words had both calmed and supported Sid.

His eyes filled with unshed tears as he nodded. 'Thanks for that. I just really want my bit to be over with and for it to be out there. Once we know who he is, and if he's got no other living relatives, I'd like the opportunity to lay him to rest myself.'

The director from BBC Scotland gestured for him to come over, but before he left, Sid turned to them, his gaze intense. 'I hope the bastard who did this gets caught. Doesn't seem right to me that he's been lying in a bloody mortuary, whilst his killer's been out there possibly living a grand old life.'

Jazzy watched as, with shoulders drooping, he approached the director. 'You know, Queenie, he's not wrong.'

But Queenie, hands on hips, glared at Jazzy. 'Something you want to tell me, JayZee? Something you want to share with your partner, eh? You know, a wee update or are you just going to leave her hanging, no' knowing what's afoot?'

When Queenie referenced herself in the third person, Jazzy knew she'd offended her badly, but her mind was still filled with her earlier combustible meeting with Simon and concern over Sid Mackie and the upcoming reconstruction. Then it hit her. The meeting she'd arranged later with the team! She'd meant to send her a WhatsApp that morning updating her and letting her know she was going to confide fully in Fenton and Geordie, but had forgotten. 'Oh, you mean . . .?'

'Aye, that's right. I mean this bloody meeting you've called. You've decided to loop them in, haven't you?' Shuffling her feet, Queenie shrugged. 'And so you should, right enough. But, you'd think you'd let me know, though. I mean us four are the Jazz Queens.' She sniffed and Jazzy understood that her friend felt sidelined. *God she's going to go ballistic when she hears that I've given Fenton jobs without clueing her in!*

'Look, Queenie, I'm all over the place and I've still got to fill you in on what kicked off with Simon this morning. It slipped my mind. I'm really sorry. Forgive me?'

Queenie, face as sour as rhubarb, shrugged, then relented.

'Aye, I ken you've had a lot on your mind and seeing Elliot when you're investigating him can't have been easy. But you owe me . . . let me think . . .'

Thankfully at that point her phone rang and Jazzy had never been so relieved to see DCI Dick's name on the screen. With a finger plugged in one ear, Jazzy held the phone between her and Queenie so they could both listen as their boss went off on one.

'You, DS Solanki, had no right. No right whatsoever to behave in the way you did. I'm surprised DI Balloch countenanced it. Need I remind you that your reinstatement to sergeant is contingent on a modicum of good behaviour and subject to a six-month probationary period? I think it's safe to assume that by acting against the investigation protocol, you . . .'

A flash of anger sent shockwaves through Jazzy's body. Her skin tingled and the lethargy that had hit her after her encounter with Simon dissipated, leaving her hot and shaking. She gripped the phone tighter, and began marching down the hill with Queenie running behind her. How fucking dare he? How fucking dare the dickless wonder tell her off. What did he want from her? Blood? Her soul? She'd sacrificed her own mental health, her peace of mind, because she wanted to catch Simon's partner in murder as much – probably more – than anyone else on the team and hearing the boss she held no respect for rollicking her over the phone was the final straw.

'Get your arse back here and bring that fat cow you call a partner with you.'

That was it. Jazzy stopped and Queenie bashed into her, almost knocking her flying. Jazzy's words were ice cold. 'I don't answer to you on this one. My actions this morning were cleared by DCS Afzal, so take it up with him. In the meantime, don't *ever* speak to me like that again or speak about my partner that way or I *will* take it up with human resources. I am not here to be treated like garbage and I won't allow you to do it. Not any longer.'

She cut off Dick's response mid-flow, flung her shoulders back and smiled at Queenie. 'That felt good. So damn good.'

For once, Queenie was speechless. She stared at her partner for long seconds, her mouth gawping, her hat awry on her head with one of the tassels dangling down over her nose. Then she launched herself at Jazzy, enveloping her in a hug until her protestations that Queenie was squashing her arm penetrated and she released her. Straightening her hat, her face a balloon of grins, she laughed out loud. 'Well, JayZee, you certainly told him. So, what the hell happened this morning? Sounds like you had a busy day.'

As the pair made their way at a slower pace back to Queenie's car, Jazzy updated her on that morning's happenings and the actions she'd asked Fenton to undertake.

Chapter 33

'You no' even got any crisps, JayZee? Since you've dragged us all here, the least you could do is supply nibbles. I mean, how do you expect us to concentrate if we're famished?'

The fact that Queenie had, after witnessing Jazzy's evisceration of Dick less than two hours ago, devoured a haggis supper had no bearing on her desire to crunch her way through a poke of crisps. Jazzy knew it was nervous energy that made Queenie want to eat, so she picked up her phone and called Geordie who, with Fenton, was on his way to her home in Bellsquarry. 'Queenie needs provisions, Geordie. Can you stop off at a . . .'

'We're just walking up to your door, but don't worry, when news of your rollicking from Dick hit, we realised Queenie would need a distraction so we stopped off at Home Bargains and stocked up on Tunnock's tea cakes, crisps and juice.'

Jazzy heaved a sigh of relief as she rushed to let them in. Hopefully, the provisions would distract Queenie from rollicking her when she revealed she'd enlisted Fenton's help without first consulting her. Bearing in mind the 'crumb risk' Jazzy directed her colleagues through to her cramped kitchen and with Queenie nodding along beside her and after promises of total secrecy she filled Geordie and Fenton in on the task she'd been assigned by DCS Afzal.

With his face scrunched up, Fenton busied himself with setting up his laptop and logging onto Jazzy's Wi-Fi whilst casting anxious glances around the room, his gaze bouncing over everyone's faces as he tried to avoid making eye contact. Geordie, not so reticent, exhaled explosively and then, hands splayed before him in a questioning manner, said, 'Elliot? Really? You're investigating Elliot for corruption?' In a dramatic gesture he jumped to his feet and clicked his fingers. 'Oh no, that's not what you're doing, is it? No, you're going one step further. You're handling an undercover cop tasked with ascertaining Elliot's corruption level – an undercover cop who Elliot thinks is his CI. God's sake, Jazzy, how messed up is that?'

Jazzy hung her head. Every word Geordie had uttered was bang on and she'd tortured herself with that knowledge since she'd taken on the task. However, in his rage, Geordie was missing something. Something crucial. She raised her head, ignoring Queenie who – chomping through her crisps – paused and winked at her as if to say, 'Go get 'em, girl,' and glared first at Geordie, who still stood, hands on hips in a pose she'd seen him do less aggressively as Misty Thistle and then at Fenton whose cheeks had taken on their telltale 'I'm uncomfortable with this discussion' hue.

'You think I'm happy with this? You think I'm jumping for joy?' She slammed her palm on the table, making Fenton's laptop jump. 'Well, I'm not. In fact, I'm anything but happy to be investigating Elliot. Not only do I know he's *not* corrupt, he's one of my very dear friends – my oldest one. This is killing me.'

Geordie exhaled again, but this time more softly, and when Fenton tugged his arm, he slid back into his chair, his gangly legs nudging the table and again making Fenton's laptop jump. Jazzy ran her fingers over her Ganesh and tried to compose her thoughts. *Come on, Ganesh, this is a big obstacle. Work your magic, eh?* Finally, all eyes on her, she exhaled.

'Look, I took this on because if I hadn't then Afzal would have signed someone from A or B team instead and . . .'

'Shite, no way you want any of them on the case. Their focus would be on finding stuff to convict not to exonerate. They'd take gleeful pride in bringing down someone whom the chief super holds in such high esteem. Nah you did the right thing, Jazzy.'

Fenton's words made Jazzy's heart sing. To have another one of her team on board was more than she could have wished for.

Geordie shuffled his legs. 'Aye, well. Maybe I spoke a wee bit hastily. I mean, as well as you having Elliot's back it gives us another way to see what's going on in Edinburgh.'

Jazzy smiled at Geordie. 'That was my second reason. We've been excluded so far and if they're so desperate they're considering that Elliot is leaking key information to Jimmy Nails, or worse is an active part of Loanie Gibbs's crew, then we need to know it. Handling an undercover officer means you have to leave your preconceptions at the door and consider every angle so you can direct proceedings to get comprehensive, unbiased intel.'

'Aye, hen, but you know that works both ways. What are you going to do if Dukesy uncovers some nasty wee secret about Elliot?' As Jazzy opened her mouth to reply, Queenie wafted her words away. 'No, I'm not for a moment saying Elliot's corrupt. Not sure he's got the balls for that – you know, he's always been a wee but uptight, a bit of a goody two shoes, an arse—'

'Queenie! I'm not going to cover up anything. If there's evidence that he's not as straight as a die, then regardless of my personal feelings on the matter, he'll go down.' As she spoke Jazzy's heart fluttered. She and Dukesy would follow the evidence and report back analytically to Afzal. Her job was to make sure that all avenues were followed, which brought her on to the tasks she'd set Fenton the previous night. 'Let's move on. So, Fenton, how did you get on with the stuff I asked you to do last night?'

Queenie frowned and slammed her half-eaten bag of crisps on the table. 'Jobs? Haggis? Still can't believe you gave that wee toad Haggis jobs to do.'

'Aw shut up, Queenie, he's the IT geek, not you.' Ignoring the wink Queenie sent in Fenton's direction she continued, 'I got to thinking that we should be proactive. Instead of trusting that everyone else's judgement is spot on, we should check, double-check and verify. Which is why I asked Fenton to do a little independent digging on all the key players – Dukesy, this retired DCS Emily Hare and the copper, Dougie Shearsby, who Dick's so close with and, of course, the Edinburgh and Glasgow gangsters. So what have you got?'

'Not had much of a chance because Dick's been on the prowl. You're not flavour of the month and he seems to think he needs to share his thoughts about you with me. I'll update you as I uncover intel. So far, though, Dukesy seems like the real deal, although I couldn't get access to all levels – but what I've found is that over the years he's been loyal to Elliot, whilst digging undercover and setting up a few stings that have intercepted huge drug distributions.'

After Fenton relayed the information he'd already shared with Jazzy earlier – which amounted to nothing much really – Geordie drummed his fingers on the table, his expression more serious than Jazzy had ever seen it. 'You know, Jazzy's right with the check, double-check, verify thing. I've been thinking this for a long time – well, since Mhairi escaped, actually.'

Jazzy frowned. What did her sister have to do with this? 'Not sure I . . .?'

'The Bitch is a devious cow and she's still on the lam. How can we be sure she's not involved in this? I think we should be vigilant. We've all got targets on our backs and a psycho killer on the loose, so maybe we should be checking and double-checking *everyone* we meet. I mean, not only the key players in these turf wars, but other folk as well. Look at this Sid Mackie character, for example. He's appeared out of nowhere and landed right at your feet – suspicious or what? What do we really know about him? Who's checking *his* credentials? The Cold Case Unit? Well, that's not good enough for me. I think we should get a full background check done on him and, just as importantly, I think we should be on the lookout for anyone else who tries to engage with us.'

He had a point. She'd been so bored with admin stuff that she'd jumped at the distraction and didn't question the fact that he'd turned up at Livingston rather than follow official channels. 'You're right. You able to take that on, Geordie? Fenton's got a lot to do as it is.'

'Yep, I'm on it. I'll leave Fenton with the juicy stuff. This should be bog-standard procedure. Besides, our beloved dickless wonder appears to have something on his mind other than keeping tabs on me. He's been creeping around, taking "private" phone calls, and leaving the office for ages at a time. He needs monitoring, too, if you ask me. Wouldn't put it past him to be smarmying up with the criminal fraternity if it kept him in expensive moustache balm.'

Jazzy remembered that weird handshake Dick had shared with Elliot's ex-boss Shearsby. Yes, keeping a closer eye on Dick might be a good idea. Jazzy caught sight of Queenie squirming on her chair. 'You all right, Queenie?'

Queenie shrugged. 'Not sure, hen. I mean it's probably nothing but, well, I did help an old fogie in distress in the Co-op in Cauther the other week – they took a funny turn, like. Wouldn't even mention it, but turns out, this auld coot has just moved in opposite me and Craig. I mean – they're at death's door and all that so Geordie's "vigilance" talk has probably got me paranoid, still . . . I've got a bairn to consider. Maybe just check that out too whilst you're at it, Fenton son.'

'Aye, just text me the address and I'll see what I can find out.'

Chapter 34

Vengeance

No idea why I bother with the news. Same old, same old – bombings, earthquakes, death, destruction – it's always those who don't deserve it who suffer. I'm about to switch it off when the digital forensic image of Cairnpapple Man flashes onto the screen. My heart lurches as that image is replaced by two men, one holding a microphone with Cairnpapple Hill looming behind, the other holding a brolly as if his life depended on it. His eyes dart from side to side as if he'd rather be anywhere other than here.

Confused, I shake my head as if that will help me make sense of what I'm seeing. Involuntarily, my hand reaches out toward the man with the brolly and a low groan escapes my lips. *How can this be?* Eyes glued to the screen, I turn up the volume and listen to the windswept reporter.

'Following the recent digital facial reconstruction of the murdered man, known only as Cairnpapple Man, found here on Cairnpapple Hill in 1990, there has been a remarkable development which might, with your help, lead to the identification of these human remains. This is Sid Mackie who, after seeing a recent appeal with the digitally reconstructed face of our deceased male – believed to be in his late teens to early twenties at the time of his death – has come forward. So, Sid, can you tell the viewers why you're here?'

Like a rabbit in the spotlight the man blinked at the reporter, then his lips – those familiar lips – turned upwards into a slightly scoffing smile.

'Well, as you can see, there is no doubt that Cairnpapple Man and I could be twins. When I first saw the digital reconstruction, I was in Turkey where I'd lived with my parents since I was small. I am an only child and since my parents died, I have no living relatives. When I spotted the similarities between myself and the facial reconstruction and the remains were discovered so close to where I was born, it just made me wonder. I thought we might be related. It felt like my duty, if I could, to help to identify him and . . .' he shrugged and looked right at the camera '. . . maybe even find myself some living relatives.'

His eyes seemed to bore right into me, their intensity so compelling they drew a tear from my eye. I struggle to reach the folded photograph that never leaves my side and I unfold it, smoothing my finger over the ridges and lines of a face I never touched in life, marvelling at the likeness to this Sid Mackie, and I'm glad I'm still alive. Glad I might have the opportunity to meet this young man – well, not so young, for he must be in his forties at least. Who is he? What strange coincidence of genes has created someone so similar to my son? It's almost as if they are siblings or cousins, yet that is impossible. Mackie? The name sounds familiar but in my morphine fog, I can't place it. Too many years have gone by, too many . . .

'As you can see, I'm wearing replicas of the clothes my relative was wearing at the time of his death. They are quite distinctive. These jeans and this short-sleeved denim jacket – both Lee brand – are replicas of those worn by Bruce Springsteen on *Rolling Stone* magazine in 1984. This BORN IN THE USA pin was attached just here. These are distinctive items. If you recognise them please come forward. The number is flashing across the screen now, I believe.'

I pause the screen, the number in bold across the bottom, Sid Mackie's earnest face pleading with me to reach out to him. Believe me, I want to. I recognise that jacket. I should do, for it was mine. The only thing I ever gave my son – other than his name, that is. I close my eyes and allow my thoughts to fill my head. Half-remembered ones, others half-forgotten bombard me. Angry words, yells of grief, shame, hatred – an assortment of useless emotions batter me – bruise my soul – my punishment for not being more. For not stepping up to the mark then. The question is, am I able to step up to the mark now, or is Vengeance all I'm good for? Something flickers in my chest, something beyond my ken. Something unidentifiable. Something that feels good and then it clicks. This emotion fluttering in my barren chest is hope.

I pick up the burner phone and dial – not the number on the screen. When he answers, I issue my instructions. 'Sid Mackie. Find me everything you can about him. Background, current whereabouts, contact details, associates – everything. And make it a priority. There's a bonus in it if you're quick.'

Chapter 35

Unsent draft email communication between Detective Sergeant Jazzy Solanki and undercover operative, Spaceman

Spaceman
Time 19:12
Subject: Back in Edinburgh. Something's afoot. LG and FJ seem antsy. Also, meeting this afternoon between LG and Dougie Shearsby. Might be nothing. Might be something. I'm on it! Watch this space.

Draft email deleted and replaced

Jazzy thought about that. A meeting between Loanie Gibbs and ex-DCI Shearsby was notable but not conclusive. Fenton had come up with nothing, Dukesy was on the ground and had nothing concrete to work with, and Afzal had told her that Lothian and Borders weren't the only division closing ranks and playing things close to their chests. It seemed that both Edinburgh and Glasgow were doing the same thing in an attempt to isolate any corruption in private. She couldn't blame them. The Met had already seen how widespread reporting of corruption within their ranks had been received by the public and no division wanted that degree of vitriol aimed at them. Still, with Emily Hare naming Shearsby as a person of interest, this couldn't be ignored.

Jazzy
Time 19:20
Subject: Any intel on what was discussed?

Draft email deleted and replaced

Spaceman
Time 19:23
Subject: Working on that. Hopefully I'll have more to report tomorrow.

Draft email deleted and replaced

Jazzy
Time 19:25
Subject: Did you break the encryptions on the V emails?

Draft email deleted and replaced

Spaceman
Time 19:31
Subject: Bounced around all over. No chance of ID on V. Got a line of inquiry to follow up on tonight regarding FJ. Sources I can contact. Not naming names till I'm sure either way, okay? Trust me!

Draft email deleted and replaced

It was frustrating that Dukesy had been unable to break Vengeance's encryption, but at least he was monitoring ongoing communications on all three targets. Who knew? Maybe something else would pop up.

Jazzy
Time 19:40
Subject: Okay. Keep safe.

Draft email deleted

The entire exchange left Jazzy with an uneasy tingle in her gut. It was good that Dukesy was settling into his role and it was still early days. The fact that he had leads to follow was promising. Shearsby's meeting with Gibbs was interesting. She wished she could have been a fly on the wall for that one. Of course, the meeting could be unrelated to Operation Towpath. It could be a routine follow-up on the murders of Loanie's cousins or something to do with one of his other criminal enterprises, but it was frustrating to still be in the dark. It was a waiting game.

Why the hell had she allowed Afzal to talk her into this?

Chapter 36

Vengeance

I'm wakened by the shrill ring of my phone. Nearly midnight! What the hell? I scramble for the phone, my heart pounding. The movement as I jolt from my sleep has set all my nerve endings on fire. The chair, so comfy when I dozed off, is hard and my bones are throbbing. Every inch of me longs for the end. It won't be long now, but I've got to hang on. I've got to see justice done. I blink a few times and even that sets off a whole wave of pain and nausea. 'Yes, I'm here. What's happened? Things are moving quickly now. The Gaffer has set a plan in action and we've no option but to bring things forward.'

I exhale. Maybe it'll be for the good. Maybe at last divine intervention is playing my way. 'But the result will be the same? I need to be there. I need to be there at the end. That's imperative.'

'Give me a few days. My people are still working on the logistics of it all. It's nearing the endgame either way, but your wishes will be respected. I know this is important to you. The Gaffer has taken the war to his enemy's door by abducting a relative.'

The voice on the other end lightens and a laugh rumbles into my ears. 'Thing is, they've not done their due diligence. It's like the Gaffer's spiralling out of control – making rash decisions, making mistakes. Still it plays into our hands.'

'Keep me informed. Oh, any word on Sid Mackie?'

The laugh from my contact is low. 'We're still working on it. But, I'll send you a partial background, current location and contact details.'

I hadn't expected so much so soon, but I'm glad. These people have been my saviours. Their reliability and efficiency have enabled me to come this far and I don't begrudge them one penny of the money they've earned. I'm indebted to them. As I hang up, a spasm contorts my body. I can't breathe. I can barely move as I press the button that will send the pain relief through my veins. The cancer is making itself felt tonight. As I lie in this paroxysm of pain, I watch the snow fall slowly outside my window and will myself to stay alive. Now that it's so close – just a matter of days till I see their faces, till I give my verdict, I will not allow myself to be too late. They will not escape retribution and my dying wish to look them in the eyes as *they* take their final breaths will be fulfilled.

Then there is Sid Mackie, and I have another decision to make. A tear seeps from my eye and as the pain eases, I allow it to trickle down, its salty taste, when it reaches my lips, somehow reinforces my spirit. I will prevail for I Am Vengeance and nothing will stop me. Nothing.

Friday 10th March

Chapter 37

The past couple of days had been difficult for Jazzy. When she'd finally faced DCI Dick in the station on Wednesday morning he'd been cold and dismissive and – as only the dickless wonder could – had taken his revenge on Jazzy by piling more and more paperwork on her and Queenie. Neither Fenton nor Geordie had discovered anything new and nor had Dukesy, despite his daily updates. According to his latest communication, word on the street was that a Glasgow criminal had been abducted, but with no confirmed ID on the abductee and no corresponding missing persons report to follow up on, the information had limited usefulness. He'd used his position as Jimmy Nails's informant to see if the gang leader would let slip an ID, but that had proved fruitless.

Thus, her reports to DCS Afzal were brief and frustrating. He'd taken the flak from the Operation Birchtree task force for her withdrawal from the Simon equation and as a result his demeanour with Jazzy was cold. So far, the only intel from Uncle Pedro was regarding Benjy's meltdown and the counselling he'd convinced both Benjy and Ivor to have. Knowing Pedro was looking after the kids was at least one weight off her mind.

The only positive development was that the stookie had been removed from her arm and replaced by a lightweight support that allowed her to do more intensive physio. Jazzy was buzzing that soon she'd be able to dispense with Queenie's chauffeuring services and drive her own Mini.

Halfway through inputting a laborious report – the suspected theft of a pedigree horse from a stables in Kirknewton – her phone rang.

She rolled her eyes at Queenie. 'Dick. Not sure I want to take this.'

'Aw, just put the wee toerag on hold. He'll only be ringing to see if we're here. You know what he's like.'

Jazzy was tempted, but there was really no escaping him. In a cool, but professional tone she accepted the call.

The DCI was in a more subdued frame of mind, when he announced that he was calling on behalf of the chief super. Although still patronising, his attitude was less abrasive than it might have been. Perhaps Afzal had warned him about his attitude, or perhaps D team's frequent threats to involve HR were paying off. Still, having to swallow her own sarcasm stuck in her craw, as she listened to his instructions.

'Right sir, I appreci— Ah, okay. Yes, I understand you've got nobody else availa—'

Alerted by Jazzy's broad grin, Queenie leaned in to hear the conversation play out.

'No, sir. We won't fuck it up! Yes, sir, I'll tell her. No, sir, no need to worry.'

Jazzy's final assurance was uttered with a grimace, whilst Queenie made boaking motions towards the phone. Too psyched to respond to her partner's juvenile behaviour, Jazzy stood up. 'Get your arse in gear, Queenie. There's a dead body, suspicious circumstances and we're the only officers free. Let's get a wriggle on.'

During their mad dash down to the car park, Jazzy filled Queenie in. 'It was phoned in anonymously. Apparently, a dead man has been found on the Lin's Mill estate near the Almond Aqueduct. CSIs and Lamond Johnston are en route.'

Queenie glanced round and lowered her voice. 'You think this is another casualty of the war of two cities?'

The same thought had occurred to Jazzy. Suspicious circumstances could mean anything from a suicide to a murder to an accident, but with Lothian and Borders being used as a body-dumping ground recently, it was logical to assume the worst. When they had an idea of cause of death and had ID'd the body, they'd have a better perspective. For now, though, she'd keep an open mind.

Chapter 38

Shuggie had tried to make peace with his old man. The atmosphere had been so bad at home that he'd been compelled to agree to this interview at Tony Macaroni's. Anything to get his dad off his back. Anything to convince his auld man that he wasn't doing anything illegal. It was only an interview, but it felt like a life sentence to Shuggie. He'd almost convinced himself that the Gaffer wasn't going to phone and that he'd be able to chalk the whole episode up to a bad experience, never to be repeated – almost, but not quite. Shuggie's dad was fond of saying 'whits fur ye'll no go by ye' and Shuggie hoped that both this bloody job and the Gaffer would jog on by. Still, if going for a waitering job at the pizza place would shut his dad up for a minute then he'd bite the bullet.

If this interview went well, maybe he'd be able to make enough to pay the Gaffer back and put it all in his rear-view mirror. *Who am I kidding? That's definitely no' how this crap works.*

Shuggie was early, so he stood in the car park near the Travelodge and paced the damp pavement. He'd his big coat on, but that didn't stop him from channelling his inner Soprano. This was an opportunity to practise his *Sopranos* repertoire, but could he pull off a New Jersey accent? More to the point, should he?

He'd decided to ditch the American accent and go in favour of one like his dad's – mainly Edinburgh with a dose of Italian flung in for good measure.

Nerves were kicking in. He always got like this before opening night or an interview – didn't matter if the interview was for an acting job or not, the butterflies always set in about ten minutes before kick-off. Of course, *that's* when his phone rang. For a second, Shuggie froze. He pulled it from his pocket and stared at it, the ring tone doing his head in. *Shit, buggery bollocks, what should I do?* He was tempted to throw it into the bushes by the side of the car park, but reconsidered. He had no choice. The minute he'd pocketed that money, his free will was gone. He owed the Gaffer and that was that.

'Hallo?' He groaned and closed his eyes. Why did he have to sound so damn scared? Why did he have to act so bloody glaikit?

'Glad you're a bit quicker answering this time, Shuggie, my lad.' The voice was all smoky cigarettes and humour. 'It's time.'

'Time?' The colour drained from Shuggie's cheeks and his breath hitched in his chest.

'Aye that's right. It's time. Best if you tell Mr Macaroni that you don't need his job after all. You'll be picked up soon. Just stay where you are.'

Shuggie glanced round as if expecting the Gaffer to materialise in front of him and an amused rumble rolled down the line. 'Don't look so scared, Shuggie. If you do this job well, there's a wee bonus in store for you. By the way – you look smart in that shirt and tie.'

As the Gaffer hung up a black Galaxy with tinted windows rolled into the car park and stopped beside the Travelodge. The driver flashed his lights and Shuggie, tie too tight round his neck now, made his way over to it, his eyes darting all over as if looking for an escape. When he got closer, the driver – the older man from the other night – gestured for him to get in. Avoiding meeting his gaze, Shuggie climbed into the passenger seat and was about to pull the seatbelt across his chest when a heavy hand landed on his shoulder and gripped really hard. Shuggie froze. Was this it, then? Had they decided he was a useless wee turd and were going to off him? Sweat dappled his brow and then a loud and familiar voice cast booze-stenched words over him. 'Shuggie, mah man. Looks like you and me are heading for the big time.'

Matty. Fucking Matty. You couldn't make this shite up.

He turned around and nearly threw up, for sitting next to Matty was a figure with a hood pulled over their head, their arms cable-tied in their lap. The stench of shite puffed up like a nuclear cloud around the prisoner and for a moment Shuggie wondered if he was dead. Then he saw the figure heave and the stink of vomit joined that of the excrement as he threw up in the hood, the vomit dripping out from the bottom.

'Oi you, you dirty fucking minger. That's gross.' Matty, with one hand over his nose, prodded the prisoner with the other and then scooted across the back seat, putting as much distance between them as he could.

Deadpan, the driver – seemingly unaffected by the fragrance – said, 'Let me introduce you to your charge, Shuggie lad. You two will babysit this fucker till further orders. Understood?'

Acrid saliva filling his mouth, Shuggie rolled the window down and breathed in the Baltic air. His chest was so tight you could have twanged it like a guitar. This was the short straw, but his only hope for survival was to carry out the Gaffer's orders to a T and pray that Matty wouldn't fuck it up for them. 'Aye, understood.'

Chapter 39

'After the discovery of the bodies of two males and one woman, on the outskirts of Wester Hailes at the weekend, a spokesperson from the Scottish parliament has emphasised the need for calm, and announced further talks with Police Scotland to formulate a plan to deal with the escalating violence. Meanwhile, in other news . . .'

'Can't believe after all this time they're no closer to getting to grips with this, JayZee. It's lawlessness, that's what it is. I mean, there was those two dumped by Tarbrax the other week, then these three at the weekend and now we've been called out to another one. Where's it all going to end, eh? I'll tell you where – Arma-bloody-geddon, that's where. The bloody Apocalypse isn't too far off, mark my words it'll be Doomsda—'

'For goodness' sake, Queenie, how many more films are you going to list? We don't even know that this death is related to the others.' Even as the words left Jazzy's lips, she knew she didn't believe them.

'Hmph, aye, you stick your head in the sand, hen. Turn the other cheek, keep the blinkers on, but we all know you're living in cloud cuckoo land.'

Queenie turned off the road and her Land Rover bounced into the car park by Lin's Mill Aqueduct in Livingston, joining the convoy of police and CSI vehicles and a mortuary van, which filled the potholed parking area that offered access to a walk across the aqueduct, which was part of the Union Canal.

Her arm throbbed, her head felt heavy and the effort of jumping out and looking ready was almost too much for her. She tightened her ponytail and exhaled. Then pasted on a smile and followed Queenie over to the officer who was directing them. She could hold it together – for a while longer.

'So' – Queenie rocked on her heels – 'we have to go down those steps and up the other side then traipse through fields and whatnot before we even get to the body – is that what you're telling me?'

The officer, stepping from foot to foot in an effort to keep warm, nodded and blew on his hands. 'Aye, and once you're over the other side you'll have to mind your step. It's slippy as fu—' His face reddened and he glanced away before finishing his sentence with a shrug. 'Really slippy.'

'Bloody no consideration, that's all I can say. What sort of idiot dumps a body in the middle of nowhere, eh? I mean, who the hell treks over the wilderness in the middle of bloody winter with a body on their back? I mean, why? Just why?' She glared at the dancing policeman. 'And more to the point, who the hell found it? I mean, who in their right minds, would be out there discovering deid bodies? It's just—'

'Anonymous phone call, I heard. Probably a dog . . .'

'Aye, a dog walker, yeah, that seems likely. Though why the hell they'd not leave a name is beyond me.' Queenie glowered at the officer and nodded towards a tree near the entrance to the car park. 'For God's sake, son, just go behind that tree. All this dancing about like a bloody dressage pony's making me need to go too. But you go first. Me and DS Solanki will hold the fort. Off you go now, son. No need to be embarrassed.'

Face as red as a beetroot, the young officer did a weird hoppy-skippy-jumpy shuffle till he was out of sight of them behind the tree and Queenie shook her head.

'They don't make them wi' bladders like they used to, Jazz. Just another sign of how bad recruitment's got. I think it should be a mandatory part of their assessment. If they can't hold their pish for five hours in icy conditions, then they don't make it.' For emphasis she drew a decisive finger across her throat.

As usual, Queenie's banter lifted her spirits. 'Aye, right. Like I've not seen you crouching behind a bush umpteen times since we've been partnered together.'

Queenie folded her arms under her chest. 'Aye, but I'm a woman of a certain age and therefore the same rules don't apply.'

Jazzy grinned as the young officer made a somewhat more dignified return. 'If you follow the tape, it'll lead you to the body, boss. There's a bit of climbing involved – grass verges and hillocks and that, so just—'

'Aye, aye, aye, aye, aye . . .' Queenie marched to the stone steps leading beneath the aqueduct with Jazzy trailing behind. 'It's slippy. I know. You said.'

At the bottom of the steps, was a huge locked gate with a sign saying LIN'S MILL. 'You'd think they'd meet us here and drive us to the site. We're going to be frozen before we reach it at this rate.'

But Jazzy overtook Queenie and jogged up the other steps leading to the opposite side of the canal where she waved to the young officer and began to walk along the towpath. The cold invigorated her and as she walked further along the canal path towards Falkirk she felt some of the tension leave her shoulders. Whatever she was presented with here, she'd be fine. She always was. She was allowed the occasional blip, but Jazzy was a fighter. Her hand crept into her pocket and her fingers moved over the smooth contours of the small glass Ganesh statue. 'Come on, Queenie, let's get moving, eh?'

Struggling to keep up, Queenie, after an acrobatic skid, slipped three times in rapid succession. 'For God's sake. Bloody ice – should be damn well banned.'

Each time amidst flailing arms and angry growls she landed on her backside on the black ice. 'Aye, that's right, JayZee. You just march on regardless. Just keep on keeping on, God forbid you help me to my feet. Just ignore me while you edge on, all leisurely while – in the interests of doing our damn job – *my* bahookie turns black and blue.'

Jazzy, struggling to keep the smile off her lips, held up her arm as far as she was able – which was about two inches. *Boy, that bloody hurt!* She'd really overdone the physio that morning, but at least her new fabric support allowed her more flexibility. She paused, waiting for Queenie. 'You knew it was slippy. The constable told you that, didn't he?'

'Aye, well, I didn't think it would be *so* slippy, did I?'

Jazzy shook her head but bit her tongue. *I'll bloody slippy her in a minute!*

Queenie squeezed Jazzy's shoulder. 'You look fair wabbit, hen. Peely-wally. As pasty as an uncooked Greggs vegan roll. You feeling all right? Your arm hurting, is it?'

Jazzy deflected Queenie's questions. 'We've got a ten-minute walk before we get to the crime scene. We should get a move on.'

The smell of moist earth and new growth was heady. A couple of months ago this trail would have been wider and less oppressive, but the resurgence of new leaves had made it sombre and threatening. In single file, they trudged across the muddy ground in silence. Neither knew what awaited them, only having been instructed to attend the scene of a possible murder on the Lin's Mill estate near the Almond Aqueduct. Whilst Jazzy prepared herself for whatever she was about to witness, she suspected that Queenie, who hated murder scenes – especially the squishy ones – was putting on a brave face too.

Chapter 40

Ahead, through the dimness, the ultra-bright lights from the CSI lamps and the muted chatter of professionals at work welcomed them. A string of Police Scotland crime scene tape dangled between two trees and a uniformed officer stepped forward as they approached, his face breaking into a grin when he recognised them. 'Good to see you both. Are you well?'

Jazzy cast about in her mind for his name, but Queenie, still rubbing her arse, stepped forward. 'Aye we're fine, Conrad, son. How's the new bairn?'

How the hell does she do that? Queenie was the most irascible, brusque, straight-to-the-point person Jazzy knew, yet here she was, not only aware of the young officer's name, but also aware he had a newborn at home.

Protocols submitted to, the pair suited up and ducked under the tape that marked the beginning of the inner cordon. A few hundred yards away the area stretched out to a shaded copse where the CSI team had already pitched a large white tent to protect the body from the elements and to prevent possible evidence from becoming degraded. Brow furrowed in concentration, Jazzy glanced round. She liked to orientate herself at a crime scene before being drawn to look at the body. She'd get only one chance to absorb her first impressions of the area chosen by the perpetrator to kill or to dump their victim and she wanted to make the most of it. Where the killer chose to commit murder or to dump a body could say a lot about them and, in Jazzy's mind, this site was a strange choice. It wasn't readily accessible and whichever direction the killer had approached from would have involved a large amount of brute strength to heft a dead body either through the trail she and Queenie had just traversed or one of the other two trails that the CSIs had marked with coloured flags.

One trail meandered for a good three miles from Lin's Mill, which was the nearest domestic property, so that seemed an unlikely choice, particularly because as Conrad had just told them, security was tight around the periphery of the property, with large fences topped with barbed wire. The only other approach was from the Almondell Visitor Centre over the Mandela Bridge and up two different sets of steps to finally reach the Almond Aqueduct. To approach the trail leading to the killer's unusual choice of dump site would necessitate a tricky trudge down to the river below, and then a bit of a hike to bypass the parking areas where Queenie had parked. Again, that seemed an unlikely choice. For one, the CCTV at the visitor centre would have picked up any vehicles parked there and for another, why trek so far when there was a perfectly good parking area with no security cameras in sight?

Jazzy was convinced that the route they'd trodden had been the same one taken by the killer and his victim, which left three burning questions. First: had they made the outer cordon wide enough to ensure that any evidence present hadn't been obscured or compromised by the arrival of the police and CSIs themselves? Second: was the victim already dead or had his killer walked him through the dark woods to his death? She pondered the scenarios that possibility created. Had he known he was heading to his death or had he been taken unawares? Had he been forced to this damp and dank place or had he gone willingly for some unknown reason? Third: had their killer been working alone or did they have help? If the victim was already dead, then two killers seemed a more likely scenario. Jazzy looked back the way she and Queenie had traipsed. It was a distance and lugging a dead body was no easy feat . . .

'Got tracks here, Jazzy. Might be worth taking a gander.'

Jazzy recognised Franny the CSI manager's voice and turned to see her crouched by a series of flags. With Queenie following, Jazzy shuffled closer – the rustle from their crime suits adding to the sensation of the woods whispering their secrets. Jazzy shuddered as she crouched beside Franny, almost toppling over when Queenie balanced herself by leaning on Jazzy's shoulder. 'What have you got, Fran?'

'Well, we've been lucky to find this, really, and we'll cast it pronto so we don't lose it. The keen frost over the past few days has meant that any tracks on the main trail are too deteriorated, but this sludgy bit here – right on the edge of the trail – has left us a couple of feet of tyre tracks. I suspect from a quad bike, which would be a good way to transport a body out here.'

Jazzy shuddered. The memory of the quad bike chase after the Bitch still gave her nightmares and, although most of her injuries had healed, that initial panic that she'd lost Elliot still caused her heart to hammer. She forced herself back to the present, because Franny was still talking.

'Of course, there's no guarantee that these tracks are anything to do with . . .' she jerked her head towards the tent '. . . but you never know. If your killer needed a mode of transport, then a quad bike's as good as any, yeah? Might be a useful bit of evidence to link the killer to the body.'

They were still a long way from that point. The body hadn't been identified yet. Jazzy sighed and looked at Queenie, whose shoulders were hunched up by her ears. 'You ready for this, Queenie?'

Queenie exhaled a long gust of prawn-cocktail-scented air and grunted. 'Aye, well, I suppose so. Let's get it over with.'

As one, the pair, sticking to the tracks laid earlier by Franny's team, walked over to the tent, which perched at an angle on the steep slope overlooking the forest beyond. As they approached the entrance flap, the low drone of pathologist Lamond Johnston's voice reached their ears. Behind her Jazzy heard Queenie mutter, 'I hope to God there's nae blood.'

Jazzy shared her partner's hope, but as she poked her head through the flap to greet Johnston, she wasn't about to bet on it. 'Hey, doc.'

Johnston, tall and cadaverous, turned towards her, the crinkles in the corner of his eyes telling Jazzy that behind the mask he was smiling at her. 'How lovely to see you again, Jasmine.'

As ever, Jazzy was momentarily thrown by his greeting, which would have been more appropriate at a social gathering than over the body of a dead man. Maybe Johnston didn't get out much? 'Eh, yeah. You too, doc.' Jazzy floundered and stuttered to a halt as Dr Johnston moved to the side revealing their dead body.

Behind her, Queenie let out a low moan and gripped the back of Jazzy's arm, her stubby fingers pinching through her overall and her outer clothing right down to the skin beneath.

'Jesus bloody hell. For once could they no' just strangle someone? Why the hell do they insist on the torture. It jams my head right up.'

Dr Johnston moved along the treads that circled the body, allowing the two detectives a better view. A lonely rectangular gravestone lay flat on the grass, its edges demarcated with weeds and brambles.

'This part of a cemetery, doc?' asked Jazzy, peering around for signs of other gravestones, but Dr Johnston was already shaking his head. 'No just this one, dear. Been here since 1645, according to the inscription.'

Dismissing the gravestone as irrelevant to her investigation, Jazzy turned her attention to the dead body lying beside it.

'As you can see our as-yet-unidentified victim has been tortured prior to death. He's . . .'

'Ned the Ned.'

The pathologist stopped mid-sentence and looked at Queenie. Jazzy extricated herself from Queenie's tenacious grip and edged closer. 'You recognise him?'

Queenie swayed, her eyes shut. 'Aye. That's Ned the Ned Moran. He's Bonnie Moran's husband. Hardass Nails's brother-in-law. Frae Glasgow like. This will not go down well with the Weegies, you know.'

Jazzy frowned. 'I've never met Bonnie Moran. Got a bit of a reputation, hasn't she?'

Still with her eyes shut, Queenie slouched closer to the body. 'Aye, she's a prize bitch that one.'

Jazzy frowned. 'Aye and Jimmy'll not be happy that his brother-in-law's been murdered, will he?'

'No, he won't but, from all accounts, there's nae love lost between him and Ned Moran. Still, the torture seems to me to point more towards Auld Reekie than an internal dispute. But, who knows with this lot?'

'You're suggesting this fella here is another one in the long list of turf war casualties being played out outside the cities, Annie?'

Dr Johnston was one of the few who refused to use his colleagues' nicknames and it took Jazzy a moment to work out he was speaking to Queenie. Hearing her Sunday name prompted Queenie to open her eyes – although she kept her gaze averted from the body. 'Aye, and he'll not be the last either, doc. Jimmy's bound to retaliate.'

Morose now, Lamont did the sign of the cross over himself and sighed out a 'God bless you, son'. With his head bowed, Jazzy was sure he was muttering a prayer and although she thought that was out of place here at a crime scene, she didn't intrude. Lamond Johnston and his fellow pathologists had been run ragged by the spate of murders ending up on their tables over the past couple of months, so she could forgive him his lapse into religion. Whatever got him through the dark times, and if saying a prayer was what worked for the elderly man, then who was she to judge? As long as he didn't try to convert her.

Queenie and Jazzy exchanged glances, both convinced that before this investigation was done they'd have learned that Ned Moran was more likely to end up in hell than heaven. Not that that would influence how they investigated.

Jazzy turned to Queenie and lowered her voice to a whisper. 'You thinking what I'm thinking?'

Queenie nodded. 'Too right I am. I think we've got a reason to pay Bonnie Moran and her big brother a wee visit.'

Jazzy cleared her throat. 'Right, doc, when you're ready, can you talk us through what you've found so far?'

Johnston straightened his shoulders, then resumed his position kneeling by the body and gestured to the pair of them, one of whom was more reluctant than the other to hunker down beside him. But Jazzy had seen Queenie's eyes drift over the body. She'd noted the vacant look, the furrow across her partner's brow and knew that Queenie had seen as much as she needed to see. Every centimetre of this crime scene would be logged in Queenie's exceptional mind, so there was no need to prolong the torture.

'Queenie, go and see what else Franny and her team have got for us, and make a few calls to get Geordie McBurnie and Fenton Heggie to set up the incident room. I'll get Afzal to okay that. He'll do it, despite any arguments the dickless wonder might offer. Now we've had an ID, Heggie can compile as much background on Ned Moran as possible and McBurnie can start to log evidence as it comes in. Get him on checking out ANPR and CCTV using the area where we parked as a starting point and spreading outwards. Maybe he'll be able to identify a vehicle; possibly one with a trailer that could hold a quad bike, although tell him not to focus solely on that, as we don't know for certain that those tracks are linked to the crime scene.'

Johnston's eyes followed Queenie as she shuffled back to the tent entrance. 'God works in mysterious ways, eh, Jasmine? What could be seen by some as a curse, when in the right hands becomes a gift. No better person could He have bestowed a gift on than our Annie McQueen.'

Jazzy – assuming the 'He' to whom the pathologist referred was God – wondered whether He wouldn't have been better placed eradicating needless violence from the world than using Queenie as a tool to thwart it after the event. Choosing to keep her own counsel, Jazzy hunkered down beside the pathologist and allowed her eyes to wander over the body of Ned Moran.

He had been stripped down to a grimy pair of greyish boxers with frayed Calvin Klein elastic at the waist and lay in a weird semblance of a foetal position on his left side. His skinny frame was mottled with bruises, his concave, near hairless white chest and puny arms telling the story of a man who took little exercise, whilst his rounded belly indicated a liking for fried foods and beer. If anyone other than Queenie had identified the corpse, Jazzy would have harboured some doubts as to the accuracy of the ID. Queenie, though, was special. In a single glance she'd have been able to conjure up every time she'd encountered this man in detail and all of those details would compute with the name she'd given. Of course, Queenie's ID would have to be corroborated by a family member and by forensic analysis, but Jazzy was convinced that the man laid out before her was Ned Moran.

His injuries were extensive and it wasn't rocket science to work out that he'd been tortured. The blackened fingernails, broken eye sockets, misaligned knees and more confirmed that. 'Somebody's done a number on him, all right.'

'Hmm.' Dr Johnston shook his head. 'Perhaps not some*body*, Jasmine, perhaps some*bodies* and judging by the state of the various bruises, not all of these injuries occurred at the same time. The post-mortem will, of course, provide more detailed information. However, for your purposes, I'm prepared to say that these bruises . . .' Dr Johnston's gloved finger drew a circle in the air over an expanse of yellow and green discolouration across his ribs and chest area and then another near his jaw '. . . occurred earlier than the others. Of course, it'll be up to you to ascertain whether the two incidents are related or not and whether, indeed, the same person or persons are responsible for both beatings.'

'Are you saying that *two* separate beatings account for all of these injuries? Not three or four?'

Johnston's eyes crinkled as he smiled. 'How astute, Jasmine. Yes, you're right. My provisional assessment is that there were two separate beatings. The former, as already discussed, proved less final for our victim than the latter. As you can see, all these injuries are more recent. The bruising is less advanced. The PM will offer a time of death and more detail on the timings of the knee capping and the fingernail extractions, et cetera.'

'So, is this the torture site or a deposition site?'

'Well, my dear, that needs to be ascertained, but at the present time, my inclination is that this is a deposition site.'

'And cause of death?'

'Oh really, Jasmine? You're going to go there? I can't tell you that with any degree of accuracy. However, the position of the body is quite revealing, don't you think?'

Jazzy studied Ned Moran again and nodded. 'The weird foetal position?'

'Yes, you see that. In as far as he was able, it appears that Ned Moran pulled his body into as near a facsimile of a foetal position as it was possible for him, bearing in mind the nature and extent of his injuries.'

'You're saying he was alive when he was dumped here? Alive and left to die in the cold, all alone?'

'I'm not saying any such thing, Jasmine. I'm merely offering thoughts and possibilities. Now, if you've seen enough I think it's time for us to take Mr Moran to my lab so we can find the answers we need, don't you? After my post-mortem, you'll get all the answers I can provide, including an accurate time and cause of death.'

Fifteen minutes later, Queenie and Jazzy watched as Dr Johnston supervised the removal of Ned Moran's remains, then left. She would have to wait for the results from that before formulating any concrete theories on what had happened to Ned Moran during his final days and hours on this planet.

'Wonder why he's been dumped here? Why this spot?'

Queenie shrugged. 'Maybe whoever killed him considered him a blight on humanity – a plague.'

'Not sure I get what you mean, Queenie.'

Queenie, looking like a miniature snowman, stared off into space. 'Well, it's no coincidence, is it? Whoever brought him here knew the significance of this site. Knew about Lin's Grave and that's got to mean something.'

'Still not with you.'

Queenie began kicking a tuft of grass. 'Well, you saw the grave? The cold stone slab next to where he was left? You saw the skull and crossbones on it?'

'Yeah, course I did. Weird, eh?'

'Lin's Grave is thought to belong to the last plague victim in Scotland. Poor bugger was dragged here by his wife and buried because no other bugger else would do it. That's what the skull and crossbones signify – that William Lin succumbed to the plague. Maybe that's why Ned Moran was left here. Maybe he and the likes o' him *are* the plague. Maybe it's symbolic. It bloody feels like it to me, anyway. The number of deaths they're causing. Addiction on the increase, weans getting hooked, selling their wares outside schools and waging war on each other all in the name o' making a quick buck. They're bloody monsters, the lot o' them. Monsters! Maybe that's why they're all being offed.'

Jazzy let Queenie's heated words hang in the air for a moment. As a dump site Lin's Grave was a strange choice – difficult to get to with a body, not commonly known about, not significant, as far as she could tell, to the Edinburgh gangs, so why here?

'You wondering if this is a vigilante killing rather than one of the turf war ones we've been called to recently?'

Queenie shrugged. 'Or maybe they're winding up to some sort of endgame. Worth keeping an open mind, don't you think, JayZee? I mean, up till now, the crims on either side have been happy to offload their carcasses in any old lay-by or field outside either city's limits. Why change now? Maybe the natives are getting restless. Maybe they're fed up waiting for us to sort it out. Maybe they're taking the war into their ain hands or maybe, like I said earlier, this is the beginning of the end.'

And with those words following them as they made their way back to their vehicle, Jazzy lapsed into thoughtfulness. This call-out might be bigger and more treacherous than she'd initially expected.

Chapter 41

Vengeance

The only thing keeping me going over the past three days is the need to stay sharp. Sharp and focused. My desire for vengeance is the only thing keeping my heart beating. They've told me I should be in hospital now, but I'm clinging to life so I can cause death. It's a weird one, isn't it? What keeps our heart beating when our body is only a dried-out old husk?

I see their faces on my wall and that pleases me, for I know that their arrogance will not last much longer. I have faith in my paid help. They will locate our trump card. The card that will pull everyone to the right place at the right time. Every one of them deserves it.

As I study the photos stuck to the wall, I force myself to sip water, but its metallic taste makes it hard not to vomit it back up. I shiver and it's as if hammers are battering against my bones. This will soon be over and then I can give in and find blessed relief from this pain.

The latest intel from my people is intriguing. Not one abduction, but two. My mind buzzes as I try to clear the fog and work out how to make this play in my favour. Some might say both are innocents, but I think the addicted junkies and their families, the raped women, the murdered innocents, the small businesses paying protection money – none of those victims would call them innocents. It's all about degrees of innocence, don't you think?

These two are merely intriguing little conundrums – a distraction from the bigger picture. An indication that the Gaffer is unravelling. I hadn't expected that, but I'll put it to good use. My mercenaries are key to the endgame but I know they'll come up trumps. For such violent people, their empathy for me is almost therapeutic. If only I'd encountered more like them during my lifetime. If only I'd nurtured those who might have loved me. Those who might have been able to lift me from the spiral of hate and self-destruction. It's been a lonely life and I have only myself to blame for it. No matter now. It's too late. I want to mix things up, so despite my brain fug, I compose an email. My fingers shake as I type. Each jab a reminder of how little time I have left to complete things.

Dear Jimmy,
You might think that I'm responsible for your recent loss, but I'm not. I know you too well to assume that those two worthless wee toerags are of value to you.
So, who else have you upset, Jimmy boy? The Gaffer? Loanie Gibbs? Wee Frankie? The list is endless, don't you think?
Rest assured, though, Jimmy, your loss won't end with your brother-in-law and nephew. I might not be responsible for their fate, but know that I AM VENGEANCE and I am coming for you.

Chapter 42

Jazzy hadn't known what Bonnie Moran née Nails's home would be like before she and Queenie pulled onto Newlands Grove, but it wasn't this. The Moran residence in Shawlands on the southside of Glasgow was an elegant red-brick detached home with delightfully quirky turreted windows peeking above the high perfectly cut hedges. It stood to reason that if your family were into criminal activity then you'd value both your privacy and your security. The thing was, Jazzy hadn't realised just how high up the pecking order Bonnie Moran's family were. Of course, she knew Bonnie's brother Jimmy was a mover and shaker in the Glasgow gang circles. But this grandiose dwelling spoke of wealth beyond what Jazzy expected for his sister. Perhaps it was Jimmy's name on the deeds and Bonnie and her family were just lodgers.

'Crime pays, eh, Queenie?'

Before Queenie had a chance to respond, Jazzy's phone buzzed with an incoming call. She glanced at Queenie and mouthed 'Uncle Pedro' before dismissing the call and setting her phone to silent. But it vibrated with a text. Whatever Uncle Pedro had for her would have to wait till after they'd done the death notification.

As Queenie stopped in front of glistening tall black gates beside the intercom, she lowered her window enough to thrust her stubby fingers clutching her warrant card through and waved it before the camera. Jazzy thrust her phone into her pocket. A fuzz of static momentarily filled the air and Queenie said, 'DC McQueen and DS Solanki here to speak with Mrs Bonnie Moran.'

Again, the fuzz of static, then the dark gates began to slide open. As they entered the Moran premises, Queenie shook her head and mumbled under her breath, 'Aye, right enough, crime does pay. It's the folk of Shawlands I feel sorry for, though. They're no sooner cited as living in one of the most desirable areas to Scotland than the Morans move in. That's bound to bring prices scuttling to the floor. Mind you, they're like dogs some of these crims, ye ken. They don't like to shite in their own backyards. So maybe they'll keep this area clean.'

Invisible from the road, the drive divided an immaculate lawn on either side and ended on a circular turning area with a gargoyle in the middle. Two cars were parked up: a Discovery Jeep and a BMW. A snazzy red sports car was visible through the open doors of a garage to the side.

'Impressive, huh?' Jazzy released a long breath. 'You met her before, Queenie?'

Queenie scowled and glared out the window with a shrug. 'You could say that. She's been no stranger to a polis station over the years. The whole family's been a blight on law and order since they were bloody weans. Bonnie was always a bitch but she was also a smarmy bitch. Teflon. Nothing ever stuck to her. First her dad protected her and then Jimmy did. She was blessed by a family that had power and was well on the way to making the big time. Her da had his eye on the main chance and had no boundaries. Prostitution, drugs, trafficking, enforcing. You name it, Ricky Nails would do it and he'd do it with a smile on his face too. Animal, he was. Glasgow breathed a sigh when he copped it. Not that Jimmy's a whole lot better, but at least while he was in control he kept the needless crap to a minimum. Had the sense to realise that it was easier to conduct his business if he buried fewer bodies. Kept the polis off his back, to an extent.'

Jazzy had never heard Queenie speak with such bitterness. Her hands gripped the steering wheel and a pulse throbbed at her temple. There was more to this than Queenie was letting on and that didn't sit well with Jazzy. Queenie was usually quite transparent. 'And?'

Queenie's frown deepened. 'What do you mean, "and"?'

'That's not the full story, is it?'

Queenie opened the driver's door and with one foot touching the expensive block paving, said, without looking at Jazzy, 'Besides, we grew up in Easterhouse together. Went to the same school. Bonnie was a couple of years older than me.'

'Oh, and you didn't think to tell me this before now? Like maybe last year when Jimmy Nails's name came up? Then might have been a good time to speak up. You never mentioned it other than to say you knew him when you were a kid. Not that you grew up together and attended the same schools.'

Queenie, still avoiding Jazzy's gaze, hopped out. Jazzy joined her and the pair took a moment to stare up at the imposing doors, before Jazzy stepped forward. 'I'm not done with you about this, Queenie. You should have told me you knew Bonnie Moran. For now, though, no matter what our personal feelings towards her are or what we think her family is involved in, we're here to give this woman a death notification for her husband. That's not to say we won't keep our eyes peeled for any useful bits of information whilst we're inside, but our priority is looking after the grieving widow.'

Turned out, though, that the grieving widow was more of a merry one – well, actually that wasn't really the case either. Bonnie didn't do merry very well. In fact, Bonnie didn't do emotion at all, as far as Jazzy could see, but whether that was due to the amount of cosmetic work she'd had done or the absence of a heart, Jazzy wasn't sure. She appeared at the doors, a vision in red and green.

Her hair bundled up in two buns on the top of her head, Bonnie looked like a horned devil in Spandex. Figure-hugging, shimmering scarlet leggings and a green crop top that displayed an enviable four-pack. Bonnie was clearly a fitness junkie.

Behind Jazzy, Queenie was muttering under her breath, only a few of her sentiments reaching Jazzy's ears. 'Spandex? Spandex? What the hell is she playing at?' Mumble, mumble. 'A woman her age?' Mumble, mumble. 'Well, I'm not going to tell her about the carcinogenic properties of Spandex. Not my job. Besides, might be an idea to encourage all criminals to invest in a full Spandex wardrobe.'

Jazzy blocked out Queenie's whingeing moans and stepped up the stairs, warrant card at the ready.

Bonnie, arms folded under her pert boobs and her eyes flashing daggers at them, shook her head. 'I don't appreciate the likes of you turning up here at my home. This could be construed as police harassment, unless you've got a valid reason for flashing your warrant card at me on my doorstep.'

Her voice was pure Glasgow, but the hardness and good nature that Jazzy associated with most Weegies was replaced by ice. There was nothing humorous about Bonnie Moran and for a nanosecond Jazzy considered just blurting out the reason for their visit, just to jolt the older woman from her high-and-mighty disdain. The sound of her partner clearing her throat galvanised Jazzy to speak. No way did she want Queenie jumping the gun and blurting out the reason for their visit. No one, no matter how objectionable, deserved that. However, before she could utter a word, Bonnie's gaze landed on Queenie and her eyes narrowed, then she flung her head back and let out a guttural laugh that startled Jazzy.

'Well, fucking hell, if it's no' Orphan Annie McQueen turning up on my doorstep like a pound of lard. Hope you don't stink o' piss like you did when we were at school.'

A flush of colour spread over Queenie's cheeks as she marched up the last couple of stairs to stand right in front of the taller woman. With her hands fisted behind her back, Queenie rocked on her feet.

'You've no' changed a bit, have you, Bonnie? Toxic as ever and enjoying doling out the venom, eh? Pity, really, because we're here to deliver some bad news. Maybe you should let us in, eh, hen?'

The word 'hen' was delivered with a slash of sarcasm that made Bonnie's eyes narrow. Then, with reluctance she stepped back and gestured for them to follow her into her home.

'What's the pillock done this time? Got himself caught with a bag of weed or something? Or is it that worthless piece of shite Ned that's in bother? Well, if he needs bailing out, ye'll need to ask someone else. I'm done bailing either of them out. The amount o' hassle them two give me.' As she spoke a whirlwind on two legs with chocolate slathered round her mouth and curly hair, ran in. 'Mummy, Mummy. Me watch *Peppa Pig*.'

The transformation on Bonnie Moran's face was epic. If the woman's lips weren't so rigid, she'd have looked like she was grinning. As it was, she held out her arms as the little girl, clearly no relation to her now-deceased husband, launched herself into her arms and dotted a series of moist chocolatey kisses over her mum's face. Wiping off the gooey mess, Bonnie replaced her daughter on the floor, laughing.

'Aye, you can watch *Peppa Pig*. Go and get Angelica to set it up for you in your playroom.' As the wee girl ran through a door on the right beyond which a massive rocking horse, a large playhouse and a humongous train track were visible, Bonnie shook her head. 'Weans eh? Didn't expect to have another one after Danny, but thank fuck ah did. Where he has the brains of his dad – which, let me tell you, amounts to a single cell shared between them – my wee Crystal makes up for it. She's as sharp as a junkie's needle and twice as clever.'

She walked down the chessboard-tiled floor and into a massive kitchen/diner that boasted a huge red AGA and designer units accented in reds and greens. If Bonnie had stood in front of them, in her current outfit, there was a strong possibility she'd disappear into them. It seemed the lady of the manor had two favourite colours. She trailed through the kitchen and took a right into a room just beyond the dining table.

Jazzy blinked as she entered. The patterned wallpaper on the fireplace wall featured a rainforest scene filled with brightly coloured parrots that looked almost three-dimensional and made Jazzy wish she'd thought to bring her sunglasses.

With a tut and an exaggerated glance at the clock above the fireplace, Bonnie gestured to two oversized sage green sofas with vermillion-coloured satin cushions adorning them. 'Sit.' The single word was more order than request, but considering the news she was about to deliver Jazzy nudged Queenie and the pair of them perched on the edge of the settee, with Bonnie Moran looming over them, her foot tapping on the carpet and her gaze intent on Jazzy as, having humiliated Queenie, she now completely ignored her.

Less sympathetic than she'd been earlier, Jazzy schooled a fake empathetic smile on her lips and, hands clasped in her lap nodded at Bonnie. 'I'm afraid we have some distressing news for you. Earlier today a body was discovered in West Lothian. We believe it is that of your husband, and it is with regret I have to inform you that Ned is dead.'

Bonnie, glacial eyes held Jazzy's gaze, then a spurt of laughter burst from her lips like a faucet exploding. 'Yeah, right. Pull the other one, would you? That bastard will be the bane of my life till he dies.' She moved her hands to her hips and jerked her chin in Queenie's direction. 'Why does it not surprise me that you've made a mistake with you employing the likes of piss-yer-pants McQueen. For fuck's sake, get yourselves out of my house. I've better things to be doing than listening to yous two.'

Jazzy ignored the jibe at her partner, but refused to stand up. 'Sit down, Bonnie. I'm afraid it's true. We had a visual ID of the body and the fingerprints taken from the deceased match those

240

of your husband. Ned Moran is dead. Now, is there someone I can call for you?'

Bonnie threw back her head and laughed again. Not hysterically and certainly not with grief. More with disbelief. 'Can ye believe it? The idiot's gone and got himself killed, that right? Murdered?'

Jazzy nodded whilst Queenie kept her head bowed, more than likely to avoid any more personal attacks from the merry widow.

'Well, that's just bloody peachy, is it no'? Like I've got time to be organising a funeral.' She whipped a phone out from her bra and hit a number. 'That you, Jimmy? You'll never guess what's happened. See that man o' mine. He's only gone and got hisself murdered. No doubt by thon Edinburgh lot. Not that he doesn't deserve it, mind. Christ, I've been tempted to off the big pillock myself.'

Jazzy couldn't hear Jimmy's response to the news, but that didn't bother her. She had a fair idea by now that Ned Moran wouldn't be considered a loss as a husband or a brother-in-law. Although that didn't mean there wouldn't be consequences to his death. Nobody got on the wrong side of Hardass Nails and lived to recount the tale. This was definitely going to be a difficult investigation to oversee and although the body had been found in her division, Jazzy assumed she'd be expected to liaise with Glasgow police. Oh, joy of joys.

'Mrs Moran, if you could just sit down for a minute.' Jazzy kept her tone neutral, but maintained eye contact with Bonnie, who stared her out for a second, before hanging up on her brother without a farewell. She shoved her phone back into her bra and flung herself onto the couch opposite Jazzy and Queenie.

'I don't know a sodding thing. Useless pillock bogged off the other night because he was in the doghouse – *again*. That's all I've got for you.' She crossed her legs and hoicked her folded arms under her chest. 'So, if you don't mind, I've got to clear my diary and arrange a sodding funeral.'

Irritated by Bonnie's uncooperative manner, Jazzy held her gaze until the other woman fidgeted in her seat.

241

'What the fuck you staring at, eh? Am I not responding in quite the way your lot expect, that it?'

Fed up with the pantomime and eager to take control of this meeting, Jazzy quirked her eyebrow. '*Your lot?* Now, I'm hoping that's not a racial slur you're using there, Bonnie. For, you know, if it is, *that's* an offence.'

Bonnie snorted. 'Aye right, hen. You've seen my wee lassie? She's mixed race, you know so, no, it's not a racial slur.' Head to one side she pursed her lips, giving her a trout-like appearance. 'Nah, if anything, it was more of an institutional slur. You know – against the polis and I don't think that's an offence, really. Just a commonly held opinion around this neck of the woods.'

'That right, eh?' After her earlier silence, Queenie seemed keen to enter the conversation now. 'Or are you mistaking your current address with your humbler childhood in the Easterhouse slums?' Queenie clicked her fingers. 'Oh, but poverty didn't affect *your* family, did it, Bonnie? Nae poverty for the high and mighty Nails family. Easterhouse royalty, you lot were. Exploiting the poor, luring weak folk with nae hope left into vices that sapped their very souls. That's what your *lot* did.' Queenie's face was flushed beetroot red, her mouth tight, her hands balled into fists by her sides. 'Wonder what your new neighbours would think of your family business? I'm quite sure they don't know what you and your clan of rogues and criminals get up to. Of course, you'll no' shite in your ain backyard, will you? No' when there's vulnerable folk in poor areas just waiting to be enticed into your world of false promises and despair.'

Bonnie jumped to her feet, arms out ready to launch herself at Queenie. 'You piss-panted wee whore. I'll bloody kill you.'

In a second, both officers were on their feet, Queenie snarling like a rottweiler. Jazzy elbowed past her to stand between the two women. The faint sounds of *Peppa Pig* drifted through from the other room accompanied by the murmured voices of Bonnie's child and the nanny, Angelica. 'For God's sake, the pair of you, just sit down.' When neither made a move to oblige, Jazzy lowered her voice, injecting it with ice. 'Now. Right. Now.'

When both women were resettled in opposite seats, Jazzy exhaled. What the hell had happened then? So much for a nice dignified, empathetic death notification. This one would go down in history the most bizarre she'd ever witnessed. Well used to Queenie's complexities – the maternal auntie figure, the avenger, the sarcastic scary lout, the skilled interviewer, the tenacious terrier and the holy terror – seeing her lose control like this was gutting. If Bonnie Moran decided to make an issue of it, then Queenie would be in big bother.

Jazzy put all of that to the back of her mind to be dealt with later. She had questions to ask and she needed answers and as Bonnie had revealed herself to be less than a grieving widow, Jazzy saw no reason to pussyfoot around. 'Right, we don't want to waste time here. Not when we've got a murder investigation to progress, so I'm just going to ask you a few questions and then we'll be on our way.'

'Aye, ye better hoof it before Jimmy gets here. He'll no' be happy when I tell him what that fat bitch said. Anyway, I've got nothing to add and I'm not under caution, so piss off, the both of ye.'

'Look, Bonnie, just a few questions, eh? That's not unreasonable, now, is it? I mean, you want to find out who murdered your husband, don't you? And the last thing you need is to be up on perverting-the-course-of-justice charges.' Both women knew that was an unlikely eventuality. But Jazzy had been unable to stop the jibe from leaving her mouth. Perhaps it was a weird desire to needle her because of the cruel way she'd treated Queenie. Or perhaps she was just knackered and fed up with pandering to a clearly not grieving criminal.

Bonnie's grin was sly as she took a packet of fags out from her cleavage and lit up. 'Aye, I'm sure you'll be on the case with that. Sure, ye'll get the killer locked up in the Big Hoose before the morning, eh?'

Christ's sake, her cleavage is like Mary Bloody Poppins' handbag. What else does she have down there? Ignoring her remarks, Jazzy reverted to script. 'You are entitled to a family liaison officer, which I will—'

'Nay bloody chance. I know what you're up to. Yous lot want to get one of your rottweilers inside my house prying into my business.' She blew out a long plume of smoke, which caught in Jazzy's throat. 'No. Yous can do one on that score. No bloody FLO.'

Wishing she had a bottle of water to wash down the acrid smoke that now hung in the air, Jazzy wafted her hand through the fug. 'Of course, that's your choice, Bonnie.'

Bonnie stubbed out her half-smoked cigarette in a used coffee mug and jumped up. 'Right then, if that's all, I'll show yous out.'

Jazzy shook her head, her false smile widening. 'Oh, but that's not all. Just a wee bit curious why you didn't ask *how* your husband died. I mean, it's almost as if you already knew.'

Bonnie's lips curled up, making them look even more plasticky than before, and her eyes narrowed. 'Don't hear a question there, hen, but if what your inferring is that I *know* who offed my hubby, then you're way off the mark. Haven't you seen what's going on? It'll be one of them scrotes from Edinburgh that did it. Mark my words.'

Changing tack, Jazzy nodded. 'Okay, so can you confirm when you last saw Ned? Earlier you said a few nights ago, but can you be a wee bit more specific?'

As if it was all a huge chore, Bonnie rolled her neck, tutted and huffed out a breath. 'Probably Wednesday. Aye, that's about right. Wednesday or maybe Monday – in the middle of *Corrie*.'

'Okay and he was in good spirits then? Good health?'

'Good spirits? Aye, the question should be when was he not in good spirits. The bugger was always pissed. Pissed or asleep, that's his two go-to positions.'

'Any idea if he got into some sort of barney about a week or so ago?'

Bonnie frowned. 'A barney?'

Jazzy glanced at Queenie. Had there been a slight hesitation? Queenie nodded too, so yes, definitely something off there. 'Yes, the pathologist noticed bruising that he dated to a week or so prior to Ned's death. Any idea what that could've been?'

'No idea. But he was always getting into bother. Disnae surprise me if he was beaten up before.'

Jazzy got to her feet, with Queenie following suit. 'That's all for now, Bonnie. Thanks for your cooperation and once more, we're sorry for your loss.'

'Aye, right,' said Bonnie, marching them through the house to the front door just as it banged open and Jimmy Nails entered.

'What the hell, they still here?' Tall and slender, Jimmy was older than his sister and had a flash of grey through his black hair. Unlike Bonnie, though, his tone was less harsh – almost genteel and quieter than hers. Despite his words, his smile was wide and widened more when he saw Queenie. 'Well, if it isn't wee Orphan Annie McQueen. I heard you were one of our girls in blue? How you doing, Annie?'

Queenie brushed past him. 'Fine, Jimmy, how's yerself?'

But before Jimmy could answer, Jazzy turned to Bonnie and handed over her card. 'We'll be back, Mrs Moran. So, if you can think of anything that might help with the investigation you just let us know.'

The sensation of their eyes on her back as she walked to the car was searing, but she'd no time to dwell on that. She was all set to give Queenie a piece of her mind. Why hadn't she mentioned she was more than passing acquaintances with Jimmy and Bonnie?

Chapter 43

Jimmy Nails watched the two officers walk out to their vehicle. Annie McQueen troubled him: full of anger and stubborn intensity, just like she'd been when she was a kid at school. She hadn't always been so angry, though. He remembered her edgy, on-the-ball observations and sharp wit, her kindness. Mind you, she'd never got on very well with Bonnie. Who did? His sister had a cruel streak that often found its mark in poor wee Annie McQueen. Jimmy put it down to jealousy. He'd always had a lot of time for Annie. Jimmy liked a fighter and Annie was certainly one of those. She'd had to be, coming from the cess pool of neglect that she had, and Jimmy respected her for holding her head high. She was tough, was Annie, and the fact that she'd dragged herself out of the poorest area of Easterhouse and reinvented herself as a police officer would be considered admirable to most people.

Jimmy wasn't most people, though. He'd much rather Annie McQueen still occupied his backyard, for she knew his history. She knew where at least some of the bodies were buried. He'd tried to get her on side when he first discovered she'd joined the polis, but Annie was incorruptible. The way she sneered at him had made him want to drive his fist right into her pugnacious wee face, but he'd refrained. He suspected she'd welcome an act of aggression from Jimmy and he feared just how far she'd go to land him in the shite if he crossed that line with her.

Queenie, her scowl darker than the thunderous clouds scurrying across the sky, glared through the windscreen at him as she waited for her lanky partner to get in. He raised a hand and waved at her. His wink was a promise of future meetings, a warning that he wasn't quite done with her. Not yet. She'd been off his radar for nearly fifteen years, but maybe it was time to test the waters again. Maybe now was the time to let her know that if she scratched his back, he'd scratch hers. After all, having another polis in his back pocket could only be of benefit and he had his trump card up his sleeve – he knew who had killed her daughter.

Until he'd seen her, he hadn't considered using the card. Of course, he'd thought about it eighteen months ago. Had even imagined how it would benefit him. But at the end of the day, he'd sensed from his cell in Barlinnie that stability in Glasgow was balanced on a knife edge. Word in the Big Hoose had been that a volcano was about to erupt and that in the interests of their survival, those not in the direct line of fire should keep their heads down and wait out the aftermath.

Despite the fragile truce he'd built with Loanie, Jimmy's usual distrust simmered beneath the surface. The whispers were becoming increasingly fervent and the sideways glances in his direction, combined with the weighty silences when his presence was noted nearby, told him that his business enterprise was involved in the unease somehow. He was glad he'd planted that Spaceman character in Loanie's camp. At least the fucker had given him a heads-up that something new was afoot in Edinburgh. Now he knew what it was. Killing his brother-in-law – much as he was a useless piece of excrement – was an act of sabotage. A direct challenge that, if not handled well, could lead to disaster.

Plus, although Bonnie didn't seem overly concerned, there was the matter of her son. Where the hell was Dan? Did whoever killed Ned have him like this Vengeance character intimated, or was that just a wind-up? In this war, his enemies would do anything they could to attack him – including this Vengeance character. Who the hell was he? Nothing he'd said in the emails indicated what his gripe was. Maybe it was all a mega piss-take – some stoater yanking his chain. Deep down, though, Jimmy knew that wasn't the case. He shelved thoughts of Vengeance for now and focused on the present.

He'd tasked his best men with locating Dan and he hoped that his nephew would turn up in some skank house, topped up on coke and oblivious to everything going on around him. Dan wasn't one for keeping his nose clean. The only thing stopping Jimmy from ordering a violent response was Loanie's denial of any knowledge of Ned's murder. Confirmation from Spaceman that the Gaffer was sidelining Loanie, combined with the arrival of another encrypted email from Vengeance, gave him pause. Who was behind all of this? This was personal. He should never have left Bonnie in charge whilst he was banged up. But who else was there?

As her hand rested on his shoulder, pulling him toward the door, he turned smiling. None of this was her fault. Bonnie's loyalty to him had never been in doubt. It was just circumstances beyond her control that had led to this. She'd been forced to take her eye off the ball and that idiot husband of hers and her even more idiotic son had taken advantage of her weakness. They were to blame. He flexed his fingers, feeling the pull at his knuckles where the scabs from beating them were at that tight, itchy stage. Maybe he should have offed the pair of them when he had the chance. Instead, he'd shown leniency and some other fucker had done the job for him. Pity, really, because he'd have made sure Ned Moran's body was never found – a couple of concrete cast shoes, a few chains and lorry to take the body down south – to Yorkshire, maybe Whitby – hire a wee boat and dump the fucker in the sea. *Auf Wiedersehen, Ned!* But that was the point really, wasn't it?

Whoever had offed Ned had maybe done him a favour. Bringing Annie McQueen to his doorstep might have been their first mistake. He already had wee Annie and her lanky mate to thank for his release from prison. Maybe she'd be at the heart of ending this stand-off once and for all. Maybe she'd find who was behind all this crap and then he and Loanie could start working on a peace agreement – not that he wanted that. Not really. Bloody Lionel Gibbs! Wee upstart with no credentials, that's all he was. Still, Jimmy had to wonder just how coincidental it was that they had both been suspects in crimes committed by that serial killer. Hell, maybe that was who Vengeance was. Maybe it hadn't been coincidental that both he and Loanie had been implicated. Now that made more sense, didn't it? That fucker was still at large and the emails had only started since they caught the Solanki bint's brother. Maybe he should reach out to Loanie and check out his thoughts on the situation. After all, it wasn't long since his cousins had been offed. Maybe Loanie and Wee Frankie had an eye on the killer. Maybe together they could work something out.

He frowned as a thought occurred. What if Loanie had had one of those Vengeance emails too? Now that would be a proper link, wouldn't it? One thing Jimmy agreed with Loanie about was that there was more to this open warfare than a turf war between the two cities. He sensed the hand of someone else at work and it troubled him.

He raised a hand to Queenie as she accelerated, sending a shower of pebbles flying into the air, glowering at him as she manoeuvred round the turning spot and down the drive. *Oh, wee Annie McQueen, I wonder just how far you'd go to find out who killed your wee lassie.*

Turning, he slung his arm round his sister's shoulders, and went inside. Jimmy inhaled deeply, savouring the floral aroma that almost, but not quite, covered the sign that Bonnie had had a wee fly smoke. Her shampoo – coconutty and fresh, her perfume musky and sensual, the faint waft of female sweat that told him she'd not had a chance to shower yet after her workout – was like nectar to him. A million times better than stale farts, the heavy metallic BO of men pumped up on steroids, overboiled veg and the repugnant fug of cigarette smoke that pervaded the Bar L.

'So, what did they say?'

Perching on the edge of the couch, Bonnie grabbed her brother's hand and dragged him down to sit next to her. An excited scream, followed by the sound of small feet pitter-pattering through the house. 'Jimmy da da, Jimmy da da, Crystal's been watching *Peppa Piggy*.'

Inside Jimmy groaned. He'd no idea why the child had taken such a liking to him and although she was cute and – unlike her half-brother, Dan – decidedly intelligent, she evoked mixed emotions in him. Plus, she insisted on using him as a climbing frame, and Jimmy was fed up leaving Bonnie's house with chocolate or (worse) snot smeared all over his clothes. Crystal, through no fault of her own, filled Jimmy with an anger and frustration he rarely felt.

In solitary moments in his own home, Jimmy had reflected on this strange antipathy he felt towards a two-year-old child. He'd never felt such rage, frustration or anger about his nephew Dan, though God knew the lad deserved it. Crystal was different, though. He suspected it was because of Bonnie's stubborn insistence in not sharing the name of the child's father with him. He'd known Dan was Ned's kid as soon as he saw him, and equally he'd realised at first sight that Crystal was not Ned's. The girl's nanny came in and extricated the child's sticky fingers from Jimmy's Armani shirt.

'Take her to the park, Angelica. She needs to run around. Maybe the ball pool or even the pictures. I don't want her back here for at least two hours, got it?'

As Bonnie's razor-sharp nails raked down his back, Jimmy flinched, not from pain but because of the embarrassed glance the nanny sent his way. He stuck his chin out, raised an eyebrow and glared the girl down. How fucking dare she judge him? Judge Bonnie? She scuttled out of the living room with a struggling, whimpering Crystal in her grip and within five minutes the door was slammed behind child and nanny.

Bonnie leaned over, rested her chin on his shoulder and flicking her tongue out, she licked his ear. 'Let's talk about Ned and the polis later, Jimmy. I can think of better things to do now we've got the house to ourselves.'

Jimmy slid round and pulled her onto his lap. Bonnie was right about that.

Chapter 44

The farmhouse was cold and dingy, but that wasn't Shuggie's immediate worry. Wee Frankie had pulled up in a muddy yard, dragged the hooded man and the now completely blootered Matty from the van and dumped them both on the ground. Neither moved so much as a finger. *Fuck's sake!*

'Oot.' The older man's voice brooked no argument as he climbed back into the driver's side. 'You're on babysitting duty now, son.'

'But . . .'

'Get the fuck oot of my car afore I land you on your arse like I did wi' those two sleeping beauties.'

Shuggie's hand moved to the door latch. He paused . . .

'Oot. Don't make me say it again . . .'

Shuggie nodded, grabbed the handle and swung the door open. *Fuck's sake! My bloody new trainers!* Still hanging on to the door handle, he gingerly stepped into the mush of mud, grimacing as it swept up over his shiny white toes. But despite his distress, Shuggie had the wherewithal to turn to question Frankie. 'What am I supposed to do wi' them? What if that one's . . .' he pointed a shaking figure at the hooded figure '. . . well, you know, like. Deid? What if he's deid?'

Frankie made a clicking sound with his tongue and shook his head. 'Don't be daft. The wee sod's breathing. If he was deid, he'd wouldn't be here. I'd have dumped him on the Lang Whang along with you and your mate.'

Shuggie swallowed, his throat dry as a camel's balls. 'But—'

'No ifs, no buts. You're in charge now, Shuggie boy. You get these two into the farmhouse and make sure you don't take the ties off that wee bugger's wrists or feet. In fact—' He rummaged in the glove compartment and came out with a handful of cable ties. 'Use these to tie the wee bastard to a chair or a bed or something. You don't want to get on the Gaffer's bad side, now do you?'

The last thing Shuggie wanted to do was get on *anybody*'s bad side, but particularly not the Gaffer's. 'But how long will I be here and what am I supposed to do with Matty?'

Frankie revved the engine, warning Shuggie that his patience was running out. 'You're going to wait here till the Gaffer contacts you. You're going to keep that wee scunner tied up inside and, if you manage to sober up your junkie mate here, you might even get some help with all of that.' Again, he revved the engine.

'Aye, but how long for? I mean, I've got obligations, you know. A life to live.'

'Aye, well, about that . . . You'll not be living a bloody life if you don't look after that piece of shit for the Gaffer, now will ye?'

Shuggie wished he could replay everything that had happened since he met the Gaffer in the Tartan Sporran. If only he'd kept his head down. If only he hadn't picked up that money. It was his greed that was to blame for all of this. His bottom lip quivered as he shook his head.

Something flickered in Wee Frankie's eyes, but Shuggie wasn't sure what. His heart picked up a beat, as the man began rummaging on the passenger side foot well. *Shite, what if he has a gun?*

Frankie tutted again and thrust a plastic bag at Shuggie. 'Here, there's some food in there. All you have to do is keep the prisoner alive. No more than a couple of days. You can do that, can't you?'

Despite being unconvinced of his ability to keep the prisoner alive and contend with Matty's nonsense, Shuggie nodded.

'Right then, I'm off.'

Shuggie slammed the door shut, then as Frankie accelerated, uncaring of how muddy his shoes got, Shuggie ran after him, grabbed the door and yanked it open again. 'Where the fuck are we, though?'

Frankie grinned, the cigar behind his ear wobbling as he did so. 'The arse-end of nowhere son. Tarbrax. That's where you are.' And he drove off, leaving the door swinging precariously for a second until the momentum slammed it shut.

Tarbrax? Tarbrax? Where the bloody hell is that?

Conscious of damp seeping through his trainers into his socks, Shuggie turned around and looked at the two dormant bundles he was now responsible for. The temptation to land his foot in their sides – particularly Matty's – was almost overpowering. Instead, Shuggie left them there and went to explore the inside of their accommodation.

The door opened at a push and with a backward glance to make sure there was no movement from the two lumps behind him, Shuggie entered the farmhouse kitchen. There on the kitchen table was a set of keys, presumably for the door he'd just entered by, and beside that was a bundle of clothes and some Lidl shower gel. *Thank fuck for that.* The thought of spending another minute, never mind a few days, with that shitty-smelling lump was unbearable. He poked about a bit and found a tiled room to the side with a huge hose attached to a tap. *That'll do nicely.* All he had to do was get his shitey arse inside, and set the hose on him, all without letting him escape. In a moment of uncharacteristic meanness, Shuggie hoped the water was cold. Yes, he knew it wasn't *actually* Mr Hoodie who was to blame for his current situation, but it felt good to be able to take his frustrations out on somebody.

He went back into the kitchen, filled a pot of cold water and marched into the yard with it. Without even an iota of guilt he flung the water over Matty and then shook him.

'Get up, you bloody stupid bastard. If I'm stuck in this mess with you, you're going to help.'

For a moment Matty's blinking eyes glazed, unfocused on Shuggie, then with a final shake of his shoulders, recognition descended. 'Whassup, Shuggie, mah boy?'

Shuggie yanked Matty to a sitting position, ignoring the water dripping down his friend's face and soaking into his clothes as he gestured to the malodorous bundle who was beginning to moan and writhe against the ties.

'That's what's up? That shitey wee bundle of crap is our responsibility till the Gaffer tells us otherwise. We're going to drag him in there.'

Matty followed Shuggie's pointing finger to the farmhouse with its open door and frowned. 'Where are we?'

'Tarbrax.'

'Tar what?'

'Never mind. Just get your arse up, we're dragging him into the wee room to the side there and we're giving him a shower. I can't stand the shitty smell a minute longer.'

Now that he'd drawn his attention to the stench, Matty began to gip again. 'Aw, for fuck's sake. That's minging.'

But Shuggie was having none of it. 'You grab an arm and I'll grab one. We'll get him cleaned up and then we'll get him dressed. We've to keep him here till the Gaffer comes for him.'

It took a lot of effort, mostly because Matty wouldn't pull his weight, but they finally got the shitey wee lad into the room with the hose. Shuggie ripped off the hood, and flung it into the kitchen thinking that they could threaten him with putting it back on if he got too cocky.

The lad lay there moaning, his eyes nearly swollen shut, with dark blue bruising almost covering his entire face. His wrists were red raw where the cable ties had dug in. Shuggie exchanged a look with Matty who, for once, was short of a smart-arse comment.

'Come on, let's get him cleaned up. There's clothes and towels through there, so we can get him changed.'

'What if he tries to escape?'

Shuggie snorted. 'Aye right. Does he look up for that?'

Matty shrugged and grabbed the hose.

It took them over half an hour to get him cleaned up and to drag the soiled clothes from his bruised and gashed body. Whoever had done this to him, they'd been thorough.

When they'd dried him and managed to yank some clothes on him, Shuggie insisted they take him through to the living room, which was filled with padded chintzy furniture and a fusty smell. He dragged one of the heavy kitchen chairs through and cable-tied the boy's hands and feet to the chair.

The lad looked at death's door. Matty and Shuggie glanced at each other, unsure what to do, then a noise erupted from their prisoner's throat. It took a few moments for either of the younger boys to realise it was laughter.

The lad grimaced and lifted his head up to look at them. His eyes were only slits, but Shuggie stepped back from them as if he'd been lasered. His voice husky, the prisoner said, 'You two are in so much fucking shite.'

That same tortured laugh rolled from his mouth and his body, despite the pain he must have been in, shook. His laughter died away as abruptly as it began. 'Do you have any idea who I am or who you're dealing with?'

Shuggie, never one for the smart comebacks shook his head. 'No.'

'I'm Dan Moran and you've just been added to Jimmy Nails's hit list. I'm his nephew.'

Shite, even Shuggie had heard of Jimmy Nails. His dad had spoken of the Glasgow gangster on numerous occasions and just when Shuggie thought the Gaffer was the worst of his worries, he felt himself land face first in a new and bigger pile of shite.

Chapter 45

'You want to tell me what all of that was about, Queenie?'

Jazzy's throat was tight with anger. Over the short time they'd worked together, Jazzy had come to rely on Queenie's integrity. God, the woman could on occasion be bloody brutal, but Jazzy had considered her honesty as one of her best characteristics, which was why she was so upset right now. That Queenie had let her walk into that death notification unaware of how close her relationship with Bonnie and Jimmy had been, was intolerable. It took Jazzy a lot to trust people and Queenie's betrayal of that trust sat like a concrete slab on her chest.

Queenie shrugged, her expression unreadable although her pallor and tense jaw indicated just how tightly she was wound. Jazzy had gleaned from that interaction with Bonnie Moran that Queenie's upbringing had been more similar to Jazzy's own than she'd previously imagined, but Jazzy was still upset. Queenie knew this was as much a fact-finding visit as a death notification and on the way to Bonnie Moran's, Jazzy had explicitly asked for Queenie's thoughts on how this might all link in with the other deaths.

Interrupted by her phone vibrating, Jazzy cursed as she glanced at it. Uncle Pedro again. He wouldn't have rung back if it wasn't important. What if his people had located the Bitch? Or, worse, what if something had happened to Benjy or Ivor? She glared at Queenie. 'I'm not done with you.' Then answered, 'Hi, mate, what's up?'

'Quick one, Jazzy, the kids are fine, but I need to talk to you about the Bitch – nothing concrete but it is of interest. You okay to talk?'

'I'm in the middle, Pedro. I'll phone back soon.'

'Understood.'

Putting her phone away, she glared at Queenie. 'You as good as lied to me, Queenie. You let me go into that situation without being fully cognisant of your history with Bonnie Moran and her brother. Hell, you should have mentioned how well you knew the Nails family last year when it came up. That could have compromised the investigation. Not only that though, you bloody squared up with the bereaved widow. What were you thinking?'

Queenie snorted, braked and indicated before screeching to a halt in a single-vehicle track just off the main road. Gripping the steering wheel, eyes flashing, she glared at Jazzy, her entire body vibrating with rage.

'Bereaved widow? Bereaved bloody widow, my arse. More like Widow Twanky, if you ask me. No, make that Widow bloody Cranky and I mean with a C not a K. She's definitely not a bloody Krankie – too lacking in humour for even that comparison, though it pains me to admit that anyone can be less funny than that duo of inanity. Besides, she's not bereaved. Not one wee bit. You need to have a heart to be bereaved and believe me, hers is on a stake somewhere, still bloody pulsating, for it's certainly not in her chest.'

She paused for breath, the air between the two women raw and febrile.

'Besides which, you've got a bloody cheek, Jasmine Solanki. How bloody dare *you* preach to me, eh? Ms JayZee, holier than thou all of a sudden, eh? I don't bloody think so. How long did you keep us – your entire team – in the dark about your past and its impact on our ongoing investigation before Christmas? Fuck's

259

sake, JayZee, we were chasing a serial killer and you kept that . . .' she pointed to her own lips '. . . zipped as tight as a duck's arse. Did you confide in us about your stalker? N.O. No! Did you tell us about your upbringing? N.O. No! Not even when it became clear that it might be all linked. No, you, Ms "I'm a team player" Solanki kept yer trap buttoned and let us flounder on like a bunch of squeaking piglets in an abattoir. So, don't you preach to me about sharing my past with you. *You* don't own my past, it's mine – in all its ignominious glory – to share or not as I see fit.'

She jabbed a pointy finger at Jazzy. 'You don't own *me*, either, so get off your high horse and let me think. Maybe I'll remember something that'll help you move your bloody investigation on a proper footing again. After all, that's the only reason I'm still on your team, isn't it, JayZee? So, I can use my memory skills on your behalf. Otherwise all I am is a washed-up liability whose main claim to fame is catching a bloody criminal and nearly blinding the bastard with a knitting needle, in the process.'

Each of Queenie's words hit Jazzy like shrapnel. There was truth to Queenie's accusations. Of course there was. Jazzy had kept secrets from her team before Christmas, but she'd thought, after all they'd been through during that investigation, that they'd moved past that. Plus she'd tried hard to keep them in the loop this time. The four of them – the Jazz Queens: Jazzy, Queenie, Haggis and Geordie – were a proper team. She'd thought they had each other's backs, that they worked together and respected each other. Now she wasn't so sure. However, what really upset her was that Queenie thought Jazzy only kept her as her partner to use her, undoubtedly useful, memory skills. That was a slap in the face. Had she given that impression to Queenie? She assumed Queenie knew how much she respected her. Just how much she cared about her and her family. Over the last few months, spending time with Queenie, her husband Craig and her grand-daughter Ruby had been her salvation. Well, that and the team's regular meet-ups in Leith to see Geordie perform as Misty Thistle.

She shook her head, Queenie's words still pulsating in the air between them, like mini drones getting ready to fire miniature arrows at them. She inhaled.

'Queenie, I'm not one for big shows of affection. You know that? But if somehow I've given you the impression that your only benefit to the team is your hyperthymesia, then I'm sorry. If you lost that skill tomorrow, you'd still be the person I'd want by my side in a sticky situation. Surely you know that.'

When there was no response, Jazzy risked a glance at her partner. Queenie, head down, her shoulders heaving, was crying. With huge, silent gulps of air, her tears flooded her cheeks and spilled onto her chest. Jazzy stared in amazement. She'd seen Queenie angry, in pain, near to breaking point, but she'd never seen her in bits like this.

'Aw, Queenie. What are you like?'

Jazzy undid her seatbelt and pulled the smaller woman into her arms. As Queenie sobbed and sobbed, it grew darker outside and Jazzy's coat got wetter and wetter, still she held tight to her friend, ignoring the way her spiky gelled hair tickled her cheeks and her nostrils, until finally Queenie pulled away from her and rubbed her sleeve over her swollen face.

'Sorry, JayZee.'

Her voice was muffled and filled with contrition. Head bowed she looked like a child who was about to get told off.

'Aw, Queenie, I'm sorry. It's just I'd no idea you'd been brought up in the roughest part of Easterhouse. You always seem so . . .'

'. . . Brash?'

'No, or at least, not always.'

'. . . Abrasive?'

'No, well, only some of the time.'

'. . . Aggressive?'

'No, that's not what I was trying to say. I think the word I was looking for was *together*. You always seem so together.

261

Like nothing fazes you. As if no matter what gets thrown at us, you'll keep us afloat.'

'Ballast! That's what I am.'

Jazzy opened her mouth to protest then realised that Queenie was smiling. Her swollen eyes sparkled – okay not as brightly as they usually did, but Jazzy would take a flicker at this stage – as if the very idea of being the team's ballast was every person's dream. Well, if that was Queenie's dream, then who was Jazzy to snatch it from her?

'Yes, Queenie. You're our ballast. You keep us balanced. Your presence keeps us on track. You are essential to our wellbeing as a unit and that is with or without your bloody quirky memory.'

The two women sat in silence for a while, then Jazzy said, 'So, you want to tell me?'

Queenie nodded and with only the lights from passing cars and the glimmer of the moon Queenie shared parts of her story with Jazzy. 'My dad was a complete dick. He would hit me and my brother with his belt when he was drunk – which was most nights – and he kept my mum so short of cash she couldn't look after us. It was worse after she died because we only had him. So, Bonnie was right. Often my clothes did smell and Bonnie Nails, as she was then, and her precious friends with their make-up and new clothes always went out of their way to make my life as miserable as hell.

'When we got a bit older and went to high school things got worse because Jimmy Nails took an interest in me. You'll no believe it, Jazzy, but I could be a gobby git as a bairn.' She looked sideways and Jazzy rolled her eyes.

'Yeah, hard to imagine you being gobby, right enough.'

'When I was fourteen – Bonnie was a couple of years older – Jimmy and I started winching. He was a lot older than me – and that's when things got really bad. One day Bonnie and her mates caught me in the park. Even in them days, the Nails family had clout. Nobody ever crossed Bonnie and Jimmy's dad. Everybody turned the other way when the Nails family were up to no good.' Queenie tapped the steering wheel as she gazed out the window, her mind right back in that park in Easterhouse with its broken swings and graffitied chute. 'The bitch grabbed a used needle off the ground. God, there were loads of them there – so many junkies, many of them with the virus or hepatitis. Glasgow wasn't as bad as Edinburgh then, but it wisnae good either. The bitch's mates held me down. If Jimmy hadn't arrived, she'd have stabbed me with it. Another time, they got me in the bogs at school and flushed my head down the loo. Once they shaved all my hair off. Needless to say, I soon learned that courting Jimmy Nails wasn't a healthy pastime. It was about then an auntie of mine from Blackford in Edinburgh turned up and took me and my brother to hers. I never went back to Easterhouse, never saw my dad again, but I have kept an eye on Jimmy Nails and his clan off and on since then.'

And as if to draw a line under the conversation, Queenie started the car up and reversed back onto the road. In silence they drove back to Livingston with Jazzy wondering what exactly Queenie wasn't telling her.

Chapter 46

As soon as she could, Jazzy phoned Uncle Pedro back. What he'd said about the Bitch was playing on her mind, and with D team – reunited for now under Afzal's instructions – she needed no distractions.

'What about the Bitch, Pedro?'

'You sure you want to go down this road, Jazz? I've heard about Ned Moran – sure you want to do this now?'

'No, but I have no choice, not knowing what you've found out is a distraction I don't need right now. Tell me what you have.'

'I pulled in a few favours and some of the most inventive operatives I've ever known are making locating the Bitch their priority.'

For a moment there was silence and Jazzy wondered if they'd been cut off. 'Pedro?'

'I'm here, hen. Seems like you're right and the Bitch isn't as far away as we'd hoped – maybe the islands, but that's not confirmed. What they've managed to do is discover who's sharing information between the Bitch and your brother.'

Jazzy's heart thudded and, for a moment, she thought she might faint. This was the closest to any reliable information on the Bitch's whereabouts they'd had and she could hardly breathe as she waited for Pedro to continue.

'It's bloody simple really, Jazz. There's a patient in there called Jock McClure. His nephew, Lance McClure, visits him every week and when he doesn't, his wife Chrissie does. They are the conduits. They're the ones exchanging messages between the two. I've sent the intel anonymously to Operation Birchtree – so at least they can follow that up. Look, I have to go, but I'll be in touch if I hear anything more. There're rumblings among my contacts and I'm waiting for corroborated intel on that other matter. Just you keep safe, okay?'

'And you, Pedro. Speak soon.'

Jazzy's head buzzed with everything she'd learned. Although she'd suspected the Bitch hadn't left Scotland, to have that confirmed sent a shiver up her spine. Somehow, she'd have to follow up and make sure to corroborate Pedro's information.

Meanwhile, it was good to see her team in the one room and working together again. It had been an awkward conversation with Afzal, ending with his confirmation that Operation Birchtree's leadership was now under review after lack of progress on locating Mhairi. Jazzy was relieved. She'd had her doubts about the apti-tude of the officers in charge, and their strategy of using her to get information from her mentally ill brother had been stressful. Hopefully, a clean sweep would set them on the right track. But for now, she couldn't focus on that.

As ever, super-keen Fenton was the first to respond. 'So, you're saying you were at school with Bonnie Moran? The deceased's widow?' DC Fenton Heggie's eyes drifted from Queenie to where Bonnie Moran's photo – taken at a recent children's cancer charity event – was pinned on the big board. Subdued, Queenie slumped over her desk, a scowl darkening her face, but Fenton didn't pick up on her mood. He continued, his words laced with disbelief. '*And* she's Jimmy Hardass Nails's sister?'

Fenton's eyes drifted back to Bonnie's photo, then he shook his head. To be fair, in this particular image, Bonnie was at her finest – busty and sexy in a skin-tight scarlet mini dress, cut so low at the front that you could almost see what she'd had for her breakfast. Her jet-black hair was bundled artistically on top of her head. Sparkling emerald teardrop jewellery gleamed from her neck, wrists and her ears. Her pouting scarlet lips, finished off by a Marilyn Monroe pout, sent the message: *I'm HOT and I know it*.

Even though her photo was fractionally smaller than that of her now-deceased husband, Bonnie dominated the screen whilst by contrast, Ned Moran – skinny, scruffy, slouching from a pub in Bathgate called the Tartan Sporran, spliff in one hand and a lighter in the other – looked like a monochrome portrait of neglect. His hair needed cutting, his skin was sallow and his hunch made him resemble a seriously ill man, although Jazzy had to admit that he looked marginally healthier here, than when she'd last seen him at Lin's Grave.

'And *she* was married to *him*?' Scepticism coloured each of Fenton's words as he shook his head, gawping at the two images, like he'd never seen a more unlikely couple in his life – which was strange considering *his* girlfriend was leggy and gorgeous whilst Fenton was distinctly average in the looks department. However, he was the nicest man you could ever hope to meet and he and Rebecca were so cute together.

With every word, Queenie's frown deepened and her face became redder. But Fenton wasn't quite finished digging his own grave. 'Boy, it's hard to believe you were at school wi' her, Queenie. Didn't realise that Easterhoose could produce such beauties. *And* you say she's older than you? Phew.' He shook his head. 'Hard tae believe really.'

Jazzy cringed and exchanged a glance with Geordie who, grinning from ear to ear, waited to witness the inevitable fallout from Fenton's unwise observations. Queenie straightened, her shoulders back, as she fixed the still-unsuspecting detective with a laser glare. The idiot had walked right into it and Queenie was not in a forgiving mood.

'What ye getting at there, Haggis?' She stood up and swept

266

her hands down her body from her substantial bosom, past her generous hips and down towards her feet which were, like Jazzy's, enclosed in Doc Martens. 'What you calling *this* package here, eh? A pile o' tripe? A crappit heid? Chopped bloody liver?'

With each sentence she advanced on her prey whilst Haggis, alerted to his mistake, rolled his chair backwards. His eyes were all wide and glaikit, his mouth a moue of disbelief at his own stupidity.

Queenie on the prowl was completely unstoppable and Jazzy had little sympathy for Fenton. He'd offended Queenie and now his jugular was well and truly in her sights. She was like a vampire, focused solely on feeding. Her words were more growled than spoken. 'At least *I'm* not mutton dressed as lamb like that tart. At least *I've* got a bit of dignity.' Glaring up at Haggis as he jumped to his feet, she prodded herself in the chest. 'I take a bit of pride in *my* appearance.' Another jab to the chest. 'Look after myself, keep myself in prime condition.'

Her final chest jab brought on a coughing fit, which thankfully served as cover for Jazzy and Geordie who were huddled in a corner trying to control their laughter. Haggis, eager to redeem himself, guided Queenie onto his vacated chair and offered her a bottle of water. Gasping for breath, she scowled at him, grabbed the bottle and waved him away. Once she got the lid off, she slurped the water, half of it trailing down her chin and landing on her bright green jumper. 'See what you've caused, Haggis? You're bloody useless. A sodden bloody liability. You've made me drench my best jumper.'

Sensing that Queenie was winding down, Jazzy stepped into the fray. 'Right, if you two toddlers have quite finished with your nonsense, *we've* got a murder to investigate and because it probably links to the ongoing turf war between the Weegie and Reekie gangs and the murders of Wee Frankie Jones's sons, I'd like to make sure we dot our i's and cross our t's before this investigation is yanked from our eager wee mitts.'

She glared at Fenton and Queenie. Both wore almost identical expressions and Jazzy rolled her eyes. *Give me bloody strength!* She waited for Queenie to vacate herself from Fenton's chair before continuing.

'Meet Ned Moran, fifty-two years old, husband to Bonnie Moran, née Nails, brother-in-law to Jimmy Hardass Nails and father of Dan Moran. Queenie and I did the death notification earlier. Two of the Glesca division's finest will bring Bonnie and Jimmy for the official ID after Dr Johnston has completed his post-mortem. According to Bonnie, she's not seen Ned for a few days. We've got officers on the ground speaking with his many known acquaintances. When we have a confirmed time of death from Lamond we can go in hard with the Moran/Nails family interviews. See what they can tell us.' She paused. 'Of course that depends on our being allowed to continue leading on this. In the meantime, Lamond suggests that we're looking at Lin's Grave as a deposition site rather than the murder scene. Again, we're trying to see if we can get any sort of intel on possible vehicles in the vicinity, but the area is secluded and CCTV is sparse. We might be better placed trying to trace the deceased's movements prior to his death. Questions?'

Geordie, his tall frame slouched over his desk, pointed a pencil at the two images on the big screen. 'We discounting the wife at this point or not?'

Queenie tutted. 'No, we're bloody not. Widow Twanky is still in the frame. She might not have got her hands dirty personally this time – although she has in the past – but she's more than capable of hiring a punter to off her husband. Particularly when her new wean – a wee lassie called Crystal – is definitely not Ned's. Mark my words, Bonnie Moran is a toxic piece of work and she'd no' even break off eating a Mars Bar tae deliver the final injury to an enemy. Do. Not. Under. Any. Circumstances. Underestimate. Her. Or she'll have yer balls in a vice and feed them tae one of her dogs before you even notice they're gone.'

The two men in the room winced, making Jazzy smirk when they crossed their legs. She nodded at Queenie. They'd agreed to keep the specifics of her relationship with Bonnie Moran between them, on the understanding that they emphasised the extent of the woman's duplicity.

'Queenie's right, though. We're not underestimating her. It may be that Ned Moran is just the latest casualty in the ongoing turf war, but then again, now *would* be a convenient time to get rid of a deadweight and set someone else up for it. Bonnie Moran is a suspect, as is her brother, Jimmy. And the son Dan.'

'So . . .' It was Geordie who spoke as Fenton brought an image of Jimmy Nails up on the screen. 'This is the infamous Hardass Nails? He went down for the Gillies murders in 2019 and served over three for them, before being released when we discovered the real perpetrator last year. That right?'

Jazzy nodded. Again, she and her partner had agreed to play down Queenie's short-lived relationship with Jimmy Nails thirty-something years ago. However, they had agreed to share that Queenie and the Nails siblings grew up on the same estate.

Queenie cleared her throat. 'Aye, unlike his sister, Jimmy Nails is a bit of a smooth operator. Bonnie's as coarse as they come – loud, opinionated, argumentative, impulsive – but Jimmy, by contrast, when he chooses, can be more quietly spoken, somewhat refined, intelligent, contemplative. He's not brash or impulsive, but he *is* dangerous. He thinks things through. Bonnie's got a history of violent behaviour – any bodies she's responsible for will be found. However, if Jimmy Nails wants you gone, it's unlikely your body will ever be discovered, got it?'

Everyone nodded and Jazzy took up the narrative. 'Right, so until we've more to go on from Lamond Johnston's post-mortem results, we're looking into Ned Moran's movements the week before he was killed. At the crime scene, Lamond pointed out evidence of healing bruises and estimated that Ned Moran had received a substantial beating a week prior to turning up dead.

Also, I've got a BOLO out for Dan Moran. It won't be long before the press release Ned Moran's name and we've so far been unable to locate his son. I don't want him to learn of his dad's death through the media – nor, if he's had anything to do with it, do I want him slipping through our fingers.'

Excited to be in the thick of things, the team focused on completing the actions Jazzy had ordered. Nobody noticed Queenie slink from the room, her gait unsteady and her head bowed.

Chapter 47

Queenie placed her mug of coffee on the table and slipped into the furthermost corner of the police canteen. Experience told her that this was the best place to remain unnoticed and right now she had to be alone. The strain of keeping her memories at bay whilst doing her job had left her exhausted, both mentally and physically. Ever since she'd seen Ned Moran's body dumped unceremoniously next to Lin's Grave, it had been like she was on a train ride moving inexorably onwards with no stops, no brakes, no reprieve, and there was little she could do to prevent it blowing up in her face.

The truth was, she'd sensed it coming before Ned had been dumped in West Lothian. Course she had. She wasn't stupid, after all. With the fallout landing firmly in their backyard, there would be repercussions. She'd seen Afzal marching into meetings with the top officers from both the Edinburgh and Greater Glasgow divisions and his entire body radiated tension.

She was desperate to know more about what was going on. Some of the names being bandied about made her hackles rise. Many of them she remembered from her childhood. It had been sheer logistics that had sent her and JayZee to the Ned Moran crime scene that morning, but now that she was involved, so many emotions and memories flooded her system. If she wasn't careful, she'd explode and she couldn't allow that to happen. She had to hold herself together, had to calm herself because she had big decisions to make.

The first and most important one being just how much of her history with Jimmy Hardass Nails should she reveal to JayZee. She'd given her partner the bare bones of it, but should she reveal more? – about the way Jimmy had groomed her. How he'd used her as a drugs mule, how she'd watched him almost kill a man. Then there was her own horrific secret. The one she couldn't share with Craig, let alone Jazzy. Shite, she'd kept it so locked up in her brain that she'd almost convinced herself that it hadn't happened. But it had and she had done it and, worse than that, she'd enjoyed doing it.

Hands cupping her cooling coffee, Queenie closed her eyes and blocked out the rest of the room, allowing the rise and fall of conversations, the smells of bacon rolls, the flicker of the fluorescent light above her head, to drift over her. As she did so, her stomach contracted and her body was racked by a long shudder as she allowed the memories from her time in Easterhouse to invade her. Jimmy Nails had been nothing but kind to her – that's how grooming worked, wasn't it? – although she had witnessed his violence first hand on more than one occasion. However, with the naiveté of her youth and the deep-seated desire to be free of the torturous comments of her peers and endless bullying, she had made excuses for his flashes of viciousness, telling herself that, unlike his sister, Bonnie, Jimmy was slow to wreak havoc and tended to use violence as a last resort. It was easy, as a kid with nothing – no friends, a useless family, no money and no hope – to pretend that the degree of retribution exacted by Jimmy was justified.

Flashes of Jimmy – before he became known as Hardass, before he took over from his dad – rolled through her head. She tried to superimpose the ones of him dancing with her, the pair of them making love under a pile of coats at a party in Gregg Street, but each image was tarnished by others. The kid, nose smashed, lying in the rain as Jimmy and his mates pissed on him because Jimmy's dad had dealt the boy's 'card', which roughly translated as he'd put out a hit on the kid. If Jimmy was involved, chances were it was a real transgression rather than one of the weird offences his dad sometimes decreed.

Trapped inside her own head with bad memories filling more and more of her thoughts, Queenie sat there nursing a long, cold drink for hours, until finally a slow tremor took over her body, rocking her to the core. She was in danger of disintegrating and this wasn't the place to do it. She had to get out of here. She had to get home to her sanctuary. To Craig and Ruby.

Chapter 48

Vengeance

Even before my contacts had activated the cameras at Bonnie's house, I'd wondered about the relationship between the pair of them. Now here it is confirmed in glorious Technicolor, wobbly bits and cellulite. My gut contracts, disgust pushing a globule of bile into my throat. I press pause, groan at the image of Bonnie, head thrown back in feigned rapture, bouncing on her brother's dick, and Jimmy, eyes closed, rutting like a hog in pig shit. I'd never met Bonnie, but the intel I had on her was revealing. She was what most folk would classify 'a piece of work'. Jimmy, though, was different. Though I wouldn't have recognised him now, I once knew him as a snotty-nosed bairn who followed me about on chubby legs. For a second, I study his face, to see if any remnants of that wee man are visible, but all I see is a self-serving murderer. The boy I'd once nurtured, the baby whose nappy I'd changed, had become a replica of his old man, but worse than that he'd killed the single precious thing I had to show for my sorry life. My son. My beautiful Billy.

I know I had no claim on Billy. I'd been the worst parent ever, but with hindsight I realise that at thirteen, ostracised by my family, sent to a foreign land, scared, and with strangers, shamed into believing *I* was dirty, that *I* was to blame – there had been little chance of a different outcome. A wail of grief erupts from my chest and I realise that the grief isn't just for Billy, it's also for wee Martha Nails whose childhood was ripped from her so abruptly the day Wee Frankie Jones came to visit.

I bend double, arms round my belly trying to stop the floodgates from opening but there's no chance: *Frankie Jones – gallus and brash, pushing me down onto my single bed, rough callused hand over my mouth as he yanks my knickers down.* I can't breathe; it's like I can smell the cigar smoke rolling from him. I struggle over to my chair as the image changes. To another nasty man.

'Only whores let men do that to them out of wedlock, Martha. Your daddy might not tell you that, but I'm the Gaffer and I always tell the truth. That's what you are. A dirty whore and that's why you and that bastard child in your belly have to go.'

Hot tears trip down my face, scalding me as, like Scrooge, I'm visited one after the other by the ghosts from my past. *'We'll come and see you, Martha. Mummy and Daddy will visit.'*

'But I don't want to go, Da. Please don't send me away.'

'Aw hen, you have to. That was the deal I made. You've got to go. For Daddy's sake. You've got to go or the Gaffer will destroy the rest of us.'

'Even wee Jimmy?'

'Aye hen, even wee Jimmy.'

'But when this thing's out of my belly, then I can come back?'

'Aye, maybe. Maybe then, but you'll like it there. You'll have a new family and you can look after that bairn just like you look after Jimmy.'

It's then I realised that I wouldn't be coming back to Glasgow. That I wouldn't see them again. 'But it won't be wee Jimmy, Daddy. I hate it already and I always will.'

I don't know how long I sit there, my face red raw, my eyes swollen, Jimmy and Bonnie's disgusting faces filling the screen, but finally I stir. I've never felt so old, never felt so poorly. I'm almost spent and I've got to sort out the ending of my story. I've got to decide what the finale will look like.

With swollen, achy fingers I press rewind. Much as my brother and sister's incestuous relationship is interesting, there is something earlier in the recording that interests me more – the arrival of the two officers at Bonnie's house. Now, *that* had been a surprise and it was certainly something worth looking at again.

According to my paid help, it had been easy to infiltrate Bonnie's home. She was disliked by most of the unfortunates who worked for her and popping the nanny a monkey-and-a-half kilo of weed was cheap indeed. She'd done a good enough job, positioning my cameras throughout the downstairs of Bonnie's home, although, until now, they'd showed nothing of note. Nothing I didn't know already. Still, having confirmation of my sister's gutter morals and the allegiances she was forming is satisfying. Who knew when one of these recordings showing interactions between Bonnie and any one of the many visitors she had might come in handy? My own staff had listed the visitors and provided annotated details of their interactions. All in all, money well spent.

Monitoring Jimmy, though, was an entirely different game. Jimmy was circumspect and although capable of extreme violence, he had recourse to this sparingly, and only when absolutely necessary. He was a fair man and on occasion would give second chances, which meant those who worked for him were loyal, making gaining access to his inner sanctum nigh on impossible. Still, today's little lapse in judgement on the sweaty leather sofa of Bonnie's brothel living room combined with the footage from last week of him battering his nephew and brother-in-law could prove useful later. Especially now Ned has turned up dead.

I rewind to an hour earlier when the black Land Rover pulled into the turning circle and parked up. I hadn't been expecting this and although the vehicle looked vaguely familiar, I was still surprised when the short woman jumped from the driver's seat, thrust her fists into her pockets and with rounded shoulders trailed the taller, leggy woman with the long dark hair pulled back in a way that she probably thought made her look severe, but actually only served to emphasise her chiselled cheekbones and long neck.

The jolt when I recognised the shorter woman as my neighbour – the one who'd helped me from Scotmid last week and who kept popping over to check on me was complete. Of course, I'd known Queenie was polis. I'd done my due diligence and although her presence in the small street I'd elected to live in had made me pause, I'd quickly dismissed my concern. Queenie worked in Livingston and had been recently demoted. My sources didn't consider her a threat. Said she wasn't taken seriously and was on the way out. She wasn't a prominent officer, nor a trusted one, and so the likelihood of her being a cause for concern was minimal. I'd ignored her occupation and had come to consider her and her small family more as friends, and had made sure to only greet her in the kitchen so she wouldn't see anything she shouldn't. I'd come to rely on her brash concern and her jaunty waves as she left in her car for work.

Now, I edge over to the window and part the blinds an inch or two. It's dark outside. Only the occasional gleam of car lights, and the cosy, blurry light from heavily curtained windows, and the white glimmer from the streetlights offer reprieve from the quiet. Her house is opposite, with the same dark Land Rover parked outside the wooden gate. A small square of garden, with a child's swing and chute taking up most of the area in front of the house, mark this as a home with a young child living in it. I like Queenie. Her brusque kindliness reminds me of my gran.

I drift back to the recording, pour myself a whisky and settle down to rewatch the interaction between Bonnie and Queenie. Boy, that Bonnie is a bitch – but by the looks of it, Queenie has a long memory too. This adds an interesting facet to the entire proceedings. I ignore the metallic taint that laces the whisky – no doubt the work of my meds – and ponder these new revelations. How can I make each of them work in my favour?

Is Queenie's involvement in Ned Moran's murder significant? I suspect not. With everything else I've orchestrated, Glasgow and Edinburgh will want to close things down pronto. There will be no time for Livingston Police, especially not a demoted officer like DC Annie McQueen to intervene before it's too late.

I reach over and home in on the other officer's face. DS Solanki – interesting. I make a mental note to have her checked out.

I refill my glass and with the help of my cane I walk over to my wall of shame. Three photos, adorn it.

Jimmy Nails – MURDERER

Wee Frankie Jones – RAPIST & PAEDOPHILE

The Gaffer – PAEDOPHILE ENABLER, MURDERER'S ACCOMPLICE & ENABLER, LIAR, DESTROYER of CHILDHOODS

Which of them is the worst? It's hard to choose, but maybe it's the Gaffer. After all, being police, you'd think they'd be on the side of the good – the victims, not the criminals. No matter. All of them will pay for what they've done.

When the call comes from my guys, I'm expecting it. 'We've located where the Gaffer is keeping him. A farmhouse in Tarbrax looked after by two gormless lads. We could sweep in right now and take control of the premises and just wait it out till the Gaffer and his men roll up?'

I consider that, but maybe I have a better plan. Maybe I have a plan for the way to end it all. 'Just watch them for now. I think I'll arrange an organised meeting between me, Jimmy, Wee Frankie and the Gaffer. How does that sound?'

Again, the low rumble reminds me that these people whom I've never met are on my side. 'Aye, that sounds like a plan. You sleep easy, now. Preserve your strength because you'll need it for the next part.'

Satisfied that things are under control, I take my glass and head upstairs. Tomorrow will be a busy day and I need to make sure I'm ready for it, for I AM Vengeance and I will prevail.

Chapter 49

Craig heard his wife's car pull onto the drive. She'd been avoiding his calls, not replying to his texts, so he knew something had happened and he suspected it was to do with that body they'd found near Almondell. He walked to the living-room window and tweaked the curtain. As Queenie flicked the headlights off and cracked her door open ready to leave the car, she hesitated. Her head bowed, she sat illuminated by the inner light, shoulders hunched as if trying to dredge up the energy to drag herself from the car and into the house.

Thank God he'd got their granddaughter off to sleep earlier. Now he could focus on tending to his broken partner. He watched her for a few seconds more, then a movement from across the road diverted his gaze. Probably just their new neighbour closing the blinds. When he glanced back to his wife, she'd shoved the door fully open and was standing, her arm leaning on the top, her gaze swung to the living-room window as if sensing him there. She was haggard, her pallor evident even from this distance and that frown was the one she wore when she had one of her meltdown migraines coming on.

He stepped back, out of sight. Experience had taught Craig that allowing Queenie the dignity to haul herself unaided into their home – their sanctuary – made her more likely to give in to his ministrations. Boy, was she a stubborn woman. He smiled, and acknowledged that obstinacy wasn't the only 'quality' she possessed. She was irascible, irritatingly confrontational, but she was also loyal and steadfast and completely and utterly dependable, beautifully caring, delightfully thoughtful, although she went to great lengths to keep that attribute hidden. She was also broken right now, and he intended to do everything in his power to fix that.

He moved from the window and began his preparations. She wasn't physically hurt – Jazzy would have contacted him if that were the case, so it must be her mind. Something had set that wonderful brain of hers into overdrive and now she was haunted by images, events and experiences that although she could pocket away a lot of the time, sometimes were too potent, too powerful to control. It was at times like these that she needed taking care of.

Chapter 50

In the quiet and privacy of her own home, Jazzy fired off a few texts. The first was to Craig asking about Queenie. By the time she'd noticed Queenie had disappeared, Craig had already said she'd arrived home in bits. When he didn't reply immediately, Jazzy knew he was looking after his wife. Queenie was in the best possible hands. Next she texted Uncle Pedro to ask if he had any more intel, but instead of a text reply, her phone rang and the big man dived right in. 'Jazzy, everything I'm going to tell you is completely off the record, agreed?'

'Of course. Any intel you give will be attributed to an anonymous source and will be shared on a need-to-know basis only. What do you have for me?'

'To be honest, hen, it's not much. Mainly uncorroborated talk and a few inspired deductions by some of my old cronies, whose identities I can't reveal.'

'Things are escalating, Pedro. If we don't get a handle on what's actually happening here, things will escalate pretty damn quickly and the fallout won't be pretty. Think nuclear-bomb-type fallout. If we can't get order restored on the streets then God knows what'll happen. We need to identify who is behind this operation.'

'Well, on the QT, my sources have heard about someone called Vengeance who has signed up a team of mercenaries to direct all the action. What's strange, though, is that none of the mercenaries employed by this person are yapping – maybe they're too feart to say anything or they're being paid mega bucks to cause chaos – I'll leave you to work that one out.' He paused and the sound of him inhaling drifted over the line. 'It's a weird one, Jazz. Typically, you'd find someone with a loose tongue, but it's like, whoever this Vengeance is, they're a ghost. There's not even a whisper of an ID. It's like they've come from nowhere and my worry is they'll disappear like that too. I'm really sorry I couldn't be of more help ID'ing this character.'

'No probs, Pedro. This information has confirmed a couple of things we've become aware of too, so it's useful. You mentioned targets earlier. Any idea who they are?'

'My sources haven't heard anything, but – and I stress that this is only them making huge suppositions – the general feel is that, with the nature of the violence being split between Edinburgh and Glasgow, this Vengeance is targeting Jimmy Nails – Ned Moran being killed sort of corroborates that – and either Frankie Jones or Loanie Gibbs or both of them. There's some talk about a bent copper called the Gaffer, but again, no ID so far.'

'Again, this is useful corroborative background, Pedro.' Intel on the ongoing violence, no matter how vague was useful. 'Just keep me in the loop, Pedro.'

She popped some painkillers and stretched her back. She still had other things to do, so she got out her burner phone and began her daily communication with Dukesy.

Unsent draft email communication between Detective Sergeant Jazzy Solanki and undercover operative, Spaceman

Jazzy
Time 22:11
Subject: You there?

Draft email deleted and replaced

Spaceman
Time 22:13
Subject: Here. Hearing word that the dirty copper is known as the Gaffer. Got a meet with ex-army contact tomorrow – hopefully get an ID then. Things not as we first thought. Jimmy Nails sent out feelers looking for his nephew.

Draft email deleted and replaced

Jazzy
Time 22:19
Subject: Still think Gaffer is polis? Activity in Edinburgh? Loanie doing anything we need to know about? Or Wee Frankie?

Draft email deleted and replaced

Spaceman
Time 22:22
Subject: Yes, still polis. Need to confirm. Strange things happening. Frankie and Loanie not acting together. Loanie Gibbs not left his house. Monitoring Frankie and Jimmy Nails's email – both receiving threatening mail from Vengeance. Still no luck locating sender. Loanie not received similar communications. Getting closer though. Keep checking mail in case I catch something earlier.

Draft email deleted and replaced

Jazzy
Time 22:29
Subject: Okay. Keep safe.

Draft email deleted

Saturday 11th March

Chapter 51

Where the fucking hell is the stupid wee bastard? After the discovery of his brother-in-law's body, Jimmy had devoted many hours to trying to locate his nephew Dan – but to no avail. The stupid wee tosser was AWOL and although Jimmy wasn't overly worried at this stage – Dan was renowned for going on day- or even week-long benders, sometimes to Europe, sometimes down south and sometimes up north – with the murder of the laddie's auld man, there was no guarantee the lad was all right. Jimmy knew some of his enemies may well consider using his nephew as a fine way to get to him, and although Bonnie's maternal streak was absent in the case of Dan, he still felt an obligation to the dozy bugger.

His thoughts turned to Loanie. Was he behind Ned's murder? Jimmy wasn't convinced either way and he hated the uncertainty. For the second time that morning he picked up his burner and dialled Spaceman's number. This time he replied. 'Whassup, boss?'

Jimmy scowled. *Whassup, boss?* Who the fuck did he think he was? A bloody mafia gangster or something? 'You didn't reply earlier and that's not good enough, Spaceman. I'm paying you to be available.'

'Aw, sorry, boss. Was on the crapper. But I was just about to call you anyway. I've got some intel. Looks like Wee Frankie and this ex-copper they call the Gaffer – still waiting on ID for him, but the rumour mill's hinting at that DI Balloch being involved somehow – anyway, seems those two are cutting Loanie Gibbs out of things.'

Jimmy's scowl deepened. Wee Frankie Jones and Loanie were family. Frankie considered Loanie to be like a son to him. Did this mean that Loanie had something to do with Frankie's kids being offed? Or at least that Frankie thought that? Jimmy wasn't convinced. Loanie was many things, but Jimmy could see no reason for him to kill his cousins. Why would he? Frankie had given him the reins and the lads had been all too happy to let Loanie take over as long as they were kept on the books. No, something didn't feel right. Jimmy could feel it in his piss. 'What's your feeling then, Spaceman?'

'No bloody idea. Only thing I can tell you is that Frankie's been getting some weird-ass emails from some punter calling himself Vengeance. Threatening like and dark as fuck. No luck so far tracing them. Don't think I'll be able to, if I'm honest. This Vengeance is a clever so-and-so.'

A cold shiver went down Jimmy's spine. This Vengeance person was emailing threats to both him *and* Wee Frankie. What the hell was that all about? He'd not spoken to Frankie Jones for years. Probably not since his da's funeral.

'What about Loanie? He getting any of these Vengeance emails?'

'Nope, all Loanie's digital activity is above board.' Spaceman gave one of his forty-a-day laughs 'Well, I mean as above board as a corrupt wee criminal's digital footprint can be. There's no indication he's got it in for you, or that he's double-crossing you. Nothing, so far anyway.'

'Aye, right, Spaceman. Keep on it, eh? Let me know if anything new comes up.' Hoping he sounded nonchalant he added, 'Oh, aye and if Wee Frankie gets any more emails from that Vengeance character, let me know pronto.'

'All good, boss. I'll do that.'

Jimmy hung up and paced the room, casting his mind back to when his dad was still alive. He'd vague recollections of his dad hating someone called the Gaffer and with hindsight Jimmy realised that what – as a bairn – he'd thought was hatred, was probably a little bit of fear too. His dad was a big talker – always had been but in Jimmy's memories, his auld man had always faltered when speaking of the Gaffer. Wee Frankie Jones, though? Nah, he was a different story. His da detested the wee man. Hated him, even – couldn't hear his name without spitting on the floor. Jimmy had never been entirely sure what it was all about, but the sense he took from his dad's deathbed ramblings was that Wee Frankie and the Gaffer had double-crossed his dad.

Of course, Bonnie would know more about that. She'd always been his da's favourite. Still, he knew that even if this Balloch bloke was the Gaffer – he wasn't the original one. He was far too young to be the same Gaffer his dad had known, so maybe he'd inherited the mantle from some other corrupt copper. Those sorts stuck together after all.

Chapter 52

Vengeance

I wake and everything is crystal clear. The fog has lifted and I'm more lucid than I've been for days. Yes, the pain still engulfs me, but that's secondary now that I know the steps I need to take. Of course, it's not the way I had envisioned it when I set out on this course of action, but no matter. This new course, incorporating everything I've experienced, the things I've learned, the people who have touched my life in whatever small way, makes this the right decision moving forward. I've learned that solace can come from the strangest of places – from the mercenaries who have become my trusted protectors. From the newest of acquaintances – my gruff yet caring neighbour, Queenie, who hides her concern behind a spiky façade. And from the hope offered by a stranger whose sense of justice and desire for resolution has drawn him to travel hundreds of miles with no desire other than to do the right thing for a man he's never met – Sid Mackie.

I've got two calls to make. Who'd have thought that after all this time on this planet, my last few meaningful communications would be with kind strangers and my enemies? The first call fills me with so many emotions. The likeness of Sid Mackie to my son is confusing and I find myself wanting to offload all my regrets and beg for forgiveness, but that won't do – he's not Billy. I take a deep breath and dial the number I've been provided with and when I hear the voice with its soft Scottish remnants, I take a deep breath.

'Hallo, Mr Mackie. You don't know me, but I've seen your interview on the TV and seen your likeness to the person they've named Cairnpapple Man. I'm phoning you to let you know that I can identify him, but before I do, I'd like to share my story with you in person.'

For long moments there's only the faint sounds of his breathing, then: 'I'm not sure how you got my personal number, but I wonder why you've contacted me direct rather than the authorities who are dealing with this investigation.'

I sigh and then, just when I don't need it, a coughing fit consumes me. When I finally catch my breath, his voice tinged with concern, he says, 'Are you okay?'

'No, no. I've only got a short time left, which is why I wanted to share my story with you personally, before it's too late. Can we meet?'

The man, so like my son, but not him, hesitates, then decides. 'Okay, when and where?'

My relief is palpable; it fills the room and brings a tear to my eye. Whilst other things – bad things – are about to happen on my orders, I can at least give this young man closure. I give him my address and arrange his visit for later. By then, everything will be in place and my confession to Sid Mackie will be the final piece in this horrible jigsaw.

Now for Queenie. Overnight, I'd been plagued by doubt and in the early hours wondered if a slight adaptation to my planned endgame might be necessary. Perhaps Queenie can help me with that, perhaps not, in which case I'll go ahead with plan A.

I struggle over to my laptop and, before I have time to regret my decision, I open my email and instead of my usual Vengeance missives, I compose a short one to Queenie adding as an attachment my diary of recollections, plans and hopes for revenge for the murder of my son. It's explosive. It names police officers, it implicates known criminals in wider criminal activity and if, as I believe she is, Queenie is on the side of justice and rightness, then she will act on this.

I've done wrong – of course I have. I won't deny it, but my maker will judge me, not the justice system. I hope Queenie judges me fairly, but it's no matter if she doesn't – I'll be gone soon anyway.

In the subject heading I type EVIDENCE OF THE CRIMES OF THE GAFFER, JIMMY NAIL, FRANKIE JONES.

The content is harder to write:

Dear Queenie,

When I needed help, you were there. You've looked after me, checked up on me and being able to see your beautiful family from my window has brightened my days.

I hope you can forgive me for not being completely honest with you, and I hope you can understand why. I attach a diary of sorts, which outlines my connections with the people mentioned in the subject line above. It explains the ways in which they have wronged me and how, as I near the end of my own life, I decided to take their destruction into my own hands.

I am weak now and won't last much longer, but as well as the diary, I attach various other documents and photographic evidence of the crimes these three have committed. I had wanted to avenge these sins personally (through my paid associates whom I am about to ask to stand down). Having met with you I am convinced that for these three monsters to spend the rest of their days in prison is a far more fitting punishment than death.

I also know where the Gaffer is holding Dan Moran – a stupid boy with criminal tendencies, who perhaps deserves a short sharp shock, but probably not the same death as his father received at the hands of the Gaffer. He is being held (guarded by two simple boys) in a farmhouse in Tarbrax – see below for the address.

I hope to meet with Sid Mackie and be able to tell him in person the story of Cairnpapple Man and why he looks so much like Sid. I hope you will allow me that single request. By this afternoon I will be in St John's hospital in Livingston as my life nears its end.

In sincerity and respect,

Yours sincerely,

Martha Nails

PS: My last act as Vengeance will be to set up a meeting with all the above at the Tarbrax location. I hope you can arrange for officers to be there at the appropriate time instead of my paid help.

Chapter 53

When Jazzy threw her door open, Queenie, breathless and red-faced – the hat Jazzy had gifted her for Christmas at a weird angle – barged inside and marched through to the living room. Although still fed up that Queenie hadn't confided in her about her previous relationship with Jimmy Nails, Jazzy was pleased to see her up and about. Yesterday had been a tough day for Queenie. The bags under her eyes testified to that.

'For God's sake, Queenie, you disappeared off yesterday, didn't answer my calls, got Craig to respond with some half-arsed excuse about a stomach bug and now here you are barging in like a bloody maniacal gnome. Are you okay?'

Dragging her hat off her head, Queenie exhaled, flung herself onto the couch – sending Winky squeaking in protest onto the floor – and cradled her head in her hands.

'I don't know what you want me to say, JayZee? I'm wabbit, that's what I am. Well and truly running on the fumes of one of Geordie's farts. Drained as a shitty cloot soaked in whisky in the possession of an alcoholic.'

Her emphatic sigh and the way her shoulders slumped made it appear like Jazzy's sofa was eating her up. Jazzy bit her lip. In the time she'd known Queenie, she'd never seen her so diminished, so completely flat, so she slumped onto the cushion beside her colleague and was about to embrace her when Queenie jumped to her feet, eyes flashing. 'What the hell do you think you're doing, eh?'

Queenie bristled. Her shoulders wiggled, her arms folded under her breasts and her chin jutted out pugnaciously. 'You think I'm some sort of charity case, eh? A candidate for a bloody pity fest like Haggis when he thought his lassie was going to dump him – is that it?'

Jazzy opened her mouth, but a ferocious glare silenced her as she ranted on.

'Somebody who needs a "there, there it'll all be all right, hen" from the indestructible, I-can-cope-with-any-crap-life-throws-at-me-including-serial-killing-siblings-a-dead-mum-and-a-bastard-dad-who-deserted-me-as-a-bairn, JAY . . . ZEE Sol . . . an . . . ki?'

Jazzy blinked a couple of times, then waited to be sure Queenie was done before shrugging. 'I was just going to ask if you wanted a coffee.'

Queenie's mouth fell open. Her eyes lost their indignant anger and before Jazzy could object, Queenie had launched herself at her, grabbed her in a bear hug and half laughing, half gruff denial she said, 'I'm sorry, hen. That was . . . well, that was me having a meltdown, you know? Going off on one. Getting it all off my che—'

Untangling herself, Jazzy pushed Queenie back onto the couch. 'Look, just tell me what the hell's going on, Queenie. We're partners, aren't we? You and me and Haggis and Geordie – we're the Jazz Queens, isn't that right?'

Queenie snorted and Jazzy was pleased to see the anguish fade from the older woman's eyes. 'Aye, you're right there, hen. We're a team. It was just—' She ran her stubby fingers through her spiky hair and exhaled, sending a waft of cheese and onion into the air. 'I left all that behind me, you know? Moved on from it all. Pretended it happened to another version of me – a less experienced, too trusting, naïve version of me.' She sniffed and, biting her lip, gazed into the distance. 'Seeing Bonnie Moran – Nails as she was then – and Jimmy brought it all back.' A half-smile flickered over her lips as she tilted her head to the side and winked. 'You ever wonder why we make such a good team, JayZee? Well, it's because we're similar, that's why. We've both had crappy childhoods and struggled to get to where we are now. And neither of us likes to broadcast that. If all that crap hadn't hit the fan before Christmas, nobody would be any the wiser about your background and that's the way you like it. It's how I like it too. But' – she shrugged – 'no matter how much we cover up the damage, punch the demons into submission, try to fit in, there's an aura about us that sets us apart from those untainted by trauma.'

Jazzy scowled, not wanting to admit it, but Queenie batted her unspoken protest away with a smile.

'It's not there for everyone to see. Oh no, they see *you* as haughty, prickly, unlikeable and they view *me* as stupid, flamboyant and crude, but we both know it's the cover we wrap round ourselves for protection. It's our bullet-proof vests, our rhino hides, our alligator scales and, we recognise it in each other – that vulnerability that lurks under the vest, beneath the hide and between the scales. That's why we work well together. So, I'm sorry I didn't confide more about Jimmy. I should have, but you and I both know that trusting another human with our deepest darkest fears is the hardest thing to do – that's why I've got Craig and you've got Elliot – they're our safety valves, but we need to be that for each other too, so I'm here to admit that seeing the Nails siblings after such a long time threw me big time. I was in bits. I disintegrated.' She narrowed her eyes and punched Jazzy on the arm. 'Mind you, I'll deny all of that if you ever—'

Queenie's phone rang. She glanced at the screen, raised a finger and answered. 'Hey, Craig, everything all right?'

Jazzy wandered through to the kitchen and popped the kettle on. Within a few minutes Queenie had joined her, her face scrunched in a frown as she flicked through her emails, her clumsy fingers making hard work of the task.

'Craig says the auld women opposite's gone off in an ambulance to St John's. You know the one I rescued in Scotmid when she took a funny turn.'

Jazzy spooned coffee into the percolator and nodded.

'Funny thing is, a bloke came to our door, as the ambulance was leaving. Craig says he was sure it was that Cairnpapple Man lookalike. Weird eh? Anyway, whoever it was he told Craig to tell me that the auld wifie had sent me an email and could I look at it now . . .'

What the fuck? Why the hell was Sid Mackie turning up at Queenie's door? As Queenie prodded at her phone with her fat index finger, Geordie's earlier cautions about trusting people echoed in her mind. She picked up her phone to instruct him to get over to Queenie's ASAP when it rang. *Geordie!* Before she could speak, Geordie spewed out a whole load of words that made her head burl. She felt the colour drain from her face as she turned to Queenie who was mumbling to herself.

'. . . Ah, there you are, you bugger.'

'I'm putting you on speaker phone, Geordie. I think everything you've found out about Cairnpapple Man and Sid Mackie is about to be confirmed. Queenie's just had an email from her neighbour.'

Queenie frowned at Jazzy, then, using her fingertips, she enlarged the text on her phone screen. As she scanned the email, she slid onto a chair, her face paling. 'Well, I fucking never, Jazz. You need to see this.'

But Jazzy already suspected what was about to be confirmed.

Chapter 54

'So, you're telling me that your elderly neighbour – a woman you assisted back to her home after she took a funny turn in the Scotmid in West Calder – has been the cause of all the criminal warfare between Jimmy Nails's gang in Glasgow and the one headed up by Loanie Gibbs in Edinburgh. Is that right?' DCI Tony Dick glared at Queenie as if he thought he could cause her to combust by the sheer force of his stare. His tone dripped with incredulity and his pursed lips underlined the message – he thought Queenie and Jazzy had lost the plot.

Jazzy cleared her throat, ready to jump to Queenie's defence to deflate the heated atmosphere in the incident room, but the chief super – tie flapping behind him – marched in, bringing a welcome Arctic breeze with him, followed by DI Elliot Balloch and Dukesy. Jazzy was surprised to see the undercover agent, but a quick analysis of both his and Elliot's body language confirmed her suspicions that Elliot knew about both their roles in investigating his integrity. This was not going to be a pleasant meeting.

Heads down at a neighbouring desk, both Geordie and Fenton sat in silence, tablets in front of them ready to take notes as this impromptu Saturday meeting took place. They were bracing themselves for a nuclear explosion. Jazzy risked an encouraging smile in their direction, whilst bracing herself for the fallout of this extraordinary meeting. When she'd phoned Waqas Afzal after she'd read the communication from Queenie's neighbour Martha, she'd hoped that he would take the lead and sideline DCI Dick, but that wasn't to be the case. So, here they were, Jazzy's 'double agent' activities, the brass's unfounded suspicions of Elliot's involvement in the Edinburgh gang, Dukesy's status as an undercover officer and the real story behind the last few months of bedlam between the Edinburgh and Glasgow gangs about to become common knowledge to the wider team.

Whilst certain that neither Elliot nor Dick would be happy that they'd been kept in the dark, Jazzy hoped that her insistence in involving them all now would mitigate their annoyance with her. Whoever was unhappy with her would have to put it aside. Right now, though, there was no time to dwell on that; their focus was needed on working out a strategy that would ensure that a captive boy, three guilty people and two stupid kids would be apprehended before the night was out.

After reading Martha Nails's email to Queenie and skim-reading the accompanying documents, Jazzy had sent a team of four officers to St John's hospital to watch over both Sid Mackie – who, according to the officers taking his statement, was still reeling from the revelations that Martha Nails had made to him that morning – and Martha Nails who was currently being treated for her pain and dehydration. Her critical illness and poor prognosis meant she was unavailable for comment at this stage. Further covert teams had been sent to monitor and report on the activities of the Nails siblings, Loanie Gibbs, Frankie Jones and the mysterious Gaffer.

With darkness rolling in and fog swirling, there was little time for the team to work out a strategy to ensure the successful apprehension of the criminals during the meeting in Tarbrax that Martha Nails under the guise of Vengeance had set up. Uncle Pedro had been in contact with Jazzy confirming that his contact

301

in the mercenary group – employed by Martha to execute her plan to destroy those she considered guilty of crimes against her and her family – had been asked to stand down after Martha reconsidered the way she wanted to end her plan. The A and B teams had been sent to scope out the land and area around the farmhouse in Tarbrax, but had seen limited activity and no sign that any ex-military mercenaries were on site. So, with no covert operators to contend with, the team and the deployed specialised firearms officers could move forward with the aim of ensuring that the guilty parties were brought in unharmed and statements taken from everyone to corroborate Martha Nails's extensive accusations, which included sexual abuse, rape, murder, criminal activity extortion and more.

'So, Dukesy, what's brought you in from the cold?' Jazzy knew her flippant words would gain her no friends, but she was fed up feeling like the pawn in everyone else's game. She hadn't chosen to keep secrets. That had been forced on her by Afzal – *another nice fatherly thing to do*. Despite knowing she was being unreasonable and that the chief super had acted as her boss not her dad, Jazzy took strength from her own pettiness.

Dukesy glanced at Afzal and after getting a 'go ahead' nod, moved to a computer, inserted a USB and brought up screen shots of two emails, which apart from the addressee were almost identical to that outlined in Martha Nails's earlier communication with Queenie.

Subject: VENGEANCE IS NIGH!

You want to end this? Well, tonight's the night. One way or another this will end.

9 p.m. MacPherson's farm, Tarbrax.

Aren't you looking forward to meeting me? To finding out what all this is about?

I AM VENGEANCE and the end is nigh!

One email was addressed to Jimmy Nails and the other to Wee Frankie Jones. The only difference between the two was that in Frankie's, Vengeance – or as they now knew her, Martha Nails – had added: *You know the address, be sure to bring the Gaffer – no show without Punch, eh?*

For long moments nobody spoke, then Fenton raised a tentative hand and clearing his throat said, 'So, we're still no clearer on who this Gaffer guy is?'

Elliot glared at Jazzy and folded his arms across his chest. 'From the other intel Dukesy's been able to gain, we've ascertained a few facts. The first is that it seems likely that, with Martha Nails's assertions that the Gaffer is or was a high-ranking police officer, more than likely now retired, he's probably a contemporary of Wee Frankie Jones and Jimmy Nails – or more likely his dad. In the interests of transparency, we've enlisted help from Grampian district to investigate the links between the Glasgow and Edinburgh mobs in the Seventies.'

Chief Super Afzal scowled, his cheeks flushed. 'We will find this Gaffer person and make an example of him. We're monitoring various ex-polis, including Dougie Shearsby. If it's him, we'll catch him. There is no room for corrupt police officers in Police Scotland, now or in the past. In light of the focus on police corruption in the aftermath of the various disgusting occurrences in the Met, Police Scotland wants to ensure that any corruption within our ranks is swiftly and effectively weeded out. Am I clear?'

Afzal waited till every one of the officers in the room had nodded their agreement before continuing. 'In the chaos of the blow-back from this, what we now know to be a "manufactured" turf war between the Nails and Gibbs gangs, we enlisted the input of many experienced retired officers from both Glasgow and Edinburgh, including Shearsby. Of course, with what we now know, these officers are under scrutiny and until their names are cleared beyond a shadow of a doubt, they will not be privy to any of this investigation. The officers in this room and a few hand-picked specialist arms officers will be the only ones privy to tonight's operation.

'Our aims are threefold. One: to remove Dan Moran from captivity uninjured. Two: to ascertain the culpability of the neds holding him at the farmhouse, and three: to apprehend the three people Martha Nails's intel says will arrive at the farmhouse, but only after they have incriminated themselves.'

Geordie stretched. 'Wouldn't it be less risky to arrest Frankie and Jimmy now?'

'Hm, I had considered that.' Afzal nodded. 'But we need the Gaffer. If we get in there early, control Moran and the two numpties holding him, and set up audio and visuals, then hopefully the three of them will fight it out among themselves. Martha Nails had initially intended to confront them herself with the backup of the militia group she hired. However, her cancer has progressed too far to allow us to use her in that way. We'll have to rely on them implicating themselves. Besides, the Gaffer's presence there will be pretty incriminating in itself.'

'That's if he turns up.'

For the first time since the discussion began, Queenie drew herself up to her full height and snorted. 'Aye, away ye go, Geordie, my wee pessimist. The Gaffer will turn up. Course he will. He'll be panting like a rutting pig to find out who's holding his balls in a vice. Mark my words, all three of them will be there.'

Dukesy grinned. 'I might not have put it quite that way myself, like, but Queenie's right. Jimmy and Wee Frankie are in panic mode. They're sending out the troops to try to ascertain who this mysterious Vengeance is. They've employed hackers to trace the emails. They'll turn up. Course they will. My guess is that they won't turn up alone, though. They'll want backup.'

'Have we got eyes on their ex-polis contacts, sir?' Fenton directed his question to Afzal, and Jazzy was proud that he held the chief super's gaze and that his nerves were only betrayed by a very slight flush across his cheeks. The Jazz Queens were holding their own and Jazzy had never been prouder of her team.

'Aye, son. We've got that covered. South Lanarkshire are helping us out with that, so we'll have ongoing intel into all their locations whilst we set up our operation. Which brings me onto our plan. Over to you, Elliot.'

Still studiously avoiding meeting Jazzy's gaze, Elliot began outlining a rough plan that would involve three cordons around the farmhouse. The inner cordon would take control of the farmhouse and its inhabitants, set up surveillance equipment around the farmhouse and surrounding outdoor areas. That team would also ensure that Fratelli and his mate wouldn't blow their cover, should Wee Frankie or the Gaffer contact them prior to the meeting. The middle cordon would involve armed officers, with eyes on the yard and farmhouse from a five-hundred-yard or so perimeter. Their job would be to identify and neutralise any backup brought by the trio of suspects. The outer cordon would provide valuable intel to the teams in the inner two cordons regarding external activity and possible risks, for example, and be on alert to provide backup as necessary. Due to the terrain around the farmhouse, the only cordon under cover would be the one located inside the farmhouse. The other two larger teams would be circling the area around the farmhouse using the natural environment for cover. Given their expertise, Elliot was content to allow the firearms teams to work out their own positions.

Fine-tuning the planning took a long time. DCI Dick wanted to sideline Jazzy's team citing unprofessional behaviour and more, but Chief Super Afzal was adamant that they deserved to be involved. Unilaterally, he decided that other than DI Balloch, he would not include any of the Edinburgh or Glasgow MIT teams, as he was uncertain just how widespread police involvement from the senior ranks was.

By 6 p.m., the plan was in place and Elliot, Geordie and Fenton, with support from the firearms team, were around the perimeter of the farmhouse. DCI Dick, the chief super and Dukesy who was monitoring the digital communications of Jimmy and Wee Frankie to ascertain what reinforcements both had enlisted, were in the command centre situated in a farmyard a mile from the target and the A and B teams, supported by additional firearms officers, made up the external cordon. Channels of communication had been checked, regular reports were updated on the locations of the targets. To ensure enough evidence to put the three criminals away, they needed to catch them red-handed and, particularly in the case of the Gaffer, Chief Super Afzal wanted the other two to corroborate Martha Nails's accusations. Because Martha was unlikely to be able to testify in person, corroborating testimony would be essential.

The last team to take their position was the team entering the farmhouse itself.

Chapter 55

Head buzzing, Jimmy paced his living room. His muscles writhed like they were possessed by snakes and he just couldn't get his head straight. The last email from Vengeance had thrown him and he was undecided what to do. Should he turn up there?

In his gut, Jimmy wanted to put an end to this. It was dragging on too long and he wanted to look this Vengeance straight in the eye and challenge them, but he was no fool.

For the life of him he still couldn't work out who the hell he'd crossed so badly they would act like this towards him. What was worse, though, was that Dukesy wasn't responding to any of his messages. He was on his own.

As he continued to pace, the squirming in his muscles became tighter and tighter like boa constrictors squeezing his biceps and triceps. He'd felt this before so he knew what it signalled. Jimmy had to keep a hold on his temper for now. He could unleash it in all its ferocious glory once he'd met this Vengeance person, but right now he needed to engage the men he trusted most to help him. At that point, Bonnie slinked into the room, wearing an indecently transparent negligée. Jimmy glared at her and she pouted.

'What's up with you? You weren't so mean last night.' She tiptoed her fingertips up his back and across his shoulders. 'Come on, Jimmy, let's release some of that tension you're feeling.'

Jimmy inhaled and grabbing her wrist, swung her round and threw her onto the couch. 'Cut the fucking crap, Bonnie. We've got a job to do, so get dressed, and I don't mean those high heels. I mean ready-to-do-murder then get your arse back here.'

Until that moment, Jimmy hadn't even considered including his sister in the evening's activity, but as soon as he saw her, it was clear that she was his secret weapon. There was nobody he knew as ruthless as Bonnie. She'd be an asset tonight.

Chapter 56

Wee Shuggie Fratelli wasn't used to being in the countryside, so cut off from civilisation, with no bloody Wi-Fi, no street-lights and the unfamiliar sounds of – well, God only knew what. The shuffling that had panicked him started up again, this time punctuated by other unidentifiable noises. In that second, he'd have given anything to hear an ambulance or even a polis siren blaring past, lights flashing and all, which, bearing in mind his dubious relationship with the po-po, showed just how far out of his comfort zone Shuggie was.

He peered into the shadows, cursing the fact that a cloud had covered the moon, making the velvet darkness even creepier. Thank fuck for the star and his phone torch. He grinned as he bounced his torch over the unfamiliar shapes, feeling his racing heart steady when, one by one, they appeared not as antagonists, but as bits of farmyard crap – old sacks, a lopsided and rusty old washing machine, a tractor with no wheels, and a tree line to his left by the side of the drystane dyke that separated him from the field with its humongous bloody coos. What the hell was he thinking? Who would be here in the arse-end of nowhere in the middle of the night in the bucking freezing cold? *It's probably just the sound of one of the coos in the next field farting, creating more of that noxious methane all them environmentalists were always banging on about. Mind you, the stench when the wind changed was pretty dire.*

He took a step closer to the field as the light of his torch showed the huge beasts doddering from grass patch to grass patch, their tails swishing and their massive arses releasing splattering pats behind them as they moved. Amused by his earlier melodrama and the weirdness of the situation, he stepped forward and with a flutter of hands made an ornate bow, one leg bending at the knee behind him as he did so.

'Good evening, kind fellows, welcome to the *Shuggie Fratelli Weird-Ass Show* brought to you from the arse-end of West Lothian.' He followed up his regal bow with a less regal curtsey, stretching his arms to the sides and bobbing down like he'd seen the wifies do on that weird show about some queen or other that his da liked to watch.

A sound from the right drew his attention. Was that a snigger? *Was that a fucking snigger?* Had that bloody tosser nipped out and seen him do his Shakespeare crap? They should've known better than to include Matty in this. Mr fucking unreliable. What the hell had they been thinking?

'That you, Matty?'

He strained his ears. Nothing, not a sound. Probably imagined it, anyway. A shiver reminded him that he'd stretched his fag break for a while now and should be heading back indoors, so he switched off his torch to save the battery. Might as well be lost on a desert island as here at the edge of Tarbrax. *Tarbrax?* Who the hell had ever heard of the place? Not him, anyway. He shrugged and exhaled, his breath creating a puff of steam in front of him, reminding him that he'd just downed three pokes of cheese and onion crisps. *God, my breath's honking!*

He sighed again and shrugged. Too late for regrets now, wasn't it? No way he could renege on the deal. Not with the prospect of more dosh at the end and definitely not when he knew what his fate would be if he pished off home. Not that pishing off home was an option – he'd no transport and no bars to call for a lift, and Shuggie was damn sure he wasn't going to hike for miles to reach civilisation – not in his new Nikes, anyway.

Thoughts darting back to the Gaffer, his smile faded as the reality of his situation struck. What if the auld man was full of pish? What if the *Shetland* promise was just a ruse to draw Shuggie into this bloody nonsense? What if Shuggie had risked everything for the promise of a grand in cash and the faint possibility that a pocket full of dosh might impress Jeanie from the Tartan Sporran? What if it all went to shite? What if he got arrested, slammed in a cell – no way would his da bail him out – he'd rather spend his benefits on a flutter on the gee-gees, never mind helping his only son.

In his darkest moments Shuggie did what he always did and channelled his inner *Trainspotting*, by stepping into Begbie's character for a moment – although minus the 'C' word – Shuggie hated the 'C word'. Made him squirm when he heard it. Disrespectful it was. So, aside from the 'C' word, being Begbie always made him feel invincible – although in his finer moments Shuggie agreed that Begbie wasn't maybe the best role model for a Scottish laddie wanting to stick to the straight and narrow. Nonetheless, he was a braw character to inhabit – for a moment, just for a moment.

Shite, Shuggie my man, dinnae be such a fucking pessimist. Instead of looking doon the crap chute afore it's been flushed, why no' picture this – you in yer best breeks, that Jeanie in a mini skirt and all made up . . . Gotta be worth the risk, son. You gotta take the chance. You've got it made, lad, got it made, eh?

Shuggie grinned. Already he felt his voice had deepened by a couple of octaves and the bum fluff on his chin had sprouted tenfold. Begbie aside, the prospect of earning the next five hundred big ones for an overnight shift was nothing to be sniffed at, even if playing babysitter to an obnoxious Weegie drug dealer wasn't high on his list of best ways to spend a Saturday night.

It was only the prospect of wining and dining Jeanie from the Tartan Sporran in Bathgate and maybe ending up getting a bit shiggy with her that made him hold his tongue every time that pipsqueak, Dan the gobshite Moran, ordered him about like he was a bloody skivvy. Wee bawbag had ended up in bother again, no doubt, and that was why he'd been shunted over here to West Lothian, leaving Shuggie to babysit.

With a heavy sigh he flicked his fag through the air creating a mini firework display that ended abruptly extinguished in a puddle two seconds later. First blowing on his chapped hands to warm them, he shoved them deep into the pockets of his skinny jeans and ambled towards the old farmhouse.

Light from the two downstairs windows guided him towards the decrepit building that hunkered in the shadows of a seamless skyline. The owners had left it to fall into disrepair, having built their own all-singing, all-dancing modern farmhouse five miles down the road. Shuggie reckoned that if they had his business savvy, they'd have done it up a bit and rented it out as one of those Airbnbs he'd read about in the *Daily Record*. That'd be a nice wee earner for them. Mind you, being in business with the Edinburgh mob probably paid well too – only thing was, when you played in their fitba team once, they expected you to be in reserve till they needed you the next time. Shuggie knew that only too well – that's another reason he'd ended up here, babysitting Moran the Moron.

At the scullery door, he paused and rooted round for the key that was on a foot-long chain attached to one of his belt hooks. It was then he heard shuffling behind him again, but closer this time. Definitely not the coos. Before he could turn around, the gun was poking right into his kidneys and the gravelly voice was right in his ear.

'Don't even think about it, ye wee bawbag. I've got you now.'

The gun prodded harder against his jacket and then a hand shoved his head right up against the door. His bowels voided, adding to the malodorous silage stench. As snippets of the events that had led him here flim-flammed through his mind, his one pervading thought was: *What the fucking hell am I going to do now?* Followed almost immediately by: *Aw no I hope I've not fucked up my new trainers.*

Chapter 57

Queenie grinned at Jazzy as she pushed the metal tubing harder into Shuggie Fratelli's kidneys and manoeuvred his stinking carcass into the farmhouse.

'Aw, don't shoot me, please don't shoot me, I'll do whatever you tell me. It was the Gaffer that made me do it and I didn't hurt him. Honest I didn't.'

Jazzy, who'd been standing three feet away from Shuggie as he'd delivered his soliloquy to the coos, pinched her nose with two fingers and shook her head. What a silly wee numpty Shuggie Fratelli was, but at least it looked like he would cooperate with them. With a gesture to the armed officers and the team whose job it was to set up the audio and visual surveillance equipment inside and around the outside of the farmhouse, she followed Queenie and the squelching lad inside.

A quick glance round showed her the shower room. She nudged Queenie who – with her pretend gun still in position – was prodding the lad, her nose curled up in distaste, and pointed to it. Queenie shoved him into the shower room. Once standing head bowed, shite soaking into his jeans and his white trainers turning a mucky brown, Jazzy directed the lukewarm spray on him whilst Queenie admonished him.

'Ye dirty wee scumbag. Ye've keched yourself and I'm damned if we're going to sit here with you when you're smelling like that. Get them filthy rags off.'

Behind Queenie and Jazzy, the authorised firearms officers entered, quickly subduing Matty, who was so stoned he barely registered their presence other than to issue a 'Wow! Cool! Guns!' before lapsing into silence, a nodding, spaced-out grin on his stupid face.

The still trussed-up Dan Moran, presumably realising they weren't his expected rescue party, scowled, 'For fuck's sake, could this get any worse? They've sent in the Krankies.'

Shuggie struggled out of his clothes, trying to cover his shrivelled-up privates, and lamented the loss of his new trainers. 'Aw, no. My trainers are fucked. How will I ever be able to replace them?'

With the last of the watered-down excrement sloshing down the drain, Jazzy switched off the hose and threw him a towel. 'Dry yourself and then get wrapped in this.' She tossed a blanket onto the floor just outside the cubicle. 'And then you'll tell us everything you know, okay?'

A short time later, Shuggie blinked up at them, his bottom lip quivering. 'All I know is that if I didn't do what the Gaffer said, my dad was going to get the brunt of it. Honest. I don't know anything. I'm just babysitting till they get here.'

With Dan Moran handcuffed in one bedroom and Matty positioned in the recovery position in another, each supervised by an armed officer, Jazzy using the kitchen as an interview room, pulled the curtains closed tight, whilst Queenie confiscated Shuggie's phone after checking through his messages.

'So, tell me again about the Gaffer. You're saying . . .'

But before Jazzy could finish her question a crackle of static, followed by 'Alert, alert. A sole occupied vehicle is approaching the farmhouse from the main road,' signalled into her earbuds.

Immediately that was interrupted by another voice. 'Eyes on three figures on foot approaching from the west. Awaiting instructions.'

Afzal's voice broke through in another burst of static. 'Monitor and observe, for now.'

A burst of activity broke out upstairs as the armed officers moved the two captives to the en-suite bathroom at the back of the house where any sounds from them wouldn't carry outside. Plunging the kitchen into darkness, Jazzy peeked through the heavy curtains as headlights swept across the room, illuminating Shuggie, wide-eyed and looking as if he was about to repeat his earlier undignified action. Outside, a Land Rover edged as close to the door as possible. The headlights remained on for a second then were extinguished, plunging them into complete darkness. Shuggie groaned, 'Aw, fuck me,' but Queenie's whispered 'Shut the fuck up or I'll bloody brain you' silenced him.

A car door clicking shut was accompanied by a warning moo from the nearby field, then silence. Jazzy's heart hammered against her chest as the armed officers took up their positions at the various entry points. Although she couldn't see or hear what the driver was doing, she knew that the command centre had eyes and ears on all activity throughout the farmhouse and the surroundings and would keep each of the officers informed. Sure enough, Afzal's voice echoed eerily in her ear.

'Single figure A, dressed in black and carrying what looks to be a baseball bat approaching entry point one.'

Entry point one was the kitchen entrance that she and Queenie had pushed Shuggie through earlier. Her eyes briefly met those of the armed officer who trained her weapon at the locked door as the handle moved silently down. Just then, Shuggie's phone lit up on the table with an incoming call. The Gaffer. *Thank God we muted it earlier.*

'Figure A circling the house to the left.'

Another voice interrupted. 'Vehicle number two approaching. Two occupants, no ID.'

Within seconds the second vehicle, also a Land Rover, nosed onto the yard with its lights out and two figures alighted. Whilst

316

Queenie kept watch on their captive, Jazzy strained to ID the figures. One was taller and skinny, the other shorter.

'Jimmy and Bonnie, Queenie.'

Jazzy heard Queenie's sharp intake of breath. This time, the rattle of the door handle was accompanied by a couple of kicks and a 'Fuck's sake, Jimmy, you sure this is the right place?'

The armed officer held their position, but whispered into her mic: 'Figures B and C identified as Jimmy Nails and Bonnie Moran. Any eyes on backup for them?'

A crackle then: 'No, nothing. But Figure A is identified as Frankie Jones and a third vehicle, single occupant, is approaching.'

Jazzy took a few deep breaths. It seemed all of Martha Nails's three targets had been hooked. This last vehicle surely belonged to the Gaffer and judging by the almost palpable silence around them, everyone was on tenterhooks awaiting a positive ID.

Elliot's voice: 'Entering the yard now. Still no ID. Headlights are off.'

Jazzy saw a tall figure jump down from yet another Land Rover.

'Any ID from the vehicle reg?'

'No, all mud-covered – they're not rookies, Solanki.'

Again, Shuggie's phone lit up, and if Jazzy strained her eyes she could make out the black-clad figure holding a mobile to his ear. Did he look familiar? Jazzy couldn't be sure. But now there were four people circling the premises, presumably Wee Frankie and the Gaffer being the two unidentified figures. As if tiring of waiting for their call to be answered, figure D thrust it in their pocket before marching to the middle of the yard, their arms extended on either side, and yelled into the night air, 'Well, I know somebody's here. I can see the cars. Show your face, if you dare, Vengeance.'

The cows, disturbed by noise in the otherwise silent night, mooed – an echo of annoyance that filled the yard. At the same time Jazzy recognised this person. The person she now realised had to be the Gaffer. She engaged her mic.

'The Gaffer is Emily Hare. I repeat ex-DCS Emily Hare is the Gaffer.'

For a moment silence reigned, then Afzal's voice. 'You're right. We've got a positive ID on her. That's her implicated in this entire mess and it gives more credence to Martha Nails's assertions.'

Elliot's 'Fucking bitch' hung in the air, ominous and threatening, and Jazzy's heart went out to him. She'd been his mentor. He'd trusted her, respected her. This was a hard blow to take and when it sank in that she'd tried to implicate him in her mess, he'd be even more hurt.

Jimmy Nails and Bonnie Moran approached from one side of the house whilst the shorter, more rotund figure of Wee Frankie Jones breasted the other side. The Gaffer eyeballed the three figures and then laughed. 'So, assuming none of you three are Vengeance, what the hell's going on here?'

Frankie stepped forward. 'Do you think that wee shite Fratelli's got something to do with it?'

'Shuggie Fratelli? Don't be daft. He's not got the brains he was born with. No, it's someone else.'

Frankie was persistent. 'Well, where's Dan Moran, then?'

Bonnie's head went up, her chin jutting out. 'My Dan? You two have had my Dan here?'

Hare snorted, then her voice rough sneered at Bonnie. 'Aw, pulease. Your Dan? You'd be happy to get rid of that wee fucker. As pleased as you were to get rid of Ned. I did you a fucking favour, hen, ordering him dead.'

'You get that?' Jazzy's voice was low as Hare continued.

'Besides, did you think Wee Frankie here would let it stand when you offed his two boys?'

But Jimmy, panting from the effort of holding Bonnie back, shook his head.

'Me and Loanie had a deal. It wisnae my crew who ordered your boys killed, Frankie. My bet's on this Vengeance character. And whilst we're here bickering among ourselves, who knows what

318

sort of trap we're in. He could be anywhere. He could have any number of weapons trained on us. We need to work together now.'

For long seconds the quartet stared at each other and then, as one, they joined in a circle back to back, each training a gun that they'd taken from their waistbands through the darkness before them.

'Who the fuck is this Vengeance you're on about?' Bonnie's head swung from side to side as she grabbed a gun from her joggers' waistband. Gripping it in a two-handed grip, she pointed it at Frankie.

With an insolent grin, Frankie shrugged. 'Aw, put the gun down, pet. I've no idea, maybe ask your brother.'

Bonnie, gun sweeping erratically between Frankie Jones and Emily Hare, stepped closer. 'None of you? None of you know? So, what the fuck's this all about.' She swung back to Jimmy. 'Jimmy? Come on, tell me what's going on here.'

Her brother sighed. 'All we know is that whoever it is seems to have initiated a turf war between our crew and Frankie – or rather, the Gaffer's Edinburgh crew. No idea why.'

Bonnie tutted. 'Bunch of idiots. If this fucker's targeting you three, then it's got to have something to do with the time when these two and oor da were in business together, Jimmy. Something that went down involving our da and these two old fogies. Any ideas?'

She glowered at Frankie, her tone derisive and challenging. 'Come on, Frankie, surely you can work that out. Unless, of course, you've lost your marbles.'

Frankie half turned to confront Bonnie then turned away. 'Nothing comes to mind.'

His tone held a note of uncertainty that made Bonnie scoff and push her point. 'Aye, right. Everyone knows about you, Frankie boy. You're not a wee innocent, so you might as well come clean. Did you dip your dick where it wasn't wanted, eh? Cause a wee scandal or was it more to do with the body parts you liked to feed to the pigs over in your cousin's farm in Torphichen? Did he get the hump at you sniffing aboot his wife all the time? What was their name now?'

Although Jazzy couldn't see Bonnie's glare she could hear the anger in her words. Frankie's rage too simmered in the air between the four of them. 'Shut the fuck up ye worthless wee whore.'

But Bonnie was on a roll. 'Aye, Mackie. That was their name. Like the ice cream. Wonder where they disappeared off to. Maybe you fed them to their own damn pigs.'

At the name, Jazzy frowned. Mackie? Torphichen? No way that was a coincidence.

'Aw away and boil yer heid, hen. You're well off base. They scuttled off abroad when his business took off. Too high and mighty to stay here in Scotland.'

Jimmy grabbed Frankie's arm and squeezed. 'You have something to do with them leaving without a word to anyone, eh, Frankie? All those years ago, was it because of you? Did you mess around with Shona Mackie when she was a bairn?'

With a brittle laugh, Bonnie plucked at her brother's arm. 'Don't worry about all of that, Jimmy. It's nothing to do with us if Frankie can't keep his pecker in his dirty broon Y-fronts, is it?'

Jazzy whispered into her mic. 'Please say you're getting all of this.'

Afzal's reply was instantaneous. 'Every incriminating word.'

In the yard, Jimmy Nails shrugged off his sister's arm and although he addressed her, his gun was on Frankie.

'It's everything to do with us, Bon. Shona was our cousin and I'm putting things together now. Mackie married her as soon as she turned sixteen, but she already had a wean. Everyone thought it was his and that he'd done the right thing by her, but now I'm thinking that with the dirt you've uncovered, maybe there was a different story to it. Maybe you were the wean's da. Maybe that's why you kept hanging around that sodding farm . . .' Jimmy paused, nodded. 'I was just a bairn myself when all of this was kicking off, but it makes me wonder.'

'Aw get a life, son. This is all a load of innuendo and rubbish spawned from the fertile imagination of your somewhat erratic sister. Hardass Nails? Soft as bloody pish, more like.'

But the Gaffer interrupted. 'Enough! The only thing that involved *all* of us that I can think of is . . . well, you know, Frankie. The thing that made our – very lucrative – deal with the Nails family redundant, and maybe Jimmy and the loudmouth aren't too far off the tracks. If it's your misdeeds that have brought us here then, Frankie, you're on your own. If this Vengeance wants you, then that's what they'll get.'

'Tell us everything.' Anger tore through each of Jimmy's words. 'What broke the deal between you and my da? Tell me now cos I'm not going to take the rap for your fucking misdemeanours.'

The Gaffer laughed a low, humourless laugh. 'Let's just say oor Wee Frankie likes them young and your big sister, Martha, was young enough to tickle his fancy . . .'

Bonnie glared at Frank, her entire body quivering as she took a step towards him, gun raised just as Jimmy broke from the tight circle and went for Frankie but just then a faint cry rent the air. 'Ma, Uncle Jimmy . . .'

Fuck, fuck, fuck, fuck, fuck. Jazzy spun round. She'd been so focused on catching what was happening in the farmyard that the faint sounds of a scuffle upstairs had eluded her. A door slammed followed by a yelp and by Dan Moran yelling louder now. How the hell had the lad got away from the officer watching him? So, what had gone wrong?

Jazzy tore across the kitchen and wrenched the door open with a 'Stay on Fratelli, Queenie.' All she had by way of a weapon was an extendable baton and a tactical vest. Halfway up the stairs, the slight figure of Dan Moran, flew at her, fingers grappling to scrape into her eyes. Jazzy, lacking the room to fully extend her baton, rammed it into his gut as he landed on her, but still the two of them landed in a heap of limbs at the bottom of the stairs with Dan on top. He jumped off her and headed for the front door.

The armed officer from the kitchen passed her, gun trained on Moran. Momentarily winded, Jazzy did a speedy mental inventory of her injuries. Her injured arm seemed unharmed, so she jumped to her feet and sped after them. Dan was fumbling with the locks when a volley of gunfire hit the door. Jazzy dived to the side but Dan fell to the ground, blood pooling around him as the armed officer spoke.

'Dan Moran down. Shots fired at front door. Urgent assistance needed.'

From the stairs the officer responsible for guarding Moran stumbled into view, a chisel sticking from his gut as he tried to slide towards her. Jazzy spoke into her mic. 'Officer down. Chisel wound to stomach. Repeat, officer down.'

She approached the officer. 'Stay there, don't move.' Ripping off her jacket, she rolled it up and padded it around the knife, then placed the injured officer's hands on it. 'Press down, as hard as you can. Help's coming.'

The officer, sweat beading across her forehead, nodded and pressed on the jacket. Jazzy's heart sank when she saw how quickly the officer's small hands became saturated in blood, but she smiled. 'Good job.'

She turned to Dan Moran, whose eyes were fluttering in his head. His blood loss seemed severe too, but at least he was conscious. Jazzy watched as the armed officer bundled up a jumper and applied pressure to the hole in his gut. *Please don't bleed out.* From her earphone a frantic static followed by: 'Weaponised drones approaching the farmhouse. Repeat, weaponised drones approaching. Clear the house. Repeat: clear the farmhouse. Weaponised . . .'

As the warning continued, activity burst out around Jazzy. Queenie and Shuggie appeared from the kitchen, and another officer dragged a still-stoned and completely oblivious Matty down the stairs.

As the drones began to release their weapons – grenades, or small bombs by the sounds of it – onto the farmhouse roof,

Jazzy, heart hammering, resisted the temptation to cover her ears and unlocked the door. Using her now fully extended baton, she stood to the side, breathing heavily, and pulled it open. When no immediate shots were fired, she said, 'We're going to have to make a run for it.'

With the help of an armed officer, she pulled Dan Moran towards the door, but it was so hard. He was heavy and her bad arm was weak. Still, together they managed it. Before the others made their way outside, she quickly assessed the situation. Officers in tactical attire flooded the area and the only shots now being fired appeared to be from further afield – from the areas designated outer and middle cordons. Trained arms officers would deal with that. 'Come on, get a move on.' She needed to get her companions out of the farmhouse before it caught light or – worse – exploded. From upstairs, cold air drifted down carrying with it the acrid smell of cordite, chemicals and smoke. Time was of the essence. 'Get out. Now. Keep as low as you can and head for the shadows.'

Queenie, dragging Shuggie Fratelli behind her, stumbled out, closely followed by Matty and his officer. Jazzy looked back. Two motionless figures lay just outside the door. Who should she take? Dan Moran or the officer? Then a figure appeared and grabbed Dan Moran. 'He's my nephew I'll take him. You get the other one. I'll come back.'

Jimmy Nails didn't wait for a reply, he grabbed his nephew, threw him onto his shoulders and ran.

Jazzy, eyes stinging from the chemicals, flinched at the ongoing sounds of firearms going off. The air thick with smoke clogged her chest and mouth. Her eyes smarted with the fumes. She crawled back to the officer. Knowing the limitations of her own weakened arm, Jazzy grabbed the moaning officer's legs. With all her strength, she pulled, ignoring the screeching pain in her arm and, inch by agonising inch, pulled the officer away from the burning building. She was almost there when two figures appeared, one dragged the injured officer to safety and the other picked her up. *Elliot – again!* And as he carried her well away from the farmhouse, flames danced from the destroyed roof.

A thunderous crash, followed by more explosions. As the remaining parts of the roof caved in and flames belched from the open door and the broken windows, Elliot dropped her, in the sopping wet yard, and fell to his knees beside her. As her heart rate slowed and adrenalin began to seep away, a wave of nausea engulfed Jazzy. She lay flat on her back, in the freezing muck, trying not to be sick and looking up at the night sky. She thanked her lucky stars that she'd survived.

'They've got them,' Elliot said. Amidst the sound of arrests being made, officers issuing instructions and emergency vehicles filling the area, the heavens opened and pounding rain beat down on her.

Still dizzy and shaking, she reached into her trouser pocket with her good hand and took solace in rubbing her fingers gently over her familiar glass Ganesh. Under her breath she whispered, 'You certainly removed one big obstacle tonight. Thank you.' She raised the elephant god to her lips and kissed his forehead before returning him to her pocket.

And then just as the thought of Queenie flashed into her mind, the woman herself, accompanied by Geordie and Fenton, appeared by her side. 'For fuck's sake, JayZee, what the hell are you playing at? We can't be the Jazz Queens if you're deid, now can we?'

A surge of relief and love and goodness knows what else rushed through Jazzy.

Geordie, face black with soot, bounced on his gangly legs. 'I've told you before, we're not the Jazz Queens, Queenie. You can say it as much as you want, but we're *not* that.'

Fenton's frown cleared when he saw her move and he heaved a sigh of relief. 'Thank God, you're okay, Jazzy. Imagine if you'd left us with her.'

324

Queenie nudged him none too gently. 'Less of the cheek, Haggis boy.'

Torn between laughing and vomiting, Jazzy remained supine on the ground, enjoying the rain, appreciating the banter. They might be weird but these three were her team and she was the boss. A giggle gurgled from her throat. 'Join me.'

'Eh?' Queenie's mouth dropped open.

'I mean it. I'm ordering you to join me, here on the mud, flat on your backs, all of you.'

Haggis exchanged a glance with Geordie who broke into a grin and plopped onto his back beside her. 'I'm in. We can make mud angels.'

With Queenie huffing and puffing, and Fenton whimpering and chittering, the D team lay next to each other in the mud, whilst a farmhouse burned to the ground, armed officers made arrests and paramedics dealt with the injured.

'Aye, yer no wrong, JayZee.'

'What?'

'It's a braw night for us Jazz Queens to make mud angels. A night to be thankful to still be alive. It's good to take a moment to savour that.'

Despite the rain and the cold, Jazzy was flooded with warmth. She turned her head to see Elliot watching her, his hair flat against his scalp, a bloody scrape down his face. 'You forgive me?'

He looked at her, his face expressionless for a good minute, then nodded. 'For what, Jazzy? Doing your job? Obeying orders? Nothing to forgive is there? Just glad I got to rescue you . . . again.'

Monday 13th March

Chapter 58

Two days had passed since the confrontation at the farmhouse in Tarbrax. Both Dan Moran and the officer had died from their injuries at the scene. Whilst the bullet that killed Moran was awaiting ballistics analysis in order to match it to one of the weapons found on Jimmy Nails, Bonnie Moran, Emily Hare and Frankie Jones, it was clear that the officer – Sergeant Leanne Brown – had been killed by Dan Moran who had stabbed her with a chisel he'd secreted down his trouser legs. It weighed heavily on Jazzy that an officer had been killed, but knowing also that the perpetrator would go unpunished felt like justice only half done. Mistakes had been made – the incomplete body search of Dan Moran being a fatal one – and lessons would be learned from that mistake. Jazzy would make sure of it.

The other big mistake was that, during the planning stages, the team hadn't considered that the use of drones could be employed to such potentially devastating consequences. It was more by luck than design that everyone else inside the farmhouse had escaped with minor injuries and slight smoke inhalation. The drones had been operated by the backup brought by ex-Chief Super Emily Hare, now revealed through her own admission as the Gaffer referenced in Martha Nails's typed statements.

Initial reports from the CSIs indicated that the drones had been fitted with firebombs that would detonate on impact and grenades that would damage the structure of the building. More detailed analysis and investigation into where such weapons were sourced would follow over the coming weeks. The audio and visual recordings implicated all four of the main players in having illegal weaponry and, in the case of Emily Hare and Frankie Jones, went a long way to corroborating the accusations levelled against them by Martha Nails.

Whilst many of the backup teams brought along by the four main suspects had scattered, Jazzy hoped that the video recordings and ongoing investigations would lead to more arrests. Some of which would lead to more corroboration of the gangsters' illegal operations. Meanwhile, with enough evidence to warrant it, Emily Hare's financials were being forensically scrutinised and already various bank accounts in tax-free havens had been uncovered, whilst in her home, it seemed the arrogance of operating unde- tected for so long had led to complacency and various documents had been seized and over the coming months the team were convinced more damning evidence would come to light.

Frankie Jones's cancer diagnosis had proven to be a blessing in disguise for them because, knowing he wouldn't spend much time in jail, he'd been more cooperative than expected about his business dealings with the Gaffer. Unfortunately, his desire to come clean didn't extend to the sexual abuse allegations levied against him. News of his arrest, accompanied by leaked stories regarding the investigation into historic sexual abuse cases, had brought many women forward to report their experiences at the hands of the criminal.

With Shuggie's previously immaculate track record and his willingness to testify, his involvement was understood to be a result of coercion by the Gaffer and as such he would get a slap on the wrist. Jazzy suspected the lad had learned a valuable and timely lesson. With Matty being under the influence of drugs during most of the operation, his testimony and statements were practically worthless and Jazzy would make sure to keep an eye on him, for – unlike Shuggie – Matty seemed less likely to learn from his mistakes.

Whilst Geordie and Fenton followed up leads in the incident room, Jazzy had volunteered to take Martha Nails's statement. Jazzy had been willing to conduct the interview under caution at St John's hospital, but, despite her specialist's objections, Martha would have none of it and insisted on coming to the police station. In the end, Jazzy was forced to give in, but it tore her heart out watching this woman suffer. It was as if Martha wanted to punish herself for her role in everything that had transpired over the past few months. After all, her actions were responsible for the bloodbath that had plagued the district and Edinburgh and Glasgow for months.

With Queenie standing silently beside her, they studied the woman from behind the two-way glass that separated the observation suite from interview room two. Even in this short space of time it was clear Martha Nails's condition had deteriorated. Her jaundiced pallor, the way her bones jutted through brittle skin, the slump of her shoulders, the effort it took for her to position her bony body on the functionally uncomfortable interview-room chairs all paid testament to how quickly the cancer was devouring her body.

Jazzy was conflicted. In her heart she had no desire to hold this dying woman to account for any of it. But the law was the law and regardless of her personal opinions it was Jazzy's job to uphold it. Knowing that didn't make it harder for those 'what if' questions to seep into Jazzy's mind. What if all those things that had happened to Martha had happened to *her*? What if it was *her* child – *her* son – who, desperately seeking a family he'd never known, was cut down so violently in the prime of his life? What if it was *her* past that had come back to bite her and had left those she loved the most exposed to lifelong hatred, fear and death?

What would she do? Jazzy chose not to dwell on that particular question – she'd had too close a shave with it only a few months earlier – and not when she was at work anyway. However, nothing could stop it from haunting her waking moments away from the job, or her sleeping moments, which were haunted by nightmares, recriminations and questions around her own familial issues. 'You okay, Queenie?'

Queenie, fists plunged deep in her trouser pockets, shook her head. The movement was slow and arduous, as if her head was too heavy for her shoulders. 'Nah, nah, I'm not okay, JayZee. This is fucking abysmal. This is nothing to do with justice and everything to do with ticking a box. It's nothing to do with what's right. Nothing to do with what best serves society. If it was, that wee bastard, Frankie Jones, down the hall, would have been strung up by his goolies long since and those women lining the halls to have their stories of his abuse documented would have been able to move on years ago, having been believed, instead of having it dragged up again now all because the cocky wee bawbag's "no commenting" like it's going out of fashion. As for the rest of them – well, between the lot of them, apart from their extensive criminal practices, they've contributed to the misery that led to all of this. They all deserve to be banged up for good. She's the only one, in my opinion, who deserves a second chance.'

There was nothing more to be said. Queenie was right, but in the here and now, in the station, in their roles as police officers, that didn't matter a jot. Jazzy squeezed her partner's shoulder, feeling the rigidity of her muscles as Queenie tried to hold it together. There would be a lot of unresolved anger issues to deal with before this was done.

'Let's find her a soft chair with some cushions. The least we can do is make her as comfortable as possible whilst we take her statement and get it done quickly.'

'She won't see a prison cell, will she?'

Jazzy shrugged, her eyes still on the shrunken woman in the other room. 'No, I doubt it. She's not going to recover enough for that and, all things considered, I doubt Afzal would push for that. Besides, her doctors wouldn't stand for it. However, we need her statement to support the other investigations. You know that, Queenie.' Jazzy flung her shoulders back and straightened her spine. 'We've got to toughen ourselves up to get through this. If you think you can't do that, Queenie, I'll get Fenton to come in with me.'

But Queenie was already shaking her head. 'No. No, I owe it to her. We'll do it together. It'll be easier for her if it's us. That way she'll know that her statement will never be lost. That her sacrifice will mean something.'

With a smile that almost broke Jazzy's heart, Queenie stepped to the door, grabbing one of the comfy chairs as she did so, and marched out.

Chapter 59

Martha's eyes held no recrimination as she met Jazzy's gaze. 'He's arrested? Locked up?'

For a moment, Jazzy was unsure which of the men currently residing in the cells or in interview rooms Martha referred to. Then she got it. Martha was a mother. Maybe not always the best mother, but still that maternal instinct was what prompted her words.

'Jimmy's been arrested for the murder of your son and will be interviewed after we're done here. Just so you know, though, when charged with Billy's murder he vehemently denied not only perpetrating the murder, but of even knowing Billy was in the country.'

Martha frowned. 'That's what he said?'

Jazzy nodded.

'Not sure what to make of that.' Martha closed her eyes and a shudder racked her feeble frame as a solitary tear rolled down her cheek. 'And the others?'

Jazzy sat down opposite her. 'We got them all and no doubt more will be implicated before this plays out, but for now, you can rest easy. They're all in custody – Jimmy Nails, Frankie Jones, Emily Hare, who we have now identified as the Gaffer, and Bonnie Moran.'

When the silence between the three women in the room dragged on, Queenie moved forward, pulling the chair behind her. 'Here, we brought you a comfier place to sit.' As gently as if she were dealing with Ruby, Queenie manipulated the drips that had accompanied Martha to the station and helped her into the other chair. Once satisfied that Martha was comfortable, she pushed two recyclable cups towards her – one of water, the other with Queenie's dark brown, overly sweet builder's tea. 'There ye go, hen. Take a few sips of that tea; it'll put hairs on your chest.'

Martha smiled, her eyes lighting up momentarily as she reached her skinny hand over to the gently steaming cup. 'You're a doll, Queenie. Thank you.'

'What about meds? You in pain, Martha? Do you want your doctor to step in? You know we can take you back to St John's, settle you in a nice cosy bed and do this when you're a wee bit stronger.'

Martha winked at Jazzy, but directed her words at Queenie. 'My time's running out now. If I'd been brave enough all those years ago, maybe a lot of this suffering would have been avoided. I'm paying my price on this earth because I don't believe I'd be punished in the afterlife. I *want* to be here. I *want* to see my statement recorded and I *want* to see all three of them put away for good. They've been free for far too long.'

As dusk settled outside the police station in Livingston and the heating kicked in, bringing with it a sense of something bigger than the four walls that contained them, Jazzy switched on the audio and visual recording system – she wanted a jury to not only hear and see, but to *feel* Martha's account in the courtroom. To have her frail appearance in mind when the paedophile who raped her at thirteen, and the criminal gang leader who abused her position as a police officer to commit heinous crimes for decades, and her brother, the gang leader who murdered her only child – were brought to trial. She settled back with Queenie to hear Martha Nails's story. Martha had declined her right to a lawyer, insisting that she was happy to clarify the sequence of events that had led to so many deaths and so much disharmony. In her calm, sincere voice that was a mix of Glasgow and New Zealand, Martha spoke, pausing only when her pain meds needed topping up or when her throat got too dry, causing her to cough for long minutes. Despite repeated entreaties to take a break, Martha – stoicism in her unflinching stare and determined smile – continued.

'I don't believe in karma. Doubt I ever did. Growing up in Easterhouse we were well loved, but also we were familiar with the feel of my dad's leather belt on our backsides. We'd been used to the ups and downs of the criminal life – not that we knew it for that then. Sometimes, when we were flush it was like we were the richest family in the world, but when we weren't we'd barricade the doors against the bailiffs and learn to keep our voices down and our rumbling stomachs quiet. That all changed when da got in tow with Frankie and the Gaffer, though. Now, we were the ones that everybody feared. Kids would hang about outside playing kerbie, desperate to run an errand for Ricky Nails. Looking back on it all now I realise his alliance with Frankie and the Gaffer had secured his place as the lynchpin of the Glasgow underworld. Even the big criminals were afraid of Ricky Nails and he made sure he kept that fear alive. I saw him do all sorts of things to those who were daft enough to get in debt to the great Ricky Nails.'

She stared into space, a frown tugging at her brow. 'Mothers greeting as one of his thugs put their fags out on their bairns' chubby legs, or a man watching as they booted his pregnant wife in the gut till she lost the bairn.' Martha blew her nose and swallowed hard before continuing. 'As my belly got bigger and bigger in the summer of 1971, I wished he'd get one of his laddies to do that to me. To kick the bastard child right out of my belly, so everything would go back to normal. But that didn't happen. Instead, my da couldn't even look at me. I was thirteen years old and he blamed *me* for the poison that was growing in my gut.'

She sniffed and blinked away a tear. 'I never saw him again after he pushed me on that plane with some woman I'd never met before. I never saw my ma again either, nor Jimmy – Bonnie wasn't even born then – not until this year. Not till I paid him back for what he did to my boy.'

Even with Jazzy's personal experience of a dysfunctional upbringing, her heart contracted at the thought of the thirteen-year-old pregnant girl being abandoned by her family and sent abroad with a woman she'd never met, but she had to push all that aside and ensure the salient details were recorded. The speed with which Martha was deteriorating made it doubly imperative that they got this right.

'Can we just backtrack a little bit, Martha. You've told us that in 1971, at the age of thirteen, you were pregnant with your first child – a claim confirmed by DNA and other forensic tests – who was registered in New Zealand in February of 1972 as Billy Chaney – Chaney being your mother's maiden name and the name under which you entered New Zealand. Is that correct?'

'Yes.'

'Can you confirm who was the biological father of your child and how did this pregnancy come about?'

'Billy's biological father was Frankie Jones. He raped me in the back bedroom of my home in May 1971 whilst the Gaffer and my father were conducting business downstairs. I told both my father and mother afterwards and they chose to send me away.'

'Again, the parentage of Billy Chaney has been forensically confirmed and the fact that you were thirteen years old at the time of the rape and Frankie Jones was an adult means that we have charged him with rape of a minor and other sexual assault charges.'

Jazzy waited as Martha, seized by a paroxysm of coughing, nodded. When she'd finally stopped, Jazzy continued, 'I know you have already given detailed and verified diaries to your solicitors as well as documentation sent to DC Annie McQueen and papers entrusted to the man, now confirmed to be your cousin's son, Sid Mackie. I want that fact noted for the recordings, so they cannot be disputed at a later date. These are being ratified by Police Scotland's legal team and will contribute to the prosecution of ex-Chief Superintendent Emily Hare, Frankie Jones and Jimmy Nails among others, should the procurator fiscal decide we have enough evidence to do so. At this point, because I can see you are struggling, I want to move on to what brought you to return to Scotland. Are you able to do that, Martha?'

'Aye, hen. With pleasure.' Martha blinked rapidly a few times, her gaze set somewhere over Jazzy's right shoulder as she began to speak. 'I wasn't a good mum. I was too young, too scared, too vulnerable, too stupid, to take care of my boy. I blamed him for everything that had happened to me. For my parents abandoning me, for me being landed in this alien place with strangers who were only interested in the baby and not the thirteen-year old mother. He grew up to hate me and I grew up to hate him. I became disruptive, got in with the wrong crowd, drank too much, snorted too much coke. Eventually when I was about seventeen and he was four years old, I just left him with the people my family had assigned to look after us. Turns out, they were distant cousins, but although they doted on Billy, they abhorred me so they were pleased to see the back of me. Can't say I blame them.'

Queenie reached over and squeezed Martha's arm. 'Did you see wee Billy again?'

Martha shrugged. 'Once. He found me when he was seventeen or so. Such a handsome boy he was. Such a polite boy, but I was too high to appreciate it. He wanted to know who his father was – who his Scottish family were – so I told him, and that was the last I saw of him alive. I snarled and sneered at him and flung their names at him, telling him his grandad might have more use for him than they had for his own daughter, and his bastard dad was probably dead by a roadside, gutted like a fish in some drug deal gone wrong.'

Her hands clasped tightly on the table before her, tightened, until Jazzy was sure she would break her fingers.

'Those were the last words I said to my boy. The last words. That boy was better off without me. No doubt about that. None whatsoever. If I'd just kept my mouth shut – if I'd swallowed those names and never uttered them, he'd never have been able to trace them. He'd never have got on that plane to Glasgow and he'd never have ended up dead and dumped in a deserted field and dubbed Cairnpapple Man for all those years.'

Tears flowed freely down her face and she brushed them away, sniffing as if her tears were an indulgence she didn't deserve. Jazzy wanted to stop the recording and comfort the woman, but the glint in Martha's eye when she finally caught her gaze warned her against it.

'You were a kid, Martha. You were a victim. A victim of the Gaffer, a victim of Frankie Jones, a victim of your father and his criminality, and perhaps most of all a victim of those times. You deserved to be looked after. To have your trauma accepted and dealt with. You are not to blame.'

Martha took the tissue Queenie handed her and scrubbed her face. 'I've not got long now, detectives. Just ask your last question, then maybe I need to go back to the hospital.'

Jazzy nodded at Queenie who said for the recording, 'I'm leaving the room momentarily to request the presence of Martha's doctor to administer any necessary medication.'

After the doctor checked her over, Martha insisted on finishing her statement.

'When I saw that photo of the man they called Cairnpapple Man, I knew it was Billy. I recognised him. And the dates told me he'd acted on my words and come to Glasgow to meet his grandad and other family. When we were kids my da used to take us to run around Cairnpapple Hill. I knew they'd killed him. I knew it. So, I planned my revenge. But then when I saw my dad was dead, I knew it had to have been Jimmy. He'd not have wanted

Billy staking any sort of claim on his business. Wouldn't have been happy to see old muck raked up. That's why he did it. I'd wanted better for Jimmy when he was wee, but seems that bad genes will out. He's proved himself to be as evil as his auld man.'

Martha's eyes fluttered and the doctor stood up. 'That's enough. She needs to rest. You need to stop this now.'

Martha smiled. 'You've got all you need. It's all with my solicitors. Queenie. It's all there. I won't last the night and I won't go to prison, but I can draw my last breath knowing they've all paid for everything they've done. I *am* Vengeance. I am Martha Nails.'

Chapter 60

'There's something bothering me about Jimmy Nails's reaction to being accused of murdering his nephew in 1990.' Jazzy leaned back in her chair and rolled her neck. All the bruises she'd sustained at the weekend had progressed from slight aches to pulsating throbs. The shoulder of her weak arm was bruised and protested every time she moved her arm, but the accumulation of other knocks made pain-free movement impossible.

It was late, nearly midnight, and only the Jazz Queens remained in the incident room. The air, alongside the usual mix of toiletries and sweat carried the remnants of smoke that – although each of them had showered and changed their clothes since then – still hung like a bad memory in the air.

Fenton clicked his fingers like a gangster.

Queenie rolled her eyes. 'Oh, here he goes – Snoop Dog on the case, or as I like to call him – Slush Puppy.'

Fenton cast a derisive snort in Queenie's direction as his fingers flew across his keyboard. 'I was watching this earlier, you know, Jazz, and something about it niggled me. Shall I play?'

Jazzy got up and, hand supporting her lumbar region, walked over so she could see Fenton's PC. After a glance at the screen she nodded. 'Yep, I remember seeing this at the farm and thinking

341

something was off with it. Whap it on the big screen. We'll all watch it.'

The night-vision footage was a shadowy grey but despite that each of the four figures in the recording were identifiable and the angle was much better than the limited view Jazzy had had from the kitchen window. Fenton pressed play at the point where Bonnie Moran was glaring at Frankie Jones. Her eyes flashed and it was clear from the way her chin jutted up and her mouth turned down that she despised the older man. But then, just as Jimmy acted, she raised the gun towards him and right then a flash of realisation skittered through Jazzy's mind. *She was one of Frankie Jones's victims too. Bonnie Moran as well as her sister Martha had been raped by this perverted piece of shit.* She'd stake her life on it – but Jazzy wondered if she'd ever get the feisty woman to admit it. The next few minutes of recording made Jazzy even more certain that Bonnie Moran was another of Frankie Jones's young victims.

When Fenton switched it off the four of them sat in stunned silence for long moments, each trying to work out what all of this meant.

'Well.' Geordie was the first to recover. 'We all know that Sid Mackie and Billy Chaney – Martha's son – are related. Now we know, or suspect, exactly how they're related. Mackie probably took Sid and his mum away to protect them from Frankie. Lucky escape if you ask me. And we know that Jimmy killed Billy Chaney to stop him trying to muscle in on the business. We've more or less got everything, don't we?'

But Jazzy was frowning. 'I'm not so sure. I still think we're missing something. I'm talking about the recording of Elliot's interview with Jimmy Nails. Why did Jimmy do a "no comment" interview with Elliot until Elliot asked about him killing Martha's son. *That* was when he exploded. He went near ballistic as if the last thing he would do was something to hurt Martha. Well, that was my take on it anyway.'

342

Fenton's fingers were again flitting across his keyboard and within moments he had isolated the section just before Jimmy Nails's explosion during his mostly 'no comment' interview.

As he was about to press play, the incident room door opened and Elliot Balloch walked in. He raised an eyebrow at Jazzy and gestured to the large screen showing the still of his interview with Jimmy Nails.

'Great minds think alike. I was puzzled by his response to that one accusation too. Before that came up, I'd pushed him hard, made sweeping accusations of things that we had no proof he was responsible for and he batted each of them away with a contained response. It niggled me so much that I had to come back and view it again.'

He settled beside Jazzy, resting his butt on a desk. The cut on his cheek had been stitched and a bruise was forming on the puffy skin around it. Fenton pressed play and, in silence, they watched the short clip.

'He didn't do it, JayZee. No matter what Martha says, Jimmy Nails didn't kill her wee laddie.' Everyone turned to observe Queenie, who was staring, face flushed at Jimmy Nails towering over Elliot, his lips pulled back in a rabid snarl, his fists clenched as two officers pulled him back to his seat.

'Nah, you're right there, Queenie. I'm finding it hard to believe that vision of passivity and placidity could harm a fly let alone another human being.' Geordie's tone dripped sarcasm.

Queenie rounded on him, her expression nearly as rabid as the one on the big screen. 'I know him, Geordie. I know Jimmy Nails. If he'd done it, he'd have smirked and no commented till Elliot's todger shrivelled up and fell off. No, that display wasn't guilt – although that's what he wants you to think. That display was a distraction. He *knows* who killed Billy Chaney – or at least he's beginning to piece it altogether. He knows it wasn't him, so there was only one other person it could've been.' Colour draining from her cheeks, Queenie turned to Jazzy. 'That no' right, JayZee?'

'Aye. It makes perfect sense. It's got to be.'

Fenton and Geordie exchanged glances, whilst Elliot grabbed his mobile and dialled. 'You two be ready. I'll set up the interview. You'll have a better chance than any of us at getting to the truth.'

'Eh, you going to tell us who you two are swanning off to interview?' Geordie asked.

Jazzy smiled. 'Work it out. You two are detectives, after all. Work it out and make us proud. That right, Queenie?'

Queenie leaned over and pinched each of their cheeks in turn. 'Aye, my wee Jazz Queens. Make us proud.'

Chapter 61

'So you see, much as I'd rather be having a haggis supper followed by a bit of rumpy-pumpy with my old man and, just so you know, like . . .' Queenie paused, folded her arms under her bosom and shoogled her breasts, a big grin splitting her face like a lurid Halloween turnip. 'Just so's you know, like. *My* old man *isnae* my brother. Nah. Nae relation at all – well, nae *blood* relation. Unlike you *I'm* no' into shagging *my* brother.'

Bonnie glowered at Queenie but remained silent, the only sign that she was irked by Queenie's taunts was the joogling of her leg. Queenie's smile widened. 'You know, incest's no' a nice word, is it? I mean here in Scotland, you can go down for at least two years, maybe more just for jiggling with yer brother – even if it's consensual like. That's you and Jimmy banged up for another two years on top of everything else we've got you for – the carrying an illegal weapon, money laundering, drug dealing . . . the list gets longer and longer as the rats jump the Nails's sinking ship. Christ, by my reckoning, ye'll no see wee Crystal till she's all grown up – aw what a shame. I reckon maybe, phew – twenty years? You do all right in a woman's nick, would you, Bonnie?'

'Aw, fuck right off, Annie. Pish yer knickers, McQueen. You've got nothing. Not a sodding jot of evidence.'

'Have I no'? Aw and there was me thinking that wee recording yer big sis took of you and Jimmy shagging in your living room was just that – evidence. Evidence of yer tawdry wee incestuous relationship.'

Bonnie regarded Queenie over the table, her eyes narrowed, her lips curled up in feigned disinterest. Jazzy stepped into the breach. 'Wonder if you're into shagging your nephew too, Bonnie? That what went wrong between you and Billy Chaney? When he found out he was your nephew and he wasn't up for a wee shag on Cairnpapple Hill with his auntie, you decided to just off him? I mean, it's not like we haven't seen evidence of your violent behaviour in the past, is it?'

'Don't rise to it, Bonnie, they're taunting you.'

Ignoring her lawyer, Bonnie rolled her eyes and tapped her fingers on the table with a muttered, 'Give me strength.'

Queenie took the baton. 'Aye, but that's it, hen; it wouldn't take a lot of strength to kill a wee unsuspecting teenager, now would it? I mean, he wouldn't be expecting his long-lost auntie to attack him, would he? And you're strong, aren't you, Bonnie?' Queenie grinned. 'Some would say masculine – no' me, like. I'm not saying that, but you got to admit with all that gym malarkey and weights and stuff, you've got muscles where most women have a bit of lushness.' Queenie joogled her boobs again and wiggled her eyebrows salaciously.

'Aw, gies a break, you old bag. I could get your husband to shag me in a wink of an eye. Not surprising, really, considering what he's had to content himself with all these years.'

Jazzy tensed, wondering how her partner would react, but she needn't have worried, for Queenie just shook her head. 'Doesn't matter anyway, hen. Jimmy's decided that *I'm* a better bet than you are.'

Bonnie's eyes faltered, her gaze flicked from her lawyer back to Queenie's grinning face. 'What you on about, you miserable hackit auld cow?'

Jazzy leaned back, leaving Queenie to bring the bacon home.

'Just like I said, Bonnie, hen. Jimmy's chosen me over you. He's not going to take the rap for you killing Billy Chaney. He's washed his hands of you and is putting in his lot with me. Of course, I wouldn't like to say it was *only* my womanly charms that convinced him to do the right thing, but well . . . I think the fact that we found digital and paper evidence that all the crap that Ned and Dan did whilst Jimmy was banged up in the Bar L was under *your* orders played an important part too. You've been working with Loanie Gibbs over in Edinburgh for years now. Jimmy's not a happy bunny. Tut, tut, tut. He's not happy at all. Seems his loyalty lies more with his older sister – the one who didnae betray him – than the younger one who did. He's squealing to us right now. Telling us about every hit you ordered, every violent act you perpetrated, every victim you abused.'

Bonnie made to lunge across the table, but her solicitor yanked her back into her chair. 'Mrs Moran, I implore you to control yourself and to give "no comment" responses moving forward.' Wide-eyed, her hand shaking as she brushed the hair form her face, the solicitor turned to Queenie. 'My client and I would like some time to consult.'

But Bonnie was having none of that. 'Shut up, you stupid fancy bitch with your stupid flowery language.' She glared at Queenie. 'The bastard's turned on me? You fucking told him about me and Loanie? You told him those two idiots were acting on my orders?' She inhaled, her eyes flashing round the room – playing for time. But in the end, she had no choice and she knew it. But, as Queenie and Jazzy expected, she had only one option if she wanted any reduction on her sentence.

'Get me a deal for manslaughter of that wee stupid bastard and write off all the other charges, including the incest and the illegal weapon charges, and I'll give you everything I know about Loanie Gibbs and Jimmy. You'll have the key to their entire operations. You'll be able to wrap it up tight, clean the streets once and for all.'

Queenie narrowed her eyes. She wasn't authorised to offer such a deal, but now that Bonnie was talking, she wanted to at least tie down her involvement in her nephew's death. It was up to the Crown Office and procurator fiscal service to do that. 'Tell me about Billy Chaney and we'll go from there.'

Shoulders slumped, Bonnie jerked her head at her solicitor. 'You can fuck off. I'm all right on my own.'

Queenie updated those present for the recording and then Bonnie Moran, no hint of remorse on her face as she stared right at Queenie, began to speak.

'Jimmy was away when the wee tosser with the Kiwi accent came over asking for him, spinning some sob story about being his nephew – didn't even know I existed, or that I was his aunt. I saw right through that. I knew the wee bastard wanted a cut of the money and the last thing I wanted was Jimmy's family loyalties split, so I lured him up Cairnpapple Hill one night on the pretext of seeing the sunset, and when we were there I bloody whapped him on the head with a boulder and then stabbed him until I was sure he was dead. I dragged him down the hill and across the field and dug a wee hole for him. To be honest, I couldn't believe my luck when nobody found him. Then I just forgot about him, until that stupid fucking farmer discovered him. Thank God he'd decomposed mostly. Nobody came forward to ID him and again I breathed a sigh of relief. Then that forensic artist came up with his face and that bloody Sid Mackie came back. This has all just been bad luck. That's all. Bad luck.'

Bonnie leaned back in her chair, folded her arms across her middle and grinned at Queenie. 'I don't care what happens now. I'll bat my eyes at the jury and get away with it. The bastard tried to rape me. I've been traumatised, especially since I've already been victimised by Frankie Jones. No jury in this land will convict a bereaved wife and mother who's been raped and abused throughout her life. They'd see it as self-defence.'

Queenie looked at Jazzy, and nodded. Jazzy stood up. 'Interview terminated at 23.33. DC McQueen and DS Solanki leaving the room. Bonnie Moran to be returned to the holding cells.'

Friday 7th April

Chapter 62

Martha had insisted on bright colours and a Humanist funeral and the small gathering had complied. Afterwards Jazzy stood with rest of D team outside the West Lothian Crematorium, off Starlow Road in Livingston. Martha, although satisfied that both Frankie Jones and Emily Hare would likely spend the rest of their lives in prison, couldn't quite – even at the end – come to terms with wrongly blaming her brother Jimmy for murdering her son.

Although Martha, had she not been terminally ill, would have spent her last days in a Scottish prison for her role in the deaths of Markie and Tommy Jones, among others, Jazzy and Queenie agreed that she too was a victim in all of this. Frankie had committed a horrendous number of rapes and abuses, all swept under the carpet by his fellow criminals and with the assistance of Emily Hare. However, numerous media appeals for witnesses and other victims to come forward had shown the extent of his depravity. Both he and Hare had been refused bail and were held in remand – Frankie in Addiewell nick and Hare in HMP & YOI Stirling.

If Jazzy dwelled too much on the extent of the abuse Frankie had inflicted on so many children, it would consume her. Instead, she and Queenie focused on expediting the interviews of the victims who had been brave enough to come forward, and making sure the procurator fiscal had sufficient evidence to ensure that Frankie Jones's victims would get justice. Bonnie Moran too had been held on remand and awaited her trial at HMP & YOI Stirling. Both she and Hare were classed as high risk and were held in separate areas of the prison.

Despite Jimmy Nails's presence at the Tarbrax farmhouse, no evidence to date had been unearthed about criminal activity since his release from jail, other than the incest charge which, due to the unlawful way in which the footage had been obtained of him and his sister, it was likely that the procurator fiscal would throw it out of court. Jazzy suspected that the time he spent in prison, wrongly convicted of murder, would play in his favour and whilst it was infuriating, she and Queenie had agreed that overall, they'd done well. Besides, now Jimmy Nails was on her radar, she'd be on him if he so much as jaywalked.

As Martha's only relatives, Sid Mackie and Jimmy Nails had organised the funeral to her specifications. Sid had given a touching speech about his short time spent with Martha and how, although misguided, her intentions had been pure. Jimmy had delivered a touching eulogy dwelling on his childhood memories of a much older sister who had fiercely protected him and how he'd missed her when she'd been sent away. Whilst Jazzy had no doubt of his sorrow over his sister's death – Jimmy was a loyal brother, after all – no amount of distress and grief could make Jazzy feel the sympathy she felt for Sid Mackie.

During Martha's final weeks, Sid had been a constant companion by her bedside. He'd read to her, devoured stories about her life in New Zealand, and her memories of his own parents. Martha had been unaware that Frankie had set his eyes on not one, but two of the Nails girls. Sid's mum had been three years older than Martha and the pair hadn't been that close because of that. Still, she'd been aware of a scandal surrounding her older cousin but hadn't equated it to what was happening to her in her own world. Whilst Sid's mum had been old enough to have her pregnancy passed off as a consensual impulsive sex act between a near-adult courting couple, which was legitimised on Shona turning sixteen, Martha had become a victim of her innocence and the misguided shame of a family who should have protected her, and ended the legacy of Frankie Jones there and then. As soon as Sid's dad had scraped enough money together, he'd left the family farm and been happy to dedicate his design skills to developing new, less traditional tartans to meet the growing international demand. Escaping to Turkey was their way of keeping his family safe from both the Glasgow and Edinburgh criminal factions.

As they waited for Sid to finish his conversation with the nursing staff who had turned up to express their condolences, Jimmy Nails approached. 'A word, Annie?' He inclined his head to the side indicating she should move away from Jazzy, but Queenie dug her heels in and scowled.

'I'd rather be tarred and feathered than talk to the likes of you.'

A pulse throbbed at Jimmy's temple as he thrust his hands in his pockets and breathed in a lungful of air. 'This what it's come to, eh? Wee Orphan Annie McQueen turning her nose up at one of her oldest friends?'

Jazzy stepped closer to Queenie, her eyes narrowing as she glared at Jimmy. Queenie snorted but said nothing.

He shrugged and turned to walk away. Beside Jazzy, Queenie's shoulders relaxed only to tense up again as he turned back, a sneer widening his lips. 'So, you'll not be wanting to know which fucker killed your wee lassie then, Annie? What was the wee bint's name again? Oh, that's it, Billi.'

Queenie's jaw dropped, but only for a nanosecond, before it snapped shut, her hands clenching into fists as she stepped towards him. Despite her lack of height, Jazzy would have put money on a raging Queenie winning a fight between them.

'Don't. You. Fucking. Ever . . .' Queenie punctuated each word with a prod to Jimmy's chest. 'Let. My. Lassie's. Name. Pass. Those. Filthy. Criminal. Lips. Of. Yours. Again.'

Jimmy splayed his arms in front of him and took a step back, his sneer widening to show just how much this amused him. 'Easy, easy, Wee Orphan Annie. Good to see being a copper hasn't drained all your feistiness from you. I'm just trying to help. Just thought you'd be interested. I mean . . . don't you want revenge?' He snorted and flung his head back. 'Nah, I forgot, Wee Piggy Orphan Annie won't want revenge. She'll want justice.' He spun on his heel, raised his hand in a final wave towards Sid who was walking over to join them. 'You know where I am if you want to know who offed your bairn, that's all I'm saying. Watch your back, though, Annie. Don't forget I know stuff about you – stuff you won't want your pig mates knowing.'

Queenie, her eyes dark, glared after him. Jazzy smiled at Sid and in an undertone for Queenie's ears alone said, 'He's playing you, Queenie. You know he is.'

But Queenie shook her head. 'Maybe, but that doesn't mean he doesn't know something, does it?' She raised her voice and yelled. 'Aye, well, maybe I've got something on you, Jimmy. Maybe you and Bonnie should have been a wee bit more careful. Wouldn't want to be leaked about your wee sister, now would you? Not with her being banged up. After all, there's nothing more *touching* than *sibling* love, is there? Maybe *you* need to watch *your* back!'

Something in Queenie's tone sent a cold shiver up Jazzy's spine. The niggling feeling that Queenie wasn't sharing everything with her made her uneasy. She sighed and tried to quell the thought. Queenie was her friend and Jazzy would return her loyalty. Although she might regret it later, she had to make the offer. Queenie had done so much for her and now it was her turn to repay her friendship.

'Look, we'll get the files, okay? We'll reopen Billi's case – unofficially like. Just us, the Jazz Queens. We'll do it in our spare time and if there's anything to Jimmy Nails's assertions we'll find it.'

Queenie blinked a few times. It was cold so her eyes were probably watering. 'Aye. We're the Jazz Queen's, JayZee, if anyone can get justice for my wee lassie then it's us.'

And with Sid, Geordie and Fenton looking on, their brows furrowed in puzzlement, Queenie launched into an adapted version of their theme tune.

'Jazz Queens. Top notch, cool and mean. Hot stuff with a killer gleam. These kids are gonna whoop your arse.'

Chapter 63

One month later

With the salty water lashing my face, its stinging droplets like acid on my flesh and the wind tugging mercilessly at my hair hard enough to yank it right out, I stand with my back to the receding island and look to the future. My future. A future that might constitute my endgame or equally a new beginning. Either way, I'm up for the challenge, ready to march onwards like the soldiers I so like to taunt. I've enjoyed shocking their sensibilities these past weeks, but know that a bit of hair dye and body-fattening disguises and the like won't protect me for much longer.

I pull my jacket tighter round my body, feeling the push and pull pound me as the freezing squall buffets me. These last months have been trying – not the end of the world, I agree; after all, living here, albeit in a basic cottage, beats being tossed in the nick. It's not been pleasant, but on a positive note, it has been safe; well, safer for me. That's what comes of having a muddied past – it's hard for them to follow all the interwoven threads that might have led them here.

I mean, who would ever link me to a step-great-great-grandad from Skye who was as canny as me when it came to putting things down on paper. No, the auld bugger, on his death bed, just slipped me the key when I was twelve. My adoptive mum – totally lame bitch that she was – had moaned and groaned about trekking up there. The only reason she made the hike, I reckon, was because she thought the auld bugger would leave her something in his will. He didn't and boy, did it piss her off. Instead he left it in trust to the community, with the proviso that his step-great-great-grandchild (no name ever stated) had the key and was entitled to use it for their lifetime. Like I said, the auld yin was well canny.

Course, I never told anyone about my windfall, not even the cowbag, and it's come in handy over the years. A bolthole to escape to when I needed it and no passport or ID necessary; although, I managed to get a fake ID using his name – McCullough – just in case and I kept up with the utilities over the years, so no one had any cause to gripe. Besides, I doubt anyone in the 'community' really wanted a battered hovel – little more than a bothy – in the middle of nowhere. Not even the village kids thought to use it for their illicit drinking or weed-smoking seshes. Too far to trek when you're high and besides, I think fear of the ghost of my cantankerous auld step-great-great-grandad Stuart McCullough was enough to frighten them off.

Every time I visited over the years, I made sure to be in disguise. I value the importance of forward planning and even at that young age, I realised that there would come a time when that hideaway would be of use. But now it's time to come back and put an end to this once and for all. Thankfully my network of acquaintances, apostles and hangers-on have been of use and the use of satellite phones for communication purpose has decreased the chances of detection.

That makes me feel so good. She's got a lot to answer for, has sister dearest – such a lot, but her time has come, so she better watch out, for this is a duel to the end.

On a whim, I raise my arms to shoulder height and stretch

them out to my sides and, channelling my inner Kate Winslet, I yell into the waves, 'I'm coming for you, Jazzy Solanki. I'm coming for you!'

A Letter from Liz Mistry

Dear Reader,

The initial idea for *The Revenge Pact* came after seeing an article on the reconstruction of Bronze Age skulls in Scotland. Subsequent research led me to understand the usefulness of these scientific processes in identifying previously unidentified bodies and the seeds for *The Revenge Pact* began to grow into a story about gangs, the desire for revenge, family history and more. Of course, the reconstructed body found in *The Revenge Pact* on Cairnpapple Hill in West Lothian is entirely fictional, although the hill itself is real as is the site of a Neolithic henge and many Bronze Age burials – a fitting place for a decades-old body to resurface, don't you think?

As ever, I've had a whale of a time in the company of the Jazz Queens and in this book, I managed to delve a bit more into Queenie and her past life in Glasgow which was enlightening for me as I learned things about her I hadn't expected.

Writing *The Revenge Pact* was an absolute pleasure and a labour of love, which at times, due to my own mental health was also a lesson in being kind to myself, which is why themes of mental ill health recur in my writing. In *The Revenge Pact* we see the repercussions from events in *The Blood Promise* come into play and hopefully they highlight these issues in a realistic and empathetic way.

I hope you enjoyed reading *The Revenge Pact* as much as I enjoyed writing it. Of course, if you loved getting to know Jazzy, Queenie and the team, then please do leave a review, shout about it to your friends or talk about it on social media.

Until the next Jazzy and Queenie adventure, keep safe. Best wishes,

Liz Mistry
X

Website: lizmistry.com

X : (Twitter) LizMistryAuthor

⬛ : www.facebook.com/LizMistrybooks

⬛ : @lizmistryauthor

The Blood Promise

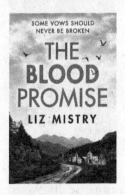

A deadly gift
Imogen Clark wakes up on her sixteenth birthday
to find her parents dead at the breakfast table,
along with a message from their killer.

A twist of fate
Detectives Jazzy Solanki and Annie McQueen join the investigation, but the more they discover, the more Jazzy suspects that the
killing is a twisted message for her. Jazzy shares the same birthday
as Imogen, and believes that this is more than a coincidence.

A race to catch a killer
When Jazzy discovers the connection between the killer and
the stalker who has been following her for years, she is forced
to confront the dark past she was desperate to keep hidden.
She must stop at nothing to solve the case, before she becomes
the next victim . . .

'Page-turning and chilling' *The Sun*

Last Request

When human remains are discovered under Bradford's
derelict Odeon car park, DS Nikita Parekh and her team
are immediately called to the scene.

Distracted by keeping her young nephew out of trouble,
Nikki is relieved when the investigation is transferred to the
Cold Case Unit, and she can finally focus on her family.

But after the identity of the victim is revealed,
she's soon drawn back into the case. The dead man is
a direct link to her painful past.

As the body count begins to rise, Nikki must do everything
she can to stop the killer in their tracks before anyone else
gets hurt – even if it means digging up secrets
she had long kept hidden . . .

**For readers of Angela Marsons and LJ Ross comes a gritty
new crime series featuring bold, brave and ferocious DS
Nikki Parekh! This rip-roaring thriller will have
you reading long into the night!**

Broken Silence

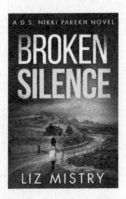

On her way home from a police training conference, Felicity notices something odd about the white van in front of her. A hand has punched through the car's rear light and is frantically waving, trying to catch her attention.

Felicity dials 999 and calls it in. But whilst on the phone, she loses control of the car on the icy road. Pinned in the seat and unable to move, cold air suddenly hits her face. Someone has opened the passenger door . . . and they have a gun.

DS Nikki Parekh and DC Sajid Malik race to find their friend and colleague. But Felicity was harbouring a terrible secret, and with her life now hanging in the balance, Nikki can only hope that someone will come forward and break the silence . . .

The next gripping crime thriller in the DS Nikki Parekh series, for fans of Angela Marsons and LJ Ross!

Acknowledgements

Writing a novel can be a solitary affair, the rest of the publication process – the editing, publicity, cover design and more is down to team work. Huge thanks to the HQ Stories team who have worked so hard to get *The Revenge Pact* through the process and into bookshops and libraries. It's always a magical feeling when that happens. In particular, I'd like to thank my editor, Seema Mitra, who stepped into the breach at short notice, got what the Jazz Queens were all about and gave such detailed and perceptive feedback, all of which has helped raise the quality of the book immeasurably. Helena Newton and Michelle Bullock also worked tirelessly to iron out my mistakes and catch my missteps – thanks very much.

Many thanks to the cover designer, Anna Sirkorska, who has truly excelled in creating a distinctive, eerie cover that matches the sinister nature of the book whilst also incorporating elements of the West Lothian landscape.

My agent, Lorella Belli at LBLA and her wonderful team have worked tirelessly to promote *The Blood Promise* and now *The Revenge Pact* too and to keep me in the loop. Thank you so much!

My many author friends, as always keep me sane during the lengthy process of writing a book and are so generous with their thoughts, support, advice and good humour. In particular, I'd like to mention Tony Forder, Andrew Barrett, Anita Waller, Mike Hollows, Neil Lancaster, J M Hall and more.

My online crimey groups, especially UK Crime Book Club and Crime Fiction Addict, are a source of constant entertainment and provide a safe space to interact with readers and fellow authors. Thanks to the Admin teams of both groups who keep them running smoothly and for the readers who are so supportive of the authors in the groups.

My family too have, as always, been amazing. They know how much I cherish being a crime writer and see the joy it brings me and are always there for me. My husband, Nilesh, in particular, goes the extra mile to make sure I can do all the writerly things I want to do. Huge thanks and much love to them.

But, my most heartfelt thanks go to you, the reader, for without you there would be no reason to write. I have enjoyed chatting with you online, receiving your feedback, meeting you at events and festivals and generally spending time in your company.

If you're reading these acknowledgements, it's because you've decided to give the Jazz Queens a chance. I hope you enjoyed your reading time with them as much as I did my writing time. Humungous thanks for taking the time to get to know Jazzy, Queenie and the team.

Dear Reader,

We hope you enjoyed reading this book. If you did, we'd be so appreciative if you left a review. It really helps us and the author to bring more books like this to you.

Here at HQ Digital we are dedicated to publishing fiction that will keep you turning the pages into the early hours. Don't want to miss a thing? To find out more about our books, promotions, discover exclusive content and enter competitions you can keep in touch in the following ways: